THE NEW

Book of

INTERNET STORIES

Recent books by Maxim Jakubowski

Past Poisons (editor)
Chronicles of Crime (editor)
Life in the World of Women
It's You That I Want to Kiss
Because She Thought She Loved Me
The State of Montana
On Tenderness Express
The Phosphorus War

About Maxim Jakubowski

Maxim Jakubowski was born in Barnet and educated in France. He is the owner of the legendary Murder One bookshop, the world's largest crime and mystery bookshop. A past-winner of the American Anthony Award for crime non-fiction, he currently writes a monthly column in The Guardian newspaper on crime fiction.

Maxim Jakubowski is author of four novels and the editor of numerous anthologies covering science fiction, crime writing and erotica.

THE NEW ENGLISH LIBRARY

BOOK OF

INTERNET STORIES

EDITED BY MAXIM JAKUBOWSKI

NEW ENGLISH LIBRARY
Hodder & Stoughton

First published in Great Britain in 2000 by Hodder and Stoughton
A division of Hodder Headline

10 9 8 7 6 5 4 3 2 1

British Library Cataloguing in Publication Data

The New English Library book of Internet stories
1. Internet (Computer network) – Fiction
I. Jakubowski, Maxim
823.9'14'080356 [FS]

ISBN 0 340 76974 2

Typeset by Palimpsest Book Production Limited,
Polmont, Stirlingshire
Printed and bound in Great Britain by
Mackays of Chatham PLC, Chatham, Kent

Hodder and Stoughton
A division of Hodder Headline
338 Euston Road
London NW1 3BH

contents

Introduction

Imagination Dot Com

A few decades ago, the Internet or its myriad literary equivalents only existed in the rarefied domain of science fiction. A nebulous if fascinating concept that would link all of us in a curious net of possibilities, temptations, crimes real and imagined and new, ever more unlikely situations.

Today, the world as we know it has changed irreversibly due to the existence of the Internet. All human activity is there, including some we couldn't even have dreamed of in our wildest fantasies. Every day, more people around the world are connecting through their computers (and already through mobile phones) to the World Wide Web, and the exponential growth rate the media is experiencing is both dizzying and extraordinary.

Take a newspaper on any given day and you will find scores of news items connected to the Internet. Traditional retailers going out of business due to the competition from e-retailers; the printed book under siege from e-books; the stock market in its speculative frenzy embracing the e-world with open arms and creating new generations of e-millionaires and, no doubt, many e-bankruptcies to follow; intense love affairs happening to people meeting on-line; virtual sex; on-line sex; new forms of interactive voyeurism (sex is, after all, always at the forefront of most technological applications when it comes to exploiting possibilities . . .); intellectual piracy through the open distribution of music and images; marriages, deaths, births and deflorations live on screen in the privacy of your own room; auctions for everything and anything, including the unfertilised eggs of beautiful model donors; fraud and crime finding new forms of creative expression; hackers, viruses threatening homes and industrial/military complexes; and so on. The list is endless and new angles to Internet innovation and development are occurring on a daily basis.

The revolution is now unstoppable and, I am confident, in another decade, we will look back with indulgent nostalgia to the years when the Internet was just a dream, as we will all be totally addicted and useless as human beings without it.

Naturally, writers have become fascinated with such an overwhelming new spectrum of potential stories, fictional and real, and this collection is an early attempt at challenging the minds of some our best storytellers by asking them to write new tales, stories that could not have come to light without the existence of the Internet.

It's a ripe ground for fabulists as many facets of the science fiction of yesteryear have come true, but never as SF writers had actually imagined or predicted. And the authors I invited to contribute to this collection have proven equal to the task, each imposing his or her own personality and obsessions on to the theme of the Internet and the resulting stories are wonderfully varied and imaginative. No two are alike, whether tackling the theme of shopping on-line, stalking, love and sex, business, human relationships, voyeurism, manipulation, ghosts and other bytes from our brand new millennium.

The whole world is here, or rather the whole worldwide web, every nook and cranny unveiling curious and fascinating concepts and characters, as a bunch of talented authors from a variety of fields, including crime and mystery, science fiction and fantasy and even erotica explore new pastures with their imagination clicking away with wild abandon.

See you on-line . . . if you dare.

MAXIM JAKUBOWSKI

crusoe.com

matt whyman

She went down like my stock shares. Fast and without warning. One minute I'm schmoozing on the sun deck, slopping my spritzer on some powerful shoes. The next I'm clinging to the guard rail with Gates himself wrapped around my ankle and the stern of the ship sliding into the sea.

Who knows what caused us to founder? It was calm. It was clement. The only icebergs were clinking in our drinks. But then we were in uncharted waters, and in retrospect the vessel may not have been designed to hold such a weighty convention. Indeed, this meeting of minds from the virtual world had only been afloat for a short time. Most of us had barely found our feet. Such was the desire to get out there and network that we hadn't even properly unpacked our bags. Choosing instead to home in on the investors in our number. Those venture capitalists who had been so keen to come on board. In the water, however, we all looked alike. Shrieking and spluttering. Stricken by panic. Fighting among ourselves for driftwood. Any purchase to keep us afloat. Every entreprenerd for himself.

I lost sight of Gates when the sharks circled in. Though I believe it was his glasses that washed up with me.

So there I am, on the island. Standing on the shoreline of this forested outcrop of rock, waiting for the choppers to spring up on the horizon. I figured I'd be rescued within the hour at most. Not a day. Or a week. A month. Then a year. At least that's how long it seemed to me. Long enough to comb the beach for treasured things, and make myself at home. I even discovered a humble cave, blasted into the scarp overlooking the sea. One that appeared to have been inhabited by some age-old lost soul, going by the hammock and the diary turned to dust beside it. Gates's glasses also proved invaluable to me. Such was the intense focus commanded by his lenses, I was able to light fires in the weakest light and roast fish speared from the shallows. In that time I went right back to basics. Grew a beard God himself couldn't better, and aimed to survive on the bare necessities of life. Food. Shelter. Laptop computer.

The PC I salvaged from a suitcase that had drifted ashore soon after me. There above the tide line, I sprung the lock with a rock and found the hardware to be in factory condition. Within seconds, in fact, I had booted it up and set my sights on home. Frantically bashing out that critical e-mail. My message in a virtual bottle. A signal of distress aimed at Lara, my PA back at base.

'I'm alive,' I began, reading as I wrote. 'Stranded on island. Middle of nowhere. Please send help. Also Nasdaq position and price.'

I hit SEND, my forefinger trembling, only to be faced by an error message. A warning that also served to alert me to the fact that all was not well with my head:

```
The modem has reported no dial tone.
Please check all connections and try again.
```

Any further attempt would be futile, I knew that. Still, it didn't stop me following instructions. On numerous occasions. Mostly at sundown when I felt the most isolated. Each time I hoped with all my heart that by some miracle I might connect, but always I would shut down in defeat. Flopping back into the sand to watch the stars emerge. Servers in their own right. Stepping stones to other worlds. It was a perspective that made my solitude seem bearable somehow. Until the suspicion slowly dawned on me that I was not alone, here on this retreat of mine, and my fragile take on fate was lost to outright alarm.

First the footprints in the sand at low tide. Then the abrupt bursts of hammering that caused the birds to spring from the trees. This unseen presence conspired to haunt me, even in my dreams, until one morning I sat bolt upright in a sweat to see a man there. Peering in from the mouth of my cave. No horns or cloven feet as I had feared. Just a ragged short-sleeved shirt and slacks. Battered attaché case in one hand. Miniature screwdrivers aligned in his breast pocket like a military decoration.

He cleared his throat, as if preparing to speak for the first time in an age. '*Salut*,' he croaked, and then drew breath sharply when his eyes fell upon my computer. '*Tiens!*'

This was no island devil, I realised with relief, but a survivor from the shipwreck. Judging by the passion with which he reacted to my laptop, I figured he had been confined below deck for the duration of the conference cruise. There to keep us in contact with our respective empires. Along with the rest of the system support staff.

'You speak English?'

He shrugged, glanced back at me. I told him my name. Motioned for the man to do likewise.

He consulted the dateline on his watch: '*C'est Vendredi.*'

Conscious of the pantomime threatened by our language difference, I simply motioned for him to stand back. Bringing the PC out into the sunshine, I then mimicked a broken gesture.

'No connection.' I pointed to his attaché case. 'Can you fix it?'

I had lost my wallet to the deep, but implored him to consider the fact that we shared a mutual goal. A desire to get home somehow, which seemed one step closer when Vendredi encouraged me to pick up my computer and follow him around the promontory. Guided by goat tracks, I followed the Frenchman on a perilous but revealing ascent. For as one elevation rose up behind the next, the horizon line receded to reveal that we were in fact just one island in a sprawling archipelago. And yet what really caused me to draw breath was the sight that greeted me at the summit. There in a clearing, lashed to the surrounding coconut trees, this technical savant had erected a relay of sorts. Some ten-foot bamboo totem, bound by vine and copper wire, studded with circuit boards and shards of solar panel. A Wicker Man gone World Wide Web.

'*L'e-mail,*' declared Vendredi, bringing two fists together.

I beamed at him. At last, we would have that connection. I opened the laptop with great reverence. Lifting the lid as if it were a chest of treasure. Meanwhile, Vendredi switched the lead from his barnacled corpse of a computer to my own and crossed his fingers tightly. This time, the e-mail dispatched smoothly. Up and away from the island. Seeking out the nearest server, then leapfrogging to the next. Closing in on my office and my PA's work station. Where Lara would stop her keyboard chattering and shriek with joy at the message on her monitor.

At least that's how I imagined things would be, in the moment before I learned how my e-business had fared without me.

By way of reply, I received my own e-mail. The bugger had bounced back at me. Address not recognised. I glanced at Vendredi. He licked his cracked lips. Scratched at his matchbox bristles. The man was plainly itching to get his own hands on the keys, but of course I forbade him outright. This was, after all, a subordinate skilled in working behind the screens. There was room for only one front-end user, and that was me.

'It would be a threat to the natural order,' I reminded him. 'Good Lord man, I'd never dream of interfering with the running of a technical department. Not without risk of an uprising.'

And there I fell quiet, mindful of what had folded in my absence. Sensing my distress, Vendredi dutifully backed away. I smiled at him bravely, then turned once more to the matter in hand. Numbed, but undeterred, I deleted Lara's name. My problem was no substitute came to mind. Since the company's launch, and steep ascent into cyberspace, I had left my friends and family behind. Lost touch with a world I now so desperately missed, just to stake my claim in another. The sound of breathing over my shoulder, just then. This time, I didn't resist.

'*Le chat room. C'est* plus *populaire.*'

He was right, though I couldn't quite bring myself to show it. Instead, I just pointed my browser to the most crowded gathering of like-minded lonely hearts on the web. Adopting the screen name **Castaway1**, we eased our way inside and silenced the masses with an urgent plea:

```
Castaway1:    Help! We're stranded on an island.
              Can't get off :o(
```

A moment passed before we got a response, and as I made the translation Vendredi clasped my shoulder as if to steady himself. At last, our ticket home appeared to be in reach!

```
HeelSpike:    Are you for real?
Castaway1:    Thank God! Can you raise the alarm?
HeelSpike:    Maybe ;o)
Castaway1:    Please. We're begging you.
HeelSpike:    Mmm, sounds good.
              What are you wearing?
```

We turned to face each other, Vendredi and I both quietly computing the implication behind this request, then made our exit without saying goodbye. I sank back against the palm tree, ready to admit defeat. Unlike my companion, whose hopes seemed to rise in inverse proportion to my own.

'Newsgroups,' he said, striking his forefinger high. '*Les newsgroups.*'

I sat up smartly, as if I'd thought of the idea myself. A well-placed posting could reach a thousand people or more. Which was what I did next, targeting alt.news.attention-seekers with just seconds to spare before a cloud slipped in front of the sun and the system went down. As the trade winds were but a breeze that day, we both agreed to break for lunch. For this was a glitch that only the heavens could fix.

I should say Vendredi had exhibited magnificent resource since washing up on the other side of the island. Without any brief or instruction, the man had made his home in a clearing and even cultivated a small potato crop. Thus we dined as he would back at work, on fries washed down with a bitter brew of his own making. *Café*, he claimed. In his department, I grimaced quietly, but not mine. For dessert, however, the sun came out and it was with high hopes that we returned to the laptop to feast on the replies.

In the space of an hour my empty mailbox had swelled so magnificently that I was forced to scroll down the screen. A whole host of e-mails responding to our SOS. Some asking us to specify what we were selling. Most telling us to quit clogging the system with spam. Junk e-mail nobody wanted. The last missive had been sent by the newsgroup host. A curt note informing us we weren't welcome to contribute without a conspiracy theory, porn pics or scurrilous celebrity gossip, and that a block had been placed on any future posting.

'But we're genuine,' I cried aloud. 'This is serious!'

Newsgroup culture. A medium for the trivial and the tasteless, it seemed. Just like the chat rooms. No place for the cerebral or sincere. My finger hovered over the exit button, and then the unthinkable happened. Vendredi, my backup boy, seized the laptop from my possession.

'*Un website*,' he said, showing me his palm to calm me. '*C'est la solution*.'

We may not have shared the same language, but I was damn glad Vendredi was fluent in a third. HTML. Hyper-text Markup Language. Computer coding, in short. We made a fine team, too. My man constructing the digital pidgin between the tags. Laying the foundations for me to compose the Queen's English that would appear on the screen. All of which amounted to a cry for help, an outline of our predicament, and an invitation to e-mail.

True to form, Vendredi refused to go live with it until he had perfected its functionality and inserted a click counter to monitor our performance. So it was that we went on-line with a comprehensive but deceptively simple menu bar and the choice to view the site without frames.

'My friend,' I beamed, as Vendredi completed the upload. 'We'll be home in no time.'

Five days later, our web page had still to claw into double clicks. Despite registering with the leading search engines, even creating a new category for 'dot com destitutes', we simply could not attract sufficient attention to ourselves. At the same time, both Vendredi and myself were struck down by fever. A virus, thought the Frenchman, but not a strain he could cure with his disc doctor. It was homesickness, I was sure, and privately I began to fear death by nostalgia.

Lolling in the shade, we watched the screen for a sign of life, attracting nothing but fleeting surfers and flies. Such was the constant buzzing around our ears that at first we were deaf to the sound of inbound propellers. Then the shadow swept over us, and in an instant our affliction vanished. Vendredi and myself both dancing in the clearing. Waving madly at the cargo plane. Wondering when it was going to turn. Then watching in disbelief when instead it made the drop. Way out in the distance. Over the island closest to ours. I looked to my feet, then across at my downcast companion.

'Reckon you can build a raft?' I asked, and was delighted to hear that he could.

Vendredi's software skills weren't much called upon that afternoon. Still, he did a fine job, and by the time the twilight tide crept forth it floated a fine-looking vessel. By our standards at least. Half a dozen lengths of rough timber held together by the remnants of his copper roll. I fashioned the oar myself. Removed every thorn so he wouldn't cut his hands on the voyage.

'*Solo?*' questioned Vendredi, and looked out across the darkening seas. I assured him that even a man of his position was up to the task. That I had been most impressed by his fortitude and invention, and that he didn't need my leadership to show him the ropes. I promised I would keep a fire burning until dawn. There to guide him back once he had reclaimed our supplies.

'You'll be fine,' I called out, as he floated into the gloom. 'Working alone after dark is what your kind do best.'

I spent a long and anxious night at the summit. Keeping watch beside the blaze. Fretting over the fate of poor Vendredi. For as the moon swung into its zenith, the sea breeze delivered the patter of distant drumming. A celebration. That's how it sounded to me. And I couldn't help but picture my island companion turning slowly on some cannibal's spit. I was beset by guilt. Overcome by the thoughtless manner with which I had dispatched him into the unknown. For the man was more than just support staff. He was *human*. In the same boat as me. Or not, as was the case just then.

Still, I stood sentinel. Leaning over a pulpit of rock. Determined not to succumb to sleep. Cursing when I awoke cloaked in dew. Then catching my breath when I peered down below. For there was Vendredi! Paddling furiously against the swell. Fighting to avoid the rocks. I called his name repeatedly. Punching the air on my way down the goat tracks. Slowing only as I scrambled over the dune and registered his lack of luck.

'The cargo?' I panted. 'Where is it?' Vendredi dropped to his knees, the raft turning in the surf beside him. His sunken eyes welling as he looked back up at me. 'What?' I said pressingly. 'Tell me what you found?'

In a husk of his former voice, the Frenchman said: '*Les femmes.*'

'Pardon me?'

'*Avec des webcams.*'

'Webcams?' I translated, chilled by a sense of dread. 'There are women over there? With *webcams*?'

'*C'est diabolique,*' he said. '*Une atrocité.*'

I agreed. It was bad. Good there were other survivors from the shipwreck. Bad none of the female contingency had chanced to wash up with us. Very bad indeed, in fact. For now it seemed we were in competition. Fighting for attention from the outside world. Women with webcams. Two chaps with no pictures on their homepage.

Yes, all websites were equal, but some were more equal than others. Far more so than ours could ever hope to be.

We were doomed, and as I contemplated the full horror of our situation a second cargo plane swung over the island. Another delivery for our nubile neighbours, I presumed. Coming in so low it kicked up sand in our face.

'That's it,' I said in despair. 'We're going to die here.'

It was then, for the first time since my arrival, that I lost command of my composure. Tears flowed down my cheeks. The salty streams serving only to reinforce our hideous predicament. Vendredi opened his arms to mine, and readily I hugged him. Pulling back abruptly, however, when something hard and uncomfortable came between us.

'A camera!' I declared, having parted his shirt to find it hanging by a strap. 'Where did you find this?'

Sheepishly, Vendredi informed me he had stolen it. Re-enacting the scene in which he crept into the outskirts of the camp under moonlight and seized this prize possession. An Olympian undertaking, so I understood, on account of the bacchanalian broadcast taking place around the fire at the time. Any other man might have turned to stone at the sight my companion so bravely resisted, and I praised him for his focus. Sadly the camera was only a basic digital model, which meant we couldn't match them with moving images. Nonetheless, we had the ability to add a visual dimension to our website. A means to entertain, as demanded by the medium.

'Can you hook this up?'

Vendredi looked at me like he owned the patent. '*Oui. Bien sûr.*'

'Good man,' I said, and clapped my hands together. 'Then get undressed.'

Without blinking, the Frenchman took one step away from me. '*Excusez-moi?*'

'Vendredi, this is the Internet.' I began to undo the two remaining buttons on my shirt. Bid my companion to do likewise. 'It's our only connection to the real world. Don't you see? How else are we going to draw attention to ourselves?'

I was right, as I prayed I would be. We were a hit. Our click count hit four, five and then six figures overnight. Quite a feat, for a site featuring only partial nudity, for Vendredi insisted his briefs stayed on when I took pictures of him, and then begged me to retain my boxers.

Admittedly our web site didn't feature as much flesh as fantasy-eye-land.com across the water, but then we depended on a very different draw. Vendredi standing proud before his relay, one hand cupped to his ear. Me in the sand at low tide, etching out another appeal. My companion even downloaded a streaming sound file, so anyone who wished could view the site to a Bontempi version of Desert Island Discs. Together, we created a cyber spectacle that solitary surfers actually *talked* about. Spreading the word around the globe via e-mail, newsgroups and chat rooms. In short, we achieved what many of my former colleagues had deemed the Holy Grail. We became a curiosity. And how the people flocked to our shores.

Virtually, at least.

One day after our relaunch, we received our first offer. A click-through banner on our site in return for a drop of supplies. Hardly the lifeline we dreamed about, but then we were competing for the catch.

'What choice do we have?' I asked myself, on reading the terms set out by this major on-line bookstore. 'If we refuse, it'll go across the water.'

Vendredi seemed not to hear me, however. His attention distracted by yet another overhead hum, for the volume of airborne traffic had increased sharply since his return, with planes criss-crossing our island on a regular basis. Feeding not only our neighbours, it seemed, but other start-ups in the archipelago. This, we knew for sure, just after our own first drop arrived, when a third party landed upon our shore.

Even without his glasses, Gates had changed beyond all recognition. Yet the emaciated wretch who dragged himself from the surf had clearly clung to his spirit. We listened to his story, from the moment he lost his grip on me to the day he realised his own island was nothing but a glorified sandbar. A platform that by his account threatened to be broken into bits by an unforgiving sea. In the wake of his traumatic bid to keep his head above water, I agreed that he could join us. At the same time I made it quite clear who was in charge. Ordering Gates to unpack the supplies while Vendredi and I continued to wade through e-mail. Sifting through the bids for interviews and film rights, searching in vain for a basic rescue package. Anything that recognised us as real people; that saw beyond the opportunity to profit from our misfortune, and offered the chance for us to get off-line.

That we were able to dine on fine food and wine was merely a distraction. Even the building materials that were parachuted in couldn't crush my desire to get home. We had the means to build quite luxurious recreational facilities, but a boat was out of the question. I negotiated hard, but our sponsors were as stubborn as they were generous. Any attempt to leave would be in breach of contract. Without our presence, they claimed, the click-counts would dry up, and so too would their revenue. Instead, they positively encouraged us to update the content and keep things looking fresh. To introduce a 'castaway of the day', endorse the books dropped for us and keep sucking in more traffic. Not just from the sky above but cyberspace, too.

We had no choice if we were to maintain our standards of survival, though still we clung to the hope that someone would visit us in person. Such was our conviction, that we took turns keeping watch from the pulpit. I even retained Gates glasses in order to fashion a telescope, putting the man himself to good use too, on account of the fact that only he could see through it. Subsequently, when he did wave us over late one afternoon, we responded to his sighting with some pessimism.

'It's probably a school of dolphin,' I said.

'I am thinking tuna,' suggested Vendredi. The Frenchman having at last abandoned his native sense of linguistic defiance and embraced our way of speaking. Gates squinted into the lens again.

'Damnedest fish I've seen,' he asserted. 'They're topless.'

They came in force. Wearing grass skirts and sun tans.

Webcams fitted to their canoes. I recognised a few from the convention cruise. Not least the webmistress who spoke on their behalf. A pert city broker who I had planned to hit on just moments before the ship sunk.

'We should merge,' she said. 'We're fighting for the same thing, and halving our chances of achieving it.'

We stood side by side. Vendredi, Gates and myself. A face-off on the beach terrace with these Internet ingénues. The westering sun cut sharply between us. Flaring through our cocktails and the pavilion windows.

'We don't need you,' I said eventually. 'We're doing fine.'

'Oh, I think you do,' she replied. 'We own the local server.'

'*Merde!*' spat Vendredi, but I could tell by the way he bowed his head that we had lost our bargaining power. For without a server, we had no web access whatsoever.

'Locating the wreck of the ship was the hardest task,' she went on. 'Salvaging the necessary hardware from it was simple. A good strip down and we were in business.'

'So it seems,' I muttered darkly. I stroked my beard, shifted my gaze along their revealing rank, only for my posturing to collapse when Gates declared her proposal to be a great idea.

'What do you say we cut in the other islands? Just imagine our position with our resources pooled.'

'*Enough* with your vision thing,' I cautioned him, and revealed that I was about to say the same thing myself.

'No need,' said the webmistress. 'We've sent a delegation to every island.' She was good. Better than Gates, it seemed, and I bowed to her foresight. What's more, I sensed she was making eyes at me.

'Vendredi,' I said turning the other way now. 'Go fetch the

Krug and some glasses. There's still a few bottles left from last week's drop.' I broke off to throw him a set of keys. 'Take the golf cart to the chair lift, it's quicker that way.'

'So we have a deal,' she inquired, extending her hand for mine.

'It's a step closer to home, I guess.'

As we shook on it, however, her grip stiffened up and she held me there. Two narrowed eyes, demanding my attention. 'It's more than that,' she declared finally. 'Today we become one island. Tomorrow we'll take on more. Increasing our advertising rates, investing in the service, expanding our horizons until we can no longer be considered an island at all. That's when we'll know that we've made it. When the rest of the world is lost without us.'

'Ambitious,' I said, aware that Gates could barely contain his enthusiasm. 'I guess ultimately you'll be seeking a flotation.'

'In a sense' she said, and swung her attention to the sea. 'But this is about so much more than money.'

I was about to press her for a share option anyway, but a reverent hush had settled over us. Everyone except me following her gaze across the water. Out to some imaginary point. Way beyond the horizon. This gathering, oblivious to the champagne cork as it rocketed from the summit behind us. Soaring over our heads. Into the boundless blue.

it came in a box

stella duffy

It came in a box. She'd seen it on the television, smooth and sleek, generous outlines coloured in with advertising gloss. She had heard them singing its praises on the radio, knew every word of each article written in its honour – knew them because they were pinned to her noticeboard, framed in wish-list glory. It was her rainbow promise and someday soon, somewhere over there was going to be right here, right now.

Once she'd decided – colour, size, accoutrements and accessories – she wrote them all up and waited. Sat beside the telephone for half a day. Each minute almost there, almost time – until the moment. Then she picked up the phone and began to call it in. She was visa-ready and the nice man was helpfulness itself. The transaction done. Phone call made, paid for and delivery the very next day. Just as they had promised on the radio, the television, the hand-delivered papers. (Everything came to her hand-delivered, car-delivered, truck-delivered. She would not leave the swollen rooms if she could help it.)

The nice man said this would help, this would open up whole new worlds for her. He said this would take her outside of herself, promised far-reaching arms and smiling faces. Promised a global warmth to envelop her cool heart. She wanted that comfort, prayed to go far beyond herself. But she did not want to leave her room. This would be a shining ark to transport her beyond fear, proof against fire, flood and acts of God. This was the same as an act of God. This was a chance to begin again.

It came in a box. Shiny, gloss-enhanced carton, sturdy with reinforced corners and heavy prophylactic polythene cover. She was waiting for the delivery all that morning. Opened the door to the postman, the rubbish collection, the electricity meter-man, smiled at each one in anticipation and hopeful expectation. The smile stayed on her face all the while they remained in her doorway, turning to a scowl with the slam behind them.

She waited four hours and then it came, arrived with the playtime bell for the children over the road, came in with a sudden summer squall and a screech of brakes, the neighbours' cat darting between the van wheels, wishing away lives four, five and six. Though she'd seen him pull up, unload the package, walk along the pavement, she held herself back, hand on the latch until he rang the bell. Only then did she open the front door to the wilderness at her gate, smile for the nice man, sign his triplicate paper and ask him, as politely as she could with crawling skin, to leave it there on the step.

He offered to bring in the box for her, carry it through to the back room where she planned to house her new universe. She refused his kind offer. She was stronger than she looked. She was stranger than she looked. He left the box on the doorstep and whistled his happy way back to the delivery van, happy man, blue van, finished early for lunch, no traffic on the drive home, it was his lucky day. Indeed.

She took a long thin knife to the outer skin of the box. Slowly, carefully sliced through the plastic layer. Lean, sharp strokes smoothly down each side, then peeled back the protective covering. Beneath the plastic the cardboard was shinier still, Christmas present glittering even after the wrapping was gone. She did this slowly, deliberately. She had cleared her life of the clutter of other people, interfering sensibilities, she knew how much time it took to offer herself the perfect balance of anticipation and reward. This one she could do slowly, this one she would breathe through.

When the plastic has gone – sliced, shredded, folded, removed – it is time to open the box. This is the gingerbread moment. The testing time between promise and delivery. It must be sweet and tart and crisp and yielding enough. It must give her everything or she will have to begin again.

She lifts back the lid. It is pulled from the body of the box with a swift shush, air escaping, vacuum freed. Her nerves are balanced on the knife edge now, she is scared to look back from the brink, knows the moment of greatest hope offers the furthest distance of failure. She feels in front of herself with blinded hands, building sense memory of this breath. Under her reaching fingers is a thick mulch of polystyrene packing, beneath that another layer of the reinforced gloss card. She lifts them both out with eyes closed, allows the packing beads to fall on the thrice-swept floor, covering her knees, her slippered feet, as she kneels before the box. Then she plunges her hands in deeper and opens her eyes as her fingertips touch. There it is. Waiting for her.

She lifted it out, careful as with a baby, held it gently to herself, pulled back on her own axis so the leverage came from herself, so she did not push against it, but brought it to her, slowly, breathing through. It was more shiny than she had imagined. She had thought perhaps they were lying, they were often lying. Had thought maybe it would be less translucent more beige, less pink more flesh. But it was perfect Barbie rose like the nail polish she once wore and now hoards in the back drawer, smooth translucent like the saliva running over her tongue as she panted with the exertion of silent strain.

She placed it on the table, centre stage, running her hands across the glossy face. Then back to the box. A list came with it; she ticked off the items one by one. Umbilical to the mains, one arm to the mouse, the other to the printer. Each extra link labelled and numbered just as she had asked for. The man on the other end of the phone was thorough indeed. She thought about sending him a letter of thanks. Then a shiver of excitement as she remembered. She no longer needed Her Majesty's Royal Mail. Now she had her own direct service to the world. She would e-mail him her thanks. It was time to switch on.

It is time to switch on. Thin and nervous fingers reach down to the mains at the wall. Two switches wait for her touch. Each one clean as the new machine though it is fifteen years since they were fresh unpacked, twice-weekly dusted, monthly disinfected, her home is perfectly preserved. She reaches down to the switches, finds she is trembling and laughs at herself, but enjoys the tremble nonetheless.

She switches on. The machine has a light. When turned on at the wall it has a light of its own, even before it has its own master switch flicked. It will sit through the night with a silent glow, a memorial light to her promise. Her promises to herself. This is part of the promise, to bring her out of herself, back to the world, re-take the promised land. It is a warm glow and she is delighted. This will be a midnight candle, a safe beacon to ward off the uninvited scare-stories lurking in her dreams. She runs her hands across the fluid face, feels a hum of potential beneath her fingers. Winds her wrists about with thin cables and pulls herself to kneeling before the machine. She is eye-level with the screen. This is a good place for greeting, meeting, making friends. Being made a friend. She fixes a smile, fingers the just-raised on-switch, flexes the eager index finger and pushes in. A note, a chord sings out in answer. Then there is light and moving picture and sound all at once. She is amazed, this is more than she had expected, televisual brilliance from a machine that is all her own, pre-programmed to know just how to talk to her. Just how to reach her.

That afternoon was one of her perfect hours. They had promised ten minutes from box to begin, but she took sixty. She drew it out and breathed through each new motion, answered the questions as if they had never been asked before, made careful and deliberate choices for colour and contrast, keys and calling cards. The password in particular was a childish delight, recalling the secret societies she had longed to be part of and was never asked to join. Now she had her own. Her own society, her own secrets. Then it was done and then she was ready. The world was waiting at her fingertips, just as they had promised. Time to take a look.

She ran her fingers over the keyboard, each fingertip touch a new greeting. She typed slowly, searching for the keys, ensuring every one was correct before moving in, joint bending to push. Each slight indent a tiny invasion. It felt good. It felt like possibility. It was better than the man had promised, he had not known what she was searching for, thought she might want to use the machine to send a letter, write lists, possibly even order up a book or extend herself to a CD, a video. It would not have occurred to him that she might stay awake for hours, sitting in the dark back room, lit by luminous blue and calling in the world.

She stayed there for eight hours, open bottle of water by her side, orange peels piling up, sticky fingers and liquid mouth wiped each time she ate another. Hands must be clean and fresh before they were allowed to reach for the keys. It was easy. Far more simple even than she had been led to believe, still less complicated than the willing salesman had told her, promises dribbling down the side of his mouth in his eagerness to pass off purchases to the unknowing lady, her credit card crediting him with more cash than truth. And she let him think so and smiled at the joy with which he took his commission. He might as well make the most of it now. The swollen confidence of youth would not always be within his fat-fisted grasp. She knew that and was prepared to forgive him. Once.

She coursed the globe that night, from the comfort of her back room, the bitter-sweet scent of orange peel on her lips. And the people out there were so willing. They made it easy for her; they wanted to talk, to play, to listen, to laugh. There were even some who wanted to make love to her. She stared for a moment, understood with a tremor of shock and slight revulsion what was being offered, and then clicked them away hurriedly. Washed her hands, swilled out her mouth with bitter rind. She was not interested in making love with strangers in the ether. Her quest was not for illicit late-night thrills in the back room, dingy sex with screen blue to light up the crevices of her unheld, self-touched body. She was not here for a virtual thrill. She was here to re-form the truth. Voyeurism and solo-pleasure were not her aim, she had had enough of the self. She intended to become a collector.

There were sites offering everything she could possibly

need, bits of everything she needed. All she had to do was put in her order and patiently wait. Then the parts would come and she would be ready to assemble her desire. She had plenty of waiting desire. From the first day she had heard about what could be bought and traded, sold and thieved, she had known this would be her path. The way she would follow back to the society of men. Not women. They scared her. Sometimes they knew too much, scented her secrets. And not really men either. Just one. The society of man.

From the Internet she would collect all the right pieces. Scanned and strained and stored and collated. There too, she would gather the words, the spells and incantations and whispers of as yet unspoken words. She would hoard them together, and then, when it was time, she would take her pieces of him and the new words she had harvested from across the globe in the pre-dawn dark and she would make him. The man. The e-male. The ultimate quest for the vir-tuous man. Virtually requested, literally hers. Superstition and ultimate technology. Twenty-first century boy-toy.

Midsummer sun rose just before five. Spilled itself in a pale arc across her scrubbed floor, scrubbed face, secret place. She spoke out loud what she had collected on her screen, named each part, whispered the charm, fingered the printed images of the talisman, talismen – men with tallis, with teffilin, with crucifix, rosary, pentacle, wand, prayer mat, evil eye, sage brush, ointment, hope. Man following boy with amulets of protection and each one thrown down, downloaded, with impossible speed, possible seed of the next man, hexed man. She made him up, brought him forth, fingered him through the keys into the keyhole. She trawled the net for the right words and images and promises, put in her orders, promised her cash and cards, accessed the sites, and whispered him into being. The global villager. It was done.

It was morning. She went to sleep. The post would take a day or two.

She waited for him to arrive. And meanwhile she began the correspondence. Replied to the offers: music to soothe, videos to enlighten, books to entertain. She ordered special dishes for their first meal together, organic and fresh – just like him. She answered unique offer questionnaires, homepage helpful hints, gave away her number time and again past the secure sender warnings.

Things began to come back. Responses that her product was on its way, acknowledgements of her data, warm welcomes to select chat-room sororities, begging petitions to free the death-row killers or stop ignorant homophobes or batter back the torturers. And she signed her name to these too, they wanted her, her identity added to a forwarded message really would make a difference. Without even stepping beyond the front door.

Then the chain e-mails began to arrive. A letter from the Dalai Lama, message from a Native American guru, promises that all her wishes would come true, financial security would be hers, love would come knocking at the door. If only she sent the e-mail on to twelve friends, forwarded within the hour, blessed the original sender with her e-dress and a fifty-pound note. She did not. She did not have twelve friends to her name, did not want twelve friends. She had but one wish and she had created it herself.

The e-mails kept coming through, dire warnings of what might befall her if she did not send them on. Each time she read it through, acknowledged the sage's wisdom and then deleted. She would make her own magic, had had sorcery enough, did not need the chain mail to tie her into old-fashioned fear. She was remaking myth through the flowing lines of beautiful modern technology. She was the delete button queen and no wish was left untrashed. She was the end point of tens, then scores, then hundreds of begging bowl offers. She un-subscribed and dumped each one. She did not have hungry desires like the senders, she had taken care of all her needs herself. He was on his way.

He came in a box. Several boxes. Pieces of him parcelled up and flown to her door from all across the world. Sometimes the postman brought him, other times a delivery van, a truck, a bicycle courier. Once a small child from three doors down brought a piece of him, mis-delivered to his mother's house, small cardboard box with squashed corner, slowly leaking thick liquid from inside. She took the box from the child's hand and slammed the door in his hoping-for-a-tip face. Lucky boy.

Then it was all there and she laid him out on the floor. Piece by piece she jigsawed the man together. Whispering promises and potential as she did so. The fossilised footbone connected to the scanned image kneebone. The kneebone connected to the plastic relic thighbone. The thighbone connected to the build-your-own soldier hipbone. Connected to the heal-your-life backbone. Joined to the sharp-as-a-knife shoulder blade. Supporting the clerical collarbone. The swan neck. The arms for giving, alms for the taking. The hands to hold you tight. The skull and unnecessary crossbones. The digitally enhanced face that launched a thousand battleships. Eyes of any hue, perfect sight and a blessed vision. The long, glossy hair you always wanted and now yours to have for the brushing. Plasma promised disease-free and cool-storage safe. The smooth skin, strong muscles, taut tummy, toned thighs, bulging biceps, perfect pecs, corporeal cock, ordered in the middle of the night with unwavering desire and certain hope.

The man. Laid out on the floor, Packing boxes piled up

behind her. She walked quietly and carefully across the room, holding in her anxiety and excitement, touched her hands to the keyboard and called up the saved spells. One after the other they flooded the split screen, some apparent order, other obvious confusion. On the monitor it was all words. In her mouth the words hardened to truth. She joined him with her speaking. Ordered the man, man made to order.

He stands. Unsteady legs; shaky. Bambi man. What are you gonna name him? He looks around, unfocused eyes at first, glazed in the half light, candle-bright. He looks to her. For solace, understanding, help. She is no help. She is astounded and delighted. And scared. He moves towards her, he knows what to do even if she does not. Bends his head to suckle at her too-clothed breast and the feel of his breath near her wakes her up, snaps her from incredulous reverie to now.

It is real. He is real. He is touching her neck, there is skin there, warmth of his just-made hand holding her neck and bringing her to him. He is almost a foot taller than she, not obvious laid out on the floor, but clear now he leans his head down to her face. He knows to kiss. Born knowing, made knowing. She did not expect he would be wise and is first surprised and then still more pleased. Pleased with herself and very pleased with him.

The touch is cool, she had thought he might be warmer, hotter. But he is new made, cold blood cool. The kiss is almost chilled and all the better for it. His lips are not the same temperature as hers. She can feel his lips, they do not meld into hers, there is no danger of mistaking her own skin for his. She has been there, the relationships and lovers that revel in the join of flesh so that there is no knowing which is her and which his. She does not want that, would not wish to be so united with any other. Here she knows who she is. He is the one holding her, lifting her feet from the floor and laying her back against the cool grain. He is knight in shining armour, in charge, and everything he does is her bidding.

There is no slow build-up, gentle sex tease and tempt. She has had the anticipation for days now, since the moment she put in her telephone order for the original box. Unpacking and ordering was her foreplay, first foray. He is the skin and flesh and cock and fuck. He is the event, she is the reason.

She is not disappointed. It has not been that long since she last laid with a man, not so many years that she has chosen to cut herself off from society. But long enough. Time enough to know he is exactly what she's been wanting, to know the taste of his skin before she bites. Her tongue on his sips the flavour of waiting, his fingers in her mouth smell of now. When they fuck he is sinew and strength, she tenses to the pulsing veins inside her, the flex of his muscles outside, the body heat difference means she feels all of him all the time. She is not lost in him, nor he in her. He is exactly what she ordered. They remain apart and fuck joined at hip, lips, hands. He comes when she comes because that was part of the deal. She falls asleep and he strokes her hair, lit by the monitor's blue glow. She has set the computer so that it does not go to sleep. Neither does he.

In her sleep she is untroubled by dreams, soothed by the cool of his hand on her head. In her sleep e-mails pile up for her, messages from suppliers, requests for confirmation of delivery, inquiries as to the safe arrival of the prod-uct. She sleeps on. It has been a tiring three days. She does not see the message come through, the chain e-mail promising her eternal happiness. As long as she answers immediately. As long as she does not trash the message. The contemporary terrors of inter-space do not disturb her dreamless sleep. Nor does his hand, lazily reaching past for the delete button, removing the message, destroying the fulsome promise of permanent bliss. And the last-line threat of tears.

When she wakes he is different. Warmer, His skin more like hers. Though he kisses her to calm she knows something has changed. His hands are rougher, her desk is a mess, looped about with cables and papers. She had not meant to leave it this long. The room is cluttered with packing boxes, bubble wrap lines the floor, clings to her feet. This is disorder and not what she wants. It is what he wants. He is playing. Touching her new screen, sticky fingers clumsy on the keyboard. Soft kisses to her breasts, her stomach when she comes close.

He is hot now, his skin clammy in the humid afternoon light. He is holding her, hugging her close, whispering love and endearments and sweet nothings that are too much of everything and she had not meant this, this is not her wish, he is too close, too much. Too real. She cannot stop him, he has hunger running through him, his touch wants to melt her resistance but sickens her instead. He is a heat rash on her body, she did not mean to grant him his own passion in her speaking. Something has gone wrong.

He left in a box. Boxes. Cardboard boxes, reinforced corners, smooth-lined with leak-free plastic. The product may be returned at any time within the first month of delivery if the user is in any way dissatisfied. The user was indeed dissatisfied. Deleted the product. Dumped it in the trash. And with deletion he was done. Temperature dropped to nothing. Sent off in boxes to the ether, everywhere and nowhere, dissemination complete.

She was disappointed. With herself, her own excesses, her stupidity at giving in to post-passion sleep and leaving him alone to deal with matters he could not understand. The superstitions of modern technology were hardly likely to be something he would comprehend in his first day out. She must work harder next time. Take more care. Take more. Meanwhile there was the mess to deal with. The fine lines of the smooth, too-fluid screen to clean. Virtual blood was no less red.

network network

james flint

The external fabric of the building ('the hull') had been built
in several sections in a boat yard by a yacht manufacturer, its
ovoid shape well beyond the capability of conventional construction techniques and this was thought very fashionable at
the time. The finished structure hovers above the great round
of the cricket ground like an ibuprofen caplet large enough,
perhaps, to relieve the muscular cramps of these isles.

On the evening in question it is dusk, past dusk, it is night,
and I don't know what you're doing there. Maybe you're
a groundsman working overtime[1] or some kind of Packer
devotee[2] performing an unauthorised searchlight viability
study or a trespassing turf collector or someone at any rate
who has some kind of reason to be hanging around at this
time, this late, after dark, and who in addition to motive has
the plain guts to brave the silent but nevertheless palpably
pulsating Quatermass-type[3] atmosphere that haunts all empty
sports stadiums in the gloaming. But as your eyes begin to

adjust so the square (the close-mown area in the centre of the ground and the site of the wicket), the dried and rolled and ultra-cut grass of which is so severely cropped it can hardly be called grass at all being less a soft carpet of shoots and blades than a holocaust of brutally amputated plant nubs looking like so many toenail clippings the way they're spaced out and set into the supercompacted mud, so the square appears to separate itself from the comparative lushness of the outfield – the nubs lending it a certain delicacy of colour – and slowly, especially if you blink your eyes a few times while those pupils of yours are dilating, slowly begins to levitate a few inches above the right and proper level of the pitch as if mirrors were being used to project it up onto some kind of giant pane of glass which owing to the onset of night and general lack of Packer-style floodlights you can't actually see in and of itself, the only clue to its existence being this hovering image, a visual effect which bears certain resemblance to that once used in Marty's excellent but now sadly unperformable teleportation illusion.[4]

All round the stadium the seats bow to this magical effect while above them, to the east, the giant ibuprofen caplet gazes down through the elliptical window of glass that runs the entire length of its inward-facing side and lends it the aspect of an alien eye. But it also still looks like an ibuprofen caplet meaning that the people moving around its terraced and violently illuminated insides are not unreminiscent of the tiny little spherical beads which spill out of such caplets in the computer-generated animations of the television advertisements and for which only people who work in pharmaceutical laboratories know the true name and also what they really contain.

One of the beads was called Marty. Being on the inside of the building it didn't look much like a caplet to him. It looked like a room, a long, high ultra-modern room walled on one side with a mirror, thanks to the light from the highly designed striplights that ran in lines overhead, bouncing off the inside of the enormous window and transforming it into a reflective surface that was quite impossible to see through, meaning that Marty couldn't make out anything of the dark stadium beyond or the pitch or the square. Even had he been able to, from that angle the square probably would not have afforded the levitation effect so familiar to groundsmen and Packer devotees and the turf collectors who travel the world with specially constructed metal cases like the ones serious diabetics carry with them but containing instead of syringes of insulin or packets of orally-administered hypoglycaemic drugs, racks of urine-sample-type phials themselves filled[5] with three-inch tubular samples of soil and verdure (or occasionally nodules of Astroturf®) stolen from hallowed sports venues all over the globe and which will be traded for unlikely sums on the Internet;[6] on the contrary from Marty's vantage point the square would have less resembled a ghostly raised plain than a hole and would therefore have looked, said hole being locked into centre of the more or less circular outfield, not dissimilar to a piece of T'ang dynasty coinage with dark patination, the relative dimensions of square and circumference corresponding in particular to those of the coins minted by the Emperor Su Tsung in 758 CE in order to finance the war with Shih Su-ming.[7] Nor did the people around him, to Marty, look much like those spherical beads to be found inside of caplets the name for which only those who labour in pharmaceutical laboratories actually know. To him they looked like gulls, they reminded him of gulls, they were dressed mostly in suits and they stood in tight little knots and bunches and were packed tightly together like gulls on the vaguely promenade-like terraces of the room and they jabbered at each other like a community of two-tone guillemots and mews discussing the fact of the sun's going down. Shoulders rounded, necks curved and extended, arms either tucked in at their sides or flapping to maintain verbal balance, weight rhythmically shifting from one leg to the other and back again and heads nodding contentedly, eyes looking out to both sides at once but never ahead. Certainly they looked like gulls, especially to someone like Marty whose great dream had only recently been totally shattered and whose life was in pieces and who was almost suicidally (almost homicidally) depressed and who really didn't want to be here at all but was here because he had to be because he had to somehow start paying off his not inconsiderable debts and who regarded the whole scene before him with a combination of cynicism and contempt, these people all being either bankers or businessmen and all therefore rather wealthier than he, Marty, was ever now likely to be. And so they were gulls, except of course that they weren't, because almost every last one of them was carrying a black record bag slung over his or her shoulder, a record bag packed with handouts and hats and booklets and flyers and free CD-ROMs and foam boomerangs and business cards and countless other items of let's-waste-the-planet's resources corporate junk which gulls never do, carry one of these bags, not yet anyway, though word is that they're working on it.

The bags were black and had the words **Network Network** machine-stitched across them in white, words which were followed by three coloured circles (yellow, green, red) and below these in blue the familiar glyphs of the various sponsors whose names, names like Oracle and Exodus and Sol, sounded vaguely hierocratic.

The dots, Magda explained to Marty when he'd arrived – early, well before the punters, so he'd have a chance to prepare – were part of **Network Network**'s unique identity profile and were crucial to how it defined itself in a marketplace already maximally niched with competing cross-fertilisation salons and business opportunity groups. 'Everyone has to wear a coloured button, see,' (she was American: she meant 'badge') 'and we've patented that.' Marty asked what the buttons symbolised, wondering if he could somehow work some kind of illusion with them, or at least a couple of good jokes. 'It's simple: red for VCs, green for entrepreneurs. And then besides that you have a white sticker with the name of your company or site. That way everyone knows who you are. It's an icebreaker. I guess it's an American thing.'

'VCs?' puzzled Marty as Magda pinned a yellow badge on his lapel and wrote him out a sticky label saying 'Magic'. He was thinking Victoria Crosses, red like poppies, or Vietcong, red again.

'Venture Capitalists,' Magda smiled. 'Money men.' She was tall and big-boned and blonde and beautiful in a slightly dazed sort of way and she had her own hand-written white sticker stuck to her blouse which read simply 'Magda' and she looked like she probably had Dutch ancestry, somewhere back there.

'Oh. Right. So what's yellow?' Marty asked, looking at his badge.

'Yellow means "other".'

'Other what?'

'Just "other".'

The magician frowned a little, pursed his lips. 'So you just want me to work the crowd, entertain people at random?'

'That OK? You can do it standing up, right? You don't need a table or anything like that?'

'It would make things easier, but no, I can do it standing up. I can do it lying down if you like.'

Magda either didn't pick up on that or didn't want to. 'So that's cool then?' she asked, trying to push the conversation into some sort of endgame.

But Marty wasn't quite ready for that. 'So,' he said, a little vacantly, 'am I it?'

'Are you what?'

'Am I the sole entertainment? I mean, are there others, fire-eaters and jugglers or anyone, or is it just me?'

'We-ll,' Magda said, 'there's you and the food icons and the wine waiters and the body ads, so you won't be all on your own.' Marty didn't ask about body ads; he already felt stupid enough over VCs.

'What time do I start?'

'Oh, whenever. Wait till the place fills up a bit. Go get a drink if you like.' She pointed over to where tuxedoed staff were setting up regiments of wine and beer bottles on white tableclothed tables.

'OK. Maybe in a while.' But he didn't move. He was looking at Magda, who was taller than he was, and really, he was beginning to think, really quite sexy.

'So what sort of tricks do you do then?'

He hated that, *tricks*. 'I'm an illusionist. I do magic,' he said pointedly, but flashing some teeth. 'Wanna see?'

'Oh, no thanks,' she said, the logos of female defensive hostility glimmering just inside her corneas. 'I don't like magic. No offence.'

'None taken.' Marty leant back against a table piled with the various pieces of gumpf people would be handed when they arrived, gumpf to be stowed in the freebie black record bags stacked up nearby, and began to study the design-award striplights suspended about five feet from his head. Then somebody called Magda's name from the other side of the room and thankful for the excuse she slipped away, leaving him to it.

A short while later the doors were opened and the room began to fill up, and as Marty watched the suits[8] begin to assemble, a terrible stage fright began to creep up over him, as bad as any he could remember experiencing. The skin of his arms and shoulder blades began to tremble and prick with a severe chemical chill that was almost paralysing. It was about then that the seagull analogy struck him, the deep cynicism at the base of it stemming neither from the feeling that the very fact of being paid to work a room like this was so far from what he wanted to be doing and knew himself to be capable of doing that he found it demeaning nor from the deep melancholy he'd been so burdened with lately and which was once again overwhelming him, but from the extent to which the (to his mind) lowly status of jobbing-magician contrasted with the (in his eyes) striking confidence of the people gathered all around, their stances and expressions and the strangely grasping hand movements they made when they were talking screaming *Succeed!* and *Acquire!* and *Believe!* until it became quite unbearable and all he wanted was to curl up into a small ball right there on the floor in the middle of them and berate himself while they didn't even notice and from time to time stepped on him.

The volume of conversation was already deafening, each knot of chat exciting the next in a kind of vocal convection until the room was fairly boiling with sound, roiling with terms that Marty didn't understand, words like WAP and leverage and hit rate and churn and IPO and metatag and frames and empeg and vermul and hacker and CEO and CFO and secure server and broadband and start-up and baud and banner and gateway and portal and OS and convergence and key escrow and chip set.

This was intimidating too: to have such an alien lingo to deal with when he was already having difficulty trying to size up the crowd made Marty nervous in the extreme. It was impossible to make jokes out of what he didn't understand or even work out a good moment to interrupt someone and start a routine – and interruption was made a necessity by the fact that everyone seemed to be talking, everyone. There didn't seem to be a single person among the assembled who wasn't engaged in animated verbiage.

Finally Marty took the plunge, picking someone pretty much at random and wandering up and fanning his cards out like feathers. 'Would you like to pick a card?' he said, hating himself as he did it. It felt so degrading, like it was pornography or something.

'So what's this then, magic.com? You need incubation?' said the man, who wore a red button alongside a name tag that identified him as Philip Deeg, Deutschebank. He took a card and looked at it. 'Hey!' he said, his accent a weird Euro-American amalgam. 'These cards aren't sponsored! You want to think about that – that's a nice marketing opportunity you're missing there.' The two men he'd been talking to laughed with him.

Marty looked mystified. 'Here,' he said, 'put it back in the pack.'

'I'm going to put it in right, then you're going to tell me what it is? How do I know I can trust you?'

'You can put it anywhere you like.'

'Can I keep it?' Another titter from the group.

'That depends on whether or not you want to see what I'm going to do with it.'

'Maybe I don't.' Marty shrugged: this was tiresome, he

couldn't deal with this shit, he'd forgotten how hard it was, how you had to continually be coming up with sharp lines. He needed to mug up on his repartee. 'OK,' the man said, slotting the card back in the deck like he was supposed too. Marty cut the pack, shuffled, then reached up and produced the card from behind the man's ear. 'Hey!' he said, genuinely surprised. 'That was cute! But how're you going to parlay that into click-through?'

What? Marty thought, returning the card and setting up a double-lift in preparation for the next stage in his warm-up routine. But the Deutschebank guy had spotted someone he must have really badly needed to talk to because he crossed in front of Marty calling, 'Hey! Hey! Doug! Hold up there, buddy!' and disappeared into the throng, patting Marty's shoulder as he passed in a patronising gesture of thanks.

Marty moved on, tried another group, enervated by despondency. 'Pick a card, any card,' he said lamely. The man did, held it there without looking, his beak shunting buzzwords towards his companions through the fermenting air while his eye saccaded through the portion of the room bordered by the axes of Marty's shoulder and neck. Marty waited, wondering whether the guy was confused and thought the card was a canapé.

'What do you expect me to do with this?' he demanded at last.

'Well, take a look at it, I'll show you a trick,' Marty unhappily replied, giving in.

'Er, thanks.' The man passed it back. 'Maybe some other time.'

Once again he moved on and was fanning his pack for another random, a wheezing gent with blubber lips and nose hair to die for, when suddenly he got shoved in the small of the back by a Greek. The Greek is a giant, wears a navy blue blazer over a white cotton shirt with English spread collar and no tie, his two top buttons undone to reveal a hairy chest, the gold links of a weighty gold chain apparently sewn into the looping black hairs. So this Greek barges Marty and Marty jolts forward, pushing out with his hands to steady himself and jabbing his proffered cards into the chest of the man to whom he's desirous of showing his trick. Being of a nervy and paranoid disposition having been bullied at school long ago the man now (over)reacts like he's being attacked and jerks his back and brings his arms up in a kind of cartoon rabbit-like bounce, fingers flopped down like a rabbit's paws, perpendicular to the floor, eyebrows arched, teeth and chin moving in opposite directions.

And as he springs into the air he knocks with his shoulder blade the head of a very short woman standing to his immediate rear who reacts by bringing her hand to her crown and crouching in a protective gesture but in the process of doing this causes her black **Network Network** record bag, which has been continually and irritatingly slipping from her shoulder all evening, to come swinging around. The bag – being full of all that corporate gumpf plus her laptop and mobile and a light cashmere sweater she's taken off because it was just too hot in here to continue to wear it – won't close, meaning that the Velcro® fastener's exposed meaning that as the bag swings around it has the opportunity to snag the hem of the wool yarn jacket worn by a fourth man standing nearby which it does. Said man, thinking someone's trying to get his attention, spins round and seeing the very short woman but not recognising her bends down to ask of her *Yes?* but in bending cracks the dome of his forehead – its dome-like quality enhanced by tight pink skin and fast thinning hair – against the skull of the guy who'd been waiting to see Marty's trick who having returned to earth after his cartoon-rabbit-like bounce has been unable to hold onto his balance and is now toppling backwards over and perhaps on to the Very Short Woman. Sensing these two men in her airspace and about to collide the VSW does what any sensible VSP[9] would do and springing out of her defensive crouch runs *forward*, black **Network Network** record bag trailing behind, thinking she'd better get well out the way.

But her running forward precipitates a whole other series of interactions too complex to describe but one of the many outcomes of which is the jolting of the arm of a waitress who has been twisting her way through the crowd seventy degrees clockwise and forward one foot, seventy degrees anti-clockwise and forward the other in the fashion of a wind-up child's toy travelling across a highly polished and no doubt extremely expensive adult-type surface while carrying aloft and trying to keep well clear of bags and bodies and beaks obstructing the way, a tray loaded with TBC[10] flutes filled to within half an inch of their rims with imitation champagne.

And now the tray, as trays will, teeters forward.

Meanwhile the Greek, who is continuing to push through the press of people only dimly aware of the complex of events his actions have conjured, catches sight first of the not unattractive waitress and then her toppling tray. It takes only nanoseconds for his finely honed and superbly supported business brain to both register the flirtation opportunity and to perform the fractal analysis of several terabytes' worth of experiential information required to deem it worthy of a few moments of his valuable time. And so to action: unleashing the highly reflective white blocks of his feta-cheese smile the Greek instantly reflects down *underneath* the tray a quantum of the energy blazing forth from the design award striplights above just sufficient to neutralise the effect of the earth's gravitational pull, the result being that the tray teeters back, righting itself.

Cute move, but not cute enough: all the glasses are safe with the exception of one: the foremost and fullest, the prow of the tray. The Greek had neglected to factor in the flex of the metal and this is powerful enough to boost the flute upwards and outwards despite his somewhat miraculous intervention and now it heels over and flips in the air, passing over Marty's left shoulder and depositing its contents all down his front, his feathers, his cards and making the point – as if it needed to be made – that Marty's career has now plummeted so far and so fast as to create a kind of a vortex, a sort of bad-shit black hole that has the power to make real any potential disaster that happens along and which will continue to do so until such time as it can either be somehow deflected away or, which is more likely, it works itself up to such a furious pitch that it actually blows itself out. Which can happen. Though believe me it's not pleasant to live through or witness. Not at all fazed by his miscalculation, not, indeed, even noticing it, the Greek now executes a full body sleight, ducking under the tray and passing between waitress and magician even before Marty's had a chance to realise he's been covered in sparkling wine. By the time our progenitor has completed his move and straightened up on the other side of the Marty-tray archway the glass has vanished, lost on the floor, and the waitress, dazzled by another flash of that wonderful smile, has not even noticed it's gone. *Thank you*, she says to the Greek, all a-tremble to be in the ambit of power, which comment Marty can hardly believe but he's too busy worrying about how to salvage his Bees[11] from their sugary shower to do anything more and by the time he's worked out that they're totally fucked and let them fall to the floor to be trampled alongside the now broken flute, the

Greek has passed the waitress his card and suggested she call his office sometime Monday a.m. so they can fix up a time to go somewhere flash and expensive for lunch and, the deed done, the initial public offering so neatly made, he's moved on, five or six feet in the direction he originally intended to go from which distance his voice, bassy and powerful and inflected with an Onassis-like burr can be heard telling some poor supplicant with black curly locks and a start-up and an unmistakably fat lower jaw that he never touches *anything* unless it's global.

Out-alpha'd and with a look of fury locked on his face Marty pushed his way away from the scene and towards what he guessed were the toilets. As he moved towards the exit and the bodies began to thin out he passed one of the many white tableclothed tables that were serving as bars, one half of its surface occupied by ranks of green German beer bottles the other half by half-litres of sparkling mineral water whose original labels had been replaced with bright orange ones bearing the eye-wink hieroglyph of a major Internet search engine. To either side of the table two girls were standing – two good-looking girls, Marty noted, his sexual sonar still operating unperturbed despite everything else. Both of the girls sported knee-length leather coats and strappy high heels; neither one of them looked much like she wanted to be there; the one to the right vaguely resembled Darryl Hannah. Marty flashed her with what he hoped was on the way to being a grin and she flashed him back, which is to say that she opened her coat and exposed herself to him.

Shortly after his racing retinas had registered the undeniable reality of the girl's breasts, Marty's cortex broadcast the disappointing news that they were breasts, yes, but that they were snugly encased in a flesh-coloured Lycra® bikini bra the cups of which were decorated with the same eye-wink logos as on the bottles of mineral water. Below these, daubed across the girl's stomach in red body paint, was the brand name of the Internet search engine she was advertising: 'Excite'.

'Er . . . hi,' Marty managed, winching his eyes like injured climbers around the dangerous overhang of her torso and up to the relative safety of her face. Then he cocked a finger at her, working it out. 'Body-ad. Right?' Her mouth windowed open to reveal a toolbar of teeth so perfect you could have clicked on them.

'What you 'ere for then?' she said, London having long ago taken her h's and given her two ellipses of glass in exchange for her eyes. 'You another of these dot-commies?'

'No – no way. I'm the magician.'

'Ohhh – you're Mr Magic Man.' The girl closed her coat and was human again. She called to her friend, 'Hey, Stella, it's the magician.' Then back to Marty: 'We've heard about you.'

'Only good things I hope.'

'Just that you were coming, that's all. Gonna show us a trick then?'

Marty shook his head.

'No?' She arched back, pretend-affronted and fluttered doe-like lashes at him.

'Well, I would do, only some twat just went and knocked Asti all over my cards didn't he, which has pretty much done for them.'

'Haven't you got another pack?'

'Yeah, of course, but my hands are all sticky. I'll muck up them up if I don't wash them off first.'

'Oh.' She looked crestfallen, and Marty couldn't bear that. It just didn't go with the heavy make-up and long crimps of blonde hair.

'Tell you what princess, I'll make you a crown,' he said.

'This is real kids' stuff. I'll bet you haven't seen this for years.' He reached into one of his many pockets and retrieved three or four long thin balloons which, after seasoning the rubber with a few hefty snaps, he boosted into long lemon tubes with his breath then tied off and twisted into a sort of tiara, which he gravely and gently placed on the body-ad's head.

'Cool,' Stella cooed, 'make us one too!'

'Yeah, go on, make her one.' And Marty obliged, squeaking and squeezing her out a similar design but in blue.

Cheered by his run-in with the girls Marty strolled off to the Gents' with restored confidence. What had he been thinking, letting himself get intimidated like that? Despondent and dickless in the wake of Terri's departure and the collapse of the act[12] he'd set himself up to be bowled over by all these businessmen cruising each other in this cute little financial stand-and-fuck bar. To begin with the scene had come over all random: the strange language, the alcohol and testosterone haze had confused him.

But while he dried off his shirt front with paper towels and washed the sticky champagne from his hands Marty began to work out the game. Just as Magda had told him, the buttons were the key. Yellows like him were irrelevant, journos and body-ads and liggers, he could forget about them. It was all about the reds and the greens, those were the boys, the reds in the minority but holding the cards, the greens playing a let's-see-what-you're-made-of-and-then-if-you're-lucky-I-might-let-you-catch-me kiss-chase-type game.

For the reds: catch what you can but don't catch a turkey, a hooker, a scam. It wasn't a million miles, in fact, from the Magicians' Convention in Blackpool, or at least from Marty's memory of it as an undignified moshpit of touting and sales. Except here it was the English who seemed to be doing the selling, the freshly spanked ruddiness of their otherwise pale faces giving them a shocked, startled look that was easily distinguished from the smooth easy tan of the Americans who made up the majority of the red button wearers.

Fine, he was remembering how to do this, he wasn't beaten yet. Unzipping the cellophane from a fresh pack of Bees and taking a waterproof marker from his pocket, Marty locked himself into one of the cubicles, a man with a plan in the can.

A short while later he strode purposefully back into the room, and sashayed through the crowd, focused and alert. He'd travelled no more than a few steps when a woman with centre-parted dark hair and dark jowls hurried up to him and grabbed hold of his arm. 'Oh,' she said, the sound a hollow West London tone, 'are you the magician?'

'Er, yes. I am.' Marty eased back a little as the woman leaned into him, nodding and tucking strands of hair back behind her right ear.

'And you do the balloon tiaras?'

'That's right. I do.'

Gripping his arm more tightly the woman deepened her frown and pointed across the room to where the Darryl Hannah body-ad was standing, Marty's construction still perched on her head. 'Do you think you could make me one that's bigger than hers?'

He tried not to laugh in her face. 'Sure, sure,' he said, digging in his pockets. 'Oh dear, looks like I'm all out of balloons. I'm sorry.'

'Oh no!'

'No – no, wait a minute. Here, I have some.' And he pulled out a handful of mismatched rubber tubes in bright condom colours which he fashioned into an enormous and garish headpiece.

'There you go. How's that for you?'

'Oh – wonderful!' And with a disdainful 'Thank you' she sauntered away, the ridiculous hat bobbing like a skiff atop the shifting brown wavelets of hair that formed part of a meniscal surface which now stretched unruptured throughout the room and lapped at the walls like they were the sides of a swimming pool.

Marty threaded in and out of the knots of nattering people, jaws rattling like wind-driven pennants, deflecting a couple of magic requests and another balloon-hat hunter as he went. He was hunting for Magda and eventually he found her over by the entrance desk, which had been divested of its flyers and promotional materials and was covered with empty glasses and bottles in their stead. She was talking with a soft-spoken, blond, bespectacled American who was dressed, unlike every other male Marty recalled seeing that evening, in corduroy and suede. Figuring that not being in a suit the man probably wasn't all that important Marty strode up to the two of them and, cleaving to his new if-you-can't-beat-'em-join-'em attitude, butted right in.

'Magda.'

'Marty.' Magda folded her arms and looked at him, not pleased by the intrusion but letting it ride. The blond man tilted his head and looked on with faint amusement, waiting to see what would happen. 'So how's it been going.'

'Hmm. Mixed. Difficult to get people's attention. So I thought since you're paying me for this I should at least make sure you get your money's worth.'

'How's that then?'

'I'd like you to let me show you something.'

'I told you I don't go in much for tricks.'

'Well that's all right then, because I don't do tricks. I create illusions.'

'What's the difference?'

'That's what I'm going to show you. Here.' He held out the pack of red Bees. 'Take these.'

'Not just one of them?'

'No, take them all. Take the pack.' Reluctantly she did so and Marty immediately turned and started to usher people back, creating a small arena in which he could move. 'Make space for Magda here, make space for Magda,' he said loudly, making sure people knew the woman's name, and while he was doing this he called out instructions, asking her to examine the pack, to make sure it was perfectly ordinary, to be certain that there was nothing unusual about it.

Embarrassed to find herself suddenly the centre of attention like this Magda fingered the cards nervously as if she was afraid they might bite. 'This is why I hate magic,' she murmured to her suede friend.

But now Marty came over and seeing that she wasn't relaxed with the cards he took them from her. Almost exactly her height, maybe half an inch taller, he stood and blocked the crowd from her view and talked into her eyes: 'OK, here we see a perfectly normal deck of cards.' He fanned them slowly and openly, let her see them, then handed them back. 'Here's what I'd like you to do. Check the pack again and then give it back to me.' This she did, properly this time. 'OK, is there anything at all weird about it that you can see?' A hesitant no. 'Good. So, now I'm going to ask you to pick a card.' He fanned the cards out and Magda chose one, held it up against her left breast but didn't look at it. 'Now, what I'd like you to do is turn around to the table here and sign your name across the face of it with this.' He produced the black magic marker from his breast pocket. 'Show it to a couple of people if you like, but don't let me see it, and when you're done slip it back in the pack.' She turned around and he turned around too, stood head–bowed–hands–clasped–at–his–groin while she did as she'd been told.

'OK. All finished?' She hadn't quite, but now she recapped the marker, blew on the card to dry off the ink, then daintily pushed it back into the middle of the pack which she then presented to Marty. 'That was quick,' he said, taking it.

'Was it?'

'Yes. Considering you did rather more than I asked.'

Magda frowned. 'What? No I didn't.'

'I told you to write your name on just one of the cards didn't I?'

'Yes, and that's what I did.'

'No you didn't,' he said smiling. 'You wrote your name on all of them.' And he threw the pack high into the air where it exploded apart, the cards not really separating until they began their descent at which point they shot away from each other on slices of air and twizzled and twirled back down to the ground like sycamore leaves, each one with the name 'Magda' scrawled on it in black. 'I told you you'd written on all of them,' Marty said, grabbing at a few of them and holding them up for everyone to see. 'And this is your handwriting, right?' Laughing, amazed, Magda nodded. 'But you say you're positive you only wrote your name on one of them? Which one was it?'

'Erm, the six of diamonds.'

'The six of diamonds. You're absolutely sure?'

'Uh huh.'

'OK well, then look up there. See if you can spot anything familiar.' Magda did – along with half the rest of the room, everyone within earshot now craning to see – and following the line of Marty's outstretched index finger she let out an involuntary gasp. There it was, her playing card, the six of diamonds, her name scrawled across it, lodged into a metal seam in one of the design award striplights that ran in bright lines over their heads.

Astonished applause.

Taking Magda's hands Marty led her forward and now she was finding coins in her hands – T'ang dynasty coins, round with a square hole in the middle and with dark patination – that definitely hadn't been there before or not in her hands when they should have been and then her watch had disappeared and now it had showed up again but on her other wrist and there was evidently a whole deck of cards down her blouse because Marty kept pulling them out from round the back of her neck when she wasn't looking which was steadily driving her nuts.

At the point when she looked most dazzled and confused he put it to her that she was still trying to work out how her name got on to all the cards in his first routine. She nodded, by now going along with anything he said.

'That was weird, wasn't it? Did you think that was weird?' She nodded again. 'Really? Did you really think that was weird?' The words were spoken, one or two of the audience noticed, with a slight iron edge, as if they were alloyed with some kind of threat. Magda didn't nod again, just gazed at Marty, suddenly a tiny bit frightened by this man. 'I'll show you something really weird. Want to see?'

'Yes,' someone in the audience said, then more voices: 'Yes! Do it! Yes!'

Marty looked round his arena then back to Magda. 'OK, here, please, clear me a space to the door.' Doing an exaggerated breaststroke with his hands he parted the people back so that they were behind him, a semi-circle with the room's entrance at its heart and Magda directly ahead – or rather, behind: because now he turned his back to her so he was facing the doorway. The crowd fell silent, exuded an anticipation so quiet and keen that the buzz of conversation in the rest of the room didn't seem like sound at all but like some other – irrelevant – kind of sensation.

He lowered his head again and counted to five before giving them what they were waiting for: holding his arms straight out as if they were wings, hands taut and dipped like ailerons at the ends, his back furrowed and lined with a peculiar geometry of tension, he rose six or seven inches from the floor and hovered in the air.

A second or two later he floated back down, turned and, feet on the ground, bowed to the semi-circle of faces, mouths open as balconies. *Bet you can't do that over the Internet*, he thought to himself as his eyes scanned across them. But somehow – and whether it was because the curved wall of bodies acted as some kind of psychic reflector or whether it was that in spite of this brief bout of success he remained filled with self-doubt – the thought came right back to him: *Bet you we can.*

NOTES

1 Unlikely.
2 At http://mdcm.arts.unsw.edu.au/students98/HammonA/innovate/lights.html it is recorded that: 'Cricket in "prime time" television had not been a viable financial decision before the invention of one-day matches. However, the new world series one-day matches allowed cricket to become a television commodity. To bring it into prime time high-powered flood lights would need to be installed at the Sydney Cricket Ground at the cost of one million dollars. Kerry Packer agreed to pay for the lights and in the 1978–79 cricket season the ground came to life at night for the first time with a capacity crowd of 50,000 people.' Kerry Packer is the richest man in Australia. His personal wealth is estimated in the billions of dollars. Kerry's young life was lonely and disrupted. He owns 60 per cent of all magazines sold in Australia including *Belle*, *She*, *Wheels*, *HQ*, *Bulletin*, *Woman's Day* and the *Woman's Weekly*. www.abc.net.au says about Kerry Packer

that: 'However difficult their relationship, Kerry admired his father and from the start he was a lot like him. "I mean I got a lot of hidings because that's the sort of person I was and the sort of person he was." [He is reported to have said].

3 Professor Bernard Quatermass, a fictional rocket scientist originally created for British television by writer Nigel Kneale. A kind of ur-*X-Files* investigator of weird extraterrestrially-linked occurrences, Quatermass appeared in four series (*The Quatermass Experiment* (1953), *Quatermass II* (1955), *Quatermass and the Pit* (1958) and then, much later, and in colour, *Quatermass* (1979)) and three films (*The Quatermass Xperiment* (1955) (US title: *The Creeping Unknown*), *Quatermass II* (US title: *Enemy from Space*), *Quatermass and the Pit* (US title: *Five Million Years to Earth*)) and various radio and theatrical releases. The plot of the 1979 series, which stars John Mills and brims with late-twentieth-century apocalyptic apprehension, concerns the rise of a cultish religion – the Planet People – whose members gather in stone age circles and sports stadiums where they are destroyed in giant conflagrations. Quatermass soon detects the operations of an alien agency: 'My evaluation, Chuck – here it is. Forget about trying to get through to it. The ripe crop can't appeal to the reaper. I think this is the gathering time. The human race is being harvested.'

4 Martin Dawes, aka Martin Mystery, a stage illusionist and the hero of this tale which is itself an extract from what will one day be an entire book which means you're just going to have to put up with the lack of available back-story and put up with a few (possibly quite irritating and unhelpful) footnotes. I'm trying to work it so that you still get a reasonably gratifying dramatic effect and some socio-psychological insight, so bear with me here.

5 And painstakingly labelled.

6 www.turfgrailauction.net

7 Source: www.calgarycoin.com/chinasal.htm

8 A very interesting piece of clothing, the suit, in that it is curiously well designed for deception. Marty's had extra pockets sewn into the lining which were primed with cards and fekes and scarves and gimmicks and coins; he had a wire attached to his right elbow and running from there across the middle of his back and down his left sleeve to a clip on his cuff to which he could attach objects in order to vanish them; and he had a button sewn over one of the buttonholes on the placket rather than onto the shirting material behind it giving the shirtfront the appearance of being completely done up when in fact it lay sufficiently open for him to slip his hand in and out of it under the convenient cover of his soberly coloured but well-kippered tie. And that wasn't the half of it: Marty's suit had all sorts of shit going on. And the businessmen and women at Network Network had deceptive suits too, suits that gave little away regarding their status or personality or intention. Plus business cards could be conjured from them and digital assistants secreted in them and bottomless wallets kept in them, wallets linked to credit lines that ran right round the whole world. The suit is an extremely handy invention. It's no accident that they're worn by playing cards, even.

9 Very Short Person.

10 Tall But Cheap.

11 'Bee'® Diamond Back Casino Quality Club Special Playing Cards, Standard Size no. 92 Cambric Finish, the US Playing Card Co., Cincinnati, Ohio 45212, USA.

12 You don't need to know all the details, but believe me, it was really fucked up. And, what made it worse, it was all Marty's own fault. Put it this way: if after years of struggling on the seaside town cabaret circuit you've developed a terrifyingly good Vegas-quality show that has every chance of making you famous and rich but which happens to be based on having available the crucial and also unbelievably rare resource of two capable and attractive female assistants who look pretty much identical to one other and, in addition, you happen to be in a long-term relationship with one of them, then it isn't the most awesomely great idea you've ever had to start screwing the other one behind her back. It really isn't. Trust me on this.

muriel the magnificent

marilyn jaye lewis

When Muriel Bing was seven years old, in the course of a single Saturday afternoon, something happened that shifted the topography of her secret inner landscape forever. The day had started out harmless enough: an afternoon in late spring, close to the end of her second grade school year. In high spirits, she and Tommy Decker, the little brown-haired boy whose family's backyard adjoined hers, played together on her brightly coloured swing set. Higher and higher they swung, until Tommy wagered with Muriel: 'I'll bet you can't swing as high as me and jump when I yell "jump."'

'Yes, I can.'

'No, you can't.'

'I can, too!'

'OK,' hollered Tommy, the bet underway. 'The loser has to do whatever the winner says,' he shouted.

Muriel's sturdy legs pumped determinedly as her swing kept pace with Tommy's. Her long auburn braids flying out behind her on the upswing, then smacking lightly against her shoulders as she swung down and back. Over and over, higher she climbed, until Muriel had reached an exhilarating height.

'Now!' Tommy Decker cried, 'Jump!' as he flung himself free of the swing, soaring several feet out over the small backyard, landing in a tumble on the cool green grass, his empty swing chink-chinking to a sudden halt behind him.

Muriel, however, hadn't jumped. The sheer height she'd reached had been too daunting. When it came time for her fingers to release their tight grip on the chains of her high-flying swing, when she'd heard Tommy's voice suddenly shout 'jump' and her eyes had taken in the full scope of empty sky she'd be forced to sail out into and the hard expanse of ground beneath her, Muriel's bowels had clenched tight. She'd been too timid to jump.

Her feet dragged the swing to a stumbling stop. Tommy had already leapt to his feet and come running over, his eyes bright with triumph. 'You lose, Muriel,' he cried gleefully. 'I won. Now you have to do whatever I say!'

Tommy Decker was only one Decker from a veritable sea of Decker boys. Unlike the Bing family, the Deckers were Catholics who'd had nothing but sons. In the Decker house, there were always boys as far as Tommy's blue eyes could see: in his bedroom at night there were boys, in the morning at the kitchen table, or in front of the television set when he came home from school – nothing but brothers. Tommy was drawn to Muriel Bing because she was an only child; a sweet, kind and smart little girl, but more because she was just that: a girl.

'Now you have to come behind the garage with me,' Tommy announced.

Bravely, Muriel slid off her swing, knowing Tommy was

fully capable of making her do something awful. Once, the summer before, he'd plucked a carrot from her father's vegetable patch, a carrot no bigger than Muriel's pinkie, and had forced her to eat it, then and there, dirt and all. Another time, he'd made her shuck unripe peas from their pods and eat them raw, giving her a churning stomach ache. Worse yet, Mr Bing didn't like Muriel and Tommy making a mess of his garden. He'd said as much, in no uncertain terms, on several occasions.

With a cursory glance back towards her house to see if anyone was watching her, Muriel followed Tommy behind the garage to her father's vegetable patch, her childish curiosity outweighing her reluctance, as usual.

When the pair were safely ensconced between the row of hedges that lined the edge of the Decker yard, and the garden at the back of the Bing's garage, Tommy told Muriel, 'Pull down your pants.'

She was stunned. 'What?'

'I said, pull down your pants. You have to do it because you have to do anything I say.'

Muriel stared at Tommy uneasily and did nothing.

'Come on,' he persisted. 'Do it. I just want to see.'

In an unfamiliar mix of interest and fear, Muriel did what Tommy wanted. She unzipped her pants, tugging them down just a little bit.

'Those, too,' he insisted, pointing at her cotton underpants.

Muriel hesitated, 'No,' she refused quietly.

'Come on, Muriel, just for one second. Just until I count "one Mississippi" then you can pull them back up, OK?'

Muriel considered Tommy's offer, her cautious hesitation giving way to a growing intrigue. She liked the way it felt, Tommy staring at her underpants in earnest, she suddenly felt eager to show him what she knew the sisterless boy wanted to see. When she tugged her underpants down just enough to reveal her smooth mound and the pouting cleft at its base, the expression of wonder on Tommy's face made Muriel almost burst with pride.

He seemed so entranced by the sight of the strange nakedness that peeked out from between Muriel's legs, that Tommy forgot to count 'one Mississippi'. In fact, the two of them stood transfixed by the magnetic pull between them for several uninterrupted moments. When they finally were interrupted, though, it happened in the worst possible way: an unsuspecting Mr Bing rounded the corner of the garage.

'Muriel Bing, what do you think you're doing?' he sputtered, as Tommy Decker took off running for the relative safety of his own backyard.

Muriel's seven-year-old mind knew instinctively that she had no satisfactory answer to her father's question. 'I'm not doing anything,' she replied weakly, hastily tugging her pants and underpants back up around her waist.

No sooner were her clothes in order, than Muriel's father grabbed her abruptly by her little arm, escorting her up the yard to the house, in through the kitchen door, down the hallway and into her room.

'You know better than that, Muriel!' he practically shouted. 'What was going on out there?'

'Nothing,' she replied timidly, realising in a panic that the most dreaded punishment was befalling her. The pants and underpants she'd pulled up to her waist only moments before, were coming down again, quickly, and her father was pulling her over his knee.

'Daddy don't!' she cried feebly, as the spanking got underway. But there was no stopping Mr Bing. The smacks rained down on Muriel's bare bottom furiously, as he unleashed a litany of reasons why what Muriel had done was bad, bad, bad.

This degree of anger was uncommon in Muriel's father and she was unnerved by it. It wasn't so much the severity of the spanking that wounded her, she was pierced to the core by the sound of his words.

'I'm thoroughly ashamed of you, Muriel,' he declared, as he unceremoniously yanked her from his lap when the spanking was over. 'What made you do a dirty thing like that?'

He stood her helplessly in front of him while he continued to lecture her harshly about the wickedness of her immodesty. Throughout the entire scolding, poor Muriel's pants remained around her knees. The little mound whose unveiling had so recently filled her with pride was uncomfortably on display and now serving as the obtrusive source of her newfound shame.

At thirty-seven, Muriel Bing was as bony as a little bird; her modest breasts, her slender waist and narrow hips, always concealed beneath the finely tailored yet conservative dress suits she wore every day to the law office, where she specialised in real estate. She wore simple silk blouses, buttoned to her throat, and durable navy pumps on her small, sturdy feet.

Muriel lived alone in a well-appointed apartment in midtown Manhattan and almost never dated. She was no longer a virgin – she wasn't as pathetic as that – still she had become an expert at repressing any unseemly urges to satisfy her drives; not just the biological urges, but the appetites of her very senses. She ate plain, unseasoned foods cooked at home, almost never drank alcohol, not even wine, and her spotless apartment held no aromas of daily living except for the distinct odour of anti-bacterial cleanser.

The law firm where Muriel had been employed since she'd

passed the New York Bar eleven years earlier, was a prestigious, well-equipped, state-of-the-art office on Fifty-seventh Street, just off Fifth Avenue. Each employee's desk had the latest model computer. They were on-line, networked, firewalled, intranetted, and secure on their dedicated server. No software program could be accessed without a valid password. Outside meetings took place in the form of on-line video conferencing. Office e-mail was monitored and noted in extensive personnel files.

At home, Muriel's fondness for technology lagged far behind the firm's. Until recently, she'd had a reasonably respectable computer, a modest printer, and the only software she'd deemed necessary was for word processing, which she did a great deal of late into the night. But gradually, the outside world had caught up with her. Only days before, Muriel had upgraded to a high-speed unit with all the frills, even free Internet access – a needless temptation Muriel had previously withstood. The only e-mail correspondence she engaged in was work-related and so it stayed on the computer at the firm. Still, acquiescing to the advancement of technology into the privacy of her own home, Muriel logged on to the Internet and set up her first personal account.

Her free Internet access included the option of maintaining a small homepage. At first, she dismissed it out of hand, having no reason to display any part of her private life on something as public as a homepage. Yet, after some consideration, it occurred to Muriel that it could help advertise the law firm. She set about learning the software to upload a humble web page devoted to her occupation as real estate lawyer, listing her experience and the contact information of the office and nothing more.

It was quite late on a Friday evening when Muriel uploaded the newly created page to her allotted space on the server.

After she'd been alerted that the files had been sent successfully, she typed the URL of her homepage into the address locator and waited for her handiwork to load into her browser.

It seemed like she waited a long time. The simple page was loading very slowly, too slowly, as if it were laden with images or those space-consuming enhancements that frequently tried her patience on other websites.

Muriel walked away from her computer and went to the kitchen to peruse the contents of her refrigerator. While the browser continued to load her homepage, Muriel reached for an apple and a diet ginger ale.

In a particularly hot pink hue, the words 'Muriel the Magnificent' blinked on and off incessantly on a pitch black background.

Muriel stared at her monitor, first in confusion, then in complete indignation, as jpeg after jpeg of a thoroughly naked woman, in all sorts of obscene poses, assaulted her vision. Clearly she had mistyped the URL. She checked the address in her browser against the address she'd been given by her service provider. It was the same.

Slightly panic-stricken, since Muriel had no ready faculties for processing lascivious feelings and the lewd images veritably bursting before her eyes in a riotous array of digitised colours aroused something primitive in her, Muriel hurriedly closed the page and prepared to resend her files to the server.

Carefully, she re-entered the ftp information, being especially observant about entering her user name and password. When the files had again been successfully sent, Muriel re-typed her URL into the browser and loaded her homepage.

This time, in only a few seconds, the page had reloaded. 'Muriel the Magnificent' flashed merrily on the screen.

A decidedly buxom, fleshy, full-figured woman in a myriad of wide-spread poses, of bending-over poses, or poses where her substantial boobs were squeezed together tightly – these assorted sordid images greeted Muriel again.

It must have something to do with our names being similar, Muriel decided. Perhaps there was a mix-up on the server because of that.

Yet there was something oddly familiar about this other Muriel, with the teased auburn hair, the heavily made-up eyes and glossy lips, wearing spiked heels and little else. Muriel scrolled down the page to the final photo: the voluptuous woman was bending over, lustily grabbing a sizable portion of her rear end in each of her well-manicured hands. Across the photo, just below a protuberance of shaved labial lips, the words 'let's make contact' flashed annoyingly, while pointing to an e-mail link.

Muriel clicked on it, only to be more horrified when the preprogrammed e-mail address turned out to be her own.

Should I? she wondered. If I do, what will I say?

Muriel didn't want to make actual contact with this other Muriel, she only wanted to know where the e-mail would ultimately arrive.

She typed the words 'testing 1,2,3' into the body of the e-mail and clicked 'send', only to receive an e-mail several moments later notifying her that her e-mail was undeliverable as addressed.

'But how could I have received *this* e-mail if my e-mail address is incorrect?' Muriel demanded of her monitor in vain.

Anxiously, she dialled the number for twenty-four-hour tech support. It was late enough on a Friday night that she wasn't on hold for more than ten minutes. After having explained her peculiar problem to the tech support person, he offered to go to her homepage himself.

'There's some information about a law firm,' he said. 'And some résumé or something for a real estate lawyer – is that what you're getting?'

'That's what I'd *like* to be getting,' Muriel whined incredulously, 'but what I'm getting is pornography!'

The tech support person was silent for a moment. 'I don't know what to tell you, ma'am. There's nothing pornographic about what I'm seeing here.'

As he read aloud, verbatim, the brief description of the law firm and work experiences Muriel had composed, Muriel was dumbfounded.

'Well, what am I supposed to do about all this pornography?!' By now, Muriel was nearly hysterical. 'I want to see my homepage. What if other people see these disgusting photos and assume it's me? That I'm *that* Muriel?'

Another uneasy silence came from the other end of the line. 'I don't know, ma'am. I don't know what to tell you. Perhaps you should try to contact this other woman.'

'But her e-mail address is the same as mine – and it doesn't work!'

'What do you mean, it doesn't work?'

'I tried sending an e-mail to her, but it came back as undeliverable.'

'Well, maybe it's a dead website. It happens all the time.'

'No, you don't understand. It's *my* e-mail address. It works just fine.'

'I'm sorry, ma'am, I really don't know what else to tell you.' The tone of the young man's voice was now edging into patronising impatience.

Muriel slammed down the phone. 'You useless piece of

. . .' Then she fumed silently for several minutes over her first personal encounter with on-line tech support.

Muriel stood rigidly in the hot shower, letting the water blast down on the back of her neck, hoping it would soothe her agitated brain. Her eyes closed in defeat and she sighed.

I must have sounded completely insane, she realised, as her conversation with tech support reverberated in her head. What the hell is going on with that computer?

In a burst of rage, Muriel had shut down the machine, overwhelmed by the extent of her unmitigated confusion. She'd elected to give it up for the time being and prepare for bed. Her anger had followed her from room to room, as she'd switched off the lights, secured the apartment, stripped off her clothes and gotten into the shower, but she was determined not to let the anxiety follow her into bed. Muriel was prone to bouts of insomnia, a state of mind she dreaded.

In a white cotton nightgown and a pair of equally white cotton panties, Muriel slid into bed. The sheets felt cool against her skin. Muriel felt noticeably calmer. With luck, she would sleep.

At 3 a.m., Muriel's eyes opened. She stared blankly into the darkness and the first thought that commanded her attention was this: why were so many grown women determined to look like parodies of little girls?

Muriel couldn't help thinking about that other Muriel; Muriel the Magnificent, with her womanly figure and shaved labia. It was absurd looking.

Muriel snuggled more comfortably into her pillow. Her hand absently playing at the stray strands of pubic hairs that poked through the leg bands of her cotton panties. As far back as she could remember, Muriel had had a generous thatch of dark brown pubic hair. She couldn't recall a time when she didn't have it.

Wait, she thought, remembering the Tommy Decker incident. But in an instant her mind skittered clear of the discomforting memory, and soon enough Muriel Bing was sound asleep.

On Saturday morning, Muriel slept in. It was uncharacteristic of her to even remotely surrender to the lure of sloth. However, her bed felt so comfortable, a cool breeze blowing in gently over the blankets, and a bird warbling merrily on a sill across the airshaft, that Muriel was lulled back to sleep before she knew it. When she finally roused herself, it was nearly noon.

She sat lazily on the edge of her bed, looking down at her loose-fitting nightgown, her skinny legs. The images of the other Muriel leapt to her consciousness.

How would it feel to be so fleshy? she wondered. What would it be like to always have one's boobs in one's peripheral vision?

She tugged open the top of her nightgown and stared down at her modest breasts. She tried squeezing them together in an unsuccessful attempt to create cleavage. She eyed her flat stomach, too. Then she noticed with interest how her cotton panties covered her slightly protruding mound so smoothly. She wondered what she looked like down there, under all that hair. And this time when her mind served her up the memory of Tommy Decker, she let it linger there.

'What's with me today?' she muttered, feeling her hormones beginning to stir. Then she realised she was thinking about her computer, about how easily salacious images could be summoned from it. Why not? she thought.

She didn't even put on the coffee pot. She went straight

to her computer and booted it up. She got on-line and went directly to the images of Muriel the Magnificent. This time, she studied the images intently. She found herself especially intrigued by the photos of Muriel spread wide, where every labial fold was blatantly revealed. There was one shot in particular where Muriel held her spread knees up to her breasts. Her tummy bulged enticingly in this position and then the smooth-shaven vulva seemed somehow more garish, even the anus was visible.

'There's something really filthy looking about that,' Muriel said quietly, realising that her pulse had quickened.

As she studied the rest of the images, she fondled her nipples through the material of her nightgown. Then she discovered that the crotch of her panties was soaking.

'Jesus,' she sighed. 'Enough!' She closed down the browser and got off-line.

Muriel was too distracted now to make coffee. She decided to go out for a cup instead. She got dressed and went down to the corner cafe. It was a beautiful sunny day, with a hint of spring in the air. Muriel surprised herself again, this time by ordering a double latte and, at the last minute, adding a cream filled, chocolate-iced doughnut to her order! She couldn't remember the last time she'd tasted a doughnut and now, suddenly, she craved it.

Muriel sat down at a small table in front of the window and watched the people on the street walk briskly past. As her teeth sunk into the gooey pastry, her mouth filling with the rich flavour of fats and sugar, Muriel barely suppressed an audible moan. It was delicious, it was the best doughnut Muriel could remember tasting. She made a mental note to have breakfast out more often.

She shifted in the seat and caught the scent of herself. She was still wet between her legs. As she drank her double latte, her mind filled with pictures of the other Muriel's shaved pussy and spread legs. She watched the girls walking past the window and wondered which ones had shaved pussies concealed beneath their jeans or under their dresses.

This is crazy, she thought. Still, she loved the feeling of surrendering to the lusty pictures filling her head. She felt hypnotised. Before she knew it, her mind was made up. She tossed her empty cup into the trash can and headed home to her apartment, to her bathroom, where she was determined she would shave herself.

Muriel stripped naked and sat on the edge of her tub. By now, she was so aroused between her legs that even something as light as shaving foam felt incredibly exciting. The steel blade, repeatedly stroking her swollen mound, caressing it, revealing more and more of her increasing nakedness, drove Muriel to ecstasy. When she washed away the final residue and admired her handiwork in the mirror, she was thoroughly enchanted with the new vision of herself. She remained naked the rest of the afternoon, studying herself admiringly in the mirror, adopting many provocative poses, masturbating herself to orgasm seven times. When she had finally exhausted herself, she collapsed on her bed and stared up at the ceiling.

What good is it to look so inviting if there's no one around to appreciate it? she wondered, coming peculiarly close to admitting that she wanted a lover.

Suddenly, Muriel realised she was starving. She pulled on some clothes and headed outside for dinner. She chose a local Italian trattoria, an establishment that had been in her neighbourhood for years but which she had never once stepped inside.

It was early enough on a Saturday evening that the host was able to accommodate a single diner with no reservation without much difficulty. He showed Muriel to a small table in the corner. The restaurant was dimly lit, a single votive flickering seductively on every table, Frank Sinatra crooning out from the speakers.

'Something to drink before dinner?'

Muriel looked up at the waiter as if in a trance. The warm timbre of his masculine voice had melted into her ears. His dark eyes were beautiful, his shoulder-length black hair pulled into a neat ponytail behind his head. Suddenly Muriel wanted wine. Red wine. The best vintage. Maybe even a whole bottle if they wouldn't serve her the best vintage by the glass. She'd drink what she wanted, without concerning herself about being wasteful for a change.

When the waiter returned with the bottle of wine, Muriel noticed for the first time that he was probably much younger than she, but she didn't care. She remained entranced. As he poured her a glass to taste, he seemed to eye her seductively, making Muriel wonder if he could smell her from where he was standing. She found herself hoping he could. Soon a busboy hovered around her with a basket of bread, then another came near to pour her some water. A different waiter came by for her food order, and, later, the host was back to see how she was enjoying her meal.

She felt flushed. Never had Muriel been surrounded by so many attentive and attractive men. She returned to her apartment reeling from the thought of so much seemingly available masculinity in the world.

She couldn't resist booting up the computer one more time.

The page was back to loading slowly, but within a few moments, 'Muriel the Magnificent' was flashing on her monitor once again. Only this time, the selection of jpegs had changed. Muriel felt slightly alarmed: this was an active web page after all. Who was this other Muriel whom she was so voyeuristically enjoying?

She studied the new photos with acute interest, for now Muriel the Magnificent was no longer solo, she had a male companion – one who was remarkably endowed. In one photo, the companion stood behind her, clutching two good-sized handfuls of Muriel's boobs, while his stiff erection poked up between Muriel's spread legs. The images became more provocative as the page continued to load. In fact, in one photo after another, a purely pornographic tryst between two rambunctious lovers was thoroughly exposed.

Oh God, this is what I *want*, thought Muriel deliriously, as picture after picture assailed her eyes and her fingers worked tirelessly down under her skirt.

The male companion looked satisfyingly familiar – much like the waiter at the trattoria who had poured Muriel her wine, who had kept her glass enticingly filled throughout the course of her incredible meal. The same waiter who had eyed her knowingly, as if he were ready to scoop up a bit of her smell with his fingers; as if he were aching to taste her.

In one photo, the lovers were passionately entwined, their copulating genitals readily captured by the camera's lens. Another pose illustrated why Muriel was so magnificent: her lover's substantial shaft filled her mouth to capacity. There were still more shots of the lovers performing intercourse in every position. The final parting shot, of course, was a daunting close-up of Muriel's snug anus stretching to accommodate every thick inch of her companion's probing tool.

When the final image loaded in front of Muriel's eager eyes, she succumbed to another orgasm. Her eighth for the day – by far, a personal record. Muriel forced herself to shut down the computer and find her way to a hot shower. But what a glorious day it had been.

Later that night, Muriel couldn't sleep. She felt too keyed-up. Finally she gave up any pretence of drifting off to slumber. She got out of bed and went in to the dark living room. Clad in her white cotton nightgown and white cotton panties, she sat on her open window sill in the cool night air and watched an occasional taxi zip across the nearly deserted street below. From where she sat, she could see the trattoria closing. It was nearing 3 a.m. The neon sign blinked off suddenly and then Muriel watched several of the employees exit the restaurant together. Most of them walked away from her building, but one walked in her direction. Muriel's heart fluttered when she realised it was her favourite waiter.

'Hey,' she called out quietly, surprising even herself. 'Hey, you – hi!'

The young man looked around curiously.

'Up here.'

'Hello,' he called back to her, seeming to recognise her immediately, even though it was dark. 'What are you doing up? It's so late.'

'I couldn't sleep.'

He crossed the street and was now standing on the sidewalk three storeys below her window. 'I was just thinking about you,' he said, reaching into his bag and retrieving a half-empty re-corked bottle of red wine. 'I swiped this from your table,' he called up to her, showing her the bottle. 'I didn't want it to go to waste, but it's too good to drink alone, no?'

Muriel's heart raced. She couldn't believe it was happening. Her mouth opened and words came out of their own volition. 'Why don't you come up? I'll buzz you in,' she offered.

'OK,' he replied, seemingly unfazed by her ready acquiescence.

He must do this a lot, she thought, as she buzzed open the front door of her building and listened to his feet hurrying up the steps in the quiet stairwell. He sounded eager, perhaps taking the stairs two at a time. When he reached her floor, she stood in her open doorway waiting for him.

He eyed her thin cotton nightgown, her skinny legs and bare feet. He smiled, a little out of breath. 'What's your name?' he asked. 'I'm Antonio – from Canarsie.'

'I'm Muriel,' she replied.

'Well, Muriel,' he said, lifting the bottle once again from his satchel, 'do you have any glasses or do you drink from the bottle?'

Antonio and Muriel sat together on the couch in her dark living room, a faint light shining in from the kitchen doorway. They were only on their first glass of the leftover wine when Antonio set his glass down on the coffee table and reached for Muriel's, setting hers aside, too. He slid closer to her on the couch.

'You know, you look really inviting in that little nightie,' he began quietly. 'Do you ask a lot of guys up here in the middle of the night?'

'No,' Muriel replied nervously. 'I haven't even been on a date in I don't know how long.'

'Well, that would explain it.'

'Explain what?'

'You have this air about you, you know? Like you're really ready for it. Am I right?' he asked, his hand sliding up her thigh, under her nightgown, his fingertips brushing along the leg band of her panties.

Muriel caught her breath and didn't reply.

'What's the matter, Muriel?' Antonio taunted her, his warm hand slipping down between her loosely parted legs, then fleetingly across the crotch of her panties.

'Nothing,' she managed to answer.

'Are you sure?' he persisted, his other hand reaching for the back of her head now.

'I'm sure,' she said, her mouth finding his in the darkness and locking on.

He tasted like wine, cigarettes, coffee. He smelled of all the robust flavours of every Italian meal he'd been in the vicinity of at the trattoria. It was a heady mixture, an unfamiliar but not unpleasant scent for Muriel, because above all, he smelled like a man, and her entire body responded.

Antonio was all over her, his hands everywhere: under her nightie to fondle her nipples, then running through her hair as they continued to kiss, then down along her thighs, then grabbing her arse. Finally he tugged her panties down and discovered the smoothness of her shaved mound with his fingers.

'One of those naughty little girls, huh?' he whispered. 'For some reason that doesn't surprise me.'

In a mere moment, he had her panties completely off, her thighs spread and his face buried between her legs. It wasn't the first time Muriel had felt a man's mouth on her down there, but it was the first time she let herself enjoy it. It was exhilarating. Antonio's tongue explored the swelling folds of her inner lips, then found her clitoris and lingered there while his fingers pushed into the sopping wetness of her hole.

She followed his lead effortlessly, her eager body assuming whatever position Antonio favoured with only the slightest word of encouragement from him; positions she'd shied away from in the past because she'd feared the lewd postures too immodest, perhaps even degrading. But now, as Antonio mounted her from behind, her knees pulled up under herself while she gripped the arm of the couch and felt the plunging fulness of his erection filling her, she found herself suddenly grateful for the happy, inexplicable accident of Muriel the Magnificent and her lurid web page.

Remembering some of the images that had filled her head earlier, Muriel found herself taking the initiative now. She straddled Antonio, impaled herself upon his substantial shaft. She explored the length of him with her mouth, sucked his erection ardently. Then squatted over his face and let his tongue go at her again.

Finally she invited him into her bed, where it was easier for him to pound into her relentlessly from behind, his thumb sliding into her anus while his thick cock tormented her. Muriel couldn't remember ever having felt so filled up, so completely appreciated, so thoroughly aroused. She took the force of his pounding as if she were born to be the receptacle of his fucking, his endless fucking, she never wanted to stop fucking . . .

Muriel and Antonio lay entwined on Muriel's bed, the Sunday morning dawn inching imperceptibly closer outside her bedroom window.

'You're too skinny, you know,' Antonio teased her quietly. 'We're going to have to fatten you up. Put some meat on your bones.'

It sounded to Muriel as if he had intentions of sticking around, that he didn't consider them a one-night stand. She wondered how she felt about that.

'You should come by the restaurant more often. I can slip you some food on the house,' he assured her, seeming to think she was thin because she couldn't afford to eat. 'What do you do, anyway, Muriel? Where do you work?'

'I'm a lawyer,' she replied.

'A lawyer? Then forget about it – you're taking *me* to dinner.'

Antonio drifted to sleep while holding Muriel in his arms.

As soon as the sun poked through her curtains, Muriel's eyes opened. Antonio was sound asleep. She was relieved that he hadn't left her. Still it concerned her that she was plunging herself headlong into such unfamiliar territory. Muriel had never done anything so rash in her life. And it had all started with that web page. Her whole life had changed simply because she'd gotten on-line.

Then her curiosity got the best of her. It was uncanny how Muriel the Magnificent's experiences were only one step ahead of her own. She studied Antonio while he slept, then decided to slip out of bed and consult her computer: what erotic pleasures did Sunday have in store? Would they include him? Was the other Muriel still cavorting wantonly with the other Antonio?

The computer booted up and Muriel got on-line. The web page loaded slowly, an indication that the jpegs had probably changed. Muriel's pulse quickened; what was she likely to see?

'Muriel the Magnificent' flashed again, as usual. The first image loaded. It was Muriel with the other Antonio, they were getting down to business. They were both facing the camera. Muriel was astride Antonio with her legs spread, making it plain that Antonio's cock was deeply imbedded up her shaved hole. But just outside of the picture stood another man, his erect penis was clearly discernible in Muriel's right hand.

'Oh my God,' she murmured breathlessly, as picture after picture revealed the other Muriel getting lewdly penetrated in every orifice by two good-looking men at once.

'Caught you!' Antonio blurted, startling Muriel, making her jump.

She whirled around in her chair to find him standing naked behind her. She blushed. 'I didn't know you were up.'

'Hey, it's OK,' he laughed. 'Don't be embarrassed. Everybody likes to look at dirty pictures. This is a nice computer,' he went on. 'It looks brand new. So you're on-line?'

'Yes,' Muriel answered sheepishly.

'Me, too. I spend a lot of time on-line. It's the wave of the future, right? Soon enough everyone will be on-line.'

Muriel looked away from Antonio and stared at her monitor distractedly. 'Yes,' she agreed quietly. 'Soon enough, everyone will be on-line.'

butt hutt

matt thorne

I first met Isobel in an Internet café. She was looking up
hardcore pornography. Normally this wouldn't have caught
my attention (especially if it was one of the places in the
centre of Soho, where no one cares what their neighbours
are accessing) but because it was the Internet Exchange in
the Trocadero and she'd already attracted the interest of the
muscular blue-shirted staff, I found myself taking the silver
seat next to her and asking,

'What site is that?'

'The bald guy. It's a sex-tracker.'

'Aren't you worried about getting in trouble?'

'Why?'

'You seem to be getting some dodgy looks.'

She swivelled round on her seat and looked at the man
coming towards her. 'Oh shit,' she said, shutting the machine
down, 'it's all right, I'm going.' I laughed. Picking up her stuff,
she asked, 'What's your name?'

'Terry.'

'Have you got much to do, Terry?'

'Not really. Just checking my e-mails.'

'Well, I'm going to McDonald's. Come join me for a drink when you've done.'

I didn't say anything, instead tapping my password into the screen. Then I turned to check out her legs as she walked away.

Isobel was looking up porn at the Trocadero because her home computer was broken. Too concerned about the secret stash on her hard-drive to take it to a repair shop (we joked about how computer repairmen should sue Gary Glitter for lost income), she was waiting for her friend to come round and fix it. In the meantime she was using Internet cafés around London, although this was the first time she'd tried the Trocadero, and had only really done so because she'd come into town to buy some CDs.

Delicately, I tried to raise the subject of why she was looking up porn, which so far she'd failed to explain. She told me that she supplemented her income from working at the Royal Bank of Scotland by putting together a weekly guide to Internet porn-sites for a small list of subscribers. She explained how most men and women (or at least those who subscribed to her magazine) tended to have one special peccadillo. Often these were quite subtle, and hard to find through uneducated surfing. The broader, grosser tastes could be easily satisfied (there were a cornucopia of coprophilia pics, and almost any single sexual word typed into a search engine would send you straight to donkey-fucking), but it was surprisingly hard to find say, softcore photos of redheads with unshaven vaginas, or even naked men alone without erections.

Not that she was only into soft stuff. If you had appetites

you were ashamed of, chances were you'd find something satisfying in Isobel's cc'd catalogue. I didn't want to seem prudish, so I told her that the service she was offering seemed a useful one. Then I mentioned an article I'd read in the problem page of *Time Out New York* about a gay man who was irritated because his boyfriend made him wank him off while he looked at pictures of amputees.

'Stumps, yes, that's quite a common one.' She looked me in the eye. 'But what about you, Terry? What are you into?'

'It's stupid . . .'

'Everyone feels like that.'

'No, I don't want to say, because it's not something that has anything to do with me sexually really, I just like it in pictures.'

She smiled. 'OK, Terry, I understand. How about I'll tell you mine and you tell me yours?'

'That seems fair.'

'OK,' said Isobel, 'I'm into dressed genitalia.'

'What?'

'You know, cunts with glasses placed on them so they look like Eric Morecambe. Cocks dressed up like Marilyn Monroe.'

I frowned, unsure whether she was winding me up. Until now, Isobel had seemed a completely normal woman. She was very attractive, with the kind of distinctive features that meant she didn't have to worry too much about clothes or make-up, wearing today a pair of blue jeans and a smart blazer over a cream top. Her hair was brown, clean, and held back by a red Alice band. There was nothing about her appearance that suggested she'd be interested in Internet porn, still less that she got off looking at photographs of comedy cocks.

'Your turn.'

'OK, I'm going to tell you, but sorry, I do have to ask. Your fetish . . . is that a serious thing?'

'Yes. And it's very popular. There's lots of sites dedicated to it. Although it sort of crosses over into insertions.'

'Insertions?'

'Yes, you know, girls with bottles up their pussies or ice creams sticking out their backsides. A lot of the funny-face cunts actually cross over into insertions. Things like Winston Churchill, for example, because of the cigar.'

'Of course.'

'So . . .'

'Yes?'

'What are you into?'

'Socks.'

She nodded. 'Any particular colour?'

'Oh, only one colour. Pink. I like pink socks. On beautiful American girls.'

'I see.'

'I don't know why. I think it's a whole eighties thing. I don't really like magazine pornography that much, but when I moved into the flat I'm in now I found a whole stack of *Knaves* from the mid-eighties. I was in seventh heaven.'

'So you go for all that eighties stuff? Madonna gloves, and legwarmers?'

'I used to, but not any more. Now it's just . . .'

'Socks.'

'Yes.'

We talked for the rest of the evening. I let slip that I was single early in the conversation, but Isobel retaliated by telling me how happy she was with her current boyfriend, Stephen. As it drew close to the time of my last tube, we swapped e-mail addresses and went home alone.

Three days later, I received an e-mail from Isobel. It told me I might like to check out a site called Butt Hutts. I typed the address into the server, and it took me to the usual page of disclaimers and a photograph of a small wooden shack. Butt Hutts was written in comic bubble-lettering, making the whole thing look like the video jacket of a Lemon Popsicle movie. With low expectations, I clicked on ENTER and waited to see what would come up.

The next graphic was a row of five huts. Each hut had a number above it but no description. Isobel's e-mail had instructed me to check hut three so I clicked that one first. The screen shivered and the next picture was of three fully dressed women. Next to each girl was their name and a small icon to click on. The girls pictured were called Amber, Candi and Helen. I clicked on Amber.

The next page was a full screen photograph of Amber. Dressed in a plain blue dress with the top two buttons undone, she had dyed red hair and a pair of sexy white boots. Beneath the photo was the following text:

Hi, my name's Amber, and I live in Butt Hutt #3 with my friends Candi and Helen. If you'd like to see me take something off, stroke now (the mouse, silly.)

Disappointed, I clicked on the photo and it was replaced by a second one which showed Amber without her boots. I'd come across these sites before, and they were always incredibly frustrating, usually consisting of a series of pictures which led up to a final one of the girl topless but still wearing knickers, and a message telling you that if you wanted to see anything more you'd have to input your credit card details, either because it was a pay site or because it operated an AVS. Still, I clicked through the pictures, wanting to see why Isobel recommended it. I expected it was probably because one of these three butt hutt babes was wearing pink socks in one of the pics. It clearly wasn't Amber, however, and after I'd got her down to her knickers I was about to move on, when, to my surprise, it seemed I could click again without resorting to a credit card.

The next picture was of Amber, fully naked. She had a nice shaved vagina and pretty tits, but the picture didn't really do it for me. I've always been pretty fussy about pornography. It only takes one detail (long, curled fingernails; ugly coloured varnish) and the picture is no longer exciting. But, and this is why I hate the tit-sites that shut off too soon, I find I am almost always aroused by a picture of a woman spreading her labium, no matter what the rest of her looks like. And when I clicked on Amber again I was amazed to find that was her next pose, lying back with her legs raised.

This was the last of Amber's pictures, so I clicked the icon that took me back to the main menu for Butt Hutt #3. I scrutinised the photos of Candi and Helen much more carefully, trying to guess which one might be wearing pink socks. But as both pictures were cropped at the calf line, it was hard to tell. Especially as it was a commonplace of almost all pornography that every woman pictured looked like she'd raided a dressing-up box, the desire to make sure every item of clothing was sexy overshadowing any concern about how the outfit looked as a whole. I decided to go with the woman I found most attractive, and clicked on Candi, a brunette with a mischievous smile and a plaid skirt. I found her sexier than Helen because she was sitting at a computer, nibbling at a pen and pulling at the shoulder of her white jumper.

I clicked on her first photograph and the next page showed her without that jumper, pleasantly plump breasts held back by a black bra. I clicked again and the bra was gone. Her hairstyle had also altered, spoiling the straightforward strip tease effect. Another mouse-tap and she'd brought her feet up onto the chair. No socks. I tapped through the other pictures anyway, aroused by the final shots of Candi sticking her green pen into her vagina and anus. Printing off copies of the last two pics, I went back to the initial menu and clicked on Helen.

She looked much more attractive in the second picture, partly because she'd rolled up her grey Butt Hutts T-shirt to reveal the bottom halves of her tanned breasts, but also because the focus was much clearer. There's nothing more disturbing than the strange visual effects that can occur when a picture has been inexpertly scanned on cheap equipment, especially the ovoid blotches that appear on the swells of arms and thighs, making the women look like they have liquid crystal skin.

Two more clicks and the T-shirt was off and she was kneeling on a bed with a metal frame, pushing her hand down the front of her panties. And there they were: the elusive socks. I unzipped my fly and took out my cock, too excited to print out the pages. I held my breath as I tapped again, hoping the photographer had realised the erotic potential of the socks and allowed her to keep them on as she divested the rest of her clothes. Another screen-shiver and there she was, entirely naked apart from the socks. But would she spread? I clicked again and there it was, the picture that did it. Helen, the socks, open legs, dildo pushed into her hole.

The following morning I e-mailed Isobel, thanking her for the tip. I didn't expect her to get back to me for a day or so, but her response came by mid-morning, asking for my phone number. I gave her the main switchboard, sensing it'd be a bad idea to mention my direct line. Twenty minutes later, she called and asked if I'd like to go on a date that evening. Surprised things were moving so swiftly, I asked after Stephen.

'Oh,' she said, 'don't worry about that. We've come to an arrangement.'

'What does that mean?' I asked.

'Well, there's this girl he wants to fuck.'

We agreed to meet at the Trocadero, then go for dinner and a movie, or a movie and then dinner, depending on programme times and whether we could find a film we both wanted to see. I hung up, and walked across the office to tell my friends about my good fortune.

We ate at McDonald's, skipped the movie, and headed to her house to fuck. I took her in the living room, from behind with her black dress hitched up. After it was over, I asked her if her friend had fixed her computer. She shook her head.

'Actually, that was something I wanted to ask you. Would you mind if I came round and used your computer while you're at work? I'll understand if you say no.'

I looked at her. She smiled sweetly. Something told me she wouldn't understand if I said no, and I even began to worry that she'd fucked me just to gain access to my computer. But that was absurd. Unless this was some kind of complex sting, and I was about to be framed as the head of a paedophile ring.

'OK,' I told her, handing over my spare key.

She said she'd come round in the morning. She'd invited me to stay over at her place, but I had to prepare my house for her arrival. I already had enough of an idea of what kind of person Isobel was to realise that to try to hide anything would be futile. No, if there was anything in my house I didn't want her to see, I either had to throw it away or take it to work with me.

The clearing operation took less time than I'd imagined, and I decided to log on to Butt Hutts again. Part of me wanted to explore the rest of the site, but once it had loaded, I was overwhelmed by the urge to visit Helen again. But when I checked Butt Hutt#3, she no longer seemed to be there. I knew I had the right number because I could see Candi and Amber, but in place of Helen was a black girl named Kelly. Trying to keep calm, I reminded myself that most webmasters are obsessive tinkerers and that he'd probably just shuffled the pictures. I checked huts one, two and four, and was about to do five when the computer crashed. Pissed off and tired, I abandoned my PC and went to bed.

I left for work before Isobel arrived, then sent her an e-mail mid-afternoon, asking her to find out what had happened to Helen. She didn't respond, and I left work early, fully expecting to come home and find my flat cleaned out. But she was still at my desk, a cup of coffee placed on my *Playboy* mouse-mat. I walked up behind her and squeezed her shoulders. She had accessed the Butt Hutt site, and was making notes in a small reporter's pad.

'Did you find her?' I asked.

'No,' she said, 'you're right, she's gone. It's very unusual behaviour for Adrian.'

'Who's Adrian?'

'Adrian runs this site.'

'You know him?'

'No, I just did a domain-search. I always do that with the sites I like. It's like trying to find out who directed your favourite film. You'd be amazed how many of these sites are designed by the same person.'

'So, what do you know about him?'

'Well, lots, but that's involved some pretty complex hacking. The domain-search only gives you the most basic information about the designer, but with the right software you can use that to do much more complicated background digging.'

'Tell me, then. Who is he?'

'He's a grad student at Princeton University.'

She clicked back to the title page and keyed in a membership identification password.

'You belong to this site?'

She nodded.

'But aren't you worried about credit-card fraud?'

'Oh, I'm part of the problem, I'm afraid. I got the password from one of those cheat-sites that break into other people's accounts.'

She moved the cursor up to the WEBCAMS bubble and clicked again. The graphic of the five wooden huts reappeared and she selected hut three. There was a short pause while various enablers loaded, and then the screen was filled with a recording of a living room. I could see a tall lamp, a long sofa and a black girl (presumably Kelly) sitting watching TV. Her hand was under her skirt and she appeared to be masturbating.

'It's quite a weird one, this site.'

'Weird in what way?'

'Well, usually, part of the appeal of these sites is that you can tell the girl what to do. You send your e-mail with your request, wave at me, flash your boobs, whatever, and she does it ... but Adrian's gone to lots of trouble to make sure there's no way you can interact with his women.'

She took a swig from her coffee cup and we both leaned

in to look at the computer screen. We watched Kelly orgasm, and then I stroked my fingers down Isobel's back.

Isobel bought the tickets over the Internet. She used a real credit-card number. Mine. It was three months since I'd first met Isobel, and although we'd never officially become boyfriend and girlfriend, and Stephen was very much still in the picture, I'd fucked her almost every afternoon since she first started using my computer.

The trip was her idea, a combination of mutual dare and birthday treat. Although I'd started out reluctant, Isobel had persuaded me by pointing out that my challenge was much easier than hers. After all, I had a choice of fifteen girls, and one of them was bound to agree to a night alone with me. And I already knew what each of them looked like, right down to the most intimate details. For all she knew, her quarry could turn out to be a complete freak.

And from the information we had so far it seemed likely that this was the case. Over the last two months, Isobel and I had befriended two lonely Princeton postgrads through regular visits to an intercampus chat room. Neither of the postgrads was friends with Adrian, but both knew him, and said that he was a visible character around campus. Although Isobel and I were being very careful not to mention the Butt Hutt site in these sessions, we'd probed enough to discover that the straighter students thought Adrian was a drug dealer. The main reasons why they believed this was because he looked a bit like James Spader in *Less Than Zero* (albeit with a weird English accent) and was extremely popular with the more outgoing female under-graduates.

Isobel thought he sounded wonderful.

★ ★ ★

Isobel and I had decided we would be much more success-ful if we worked separately. Although my PC pal (Eric) was driving to Newark to collect me, Isobel's connection (Wendy) had told her to take the shuttle-bus. In order not to be spotted together, Isobel took the slow queue through Immigration.

I spotted Eric immediately. He was wearing a black vest, blue jeans and what looked suspiciously like slippers. In his hands was a cardboard sign with Terry written on it, the 'e' turned into a smiley face.

'Eric?'

'Terry? Good to see ya.' He clapped me on the back. 'That all you brought?'

'Yeah,' I told him, thinking he looked much older than twenty-eight, and wondering whether he'd lied to me about his age, 'travelling light.'

'No problem. I have some old shirts if you get stuck for clothes.'

About a year before I had spent three weeks working in New York. That had been just long enough to get a general sense of Americans, although I had a suspicion that graduate students would turn out to be quite different to the people I'd been working with.

'This isn't that great a drive, Terry,' he told me, 'but it's best to do it quick. We can get something to eat once we get to Princeton.'

'OK.'

We walked to his car. It was a great car, a huge monster-mobile that had no doubt served someone's family well before Eric picked it up. I sat in the passenger seat, wondering why we'd never been allowed those weird self-fastening seat-belts in England. Eric looked at me.

'Did you bring the tapes?'

I nodded, unzipped my bag and handed him a yellow Tower Records carrier. He took out the tapes, looked through them, growled his approval and pushed *Generation Terrorists* into the car-stereo.

Eric was right. It wasn't much of a drive, and even the excitement of being in America didn't make the passing scenery any more interesting. Reaching Princeton was a real relief, and when Eric asked me if I was hungry, I nodded enthusiastically.

'Is there anything you'd especially like? We have pretty much everything here.'

'I don't mind.'

'OK,' he said, 'let's take a walk. Stop me if you see somewhere.'

We ate in a place called 'Tiger Noodles'. I had Sesame Chicken, a meal that seems a staple of Chinese cuisine in America, but is rarely found in English Chinese restaurants. I'd developed a taste for this main course when I'd been working in New York, and eating it now took me back to that turbulent time.

'More rice, Terry?' Eric asked me as the waiter refilled our water jug.

'Mmm. Thanks.'

'I gotta say, Terry, it's so good to have you here.'

'Thanks, Eric. It's kind of you to put me up.'

'Forget about it. I don't have that big a place, but it's a damn sight better than a butt hut.'

I looked at him, amazed. 'A what?'

'Butt hut. The Butler Apartments, if you want to get prissy about it. A bunch of prefabricated buildings on the edge of campus. I was stuck in one of those for my first two years here.'

'Can you show me the huts?'

'Of course. Why?'

'No reason. I'm just interested in how they house students here.'

'Well, Terry, if that's what gets you going. But, listen, a girl from my department is having a party tonight in her butt hut. Why don't we wait till then?'

'OK,' I said, 'that sounds great.'

'Cool. I wasn't planning to go, but it'll be a good opportunity for you to meet some of the other students. And that guy you asked me about will probably be there.'

'Adrian?'

'Yeah. He's at pretty much every party in Princeton.'

'Great.'

'You done there?'

'Yeah.'

'Come on, then, let me show you my place.'

Eric's room was revolting. I'm not an especially fastidious man, but this went far beyond any depths of student squalor I'd previously witnessed. The main reason why I found this mess so distasteful was that this was clearly the apartment of a relatively wealthy individual. All kinds of gizmos and gadgets were scattered around the apartment, including a complex laser system that sent cross-cutting red beams at just above ankle-level.

He spent the afternoon telling me about his studies. They seemed abnormally fascinating to him, which surprised me, as our chat-room exchanges had indicated that he devoted all his time to devouring popular culture. Discovering that he was much more interested in mediaeval music made me wonder when he found time to sleep.

I persuaded him to go out for food again before we

went to the party, although it was obvious he would've clearly preferred to finish up the leftovers in his fridge. I knew from experience that while most Americans (especially those who want to be your friend) initially seem easier to push around, they also tend to turn on you more suddenly than English people, the switch from complete compliance to unwavering resistance often surprisingly violent. Usually I'd be more careful to avoid a future confrontation, but as I didn't intend to stick with Eric for long I was prepared to take advantage of his goodwill.

We ate in The Annexe, a pleasant bar-restaurant that served good veal. At the table next to ours was a group of Eric's fellow students. Although they didn't seem to like him that much, they were curious about his new English friend and invited us to join them for a drink in the D-Bar.

'You want to, Terry?' he asked.

'Sure,' I replied, 'it's still early, after all.'

The D-Bar was like every other college bar I'd ever been in, no doubt the same the whole world over. A depressing day-after-the-party atmosphere, puddles of flat beer on every surface. An insufficient cash register, pool table with two broken pockets. A few stray souls surrounding a table with too many empty bottles. We stayed long enough to hear the last Wilco album and the first Liz Phair, leaving just as they were putting the Wilco back on again.

I hadn't thought about Isobel that much since arriving in Princeton, but as we began walking down towards the butt huts, I wondered whether she'd also found out about the party. Given her formidable investigative skills, it seemed fairly likely, but maybe her contact was too much of a social outcast to have been told.

'Do we need to bring drinks?'

'You haven't told him then,' one of the girls said, giggling.

Eric looked at her. I looked at Eric.

'What?'

'The woman who's organised this party always does a huge bowl of this fatal blue cocktail. Everyone has to give five bucks when they go in.'

'She'll probably let you off,' Eric told me, ''cause you're a guest.'

The two women in our group were far too plain to be Butt Hutt babes. They were also dressed in Princeton sportswear, something absent from Adrian's Internet site. I tried to image both the girls naked, just to be certain, but the thought was too repellent to consider for long.

It was a pleasant evening, and everyone we passed seemed to be walking down to the huts. The huts looked quite different from the graphic representation on the title page of the site, and made me think that the photograph was probably a deliberate red herring. It seemed strange that Adrian would use this phrase as the name of his site at all, given that it was such a well-known euphemism on the Princeton campus. Surely this was the sort of thing that could get him kicked out of college if the authorities found out.

There was loud industrial music coming from the party hut, although I wasn't sufficiently schooled in the genre to know if it was Ministry or Nine Inch Nails or some smaller band. The woman I'd been seeing in New York had liked this sort of music, and while I had no problem with it and it certainly made for a lively party soundtrack, I found its popularity hard to fathom.

By now, I was fairly certain that most of the other students thought Eric was a geek. If I was to have any success seducing a butt hut babe (assuming there were any at the party) I'd have to separate myself from him early on. From the attention I'd been drawing at the D-Bar, it seemed that being English was something of a secret weapon, and I'd already begun to exaggerate my accent.

A tall, skinny guy in a blue shirt was walking next to a bald man up ahead of us. The bald man had a Sesame Street voice and was getting extremely agitated. The skinny guy recognised Eric and raised his arm.

'He's another English guy,' Eric explained, 'do you want to ask him about Adrian?'

'No,' I said, 'that's OK.'

Eric shrugged. 'Suit yourself. Let's go say hello to the host.'

He dragged me across to the doorway of the butt hut. The girl standing in the entrance had a large glass bowl into which she was depositing collected five-spots.

'Terry, I'd like you to meet . . .'

'Candi.'

The girl looked at me, shocked.

'No, dude, this is Lisa.'

It was Candi. After Helen's disappearance from the Butt Hutt site, I had spent many nights masturbating to my print-outs of Candi, and didn't need to see her poking a pen into her private places to know I had the right girl.

'I'm sorry,' I said, 'my mistake.'

We went inside the hut and Eric scooped us both a glass of the blue stuff. Lisa kept looking at me, and I couldn't help worrying that I'd blown my cover too early. I was also anxious that I wasn't taking this whole thing seriously enough. After all, even if the very least these people had to worry about was being kicked out of college I'd spent enough time around Eric to know that was a pretty big deal. I tapped Eric on the shoulder.

'Is Lisa going to be collecting money all night?'

He grinned. 'Unless some poor sap takes over for her.'

'Eric?'

'Yes, Terry?'

'Would you be that poor sap for me?'

'Oh,' he said, 'you wanna talk to Lisa?' He looked around, then smiled and nudged me, 'OK, but not for long.'

'Sure,' I said, 'thanks.'

Eric walked over to Lisa, took the bowl, and pointed in my direction. I smiled, and she walked across.

'What was your name again?'

'Terry. Look, I'm sorry about earlier. I didn't mean to embarrass you.'

'Why would I be embarrassed about you getting my name wrong?'

'Right. I just wanted to say that I'm a friend of Adrian's and a big fan of your site.'

Her mouth opened and she looked at me again. *Shit. Why had I said that? Another stupid mistake.*

'You?' she said slowly. 'A friend of Adrian's? I don't think so.'

'OK, I'm not really his friend, but I know some people he knew in England.'

'Look, Terry, I don't know what you're doing here, but I don't think you realise what you're getting yourself into. And if you don't want to take my word for it, stick around and let Adrian warn you himself. Only don't expect him to be so nice about it.'

Shooting me one last look, Lisa turned away and walked back across to Eric, angrily tugging the dollar-filled bowl away from him. He looked back at me, shrugged, and came over.

'Got shot down, did you? Don't worry, Terry, she's like that with everyone.' He paused. 'Except Adrian.'

'Is she going out with him?'

'Oh no, I don't think so. She's probably fucked him once or twice, but then again so has almost every girl on campus. Let's go outside.'

I followed Eric out of the already humid hut and joined the revellers on the grass outside. The English guy and his bald friend were still arguing about something, and after a few minutes of watching them I realised the source of the conflict was that the English guy didn't really want to be here. A few of the men outside smiled at Eric, but no one seemed interested in talking to him.

I was still checking the girls' faces for any other representatives from the Butt Hutt site. But most of the girls looked more likely to appear on some nihilistic bondage site. It seemed strange that the students of such an elite institution would go for an outdated fashion-phase like goth in such a big way, but maybe that was their form of rebellion. I also wondered why Adrian didn't have a goth hut on his site, as I'm sure he would have got plenty of volunteers, and that the girls would've thought it a totally punk thing to do.

I sat down next to one of the goth girls. Unlike most of the goths I'd seen in England, who seemed to take to that fashion as if it was the only way of making themselves sexy, most of these girls seemed gorgeous. The girl I'd sat next to could've passed for a film star if it wasn't for the purple hair.

'Hi, I'm Terry,' I said, holding out my hand.

She laughed, and then said something to her friend. I couldn't work out what she said because she covered her mouth with her hand. The friend, who was slightly overweight and wearing a black lace dress leaned in to ask me, 'Are you a friend of Eric's?'

I looked up at Eric, who looked embarrassed and on the verge of tears. 'Am I your friend, Eric?'

He nodded, moving back and forth on the spot as if he needed to urinate.

'We met over the Internet,' I explained. 'I'm from England.'

'Duh,' said the girl next to me. Her friends laughed.

'Come on, Terry,' Eric said, looking from side to side and pulling at my shoulder.

'What?' I asked.

'They don't like me.'

'Who doesn't like you?' I asked. 'These girls? That's not true, is it?'

I looked round their faces, enjoying the feeling of being back in control after Lisa had embarrassed me. Then I looked up at Eric.

'Sit down, Eric.'

He shook his head. 'I'll get some drinks. You want another drink, don't you?'

'Thanks, Eric, that would be lovely.'

The girls handed over their empty cups, although I was fairly certain they were only doing it for the entertainment of watching Eric struggle back with so many drinks. I sensed the girls were beginning to relax in my company, so I asked, 'Why don't you like Eric?'

The lace girl laughed. 'We don't like anybody.'

Isobel arrived at midnight. It was dark and I only noticed her because she was on Adrian's arm. Everyone at the party was in a hurry to greet him, rushing over to pat his shoulder. Eric had been completely wrong about Adrian's appearance. He looked nothing like James Spader. Instead, he looked like a cross between Malcolm Maclaren and John Lydon, albeit clad in a stained blue blazer. He had a shock of bright red hair, like a punk Tintin, and white, almost translucent skin.

I waited until the greetings had finished, then went over to say hello to Isobel. Adrian raised an eyebrow at her, and she introduced me,

'Adrian, this is my friend, Terry, the one I told you about.'

'Ah, Terry,' he said in a fruity English accent, 'it's a pleasure to meet you.'

After being seen with Adrian, my stock rose considerably. Lisa came back across to me and told me that her real name was Lisa, not Candi, although it was her in the pictures. I told her she was my favourite butt hutt babe, and then asked her what would be showing on the site tonight.

'Oh, it's Amber's night tonight,' she said. 'She's doing a home alone thing.'

'Didn't she want to come to the party?'

'Yeah, but she needs the money. And Adrian's paying her double tonight.'

We talked for a little while longer, and then Lisa invited me to a private party at Adrian's place. It wasn't due to start until two, but she promised me it'd be lots of fun.

'There'll be, y'know,' she said, gently tapping the side of her nose, 'and Adrian's got a hot tub.'

The party had thinned out considerably by two, but Adrian was still careful to make sure we didn't pick up any uninvited guests. Eric had left at about midnight, after we'd had a brief argument. He told me that he needed seven hours sleep a night and couldn't stay any longer because he had breakfast commitments. I told him I understood, but still wanted to stay.

'Can't you leave a window open?'

'No way, Terry, I can't do that. Not with all my equipment.'

'But Princeton seems a pretty safe place.'

'I'm sorry,' he said, shaking his head, 'why don't you come back with me?'

'Because I've got something I need to take care of.'

'Give it up, Terry. She already shot you down once.'

'Things are different now I'm friends with Adrian.'

'Let him put you up then. I'm sorry, buddy, I'll see you in the morning.'

I wasn't too worried, knowing that Adrian's party was likely to last all night. But I did feel a little nervous now that I no longer had an escape route, especially as I knew I wasn't really in the same league as Adrian and Isobel, and worried that they might use this fact to humiliate me in some way.

'How are you doing?' Adrian asked as he sidled up alongside me. 'Still up for another party?'

'Of course.'

He patted my shoulder. 'Glad to hear it.'

'Which way is it?'

'Hang on a mo. Lisa's just rounding up the stragglers.'

We turned and watched Lisa talking to two women and the skinny English guy. I was surprised that he'd been chosen for this select gathering, especially after his earlier protestations to his bald friend.

'Who's that guy?'

'Glenn? President of the Rocket Society. That's an unofficial position, of course. Why? Do you know him?'

'No, no, I'm just surprised he's coming. He seemed very reluctant about the party earlier.'

'My party?' Adrian asked, frowning.

'No, the blue drinks do.'

'Oh, that's just his way. And I expect he didn't want to upset Donald.'

'Who's Donald? The bald guy?'

Adrian nodded. 'The two of them are very close.'

I hadn't realised how tired I was until we started walking to Adrian's. I suppose it wasn't that surprising, given that I'd now been up for almost twenty-four hours straight. I tend to always run on New York time, even when I'm in England. But the flight and excitement (and, oddly, the fresh air, not to mention the blue cocktails) had taken it out of me, and I could feel myself starting to flag. My eyes were closing when I felt someone take my hand.

'Tired?' Isobel asked.

'Exhausted. Aren't you?'

She nodded. 'But I'm too excited to back out now. And I don't have anywhere to sleep.'

'What happened to Wendy?'

'I've no idea. When I went to the address she gave me there was no sign of her. And no one I've spoken to seems to know who she is. Apparently, there's no one with her name at Princeton. The whole thing must've been a hoax.'

'Probably some horny guy pretending to be a girl.'

'I suppose so. It was stupid of me not to be more careful about checking her out.'

'How did you find Adrian?'

'He found me,' she giggled.

'Really?'

'Yes, it was ridiculous. I got off the bus and there he was. And, of course, he started trying it on straight away.'

'What did you say?'

'That I'd be more than happy to be a butt hut babe. Apparently an opening's just about to come up.'

She released my hand and skipped over to Adrian. We'd reached the road now, and began walking towards the main streets where Eric had taken me to eat earlier. I looked over at Lisa and she smiled back at me.

'Not far now,' she said, 'and I promise you it'll be worth it.'

Adrian strode into his home, immediately heading for the dining room. The rest of us followed and stood in an awkward cluster at the far end of his large table. He rang a small bell and two maids appeared. They were both attractive women with long dark hair, dressed in a uniform that left their breasts and buttocks exposed. I chuckled to myself, thinking that Adrian had probably watched *Story of O* more often than was good for him.

'Champagne, everyone? I know I need something to wash away the taste of that horrible Harpic. Now does anyone want something more substantial to eat? Say now, because I predict in a short while you're all about to lose your appetite.'

I looked up at him, feeling scared. Then I saw him bring out a small vial from his blazer and relaxed. I had no problem with drugs. Or sex, for that matter. But I've always shied away from violence, and hate it when S&M gets too serious.

We sat at the table, waiting while Adrian prepared the lines. I took this opportunity to check out the other two women that Lisa had brought back from the butt huts. They didn't look like they were the stars of his site, although it was true that I didn't remember the exact appearance of every girl.

The maids returned. On closer inspection I realised that one of the maids was blindfolded. She was the one with the bottle. The other girl arranged the glasses and guided the blindfolded girl's hand as she poured on the champagne. Adrian looked up from his chopping and smiled at this, before checking that everyone else was enjoying the performance.

'OK,' he said, 'who wants to go first? Terry?'

He passed the tile to me and I took out a ten-dollar bill from my pocket. Adrian noticed and shook his head.

'Oh no,' he said, 'there's a straw there. And you're the first to use it so there's nothing to worry about.'

I picked up the thin straw and snorted the line. Aware that everyone was watching me, and wanting to make a good impression, I dabbed my fingers on the small crumb that was left and rubbed it on my gums.

'Jolly good,' said Adrian. 'Isobel?'

She snorted a line, and then passed it across to the skinny English guy. He grimaced.

'Problem, Glenn?' Adrian asked.

'No,' he said, leaning down to snort the line.

The tile went round the table, and ended up with Adrian. He chopped out some more lines and it went round again. Two more times and I was feeling awake again, and oddly enthusiastic to see what happened next.

'OK, everyone,' said Adrian, 'how about a game?'

Lisa laughed. 'Perfect.'

'It's a very tame game, but seeing as we do have two new people with us tonight, I think it'll serve as a very good way of breaking the ice. It's a Swedish game, although for some reason it's called The Russian Post Office. Now, the rules are very simple, although we should probably move into the sitting room if we're going to have enough space to play.'

Adrian stood up. Everyone else copied him, giggling and smiling at each other. He took Isobel's hand and pulled her behind him. The two maids retreated and I sensed that'd be the last we'd see of them for the evening. We walked through into the other room, which looked like Tony Scott's idea of an opium den, with billowy curtains with a fan behind them and cushions for everyone to lie out on.

'Music?' Adrian asked, as he walked across to the stereo. He placed three new CDs in a multidisc carousel and then brought the remote back with him as he sat down.

'Lisa,' he said, 'would you like to explain the game?'

She stood up, brushing a hand down over her top and looking at me. 'What happens is, we each take turns to be the postman. The postman goes outside and knocks on the door. He then says he has a delivery. Adrian then asks him what sort of delivery he has. The delivery can be a kiss, which is just a kiss, a French kiss, a touch-up, which is a touch-up *under* the clothes, or a hamburger, which is where the postman lies on top of the chosen person and makes out with them, but is not allowed to do anything under the clothes.'

'You missed a bit,' Adrian told her.

'Hang on, I was getting to that. When the person knocks, Adrian also has to ask who the delivery is for. He points at a person at random and says, "is it for this person?" and then moves round the room until the postman says yes.'

'OK,' said Adrian, 'Glenn, you've played this before. Why don't you start us off?'

Glenn smiled and got to his feet. He went outside the door and ended up giving a hamburger to Isobel. Although she was perfectly willing, the way they arranged themselves on the floor was awkward and he ended up kneeing her in the crotch.

'Christ,' she said, pushing him off.

'I'm sorry,' he told her, immediately standing up, 'shit.'

Adrian laughed. 'OK, Lisa, your turn.'

Lisa stood up and went behind the door. Adrian's head was lolling backwards. The maids had left two or three bottles of champagne and I refilled his glass. Lisa knocked.

'Yes?' Adrian called out.

'I have a delivery,' she replied.

'What sort of delivery?'

'A touch-up.'

'Ah,' said Adrian, 'but who's it for?' He pointed to Isobel.
'Is it for this person?'

'No.'

He pointed to one of the girls. 'This person?'

'No.'

He pointed at me. 'This person?'

'Yes,' she said, and opened the door.

We played The Russian Post Office for about an hour, by which time everyone had been comprehensively kissed and groped by everyone else. The only awkward moment came when I had to deliver a hamburger to Adrian, mainly because I didn't want him to know I wasn't really into it. After the last time round, Adrian said,

'OK, that's enough. Who wants to stay and fuck?'

Everyone did apart from one of the girls, who chose this moment to leave. This evened the numbers, but seemed surprising given that we could've easily coped with another woman. Unless she didn't like the look of the men on offer.

The six of us went through to Adrian's hot tub. He'd prepared some more lines and we did those before stripping and climbing into the water. Adrian looked at my erection and smiled at me as I slid into the tub. He had his arm around Isobel and was absent-mindedly stroking the tips of her nipples. There was something lazily proprietorial about this gesture that really irritated me, even though my claim on Isobel was slight. I knew I should be more excited about being coked up in a hot tub in America, seconds away from sex with an amateur porn star. But my libido was dulled by the fact that I'd also have to witness a woman who'd become one of my best friends being fucked by a gamy English pervert. There was also the worry of safety, as no one seemed about to put on a condom. I looked at Lisa as she moved through the bubbling water, trying to convince myself I was getting a fair trade. She had a better body than Isobel, muscular without being off-putting. But it was her smile that really got me excited; the look in her eyes that reminded me of the girls in my high school that I'd lusted after but never actually fucked.

Glenn's glasses were steaming up, but when his girl tried to take them off he barked at her to leave them alone. I could sense we were all waiting for a signal from Adrian that it was OK to start fucking, and it came when he pulled Isobel onto his lap.

I found it surprisingly easy to penetrate Lisa, even though I wasn't that used to underwater fucking. I sat back with my arms stretched across the tub while she moved up and down on my cock. Adrian and Isobel were facing each other, him underneath and her gripping his wet neck. I kept trying to look over Lisa's shoulder to see what Glenn and the other girl were up to, and was confused and distressed to see four feet sticking out of the water.

Adrian finished first, pushing Isobel off and standing up. Climbing out of the tub, he wrapped a towel around his skinny white frame and made straight for the cocaine. Lisa looked at him. Scared she was going to follow his lead and stop, I gripped her shoulder hard and sped up until I came.

'Who wants downers?' Adrian asked. 'Everyone right, unless you're keen to see the sunrise.'

He moved among our still dripping bodies, handing out pills from two different bottles.

'Is it safe to mix them?'

'Safe? I'd recommend it. It's taken me years to find a combo that cancels out each other's side-effects. But maybe we should all go upstairs first.'

It seemed the arrangement was that we'd sleep in couples. Adrian and Isobel had the biggest bedroom, Glenn's and mine being of a similar size. Adrian gave Lisa a long kiss goodnight and then retired. I shook hands with Glenn, and then Lisa and I were alone.

We popped our pills.

'How long have we got?'

'Ten minutes max.'

'Then I'll be brief. What happened to Helen?'

'Who?'

'The girl who was in your butt hut before Kelly replaced her.'

'Oh, Amanda. Why, did you like her?'

I looked at her. 'Yes, but that's not what this is about. I want to know what happened to her.'

'OK,' she said, 'get into bed and I'll tell you.'

The bed was only a queen size, and the two of us had to hold each other tight to be comfortable. Her fingers found my penis and she looked at me inquisitively.

'Oh no,' I said, 'I'm completely dead down there. And don't try to distract me. What happened to that girl?'

'Nothing happened to that girl. You know what people are like when they go to college. They experiment with sex, they experiment with drugs . . . and some people discover that they love that lifestyle, while others get scared and turn to something else.'

'What d'you mean?'

'I mean Amanda found a boyfriend. She was never really that interested in appearing on the site in the first place. Adrian

. . . preys on people at their weak moments, and makes it seem like everyone around him is having the most incredible fun. But he gets bored of people pretty quickly.'

'OK,' I said, 'so explain this to me. What did Adrian mean when he told Isobel that there would be an opening on the site soon.'

She looked at me. 'Did Adrian say that?'

'Yes.'

'And those were his exact words? There would be an opening?'

'Yes. What did he mean?'

She shook her head. 'Nothing. Another one of the girls has probably dropped out is all.'

I wanted to question her further but the sleepers had already kicked in and I drifted off into a dark, blank place.

The following morning I was awoken for breakfast by Isobel. She came into our bedroom and shook me awake, making me get out of bed and come outside onto the upstairs landing.

'I'm going to stay,' she told me. 'What about you?'

'I'm going home. Just as soon as I've found Eric and got my stuff back. And I think you should come with me.'

She shook her head. 'I knew you were going to say that. But listen, it's just an experiment, OK? This is something I've always wanted to do, and I'm desperate to experience it for myself.'

'But, Isobel, I don't think you realise what's involved here. I'm convinced there's something sinister going on.'

'Oh, come on, Terry, don't be stupid. It's just sex, OK? Just sex.'

Eric was waiting for me. He opened the door on my first

knock and gave me a hug. Surprised, I gripped him back. Then I realised he was crying.

'I'm so sorry, buddy.'

'What for?' I asked, surprised.

'Last night. I shouldn't have left like that.'

'It's OK. I got Adrian to put me up. Like you suggested.'

'Still, I did a bad thing.'

'Don't be stupid. But listen, Eric, I have to go back home.'

'It's because of me, isn't it?'

'No, Eric, it's nothing to do with you. It's just that coming out here was a spur of the moment thing.'

'And now you regret it?'

'No, of course not.'

'Are we still friends?'

'Of course.'

'And you'll carry on sending me e-mails.'

'Definitely. Now, Eric, could you drive me to the airport.'

'Sure thing, buddy. Just let me use the bathroom and we'll go.'

The flight back was horrible. Although I hadn't suffered too much from my indulgence the night before, my body clock was out of whack and I couldn't tell whether I wanted to sleep or stay awake. So I tried to sleep, then got irritated and watched a bit of a bad movie, then played computer games for a while (unsuccessfully, due to my faulty handset) before trying to drink myself into a coma.

I don't know how to tell the last part of this story. Just writing this down, and ordering these events into a narrative makes me feel as if I am in some way culpable; as if I'm inviting my own punishment. I haven't said any of this to anyone, and sat in silence when Stephen came round to find out what had happened to his girlfriend.

I know that once I've written this I won't be able to stop myself feeling guilty, and maybe I'll even feel forced to report this to someone, although exactly who I don't know. Maybe I'll even have to conduct my own private investigation, fly back to Princeton and sort things out myself. But I can't help feeling that it's just a bad joke, and I've done nothing more serious than accidentally access a disturbing website.

I was feeling edgy from the moment I got off the plane. Certain I would be pulled over and strip-searched, I made little effort to disguise my dishevelment as I shuffled past the customs officers. But, for almost the first time ever, they let me through unmolested. Going down to the luggage carousel, I collected my bag and took a Piccadilly line tube home.

I fell into bed the moment I got through the door, telling myself I'd check on Isobel's progress as soon as I'd had some proper sleep. In spite of my intentions, it was two days before I returned to the butt hutts. Now I was no longer with Isobel, I felt my past few weeks' indulgence all the more keenly, and felt eager to reconnect with my family and friends.

The only time I came near to telling anyone what'd happened was when two of my mates at work asked me about the girl I'd been seeing, the one I'd told them was 'up for anything'. But I knew if I described my time in America, they would think I was either boasting or lying, or, if they did take me seriously, this rumour would be something I'd have to live down if I ever introduced them to any of my subsequent girlfriends. And that would definitely be it for me with any of the women in the office.

I had known for ages that a time would come when I'd have to clean up my act, although I always thought it'd be a new girlfriend that'd prompt me to change. But now I'd begun to suspect that it didn't work like that. Most men didn't meet women like Isobel because they didn't spend their evenings in Internet exchanges, and even if they did, they didn't strike up conversations with odd-looking women accessing hardcore porn. If I altered my lifestyle, it would put me back in a world where I could meet normal women.

By the time I went back to the computer, I'd decided that I was glad Isobel had gone, and that rather than using this site to monitor her progress, I would just check it once and then forego Internet porn forever. It didn't really do that much for me, and if I went back to using my imagination for masturbation, it'd stop me feeling like I was hiding some terrible dark secret. So I clicked through the huts and there she was, the new girl in hut #5. And as I went through the pictures with a sense of finality, I felt pleased that she was wearing pink socks, thinking this a nice gesture and wondering whether they were the same pair that Helen had once worn.

I printed out paper copies of the pictures of Isobel, then did the same for the rest of the girls on the site. I tried to forget that I had fucked Isobel and Lisa, and found that at least for the moment this was surprisingly easy, and the fact that they were naked in the photos made me feel less emotional than I might have done if they were fully clothed. I shut down the computer and went to bed.

Putting the pages on top of a cupboard, I made myself think about an ex from a few years ago as I masturbated on to the sheet. But after I'd come I didn't feel satisfied, and, hating myself, returned to my PC. I looked through the pictures of the girls again, then accessed the webcam. What I saw there scared me as much as if I'd been directly connected to a disapproving god. Filling the screen was a huge close-up of Adrian's luminous face, staring straight into the camera.

Within seconds he looked right at me, as if making sure I was there. I knew he couldn't really see me, but it felt as he was peering straight into my soul. Then he walked back from the camera, turned round so that his back was facing me, and pulled down his chinos. He wasn't wearing underwear, and he turned his backside towards me. Squatting, he began a bizarre sideways herky-jerky dance, fingers flipping as he crouched and shuffled.

He kept this up for about five minutes, before he stopped, stretched open his bum-cheeks and squeezed out a thick black turd. As he did this, the hut door opened and Lisa wheeled in a bed. Strapped to the bed was Isobel, naked apart from a pair of knickers. With the slow, halting nature of the webcam, it was hard to make out all of the action, but while I watched Lisa seemed to do something unpleasant and gynaecological to Isobel, the image on my screen changing without warning to a bloody close-up. Then the server disconnected. I kept trying to get back on, but every time I attempted access of the Butt Hutt site it flashed me a 404.

That was three months ago.

It's the only ending I have.

I'll let you know if anything changes.

the proxy

paul j mcauley

Oz Hardy was in his flat, chair cocked back and feet up on the desk next to the humming computer, listening to the D'Oyly Carte recording of *Ruddigore* while sleepily digesting a chicken pie and two pints of Strangeways Ale after his lunchtime session at the Branch, when someone rang the doorbell. Oz nearly fell out his chair. Customers didn't come to his flat these days. That wasn't how he did business. No one visited his flat, except people who came to take things away: swarthy leather-clad bikers; wiry Lycra-clad cyclists; off-hand van drivers in nylon windcheaters. But someone had rung the bell, and, after a measured pause, they rang it again. Expecting bad news, Oz threw open the window and looked down.

The old gent in the pinstripe suit lifted the horn handle of his furled umbrella from the bell push and said, 'Mr Hardy? I'd like you to find something for me.'

★   ★   ★

Colonel Leslie Salisbury explained that Oz had been recommended to him by a mutual friend, Teddy Bannister, the owner of a second-hand bookshop in Islington.

'Teddy's an old chum,' Colonel Salisbury said. He was as thin as an Egyptian mummy, with fine dry hair the colour of tobacco, combed sideways across his freckled scalp, but his blue eyes were clear and sharp. He leaned forward, using his umbrella as a pivot, and added, 'He came to my rescue twenty years ago, when I was financially embarrassed by death duties. Gave a fair price for what he took and suggested that I should send half a dozen items to auction. He said that you might be able to help me.'

Oz said cautiously, 'My interests are pretty specialised.'

Colonel Salisbury looked around. They had retired to the Branch, where the Colonel had bought a pint of Strangeways for Oz and a double Bell's for himself. The Branch was an old Victorian barn of a pub on the eastern border of Islington, close by the Grand Union Canal. There was a little theatre on the first floor, and it was popular with drama students and resting actors, none of whom ever commented on Oz's fashion sense. Apart from Ken the barman the place was deserted, but the Colonel leaned so close that Oz could smell the whisky on his breath, and said, 'This is rather a confidential matter.'

'You have something special you want to sell?'

'Not to sell: to buy. And Teddy said you were the man to help me.'

'I quit the book-running business a while back, Colonel.'

The Colonel drummed his bony fingers on the beak of his umbrella. 'You don't have to search for this particular item. I know just where it is. But I do need your help to buy it.'

The Colonel was the younger son of a Kentish family which had fallen on hard times. His elder brother had squandered the family fortune, losing heavily in Lloyd's syndicates, and at Kempton, Sandown and Cheltenham. When his brother died, the manor house had to be auctioned off to meet the debts and death duty; that's when the Colonel had moved to London, and sold much of the library to Teddy Bannister.

'But not everything, you understand. I kept my favourite volumes, and of course, the Eccham Incunabula.'

'The Eccham Incunabula,' Oz said, trying to look as though he had heard of it.

'You won't have heard of it,' the Colonel said, twinkling over the rim of his whisky glass. 'The man who built Eccham Manor, Sir Toby Eccham, compiled it. He was something of an alchemist, and also a Monarchist. When it was clear which way the Civil War was going, he walled up the Incunabula for safekeeping. But he never came back – he was killed at the siege of Oxford. His sister's family – my family – took back the Manor after the Restoration. The Incunabula turned up again when my grandfather was extending the Manor. Made his fortune out in India. Jute. Anyway, it's been a secret family treasure ever since, and I kept it through the recent troubles. But then I recently learned that it was for sale.'

Oz said, 'It was stolen?'

'My thought exactly. I went straight around to my bank, in fact. That's where I keep it. Far too valuable, you see, to have in the house. No, I still have it. But so, it seems, does someone else.'

'A copy,' Oz said.

'Not very likely. Only the immediate family knew about it, and it has always been locked away. And what's advertised for sale is a printed volume, dated 1818. Made when the original was still walled up in Sir Toby's hiding place.'

Oz sipped his beer. He said, 'It could have been set from a copy made before Sir Toby hid the original.'

The Colonel nodded vigorously. 'Perhaps, perhaps. In any case, the mystery will be clearer once I've bought the damned thing. It's up for auction. That's why I came to you.'

'Why not bid for it yourself?'

'Because it is up for auction on the Internet. At somewhere called . . . just a minute . . .' The Colonel reached inside his jacket, took out a piece of paper and unfolded it and held it close to his eyes. 'Haystack full stop com. My great-niece saw it and told me, and Toby told me that you conduct most of your business that way. So, young man, will you do it?'

'It's simple enough. Your great-niece could—'

The Colonel laid a hand on Oz's sleeve. 'Ah, but there's one other thing. I want you to be my proxy in this auction, and I also want you to find out about the person who is selling it.'

They agreed on a fee of one hundred pounds a day plus expenses; the Colonel handed over a retainer of five hundred pounds. He said that he wasn't such a silly old fool to trust everyone he met, but he liked the cut of Oz's jib. 'Not many people your age appreciate Gilbert and Sullivan. And not many have the sense to dress properly either.'

Oz was hardly the showiest character in the book trade – Lawrence Ackroyd, for instance, wore a red leather jumpsuit and went about without a shirt even in the depths of winter – but people often commented on his clothes. That day, for instance, he was wearing a high-collared white shirt with a ruffled front, a white silk cravat, a red and gold waistcoat, a black jacket and black trousers with a black velvet stripe, and a practical pair of Dr Marten's. He habitually carried an ebony cane with a silver fox's head, which he had picked up for a song on one of the stalls in Camden Passage, and his blond hair was worn in a shoulder-length Richard the Lionheart bob.

It had started after he had joined the chorus of the Cornish Gilbert and Sullivan Society. He'd sung in *Iolanthe*, in *HMS Pinafore*, in *The Yeoman of the Guard*. He'd sung in *The Pirates of Penzance*, in Penzance. And he'd taken to wearing the clothes of the period, cutting such an eccentric figure at school that he had never been troubled by bullies. His parents were artists – his father American, his mother English – who had moved from San Francisco to a commune in Cornwall in 1970, two years after Oz had been born, and Oz's adoption of Victorian formality might have begun as a typical rebellion against his parents' values, but it had lasted half his life, for so long that it was no longer an affectation.

Oz had been in the book trade since leaving university. He'd lived off book reviewing (exhaustive biographies of minor poets and obscure nineteenth-century politicians) and social security for a few years, but eventually dropped out of the reviewing game because it took too much time from what had become his real job: a book-runner.

He'd fallen into that through contacts made when, every week, he staggered down to Charing Cross Road or Chancery Lane with a cardboard box of review copies. A book-runner ran after books. A customer would come into a bookshop and ask for some long-out-of-print rarity. If the bookshop didn't have it, it would add the title to its want list. Oz and all the other book-runners ran around London looking for those wanted books. It was a little like bounty hunting, although hardly as dangerous, considerably less exciting, and very badly paid. Oz developed a talent for sniffing out rarities in the marginal bookshops of Tilbury and Greenwich, in charity shops, in church sales, in the bargain bins of department stores whose buyers didn't have a clue. He sold on his finds, developed his own list of customers with their obscure wants and desires.

But the Internet was bringing an end to the book-running trade. You could enter the rarest title in an Internet search engine and be presented, at once, with choices from half a dozen booksellers. You paid by credit card and received your prize by post or by courier a couple of days later.

Collectors were shortening their want lists; booksellers were buying books off other booksellers rather than go to the bother of looking for fresh stock.

Oz was trying to adapt. Apart from the time spent dredging the benthos of the city for saleable items, he did most of his business on-line. He had his own web site, specialising in genre fiction because genre writers often had low print runs but rabid fans, and he used an Internet auction house for his other business, selling historical documents and autographs.

The problem was that anyone could now, in theory, sell anything to anyone else. The auction sites on the Internet were like global yard sales; sellers and buyers were cutting out the middlemen. The six months Oz had spent selling, page by page, the autograph album of a particularly tenacious pre-First World War stagedoor Johnny, now seemed like a golden age. His rusty Morris Minor, that most Victorian of car designs, had comprehensively broken down on the Westway two months ago, and it had cost him twice its scrap value to get it towed away.

So although this job was out of the ordinary, he couldn't pass up the chance. He really did need the money. Oz explained to the Colonel how the auction system worked, and how proxy bidding could automatically top any counter-bid to an agreed level, and the Colonel told Oz the ridiculously high price he was prepared to pay.

They shook hands on the deal in the windy sunlight outside

the Branch. Oz went back to his flat, fired up the modem, logged on to the auction web site, trawled its lists and indices, and found the relevant page.

The auction had been under way for more than three days and was scheduled to expire at midnight; there were only six hours left. Oz initiated a proxy bid and entered the Colonel's ceiling price – more than a hundred times the highest current bid. It took him two minutes. He wrote down the e-mail address of the sellers and went off to catch a No. 38 bus.

'Looks like they've got their own server, man,' Gabriel Day told Oz.

'How is that a problem?'

Oz was standing at Gabriel's shoulder, because Gabriel was sitting at the computer on the only chair in Gabriel Day's studio flat. The small room, in a housing association block on Rosebery Avenue, was crowded with dead tech. Vocoders, Betamax video players, video disk players, record decks, cyclostyles, ancient computers, battered printers. Boxes of 8-inch, 5¼-inch and 3-inch disks. Shelves of gutted electronics, sheaves of wires, the multicoloured pips of transistors, the beautiful acorns and thimbles and pods of electronic valves.

Gabriel Day was a forty-something university drop-out, with a greasy ponytail pulled back from his bald patch, a permanent hunch, and slab-like glasses with thick black plastic lenses. He specialised in fixing obsolete hardware, but had a sideline in sourcing obscure information.

He told Oz, 'If they were using a commercial service provider to get access to the Internet, I could probably get their address through the subscriber list. A simple hack, or even easier, a little bribe to an under-paid clerk. But this will take a little time.'

'But you can do it?'

'I'll have to lay it off on a real black–hat hacker, but it shouldn't take long. He'll use a trojan program to get into their computer through their e-mail, and it'll look around for their phone number or find some file with their address.' Gabriel sucked at his stained teeth. 'Two days at the most. Why do you want to find them?'

Oz laid out the story over a cup of black coffee. Gabriel made good coffee in a battered electric percolator, but spoiled it by adding powdered milk if you wanted it white.

'It might be a scam,' Gabriel said, when Oz was finished.

'I did wonder. That's why you might get your hacker friend to check the people making bids, too.'

'In case they're fake bids, artificially jacking up the price for something which might not exist.'

'Exactly.'

Gabriel grinned, showing coffee–stained tombstone teeth. 'Like the Australian virgins.'

'There are virgins in Australia?'

'Some guy in Perth, man, offered virgins for sale through one of the net auction houses. He wasn't really selling virgins, of course. He was collecting names and addresses of everyone who made a bid. And then he posted them on his web-site. It's the fourth wave.'

'The fourth wave?'

Gabriel adjusted his heavy glasses with finger and thumb. 'The first wave was hardware – actual machines, IBM, the telcos. The second wave was software – that's what Bill Gates realised, that's why Microsoft beat out Apple, because Apple was as much about beautiful machines as it was about software. The third wave, that's now, that's concepts, dot coms, ideas about how to use the Internet to connect people and things in the real world. But soon there'll be the fourth wave: stuff that never leaves the Internet, stuff that only exists in cyberspace.'

'Oh. You mean virtual reality.' Oz had read some of the sci-fi books he sold: he knew about virtual reality.

'I mean fairylands, dreams, ideals. And scams, spoofs, pranks. Fairy gold, man. Looks like gold when you find it, but turns out to be cobwebs or leaves when you get it home. That's what this book might be. You could be chasing the grail.'

'But you can find the grail's telephone number.'

'Don't worry about that, man. Everyone has to live somewhere.'

'You have it?' the Colonel said. 'I must say that's amazingly quick.'

'We won the bid. Now you have to pay for it.' Oz gave the details.

'That's the Queen's bank,' the Colonel said.

'Yes, and they wouldn't give up the name of the account holder.'

'I pay the money into this account, and the book will be delivered?'

'To me, yes. I gave them my address.'

'I'll do it right now,' the Colonel said.

'Use a credit card. It'll go through at once.'

'I knew I could rely on a chap like you.'

'We're not done yet, sir,' Oz said, and rang off.

Although Oz was fairly sure that Gabriel's hacker would be able to dig out a telephone number, he planned to interrogate the courier who would bring the book to his flat once the Colonel had settled the bill. Couriers were physical extensions of the Internet, their routes an analog of the Internet's web. The courier who brought the Incunabula would have to have picked it up from somewhere, and the right question (or bribe) might help Oz trace it back to its source.

So Oz sat in his flat all day, waiting for the courier. He checked the various auctions he was conducting. He got his accounts up to date. A can of oxtail soup took care of lunch. He waited until eight o'clock in the evening, then put his hat on his head, took up his cane, and went out.

There was a lock-in at the Branch: five-card stud poker at a penny a point, played upstairs on the tiny stage, amidst the props of the latest play, an adaptation of a minor but classic noir movie, *Detour*. At midnight, Oz was holding two sevens and two fives, and was pretty sure that Ken the barman was yet again bluffing on a high card pair, when he heard the throaty roar of a motorcycle. He threw in his hand, made a hasty farewell, and clattered down the stairs and shouldered through the fire door just as the motorcycle roared past again, heading back the way it had come.

It was a big black beast, its black-clad rider bent low as it raced past, raising a wind that sent litter swirling high in the air. Oz glimpsed the insignia on the motorcycle's tool box – an old-fashioned posthorn with a single loop of cord, white on blue – and then twin red flames stabbed from the exhaust pipes as the bike put on speed and flew across the bridge that arched over the canal, the throaty snarl of its engine rising and then cutting off as abruptly as if the motorcycle had hit a brick wall on the far side.

Oz walked to the crown of the bridge, but saw only the empty street stretching away beneath the double chain of orange streetlights.

The posthorn insignia wasn't the badge of any courier

service he knew, but when he got back to the flat he found that the book had been delivered. Not to his door, but to his flat: to his desk.

The package sat on top of his computer. A big padded envelope, sealed with staples and parcel tape, his address printed on a stick-on label, with the name of the courier service in cursive script below. *Thurn und Taxis*. Befuddled by Strangeways Ale, Oz sat on his swivel chair for some time, looking at the package. After a while, he got up and went downstairs and looked at the locks on the front door, and then at the locks on the door to his flat. There seemed to be fresh scratches around the keyholes, but he wasn't enough of a locksmith to know if that meant anything. But, indisputably, the book existed. It had been delivered.

'You didn't open it,' the Colonel said.

'No, sir. It's your package.'

It was the next day, in Colonel Salisbury's tall, narrow house in a quiet Camden square. It was crammed with old furniture designed for much bigger spaces. The living room was carpeted with three overlapping Persian rugs, and two big sofas faced each other amidst a profusion of side tables which held art deco lamps with stained-glass shades, vases, and family photographs in silver frames. Portraits in heavy gilt frames were hung cheek by jowl on the walls.

The Colonel did the thing with his eyes which made them look like they were twinkling, and said, 'I knew I could rely on you, young man.' He weighed the package in both hands, then turned it over and ripped the tab of the envelope and pulled out a slim octavo volume bound in faded red calfskin with stamped gilt lettering.

A silence fell as the Colonel stared at the cover, and at last Oz ventured, 'It is the right book?'

'What? Oh yes, yes. Would you excuse me for just a moment . . . ?'

After the Colonel had wandered out, not taking his eyes from the book, Oz sat in one of the sofas, sipping the driest sherry he had ever tasted, so pale it was almost colourless. He'd woken early, and had spent a lot of time on the Internet, where he had learned that the family of Von Thurn und Taxis had had a stranglehold on postal services in Western Europe from the fifteenth to the nineteenth century. At the height of its power, it had employed more than twenty thousand mail-boys, and its monopoly on mail extended from the Baltic to Gibraltar. But after the French revolution, Napoleon allowed some of the German states to start up their own postal services, and by the nineteenth century nationalisation of mail transport in most European countries shrank Thurn und Taxis's empire to a few German territories and cities – and even that rump had been lost after the family had supported the losing side of the war between Prussia and Austria.

Oz used half a dozen web search engines, plundered the Internet white pages, even phoned Company House. No courier service by the name of Thurn und Taxis was registered in any European country. The family still existed – you could visit their palace in Frankfurt – but the courier service had expired at about the same time as the passenger pigeon.

A courier service which did not exist had delivered a book which should not exist.

Oz had gone back to the auction site, poked around, and discovered that the same person (or at least, someone using the same e-mail address) who had sold the printed copy of the Eccham Incunabula was a fairly active buyer and seller of antiquarian books. He'd made some phone calls, and at last discovered that Lawrence Ackroyd (he of the red leather jumpsuit) had sold the mystery man several items.

'All late eighteenth- and early nineteenth-century stuff. French, mostly, and mostly commonplace stuff in no more than fair condition. Hardly your sort of thing,' Ackroyd added, clearly suspecting that Oz wanted to edge into his business.

Oz said, 'I leave the gilt and leather trade to experts like you, Larry. But I have a friend who has something your client might be interested in.'

'I'd be happy to take a look at it, but between you and me, I can't guarantee anything.'

'You don't know your client?'

'I've never met the man. He keeps in contact by mail or by e-mail, pays by banker's draft, and the books are collected by courier.'

'Thurn und Taxis, I suppose.'

'I wouldn't know. I leave the books outside my door at night, and in the morning they're gone. If your client has something to offer, I'd be happy to help out.'

Oz said that he would bear it in mind, and called Gabriel Day, and learnt that Gabriel's tame hacker had found the telephone number associated with the e-mail address of the mystery man.

'But it won't be much use,' Gabriel said, 'because it isn't real. See, the telcos keep back certain numbers. Fake numbers, the way every number in an American movie starts with the 555 area code. And this number, man, is from 555 land. I looked it up on this reverse directory I happen to have, and it doesn't exist.'

'It's ex-directory.'

'It's ex-everything, man.'

Oz was looking at the time-darkened portraits when the

Colonel came back. He had the dazed look of a man who has opened his own front door one morning to discover not the accustomed street, but a jungle or a cratered moonscape. He poured himself a sherry, drank it in one go, and said, 'It's the same text, more or less.'

Oz said, '"Things are seldom what they seem, Skimmed milk masquerades as cream."' It was a famous couplet from HMS *Pinafore*. 'Whoever sold you this has been buying old books, mostly battered and foxed volumes. But condition doesn't matter if all you want to do is make pristine copies. You age them with tea, you bake them in an oven. I know this little maniac who can knock up a perfect copy of any modern edition overnight. He'll be able to tell if what you've bought really is nineteenth century.'

'I don't want anyone else involved.' The Colonel poured himself another sherry, and said, 'Might there be more than one copy?'

'It's possible.'

'I was afraid of that. And I'm afraid that I haven't been entirely frank with you, young man.'

The Colonel crossed to the window, looked out in both directions, then drew the heavy curtains and said, 'Sir Toby Eccham was not just an alchemist; he was also a practitioner of black magic. The Eccham Incunabula contains descriptions of his ceremonies. Many of them involving dead bodies or parts of dead bodies. And molestation of children. Of babies.'

Another silence, into which a clock under a glass dome threw three silvery chimes.

Oz said, 'Every family has its black sheep.'

'It doesn't matter to me, young man, but my nephew, you see . . .'

The Colonel mentioned a minor cabinet minister, well known for his promotion of Christianity and family values.

As far as the Colonel was concerned, it wasn't a political matter. He was an old-fashioned Tory and disliked New Labour because they had stolen the ideas of the Conservative party (Oz, a socialist by upbringing and inclination, disliked them for exactly the same reason). It was a matter of family honour, the Colonel said: that was why he had to be sure that there were no more copies of the Incunabula.

'His daughter told me about the auction, and I promised her that I would do something about it. *He* doesn't know about this, and I hope he never does. But if a newspaper should get hold of this . . .'

Oz promised that he would do his best, and walked all the way home. It was raining lightly, and he turned up the collar of his raincoat and pulled down the brim of his hat, just like a proper detective. By the time he reached his flat, he knew exactly what he had to do. No more sneaking around. Time for some direct action. He hung up his raincoat and his jacket, rolled up his sleeves, and dialled the number Gabriel Day had given him.

It rang a long time. Oz sat in his chair, his feet cocked beside his computer, and listened to it ring. He was beginning to think that it would ring for ever when someone picked up.

A sound like the ocean roar in the seashell of his ear, and then a whisper, hoarse and curiously intimate.

'There's no one here.'

The line went dead. Oz redialled.

It rang for five minutes, ten. At last a click and the sigh of distant waves. Oz said quickly, 'I know about Thurn und Taxis.'

No reply. Oz said into the roar of the sea, 'I know what you're doing. I know why you're buying copies of old books.' He said, 'We need to talk.'

The line clicked, and there was only the burr of the dial

tone. Oz redialled. The phone rang and rang, but no one picked up again.

They came for Oz that night.

He was on the way home after sinking one too many pints of Strangeways at the Branch. They rushed him from behind a double-parked white van, two figures all in black, their heads swollen globes. Oz swung at one with his cane, but his arms were seized and something cold and wet, with a piercingly sharp chemical reek, was pressed over his mouth and nose.

The world receded. When it came back, everything was in motion. Oz was lying in a swaying, rushing metal box stroked by flashes of light. The back of a van, a van making speed. A figure loomed over him, braced against the van's sway. The swollen head was nothing more sinister than a black crash helmet, but behind the darkly tinted visor were two red sparks where the eyes might be, and the fingers of the hand which pushed the wet cloth against his face were tipped with strong curved claws.

The strong reek: the van's rush rushed away.

Oz woke, his mouth dry, his head pounding, bathed in the cold light of three widescreen Sony TVs stacked on top of one another like a piece of modern art, all tuned to a dead channel. Oz sat up in stages and at last managed to get to his feet, fairly sure that he wasn't going to throw up, dusted off his black jacket, straightened his cravat. His cane lay at his feet, and he picked it up and tucked it under his arm.

The huge room was lit only by the TVs. Bare concrete walls, a poured concrete floor, no windows, metal double doors big enough to admit a truck. There was a row of bookcases behind the stack of TVs, a ticking as of many clocks in the darkest corner, beyond the caravan which sat on blocks in the middle of the dark, lofty space, a streamlined aluminium cylinder like a spaceship from a fifties B-movie. Luminescent TV snow sparkled on its side like rushing stars. A thick cable ran up from its curved roof into the darkness. Its windows were shuttered with black blinds and its door was locked; no one answered when Oz rapped on it with his cane.

The big doors were locked too.

There was a bog standard Panasonic video recorder on top of the three TVs, but on top of that was a silvery box from which half a thick black glass disc protruded, and on top of *that* was something like a reel-to-reel tape recorder that used inch-wide transparent tape. All cabled into the back of the TVs, from which three black cords rose up into darkness.

The bookcases were ordinary enough, fibreboard and white melamine, but the books were anything but ordinary. Oz squinted at volume after volume in the TV light. There were leather-bound books in French and German and Italian. There were books which should not have existed because they had never been written. Charles Dickens's *Martin Sweezlebugg*. Raymond Chandler's *The Poodle Springs Mystery*. J.R.R. Tolkien's *The Lost Road*. H.G. Wells's *The Return of the Time Machine*. James Joyce's *A Dublin Fairy Story*.

Oz thought that he'd been right all along. The Colonel's dissolute brother had let someone take a long look at the Eccham Incunabula. He'd had debts, and there were crazed scholars who'd pay well for access to a suppressed book of the black arts. A copy had been made, and it had fallen into the hands of these people. They were forgers all right, but with a lot more style than most. They didn't just copy books: no, they actually wrote *new* books . . .

Here was a book in what looked like Babylonian cuneiform, but with pictures of what looked like airships. Here was a rack of pornography: men and women; women and women; men and men; men and animals; men and really *strange* animals . . .

The biggest book of all stood on a brass lectern, a folio volume bound in heavy leather with iron corners. Oz heaved it open.

Fiery letters hung on pages of infinite depth, burning through his eyes into his brain.

He slammed the heavy cover shut: the crash echoed around the huge, stark room.

A moment later, lights came on all around the walls: the ordinary miracle of electric light.

The first thing Oz saw, through swelling tears and the fading brands of backwards-slanting script, was that the clocks ticking at the far end of the room were not clocks at all, but tickertape machines. There were more than two dozen, standing under glass domes like bird skeletons modelled in brass and meccano, pecking and clucking and scratching, busy with gears and pinwheels, extruding henpecked ribbons of paper that made untidy nests as they spilled on to bare concrete. The smallest, elevated on a mahogany table, could easily have fitted into the palm of his hand; the largest was twice as tall as a man. There were other machines on a bench, things like teletypes, thing with mirrors or crystal spheres, a tangerine iMac. Every machine connected to a thick black cord, and all the cords running up into the ceiling.

Oz's first thought was that Gabriel Day would definitely feel at home here.

His second was that these maniacs weren't forgers after all.

'You are a traveller,' someone said.

'By your clothes we can see that you are not from this place,' someone else added.

Oz turned. Two people stood in front of the big doors. They were slight and slender, fine-boned and white-haired. They might have been brother and sister. They were holding hands, and dressed identically in black roll-neck sweaters and black jeans, like two beatnik elves.

The man said, 'You said that you know about Thurn und Taxis. We do not know about you.'

The woman said (hers was the hoarse whisper Oz had heard on the telephone), 'We know nothing about you, but your strange clothes show that you are obviously a traveller.'

Oz laughed.

The two looked at each other.

'He looked in the Book of Uriel,' the man told the woman.

'If he looked too long, his mind will have been turned,' the woman told the man.

Oz said, 'People make all kinds of comments about my clothes, but I think it's the first time they've saved my life.' He was trying to regain his equilibrium. It was like walking on to the stage: you had to leave your fear behind. He said, 'I thought it was an elaborate hoax, but it's all real, isn't it? The books are real. Thurn und Taxis is real, too. I think it links all kinds of places together – including places which don't really exist.'

'Of course they exist.'

The two spoke together.

'I bought a book from you, on behalf of a client. It was a printed copy of a unique handwritten manuscript that was a closely guarded family secret. A secret in this world, in this line of history – but perhaps not a secret in other histories. My client is anxious to know whether you might be selling other copies.'

The man said, 'Is that why you contacted us?'

'That's how it started,' Oz said.

'We sell unique items,' the man said.

'You mean, no more than one of a kind?'

'We mean what we say,' the woman said.

'My client will be pleased.'

The man and the woman looked at each other. The man said, 'We think that you are not a traveller after all.'

The huge metal doors swung back. The space beyond seemed as infinite as the sky. Figures were slowly advancing out of it, seeming to cover many miles with each step. It hurt Oz's eyes to look at them, and he forced himself to look away, to look at the man and the woman.

He said, 'Perhaps I've read too much of my own stock, perhaps it's the stuff you dosed me with, or perhaps looking in that book really did drive me crazy, but I think that Thurn und Taxis didn't fade away where you come from.' He was talking quickly. He felt that he was talking for his life.

'Perhaps Napoleon didn't start to dismantle their empire; perhaps Napoleon never existed, or never became emperor of France. Thurn und Taxis kept growing, and grew bigger than the world. It buys quite ordinary items in one place, and sells them in another to collectors who want things which don't exist — at least, not where they live. I know how it works: I'm in the same trade. Christ, what *are* those things?'

The advancing figures seemed to be giants, but it hurt too much to look at them — like staring at a welder's torch — to make out any details.

The woman said, 'In some places, people are not like you or me.'

Oz said, 'I want to help you. Do you think I'm the only one who can put this together?'

'Most people do not ask questions,' the man said calmly.

'You haven't been using the Internet for long,' Oz said.

'You've been relying on deals with people who were happy to take your money and ask no questions. But the thing about the Internet is that it is transparent. Anyone can find out about you because anyone can see what you buy and what you sell. You've to set up a point of contact, and that allows anyone to find you. Anyone in the world. I'm the first. There'll be others.'

The man and the woman looked at each other, looked at Oz.

Oz said, 'OK, perhaps I'm not the first to find you. But I'm the first who can help you. Do you know what a proxy is?'

The two looked at each other again. After a long moment, the great doors swung shut.

The woman said, 'You told us that you are in the same trade?'

If anyone asks (hardly anyone does), Oz is in the import/ export trade. He handles all the work himself, with computer and modem, telephone and fax. No customers ever come to his house. That isn't how he does business. No one visits his house except for the people who come to take things away, and he is careful never to see them.

His imports are exotic, peculiar, unique, one of a kind, but he earns exactly the same commission from exports as mundane as skimmed milk: a complete set of Jeffrey Archer's first editions, the Athena print of the map of Middle-Earth, a Monopoly set, a 3-D postcard of da Vinci's *Last Supper*, the London telephone directory for 1953 . . .

when larry met allie

val mcdermid

We'd done virtually everything before we even met.

Let me rephrase that. We'd done, virtually, everything before we even met.

Or perhaps, we'd done virtually everything, virtually, before we met.

Amazing what a difference a couple of commas can make. The difference between life and death, sometimes.

I chose her very carefully. I knew what I was looking for. Distance was a key factor; I didn't want there to be any possibility of her appearing in my world. No witnesses, you see.

That she already had a lover was also important; there had to be a good reason for her to keep me clandestine.

I didn't want her beautiful, either; beautiful women are accustomed to having men come on to them. They know how to brush us off and they don't think twice about it. As every teenage boy knows, the ugly girls are always grateful for attention.

The other vital element in the selection process came from her work. I was looking for a writer who revelled in sensuality, whose work displayed a hunger for the wilder shores of sexual experiment, whose prose had the power to inflame a flicker of desire. There's no shortage of sex in crime fiction these days, but most of it is about as erotic as the Encyclopaedia Britannica. I had to plough through a lot of depressingly grim attempts at arousing the reader before I found her.

Allie James. Author of four psychological thrillers featuring FBI profiler Susan Sondheim. None of them had been *New York Times* bestsellers, but she had respectable sales and a growing fan base, if her sales ranking and reviews on amazon.com were to be trusted. I read the books and felt a prickle of excitement run up the back of my neck.

On the face of it, she was a prime candidate. Her protagonist had two lovers during the course of the four novels. Allie's descriptions of their encounters managed to walk the tightrope between graphic mechanics and sentimental euphemism. There was a genuine erotic charge in what she wrote, a sly, knowing sensuousness that tightened my stomach, dried my mouth and made me want more.

The brief author biog on the back flap was encouraging too. 'Allie James was born and raised in rural North Carolina. She trained in graphic design and worked for ten years in advertising in Chicago. She now lives in Virginia with her partner.' There was no photograph, which made me think that Allie James didn't have a high opinion of her looks. And with her background, she probably wasn't as sophisticated as a big city girl. She'd be easier to flatter, to convince and to capture.

I needed more information, however. Next stop, the search engine. Google.com gave me a couple of hundred hits, and I worked my way through reviews, through on-line booksellers, through newsgroup discussion strands on her work until eventually, I found a couple of lengthy interviews that coloured in the picture more fully. Allie was thirty-seven, a Gemini only child who professed to be fascinated by the extremes of human psychology. Her partner taught English literature in a small college in Virginia. They'd been together for eight years. They had no children, but doted on their Labrador bitch. And still no photograph anywhere.

I headed off to a site I'd discovered where it's possible to track down who owns domain names. I typed 'alliejames.com.' into their search engine. As I'd expected, I was told that the site was already owned. Any writer with any sense has figured out the importance of owning their domain name, even if they're not doing anything with it yet. If they don't register it themselves, they run the risk of being held to ransom by some nerd who's seen the potential of selling it back to them. Or worse, having their name bought by their publisher, to do with as the parent company wishes.

I chose the option that allowed me to find out the site's owner. Most people don't realise this information is readily available, so they don't bother to hide behind their agent or a box number. Allie was one of those who hadn't. Within seconds, I was staring at her address and the phone number I'd already discovered was unlisted. I printed out the details for future reference, then went on-line to set my bait.

From: Lawrence Ryan, Lr25478@hotmail.com

To: Allie James, ajva@alliejames.com

Re: Your books

Dear Allie,

I wanted to write and tell you how much pleasure your books have given me. Few writers achieve the insight

into the human condition that you seem to manage so
effortlessly. I love the depth of characterisation in your
work, and the way you convey the passion of the hunter
for her goal. Susan Sondheim is one of the best-rounded
protagonists in the genre, a woman with a heart and soul
as well as a brain.

As one who toils in the same part of the garden as you,
I know how difficult it is to create something genuinely
fresh in the genre. I just wanted to tell you how much I
respect what you do.

Best wishes,

Larry Ryan.

I had few doubts that my approach would provoke a response.
And I was right. Within twelve hours, I had her reply sitting
in my in-box.

Dear Larry,

Wow! What an honour to get fan mail from a fellow writer of
your achievement! I've been a huge – albeit silent – fan
of your work since The Lazarus Angel was first published
over here. Since when, I've had to break the bank to
import the UK editions, because I just don't want to wait
for your US publisher to catch up :-)

I'm so thrilled that you enjoy my adventures with Susan.
All fan mail is great, of course, but it means so much more
to hear it from someone I admire. So, where are you up to?
When can I expect my next fix?

Yours, in awe,

Allie

Of course, I was straight back on to her. There would be a
time to keep her hanging on, but not yet.

Allie,

What a charming reply. You certainly know how to flatter!
I didn't expect you even to have heard of me, never mind to
have read my books, given the complete lack of promotion
my US publishers throw my way. So it goes.

<So, where are you up to? When can I expect my next fix?>

I've just finished the proofs for my new book, *Night
Sweats*, which means I have a blessed period of about three
weeks before I begin the next book. I'm afraid *NS* won't
be out for another five months, so you'll have to possess
your soul in patience.

Unless, of course, you'd like me to e-mail it to you? I
know there's nothing more tedious than to read a book in
typescript, but if you can bear it, I'd be happy to let
you see it. You can be the first person to read it cold,
knowing nothing at all about it . . .

Best

Larry

It was, of course, an offer she couldn't refuse. I'd known
that when I made it. This hadn't been part of my original
plan, but the fact that she'd read my work short-circuited
the long game I'd initially had in mind. It was a gambit that
accelerated the pace enormously, and within days we were
deep into exchanges about the craft of writing, the business
of publishing, the process of getting a book together, and all
the other things that outsiders imagine writers talk about all
the time. Although, in fact, we seldom do. But it built bridges
between us, principally because I let her do most of the
running then made sure I agreed with almost all she said.

Inevitably, the small details of her life began to slide
into the e-mails. I discovered the lover was called Jeffrey,
that he was a self-obsessed Aquarius who resented Allie's

success. Not that she told me this directly. But it wasn't hard to read between the lines. I avoided criticising Jeffrey, concentrating rather on making myself seem the considerate and supportive type. I let slip that my lover had died a couple of years before and that I hadn't felt able to open up to anyone since.

From there, it was a short step to gentle flirting. Given that we were by then exchanging between twenty and fifty e-mails a day, ranging in length from a few sentences to 20k messages, it didn't take long to escalate into something much more intense. We even swapped our favourite porn sites. Which, of course, both of us only ever accessed in the interests of research.

One of us might have been telling the truth, but it certainly wasn't me. When I had to leave town for a couple of days, I told her I wouldn't have my laptop with me. She sent seventeen messages, regardless.

Of course, we got to the inevitable point where Allie said Jeffrey was beginning to wonder if she was having an on-line affair, she was spending so much time on her computer. :-}

So what constitutes an on-line affair?

I think cyber fucking.

Phew. Well, that's all right, then, we've never been in a private chat room together . . .

I certainly don't feel as if we've crossed a line. I'm
very open with you and I share my feelings, but that's
what friends do, right? Do you feel like a line has been
crossed?

No, I don't feel we've crossed a line. I think we've
both danced kind of close to it, but we use humour to
bounce back from the danger zone. This is not an easy
thing to discuss in e-mail. Face to face or on the
phone, you get the verbal and non-verbal cues from
the other person as to whether they're thinking <Yes,
I want to hear more about what you feel about this>
or <DON'T GO THERE>. In e-mail, if you get into these
complex zones, somebody has to put their toe in the
water first then bite their nails till the other party
has the time to deal with it. So, here goes . . . We are
very open with each other and we go places we would
neither of us go with anyone else. We miss each other
when we're not in touch. We've got a lot in common
and we connect on many different levels. We've got
mutual respect and we laugh a lot together. It would be
disingenuous to deny there is some sort of attraction
between us. But we're neither of us up for taking
chances with your relationship with the man you live
with. So we've found a way to relate that walks that
tightrope.
I think.
What do you think/feel?

*I think/feel the same as you. I'm glad this is cleared
up. I really do enjoy our friendship. It's become
very, very important to me. I can't imagine what life
was like before. Or what it would be like without
you and your crazy humour that gets me through the
days. You are the best thing that has happened to me
for a very long time, Larry. And that's not to say
anything against Jeffrey. Though I don't think he'd be
comfortable with the way we're so open about sex. ;-)*

*I mean, it's kind of like with porn, isn't it? It's
hard to explain it to someone who doesn't like it. What
about you?*

I think I'm in more or less the same place as you on this.
I don't want there to be barriers between us, though.
That's really important to me in terms of my relationship
with you.

Same here.

Consciously or not, it was her way of seeing whether the ante was about to be upped. I nearly danced round the room. Hook, line and sinker. I let a couple of weeks go by, then, when I knew Jeffrey was out of town for a couple of nights at some post-modernist seminar, I started to reel her in. First, I planted a couple of lures in that morning's e-mail. Then I called her number.

'Hello?' She sounded more assertive than I'd expected.

'I bet you can't guess who this is,' I said.

'Larry?' Her voice rose an octave.

'Right first time.' I laughed. 'Amazing.'

'How did you get my number?' She sounded bewildered. 'It's unlisted.'

'What kind of stalker would answer a question like that?' I teased.

Now it was her turn to laugh. 'No, but really, tell me how you tracked me down.'

So I did. I could hear the mixture of delight and unease in her voice. She didn't mind me finding out, but it worried her that other, weirder people might be able to find her so easily. 'I need to change that,' she said.

'You really should. After all, the only person who needs to be able to find you already has.'

The ice was broken. We started talking about things we'd been discussing in our recent posts, and I let the conversation glide round to the fresh bait I'd laid that morning. 'Like I said, I wish I had your ability to write credible sex scenes,' I complained. 'I really need to show the interaction between Guy and Zoe, but the more I work on it, the more wooden it gets.'

She bit. Within seconds, we were talking each other through what I needed to write. Within minutes, we were practising method writing. 'I can't believe you're making me so horny,' she sighed.

'Oh God. Me too . . .' I let the pause hang for a moment while our breathing crossed thousands of miles. 'It would be very bad manners of me to leave you in that state,' I said, aiming for that ironic English politeness that Americans love so much. And of course, she didn't demur when I moved the conversation up another gear. I told her exactly what I knew she wanted to hear. The deliciously dirty things I was doing to her. The forbidden fantasies she was unleashing on me. At first, she said almost nothing, but that didn't last. When the dam broke, it was as if we were playing a new Olympic sport of competitive arousal.

The thing about phone sex and cybersex is that anyone can be the perfect lover. I'd studied everything Allie had ever said to me about sex, pondered carefully the porn that turned her on. Because I was interested only in impressing her with how perfect a fit we were, I could give her everything she had ever wanted without having to consider for a moment whether or not it aroused me or turned me off. Women can fake it anywhere; men need to be invisible to achieve the same result. That first time on the phone, I really didn't care whether I came or not. What I was concerned with was keeping Allie on the hook.

That I did come with such intensity only confirmed for me how right I'd been to choose her.

We made the most of Jeffrey's absence.

What I hadn't bargained for was that term was almost over. Jeffrey was spending an increasing amount of time at home, marking exam papers, writing up his latest research papers. But in a funny kind of way, that worked to my advantage too. It meant we couldn't call each other as much as Allie wanted to. There's nothing like scarcity to push up the value of a commodity.

After three weeks of this, she was going crazy.

> I didn't plan to feel this way, Larry. But all I can
> think about is being with you, in cyberspace or on
> the phone. I don't understand this; it's not like I
> suddenly stopped loving Jeffrey or anything. It's not
> that I want to leave him and run away with you. We
> both know that two writers under the same roof is a
> recipe for disaster. But whatever it is that's glowing
> between us needs resolution, and I don't see how we
> can achieve that without we spend some time together.
> I know I'll see you in October in Washington at the
> convention, but that's not the right environment for
> us to find out what's really going on here. What do
> you think?
> A xxx

> Darling Allie,
> <that's not the right environment for us to find out
> what's really going on here.>

```
You're right. So here's what we do. You tell Jeffrey
you've been invited to a conference in Europe to talk
about your books. Make it somewhere he won't be desperate
to visit, and make it on dates when he's got something in
his diary it would be impossible to cancel. I'll send you
the air tickets and the hotel reservation, and you come
over here. We'll have five days or so together. One way or
another, we'll know where we're going.
I know I shouldn't say this, Allie. But I love you.
Larry
```

Of course, she couldn't resist. We settled on five days in Brussels. Now I had to start being very, very careful. There must never be any grounds for suspicion. I took the car over on the ferry from Harwich to the Hook of Holland and drove down to Brussels. I bought an air ticket in Allie's name in a busy travel agency, paying in cash. I made a hotel reservation, also in her name, and paid a deposit in cash. I FedExed the ticket and the hotel reservation to her from Brussels along with a letter I'd faked up on the computer, so that her story would hang together for Jeffrey's benefit.

The intervening two weeks were torture. It was easier for Allie; she'd already had a lot more than a taste of what it felt like to have your fantasies become reality. But the burning desire that had pushed me into this conspiracy was growing stronger in me day by day. She'd had satisfaction; mine was still to come, and the need ate at me like an incessant heartburn of the soul.

The night before she was due to fly out, I composed a very careful e-mail.

```
Dearest Allie,
I know you're going to think this is paranoid, but I'm
```

thinking here of the future for you and Jeffrey. I know
you're not certain what that future is going to be, but
it's entirely possible you will want your relationship to
continue. So it's important that he doesn't find anything
while you're gone that might indicate to him that there is
any reason for him to doubt your feelings.

I know from what you've told me that you keep our exchange
of e-mails in a separate folder in your comms program's
filing cabinet.

What you need to do is delete the whole folder. I know you
don't want to destroy our correspondence, but I've got
everything on file here, and I'll send you a copy of it
all as soon as you get home. I just don't think we should
tempt fate.

It has a horrible way of biting back.

What do you think?

Love, always,

Larry

*Oh God, babe, you don't know what you're asking. I know
deep down you're so right, but it feels like cutting out
my heart to delete all the beautiful things you've said
to me. (not to mention the down and dirty ones, heh heh
heh). I'm going to do it, though. Last thing before I
leave. What I never told you is that I printed out all
your e-mails to me. While Jeffrey's out at the gym this
afternoon, I'm going to shred them. I hate to do it, but
I know it makes sense. Like the song says, I can't wait to
meetchu . . .*

Love, love, love,

A xxx

I only realised I'd been holding my breath when I got to the end of the e-mail. I couldn't help smiling. Good girl, Allie, I thought. Now there would be no obvious trace of me on her computer. Nothing for nosy Jeffrey to find if he started looking for reasons why Allie had gone off sex with him.

That night, I made the crossing to Holland again. I booked myself into a hotel near the ferry port. I plugged my laptop into the phone socket and set it up so that it would make a <send and receive mail> call every seventy-three minutes until midnight. That way, there would be a record of me making phone calls from the room throughout the day, should I ever need to convince Jeffrey that I'd been nowhere near his beloved Allie. I took the stairs down and slipped out while the foyer was busy with a coachload of pensioners from Ipswich.

I took my time driving down to Brussels. I was conscious of how edgy I was and I knew that could easily translate into the kind of bad driving that picks up a ticket from the traffic police. I arrived at the hotel around the same time Allie's flight was due to land. I found a legal parking slot about fifteen minutes' walk away and left the car there, carrying nothing with me but the laptop case containing a lightweight raincoat I'd bought in Holland. With cash, of course.

There was a busy bar on a corner opposite the hotel, and I wedged myself into a spot by the window where I could watch the entrance. I knew what she looked like now; although she'd always refused to send me a photograph, claiming I'd only be disappointed and wouldn't want to meet her, I'd finally tracked down an article on the internet from her local paper. They'd published a photograph of her at a book signing. As I'd thought, she wasn't beautiful. She wasn't ugly either; but you could see she'd have gone through her teens as a wallflower. The fat kid that nobody wants to dance with.

I'd been there about an hour when she climbed out of one of the regular stream of taxis. I watched as the bellboy took her suitcase, catching a glimpse of her nervous frown. I left it about ten minutes, then I called the hotel from the bar and asked for Ms James in my best American accent.

When I heard the familiar, 'Hello?' my heart rate shot up. I was so close now. I'd been rehearsing this scenario in my head for so long, the thought of it coming to fruition was enough to make me hard.

'It's me,' I said. 'I'm about twenty minutes away.'

'Oh God,' she said, her voice cracking. 'Larry, I'm so scared. I'm going to be a major disappointment.'

'No way,' I said. 'I know the woman inside. And she's beautiful. I'm so glad you made it.'

'Me too. Twenty minutes, you said?'

'Less, if I can make it.'

She chuckled. 'No. I need to shower and get into something a little more alluring.'

'Twenty minutes,' I said firmly.

'You're so masterful,' she teased.

'Believe it,' I said.

She opened the door so swiftly I wondered if she'd been standing behind it. I suppose if I'd been in love, it would have been a breathtaking sight. She was wearing a black lace basque with push-up cups. Her stockings were sheer and black, her heels high and spindly. She stood with one leg cocked at what's generally assumed to be a coquettish angle, one hand on hip, the other on the door. She'd done her best. It was as good as it was ever going to get, given what genetics had handed out to her.

Believe me, it wasn't what I saw that was reviving my erection. It was the realisation that all my careful planning had worked out in fact as precisely as it ever had in my fantasies.

Her smile was tentative, the ultimate oxymoron in the light of the brazen nature of her pose. I stepped forward and gently closed the door behind me. 'Wow,' I said.

'You mean it?'

I nodded, dropping my bag and moving into her. 'I mean it.' I buried my face in her hair. She hadn't had time to shower, and it had that musky, animal smell that women spend fortunes trying to erase. I wrapped one arm around her, easing her back towards the king-sized bed I'd specifically asked for when I booked the room. Her lips were all over my face as we inched backwards. I nibbled her ear, moaning softly. This time, there was no calculation. My response was for real.

She fell back on to the bed and I let myself fall with her, my knee between her thighs. I could feel her wetness through the fine wool of my trousers. Her hand was groping for my cock, pushing my jacket aside. With one hand, I reached for her face, pushing her hair back so I could look into her eyes.

With my free hand, I reached behind me and pulled the knife from the waistband of my trousers. As I plunged it into her side again and again, her hand closed convulsively against me.

I think I was coming as she died.

As I said, we'd done virtually everything before we met. But not quite.

myflesh.com

stewart home

Have you ever tried to find God using a search engine? I have and this is my story.

I knew there was something missing from my life. When I'd first worked for the record company that employed me I'd imagined what I did was glamorous. However, it didn't take me long to discover that what I held down was just a common or garden office job. Nonetheless, I needed a wage and I'd stayed with the company for the best part of five years.

I'd seen some changes in Shoreditch while I'd been working in the area. Numerous wholesalers had been forced out of business by rent hikes, and they were replaced by fashionable cafés and bars. Then, one weekend, the storefront church opposite my office disappeared. As I went in to work on Monday morning I saw that the altar had been ripped out and dumped in a skip. The building was being redecked as an art gallery.

When I'd first clocked the Church Of Jesus Christ Socialist, I'd thought it was some kind of joke. But over the ensuing weeks I noticed that the congregation was mainly black, principally middle-aged and overwhelmingly female. The church wasn't an art world jape. Father Pellucid who ran this house of worship was attracting the oppressed and downtrodden. The congregation was always neighbourly and I would sometimes chat with people going into or coming out of a service.

I got on particularly well with a girl in her early twenties. Sister Gloria was not only very close to Father Pellucid, she dressed impeccably and was incredibly good looking. Gloria invited me to attend a Christian love-in but I was reluctant. Just before the church disappeared, she began to turn up in the sandwich bar where I ate my lunch. Gloria told me to forget all my prejudices about religion. There was an inner circle around Father Pellucid and given his desire not only to serve the entire human race, but to be seen to be doing so, there were vacancies among this elect for foxy chicks like me.

While the majority of those attending the Church Of Jesus Christ Socialist imagined they were following doctrines inspired by the depression era American social reformer and religious leader Father Divine, the inner circle of the sect practised a form of Bible Communism based on the teachings of the nineteenth-century schismatic John Humphrey Noyes. This inner circle of perfectionists believed morality was for those lacking grace and that the rule of law did not apply to individuals who had been saved by Jesus. Gloria showed me a pledge she'd signed, it ran as follows:

1. I do not belong to *myself* in any respect, but I *do* belong first to God, and second to Father Pellucid as God's true representative.

2. That I have no rights or personal feelings in regard to child-bearing which shall in the least degree oppose or embarrass Father Pellucid in his choice of scientific combinations.

3. That I will put aside all envy, childishness and self-seeking, and rejoice with those who are chosen candidates, that we will, if necessary, become martyrs to science, and cheerfully resign all desire to become mothers, if for any reason Father Pellucid deems us unfit material for propagation. Above all I offer myself as a living sacrifice to God and true communism as outlined in the Holy Bible.

I shuddered as I read this. With his shock of carrot-red hair and heavily freckled complexion, Father Pellucid simply wasn't my type and I found the idea of letting him organise my sex-life really gross. Seeing that I hadn't been won over, Sister Gloria inveigled me to promise that I wouldn't discuss her revelations with other members of the church. That was the last time I spoke to Gloria and the following week the entire congregation disappeared.

Don't get me wrong, I don't have a problem with people practising free love, but I do object to secret doctrines and the cynical manipulation of belief. Even if the Church Of Jesus Christ Socialist was rotten at its very core, that didn't invalidate the desire for spirituality and personal growth the more innocent of its members professed. So after glancing through a window at the skip containing the remains of Father Pellucid's Shoreditch ministry, I called up a search engine on the office computer and entered the word God.

I quickly realised that finding God on the net wasn't going to be easy. He had thousands upon thousands of entries ranging from the Church Of God to a pop group called God Is My Co-Pilot. I looked at a few dozen listings and eventually decided to try a Christian chat room. My credit card had been cancelled due to my failure to meet the repayment schedule, so to subscribe to the service I required, I availed myself of my employer's flexible friend. The discussion in the chat room was fast and furious but far from satisfying. There must have been a dozen people on-line. I asked where I could find God and in response I was love bombed with one-sentence testimonials about the power of Jesus to save me.

The testimonials kept coming but there was little rational discussion or practical advice. Eventually, an advocate of Bible exegesis came on-line and drew the attention of all those present – in the spirit, if not the flesh – to 1 Corinthians iii, 16: 'Know ye not that ye are the temple of God, and that the spirit of God dwelleth in you?' According to the heretic who'd joined our discussion, this piece of biblical text made it clear that God was everywhere and therefore we were all God. He then added that heaven was already established on earth and there could be no sin.

Most of those involved in the theological discussions immediately denounced the free spirit advocate as mad, but he worked his corner well and outwitted them all. While everyone using the chat room appeared to be a Christian, those involved came from many different denominations. So the heretic got a Holy Roller to censure as pure madness the Baptist convictions of another visitor and vice versa. Before long a Methodist had pronounced a Catholic insane, while a Seventh Day Adventist attacked the beliefs of the Russian Orthodox Church as crazy, and so on.

I decided to cut my losses and try another site. Eventually I hit upon myflesh.com, where for a small fee my sins would be absolved and my questions answered. I gave my employer's credit details and then asked where I could find God. The reply I received was short and cryptic. I was told to have patience and all would be revealed within the space of a few weeks. In the meantime my membership fee gave me access to all areas of the myflesh.com site. I thought I'd better get back to work before someone noticed I was skiving, so I never did get around to looking at the pay-to-view areas of this enterprise.

However, all was revealed seven days later. I was advised by my boss that I was dismissed without notice. A substantial sum had gone missing from a company account. An investigation showed that most of the missing money had been paid over as a subscription to myflesh.com for on-line pornography. I was brusquely informed the music business had no use for a dozen Victorian porn novels that existed in cyberspace as badly scanned e-texts. I tried to explain I'd been searching for God and was under the impression I'd done no more than make a £5 love offering to a Christian ministry, but my boss wouldn't listen.

I'd rather despised Sister Gloria for being conned by a sharper like Father Pellucid, but I'd been done good and proper by an operator whose technique was just as crass. I'd gone on-line searching for God only to be diddled by a grifter who'd sold me second-rate pornography at a hugely inflated price. Looking at what I'd been offered, the ambiguities in the wording no longer appeared accidental. The conman responsible for them was playing it safe. While the cops might pursue a self-styled minister who exploited the gullible, they were unlikely to hammer someone charging way over the odds for out-of-copyright pornography. What the episode taught me was that we've taken the ways of the world with us onto the net. I guess the free spirit heretic I encountered in the Christian chat room was right, and I should have looked for God in my heart.

is there anybody there?

kim newman

'Is there a presence?' asked Irene.

The parlour was darker and chillier than it had been
moments ago. At the bottom of the heavy curtains, tassels
stirred like the fronds of a deep-sea plant. Irene Dobson –
Madame Irena, to her sitters – was alert to tiny changes in a
room that might preface the arrival of a visitor from beyond
the veil. The fizzing and dimming of still-untrusted electric
lamps, so much less impressive than the shrinking and bluing
of gaslight flames she remembered from her earliest seances.
A clamminess in the draught, as foglike cold rose from
the carpeted floor. The minute crackle of static electricity,
making hair lift and pores prickle. The tart taste of pennies
in her mouth.

'Is there a traveller from afar?' she asked, opening her
inner eye.

The planchette twitched. Miss Walter-David's fingers
withdrew in a flinch; she had felt the definite movement.

Irene glanced at the no-longer-young woman in the chair beside hers, shrinking away for the moment. The fear-light in the sitter's eyes was the beginning of true belief. To Irene, it was like a tug on a fishing line, the satisfying twinge of the hook going in. This was a familiar stage on the typical sitter's journey from scepticism to fanaticism. This woman was wealthy; soon, Irene would taste not copper but silver, eventually gold.

Wordlessly, she encouraged Miss Walter-David to place her fingertips on the planchette again, to restore balance. Open on the round table before them was a thin sheet of wood, hinged like an oversized chessboard. Upon the board's smoothly papered and polished surface was a circle, the letters of the alphabet picked out in curlicue. Corners were marked for YES – 'oui', 'ja' – and NO. The planchette, a pointer on marble castors, was a triangular arrowhead-shape. Irene and Miss Walter-David lightly touched fingers to the lower points of the planchette, and the tip quivered.

'Is there anybody there?' Miss Walter-David asked.

This sitter was bereft of a fiancé, an officer who had come through the trenches but succumbed to influenza upon return to civilian life. Miss Walter-David was searching for balm to soothe her sense of hideous unfairness, and had come at last to Madame Irena's parlour.

'Is there—'

The planchette moved, sharply. Miss Walter-David hissed in surprise. Irene felt the presence, stronger than usual, and knew it could be tamed. She was no fraud, relying on conjuring tricks, but her understanding of the world beyond the veil was very different from that which she wished her sitters to have. All spirits could be made to do what she wished them to do. If they thought themselves grown beyond hurt, they were sorely in error. The planchette, genuinely independent of the light touches of medium and sitter, stabbed towards a corner of the board, but stopped surprisingly short.

Y

Not YES, but the Y of the circular alphabet. The spirits often used initials to express themselves, but Madame had never encountered one who neglected the convenience of the YES and NO corners. She did not let Miss Walter-David see her surprise.

'Have you a name?'

Y again. Not YES. Was Y the beginning of a name: Youngman, Yoko-Hama, Ysrael?

'What is it?' she was almost impatient.

The planchette began a circular movement, darting at letters, using the lower tips of the planchette as well as the pointer. That also was unusual, and took an instant or two to digest.

M S T R M N D

'Msstrrmnnd,' said Miss Walter-David.

Irene understood. 'Have you a message for anyone here, Master Mind?'

Y

'For whom?'

U

'For Ursula?' Miss Walter-David's christian name was Ursula.

N U

'U?'

'You,' said Miss Walter-David. 'You.'

This was not a development Irene liked a bit.

There were two prospects in his chat room. Women, or at least they said they were. Boyd didn't necessarily believe them. Some users thought they were clever.

Boyd was primarily MstrMnd, but had other log-in names, some male, some female, some neutral. For each ISDN line, he had a different code name and e-address, none traceable to his physical address. He lived on-line, really; this flat in Highgate was just a place to store the meat. There was nothing he couldn't get by playing the web, which responded to his touch like a harpsichord to a master's fingers. There were always backdoors.

His major female ident was Caress, aggressively sexual; he imagined her as a porn site Cleopatra Jones, a black model with dom tendencies. He kept a more puritanical, shockable ident – SchlGrl – as back-up, to cut in when Caress became too outrageous.

These two users weren't tricky, though. They were clear. Virgins, just the way he liked them. He guessed they were showing themselves nakedly to the chat room, with no deception.

IRENE D.

URSULA W-D.

Their messages typed out laboriously, appearing on his master monitor a word at a time. He initiated searches, to cough up more on their handles. His system was smart enough to come up with a birth-name, a physical address, financial details and, more often than not, a jpg image from even the most casually assumed one-use log-on name. Virgins never realised that their presences always left ripples. Boyd knew how to piggyback any one of a dozen official and unofficial trackers, and routinely pulled up information on anyone with whom he had even the most casual, wary dealings.

IRENE D: Have you a message for anyone here, Master Mind?

Boyd stabbed a key.

Y

IRENE D: For whom?

U

IRENE D: For Ursula?

N U

IRENE D: U?

URSULA W-D: You.

At least one of them got it. IRENE D – why didn't she tag herself ID or I-D? – was just slow. That didn't matter. She was the one Boyd had spotted as a natural. Something about her blank words gave her away. She had confidence and ignorance, while her friend – they were in contact, maybe even in the same physical room – at least understood she knew nothing, that she had stepped into deep space and all the rules were changed. IRENE D – her log-on was probably a variant on the poor girl's real name – thought she was in control. She would unravel very easily, almost no challenge at all.

A MESSAGE FOR U I-D, he typed.

He sat on a reinforced swivel chair with optimum back support and buttock-spread, surveying a semi-circle of keyboards and monitors all hooked up to separate lines and accounts, all feeding into the master monitor. When using two or more idents, he could swivel or roll from board to board, taking seconds to chameleon-shift. He could be five or six people in any given minute, dazzle a solo into thinking she – and it almost always was a she – was in a buzzing chat room with a lively crowd when she was actually alone with him, growing more vulnerable with each stroke and line, more open to his hooks and grapples, her backdoors flapping in the wind.

I KNOW WHO U ARE

Always a classic. Always went to the heart.

He glanced at the left-most screen. Still searching. No details yet. His system was usually much faster than this.

Nothing on either of them, on IRENE or URSULA. They couldn't be smart enough to cover their traces in the web, not if they were really as newbie as they seemed. Even a netshark ace would have been caught by now. And these girls were fighting nowhere near his weight. Must be a glitch. It didn't matter.

I KNOW WHAT U DO

Not DID, but DO. DID is good for specifics, but DO suggests something ongoing, some hidden current in an ordinary life, perhaps unknown even to the user.

U R NOT WHAT U CLAIM 2 B

That was for sure.

U R NOT WHAT U CLAIM 2 B

'You are not what you claim to be?' interpreted Miss Walter-David. She had become quickly skilled at picking out the spirit's peculiar, abbreviated language. It was rather irritating, thought Irene. She was in danger of losing this sitter, of becoming the one in need of guidance.

There was something odd about Master Mind. He – it was surely a he – was unlike other spirits, who were mostly vague children. Everything they spelled out was simplistic, yet ambiguous. She had to help them along, to tease out from the morass of waffle whatever it was they wanted to communicate with those left behind, or more often to intuit what it was her sitters wanted or needed most to hear and to shape her reading of the messages to fit.

Her fortune was built not on reaching the other world, but in manipulating it so that the right communications came across. No sitter really wanted to hear a loved one had died a meaningless death and drifted in limbo, gradually losing personality like a cloud breaking up. Though, occasionally, she had sitters who wanted to know that those they had hated in life were suffering properly in the beyond and that their miserable post-mortem apologies were not accepted. Such transactions disturbed even her, though they often proved among the most rewarding financially.

Now, Irene sensed a concrete personality. Even through almost-coded, curt phrases, Master Mind was a someone, not a something. For the first time, she was close to being afraid of what she had touched.

Master Mind was ambiguous, but through intent rather than fumble-thinking. She had a powerful impression of him, from his self-chosen title: a man on a throne, head swollen and limbs atrophied, belly bloated like a balloon, framing vast schemes, manipulating lesser beings like chess pieces. She was warier of him than even of the rare angry spirit she had called into her circle. There were defences against him, though. She had been careful to make sure of that.

'Ugly hell gapes', she remembered from Dr Faustus. Well, not for her.

She thought Master Mind was not a spirit at all.

U R ALLONE

'You are all one,' interpreted Miss Walter-David. 'Whatever can that mean?'

U R ALONE

That was not a cryptic statement from the beyond. Before discovering her 'gift', Irene Dobson had toiled in an insurance office. She knew a type-writing mistake when she saw one.

U R AFRAID

'You are af—'

'Yes, Miss Walter-David, I understand.'

'And are you?'

'Not any more. Master Mind, you are a most interesting fellow, yet I cannot but feel you conceal more than you reveal. We are all, at our worst, alone and afraid. That is scarcely a great insight.'

It was the secret of her profession, after all.

'Are you not also alone and afraid?'

Nothing.

'Let me put it another way.' She pressed down on the planchette, and manipulated it, spelling out in his own language.

R U NOT ALSO ALONE AND AFRAID

She would have added a question mark, but the ouija board had none. Spirits never asked questions, just supplied answers.

IRENE D was sharper than he had first guessed. And he still knew no more about her. No matter.

Boyd rolled over to the next keyboard.

U TELL HIM GRRL BCK OFF CREEP

IRENE D: Another presence? How refreshing. And you might be?

CARESS SISTA.

IRENE D: Another spirit?

Presence? Spirit? Was she taking the piss?

UH HUH SPIRT THAT'S THE STUFF SHOW THAT PIG U CAN STAND UP 4 YRSELF

IRENE D: Another presence, but the same mode of address. I think your name might be Legion.

Boyd knew of another netshark who used Legion as a log-on. IRENE D must have come across him too. Not the virgin she seemed, then. Damn.

His search still couldn't penetrate further than her simple log-on. By now, he should have her mother's maiden name, her menstrual calendar, the full name of the first boy she snogged at school and a list of all the porn sites she had accessed in the last week.

He should close down the chat room, seal it up forever and scuttle away. But he was being challenged, which didn't happen often. Usually, he was content to play a while with those he snared, scrambling their heads with what he had found out about them as his net-noose drew tauter around them. Part of the game was to siphon a little from their bank accounts: someone had to pay his phone and access bills, and he was damned if he should cough up by direct debit like some silly little newbie. But mostly it was for the sport.

In the early days, he had been fond of co-opting idents and flooding his playmates' systems with extreme porn or placing orders in their names for expensive but embarrassing goods and services. That now seemed crude. His current craze was doctoring and posting images. If IRENE D was married, it would be interesting to direct her husband to, say, a goat sex site where her face was convincingly overlaid upon an enthusiastic animal-lover's body. And it was so easy to mock up mug shots, complete with guilty looks and serial numbers, to reveal an ineptly suppressed criminal past (complete with court records and other supporting documentation) that would make an employer think twice about keeping someone on the books. No one ever bothered to double-check by going back to the paper archives before they downsized a job.

Always, he would leave memories to cherish; months later, he would check up on his net-pals – his score so far was five institutionalisations and two suicides – just to see that the experience was still vivid. He was determined to crawl into IRENE D's skull and stay there, replicating like a virus, wiping her hard drive.

URSULA W-D: Do you know Frank? Frank Conynghame-Mars.

Where did that come from? Still, there couldn't be many

people floating around with a name like that. Boyd shut off the fruitless backdoor search, and copied the double-barrel into an engine. It came up instantly with a handful of matches. The first was an obituary from 1919, scanned into a newspaper database. A foolish virgin had purchased unlimited access to a great many similar archives, which was now open to Boyd. A local newspaper, the *Ham&High*. He was surprised. It was the World Wide Web after all. This hit was close to home – maybe only streets away – if eighty years back. He looked over the obit, and took a flyer.

DEAD OF FLU

URSULA W-D: Yes. She knows Frank, Madame Irena. A miracle. Have you a message from Frank? For Ursula?

Boyd speed-read the obit. Frank Conynghame-Mars, 'decorated in the late conflict', etc. etc. Dead at thirty-eight. Engaged to a Miss Ursula Walter-David, of this parish. Could the woman be still alive? She would have to be well over a hundred.

He launched another search. Ursula Walter-David.

Three matches. One the Conynghame-Mars obit he already had up. Second, an article from something called *The Temple*, from 1924 – a publication of the Spiritualist Church. Third, also from the *Ham&High* archive, her own obit, from 1952.

Zoiks, Scooby – a ghost!

This was an elaborate sting. Had to be.

He would string it along, to give him time to think.

U WIL BE 2GETHER AGAIN 1952

The article from *The Temple* was too long and close-printed to read in full while his formidable attention was divided into three or four windows. It had been scanned in badly, and not all of it was legible. The gist was a testimonial for a spiritualist medium called Madame Irena (no last-name given). Among her 'sitters', satisfied customers evidently, was Ursula Walter-David.

Weird. Boyd suspected he was being set up. He didn't trust the matches. They must be plants. Though he couldn't see the joins, he knew that with enough work he could run something like this – had indeed done so, feeding prospects their own mocked-up obits with full gruesome details – to get to someone. Was this a vengeance crusade? If so, he couldn't see where it was going.

He tried a search on 'Madame Irena' and came up with hundreds of matches, mostly French and porn sites. A BD/SM video titled *The Lash of Madame Irena* accounted for most of the matches. He tried pairing '+Madame Irena' with '+spiritualist' and had a more manageable fifteen matches, including several more articles from *The Temple*.

URSULA W-D: Is Frank at peace?

He had to sub-divide his concentration, again. He wasn't quite ambidextrous, but could pump a keyboard with either hand, working shift keys with his thumbs, and split his mind into segments, eyes rolling independently like a lizard's, to follow several lines.

FRANK IS OVER HIS SNIFFLES

Among the 'Madame Irena'/'medium' matches was a *Journal of the Society of Psychical Research* piece from 1926, shout-lined 'Fraudulence Alleged'. He opened it up, and found from a news-in-brief snippet that a court case was being prepared against one 'Irene Dobson', known professionally as 'Madame Irena', for various malpractices in connection with her work as a spirit medium. One Catriona Kaye, a 'serious researcher', was quoted as being 'in no doubt of the woman's genuine psychical abilities but also sure she had employed them in an unethical, indeed dangerous, manner'.

Another match was a court record. He opened it: a

declaration of the suit against Irene Dobson. Scrolling down, he found it frustratingly incomplete. The document set out what was being tried, but didn't say how the case came out. A lot of old records were like that, incompletely scanned. Usually, he only had current files to open and process. He looked again at the legal rigmarole, and his eye was caught by Irene Dobson's address.

The Laburnums, Feldspar Road, Highgate.

This was 26, Feldspar Road. There were big bushes outside. If he ran a search for laburnum.jpg, he was sure he'd get a visual match.

Irene Dobson lived in this house.

No, she had lived in this house. In the 1920s, before it was converted into flats. When it had a name, not a number.

Now she was dead.

Whoever was running this on Boyd knew where he lived. He was not going to take that.

'This new presence,' said Miss Walter-David. 'It's quite remarkable.'

There was no new presence, no 'Caress'. Irene would have felt a change, and hadn't. This was one presence with several voices. She had heard of such. Invariably malign. She should call an end to the seance, plead fatigue. But Ursula Walter-David would never come back, and the husbandless woman had a private income and nothing to spend it on but the beyond. At the moment, she was satisfied enough to pay heavily for Irene's service. She decided to stay with it, despite the dangers. Rewards were within reach. She was determined, however, to treat this cunning spirit with extreme caution. He was a tiger, posing as a pussycat. She focused on the centre of the board, and was careful with the planchette, never letting its points stray beyond the ring of letters.

'Caress,' said Miss Walter-David, a-tremble, 'may I speak with Frank?'

'Caress' was supposed to be a woman, but Irene thought the first voice – 'Master Mind' – closer to the true personality.

IN 52

'Why 1952? It seems a terribly long way off.'

WHEN U DIE

That did it. Miss Walter-David pulled away as if bitten. Irene considered: it seemed only too likely that the sitter had been given the real year of her death. That was a cruel stroke, typical of the malign spirit.

The presence was a prophet. Irene had heard of a few such spirits – one of the historical reasons for consulting mediums was to discern the future – but never come across one. Could it be that the spirits had true foreknowledge of what was to come? Or did they inhabit a realm outside time and could look in at any point in human history, future as well as past, and pass on what they saw?

Miss Walter-David was still impressed. But less pleased.

The planchette circled, almost entirely of its own accord. Irene could have withdrawn her fingers, but the spirit was probably strong enough to move the pointer without her. It certainly raced ahead of her push. She had to keep the planchette in the circle.

IRENE

Not Irena.

DOBSON

Now she was frightened, but also annoyed. A private part of her person had been exposed. This was an insult and an attack.

'Who's Dobson?' asked Miss Walter-David.

SHE IS

'It is my name,' Irene admitted. 'That's no secret.'

ISNT IT

'Where are you?' she asked.

HERE THERE EVERYWHERE

'No, here and there perhaps. But not everywhere.'

This was a strange spirit. He had aspirations to omnipotence, but something about him was overreaching. He called himself 'Master Mind', which suggested a streak of self-deluding vanity. Knowledge wasn't wisdom. She had a notion that if she asked him to name this year's Derby winner, he would be able to furnish the correct answer (an idea with possibilities) but that he could reveal precious little of what came after death. An insight struck her: this was not a departed spirit, this was a living man.

Living. But where?

No.

When?

'What date is it?' she asked.

Good question. Since this must be a sting, there was no harm in the truth.

JAN 20 01

IRENE D: 1901?

N 2001

URSULA W-D: I thought time had no meaning in the world beyond.

IRENE D: That depends which world beyond our guest might inhabit.

Boyd had run searches on 'Irene Dobson' and his own address, independent and cross-matching. Too many matches were coming up. He wished more people had names like 'Frank Conynghame-Mars' and fewer like 'Irene Dobson'. 'Boyd Waylo', his birth-name, was a deep secret; his accounts were all in names like 'John Barrett' and 'Andrew Lee'.

Beyond the ring of monitors, his den was dark. This was

the largest room in what had once been a Victorian town house, and was now divided into three flats. Was this where 'Madame Irena' had held her seances? His raised ground-floor flat might encompass the old parlour.

He was supposed to believe he was in touch with the past.

One of the 'Irene Dobson' matches was a jpg. He opened the picture file, and looked into a small, determined face. Not his type, but surprising and striking. Her hair was covered by a turban and she wore a Chinese-style jacket, buttoned up to the throat. She looked rather prosperous, and was smoking a black cigarette in a long white holder. The image was from 1927. Was that when she was supposed to be talking to him from?

WHAT DATE 4 U

IRENE D: January 13, 1923. Of course.

Maybe he was supposed to bombard her with questions about the period, to try and catch her out in an anachronism. But he had only general knowledge: Prohibition in America, a General Strike in Britain, talking pictures in 1927, the Lindbergh flight somewhere earlier, the stock market crash a year or two later, *Thoroughly Modern Millie* and P.G. Wodehouse. Not a lot of use. He couldn't even remember who was Prime Minister in January, 1923. He could get answers from the net in moments, though; knowing things was pointless compared with knowing how to find things out. At the moment, that didn't help him.

Whoever these women were – or rather, whoever this IRENE D was, for URSULA W-D plainly didn't count – he was sure that they'd have the answers for any questions he came up with.

What was the point of this?

He could get to IRENE D. Despite everything, he had

her. She was in his chat room; she was his prey and meat and he would not let her challenge him.

I C U

I see you.

Irene thought that was a lie, but Master Mind could almost certainly hear her. Though, as with real spirits, she wondered if the words came to him as human sounds or in some other manner.

The parlour was almost completely dark, save for a cone of light about the table.

Miss Walter-David was terrified, on the point of fleeing. That was for the best, but there was a service Irene needed of her.

She did not say it out loud, for 'Master Mind' would hear.

He said he could see, but she thought she could conceal her hand from him.

It was an awkward move. She put the fingers of her left hand on the shivering planchette, which was racing inside the circle, darting at the letters, trying to break free.

I C U ID

I C U R FRIT

She slipped a pocket-book out of her cardigan, opened it one-handed and pressed it to her thigh with the heel of her hand while extracting the pencil from the spine with her fingernails. It was not an easy thing to manage.

U R FRIT AND FRAUD

This was just raving. She wrote a note, blind. She was trusting Miss Walter-David to read her scrawl. It was strange what mattered.

'This is no longer Caress,' she said, trying to keep her voice steady. 'Have we another visitor?'

2TRU IM SNAKE

'Im? Ah-ha, "I'm". Snake? Yet another speaker of this peculiar dialect, with unconventional ideas about spelling.'

Miss Walter-David was backing away. She was out of her seat, retreating into darkness. Irene offered her the pocket-book, opened to the message. The sitter didn't want to take it. She opened her mouth. Irene shook her head, shushing her. Miss Walter-David took the book, and peered in the dark. Irene was afraid the silly goose would read out loud, but she at least half-understood.

On a dresser nearby was a tea-tray, with four glasses of distilled water and four curls of chain. Bicycle chain, as it happened. Irene had asked Miss Walter-David to bring the tray to the ouija table.

'Snake, do you know things? Things yet to happen?'

2TRU

'A useful accomplishment.'

NDD

'Indeed?'

2RIT

There was a clatter. Miss Walter-David had withdrawn. Irene wondered if she would pay for the seance. She might. After all, there had been results. She had learned something, though nothing to make her happy.

'Miss Walter-David will die in 1952?'

Y

Back to Y. She preferred that to 2TRU and 2RIT.

'Of what?'

A pause.

PNEU

'Pneumonia, thank you.'

Her arm was getting worn out, dragged around the circle. Her shoulder ached. Doing this one-handed was not easy. She had already set out the glasses at the four points of the compass, and was working on the chains. It was important that the ends be dipped in the glasses to make the connections, but that the two ends in each glass not touch. This was more like physics than spiritualism, but she understood it made sense.

'What else do you know?'

U R FRAUD

'I don't think so. Tell me about the future. Not 2001. The useful future, within the next five or ten years.'

STOK MRKT CRSH 29

'That's worth knowing. You can tell me about stocks and shares?'

Y

It was a subject of which she knew nothing, but she could learn. She had an idea that there were easier and less obtrusive fortunes to be made there than in Derby winners. But she would get the names out of him, too.

'Horse races?'

A hesitation.

Y

The presence was less frisky, sliding easily about the circle, not trying to break free.

'This year's Derby?'

A simple search (+Epsom +Derby +winner +1923 −Kentucky) had no matches; he took out −Kentucky, and had a few hits, and an explanation. Papyrus, the 1923 winner, was the first horse to run in both the Epsom and Kentucky Derby races, though the nag lost in the States, scuppering a possible chance for a nice long-shot accumulator bet if he really was giving a woman from the past a hot tip on the future. Boyd fed that all to IRENE D, still playing along, still not seeing the point. She received slowly, as if her system were taking one letter at a time.

Click. It wasn't a monitor. It was a ouija board.

That was what he was supposed to think.

IRENE D: I'm going to give you another name. I should like you to tell me what you know of this man.

OK

IRENE D: Anthony Tallgarth. Also, Basil and Florence Tallgarth.

He ran multiple searches and got a cluster of matches, mostly from the twenties, – though there were birth and death announcements from the 1860s through to 1968 – and, again, mostly from the *Ham&High*. He picked one dated 2 February, 1923, and opened the article.

TYCOON FINDS LOST SON.

IRENE D: Where is Anthony? Now.

According to the article, Anthony was enlisted in the Royal Navy as an Able Seaman, under the name of T.A. Meredith, stationed at Portsmouth and due to ship out aboard the HMS *Duckett*. He had parted from his wealthy parents after a scandal and a quarrel – since the brat had gone into the Navy, Boyd bet he was gay – but been discovered through the efforts of a 'noted local spiritualist and seeress'. A reconciliation was effected.

He'd had enough of this game. He wasn't going to play any more.

He rolled back in his chair, and hit an invisible wall.

IRENE D: I should tell you, Master Mind, that you are bound. With iron and holy water. I shall extend your circle, if you co-operate.

He tried reaching out, through the wall, and his hand was bathed with pain.

IRENE D: I do not know how you feel, if you can feel, but I will wager that you do not care for that.

It was as if she was watching him. Him!

IRENE D: Now, be a good little ghostie and tell me what I wish to know.

With his right hand lodged in his left armpit as the pain went away, he made keystrokes with his left hand, transferring the information she needed. It took a long time, a letter at a time.

IRENE D: There must be a way of replacing this board with a type-writer. That would be more comfortable for you, would it not?

FO, he typed.

A lash at his back, as the wall constricted. She had understood that. Was that a very 1923 womanly quality?

IRENE D: Manners, manners. If you are good to me, I shall let you have the freedom of this room, maybe this floor. I can procure longer chains.

He was a shark in a play-pool, furious and humiliated and in pain. And he knew it would last.

Mr and Mrs Tallgarth had been most generous. She could afford to give Master Mind the run of the parlour, and took care to refresh his water-bindings each day. This was not a task she would ever entrust to the new maid. The key to the parlour was about Irene's person at all times.

People would pay to be in contact with the dead, but they would pay more for other services, information of more use in the here and now. And she had a good line on all manner of things. She had been testing Master Mind, and found him a useful source about a wide variety of subjects, from the minutiae of any common person's life to the great matters which were to come in the rest of the century.

Actually, knowing which horse would win any year's Derby was a comparatively minor advantage. Papyrus was bound to be the favourite, and the race too famous for any fortune to be made. She had her genie working on long-shot winners of lesser races, and was sparing in her use of the trick. Bookmakers were the sort of sharp people she understood only too well, and would soon tumble to any streak of unnatural luck. From now on, for a great many reasons, she intended to be as unobtrusive as possible.

This morning, she had been making a will. She had no interest in the disposal of her assets after death, when she herself ventured beyond the veil, for she intended to make the most of them while alive. The entirety of her estate was left to her firm of solicitors on the unusual condition that, when she passed, no record or announcement of her death be made, even on her gravestone. It was not beyond possibility that she mightn't make it to 2001, though she knew she would be gone from this house by then. From now on, she would be careful about official mentions of her name; to be nameless, she understood, was to be invisible to Master Mind, and she needed her life to be shielded from him as his was from hers.

The man had intended her harm, but he was her genie now, in her bottle.

She sat at the table, and put her hands on the planchette, feeling the familiar press of resistance against her.

'Is there anybody there?'

YYYYYYYYYYYYYYYYYYYYYYY

'Temper temper, Master Mind. Today, I should like to know more about stocks and shares . . .'

Food was brought to him from the on-line grocery, handed over at the front door. He was a shut-in forever now. He couldn't remember the last time he had stepped outside his flat; it had been days before IRENE D, maybe weeks. It wasn't like he had ever needed to post a letter or go to a bank.

Boyd had found the chains. They were still here, fixed into the skirting boards, running under the doorway, rusted at the ends, where the water traps had been. It didn't matter that the water had run out years ago. He was still bound.

Searches told him little more of Irene Dobson. At least he knew someone would have her in court in four years time – a surprise he would let her have – but he had no hopes that she would be impeded. He had found traces of her well into the 1960s, lastly a piece from 1968 that didn't use her name but did mention her guiding spirit, 'Master Mind', to whom she owed so much over the course of her long and successful career as a medium, seeress and psychic sleuth.

From 1923 to 1968. Forty-five years. Realtime. Their link was constant, and he moved forward as she did, a day for a day.

Irene Dobson's spirit guide had stayed with her at least that long.

Not forever. Forty-five years.

He had tried false information, hoping to ruin her – if she was cast out of her house (though she was still in it in 1927, he remembered) he would be free – but she always saw through it and could punish him.

He had tried going silent, shutting everything down. But he always had to boot up again, to be on-line. It was more than a compulsion. It was a need. In theory, he could stop paying electricity and phone bills – rather, stop other people paying his – and be cut off eventually, but in theory he could stop himself breathing and suffocate. It just wasn't in him. His meat had rarely left the house anyway, and as a reward for telling her about the extra-marital private habits of a husband whose avaricious wife was one of her sitters, she had extended his bindings to the hallway and – thank heavens – the toilet.

She had his full attention.

IRENE D: Is there anybody there?

Y DAMNIT Y

the beacon

christopher fowler

Mr Canvey lived on a wild Cornish clifftop where the trees could barely stand, and where the hedgerows were hobbled by the pounding gales that blasted up from the sea. His tough little box of a house was one of only four left in a village that had been shrinking for a hundred years. You could still see the flint foundations of the old churchyard, the post office and the schoolhouse, left like tidemarks around the remaining homes.

For five months of the year it was too inclement to venture far from the house, so Mr Canvey watched the world from his window, what he could see of it, which chiefly consisted of the sea from the lounge and kitchen windows, and from the sitting room, the back of the derelict church. In high summer a few tourist cars passed, and bickering seagulls alighted on the headstones, but all in all it was a lonely existence, one that required you to keep a tight grip on life lest it tore itself free and blew away into wildness. Everything clung on to the land. Even the orange lichen that bedded into the roof tiles had to be removed with a chisel. In a less severe climate the spirit could rise and drift in warm air currents, but here it dug in its heels and refused to budge. The land bred a certain type of people; self-sufficient, kind but suspicious of generosity in others, dry and hard as stone.

Mr Canvey was of this stock, but lonelier and somewhat gentler, although he attempted to dismiss these newly recognised feelings. He had moved here from Truro after the end of his marriage. Now he led a very ordered life. The drawing of the curtains at dusk, the turning of the key in the mantelpiece clock, the lighting of the gas fire, Chopin or Handel in the CD player, a favourite old book from the shelf in the lounge. He was fifty-three, but he felt much older. Men often do when they think they have reached the end of being useful. Mr Canvey had lived, to a degree; he had travelled and worked and fallen in love. He had fathered a child, lost it and lost his wife as well. He had seen his fortunes wax and wane, survived accidents and illnesses. And although dissatisfaction sometimes gnawed at him, he had come to accept his lot, and to appreciate his time on earth. As he watched the restless sea from his window, he was aware that he had been forgotten.

An ashthmatic condition had forced Mr Canvey into early retirement, and as his isolation grew he decided, if not exactly to break out of his shell, then to crack it open a little.

Just before Christmas, on a morning bogged in browns and greys, and capped with a slippery silver sky, he drove into Truro to buy himself a computer. If the adverts were to be believed, the Internet would expand his shrunken world. Mr Canvey did not consider himself to be resistant to change, but his lack of experience with technology made him feel prehistoric compared to people he watched on television, navigating their way around the electronic universe with fleet fingers. He was capable of setting his video recorder and tuning his satellite stations. He understood the basic principles of computing. He liked the idea of having the world at his fingertips. He'd made a note of the model he wanted, and the software he would like to go with it. He had carefully compared prices, then made his purchase.

Later in the week, a young technician arrived at the house. He wore black overalls with the name of the store on the back and his own name – Danny – stitched in gold thread over his heart. He quickly set about unpacking the equipment. Then he installed various items of software and registered his new customer as the user.

Men of Mr Canvey's age had, supposedly, seen more changes in their lives than anyone who had ever lived. Post-war rationing, the rebuilding of bombed cities, the loss of empire, the end of monarchy, the collapse of the class system, the disintegration of the family, raised living standards, lowered sexual inhibitions, space travel, mass transit, and electronic communication, which shrank the world from something vast, alien and mysterious down to a more manageable size. Now here was something completely new. A world within a world, he thought as he waited for the technician to finish.

It was becoming dark. He drew the lounge curtains and turned on the television, but was bored by what he saw. The channels were filled with the obsessions of youth. Sex, cars, clothes, music; girls becoming aroused by hair care products, boys stroking their chins as they compared triple-blade shaving to piloting jet fighters. The dream market, spending power coupled with inexperience. Pity today's youth, he thought. Lambs being readied for slaughter. *Tanquam ovis*.

Mr Canvey sat back in his chair as Christmas commercials blurred before him. In a world where there's less and less to discover, you have to be contented with small pleasures, he thought. In the next room, the technician tapped away at the keyboard. Outside, the wind flounced against the hedgerows.

'Nearly finished. I'll explain the set-up to you.'

The technician pulled up a second chair and sat Mr Canvey down beside him. He ran through the basic procedures, but forgot that his customer had never used a computer in his life, and went too quickly to be fully understood. Mr Canvey attempted to keep up, but it seemed that few concessions were made for neophytes. The stream of information finally washed over him, and he knew that he would have to resort to the manual for help.

He made the technician a cup of tea, and they sat dunking biscuits as little coloured boxes scrolled across the screen.

'Man, I hate Christmas. See, I hardly ever take a drink, don't like the taste of beer, an' it bores the arse off me watching my friends get drunk, and I'm always the designated driver, so I just hate the whole thing.'

'You should try tea with a shot of whisky in it. I often have one at the end of the day, if I'm feeling good about something.' He looks a little like my Tony, thought Mr Canvey. When he reclines his head in that fashion. 'So, what do you do instead?' he asked.

'Spend most of my time on the net.'

'Doing what, exactly?'

'The usual. Lookin' at websites, sendin' messages, stuff like that. Stuff you'll be doin' soon.'

'Have you always done this kind of work?'

'No. I've been a postman and a poet.' The technician chuckled. 'In some ways this isn't so different.'

'But now you teach.'

'I suppose so. I've got a natural aptitude for it, see. I learn fast.'

'Do you ever get anyone who can't learn?'

'How do you mean?' Danny barely heard the question as he reached forward to tap the keyboard. He had the distracted air of someone taking a phone call while trying to watch a television programme.

'Your company runs management training classes, doesn't it? Are there ever any people who simply fail to understand how it all works?'

'Oh, yeah.'

'Then what do you do?'

'We have a special programme for them. It's a kind of electronic colouring book. Stops them from looking stupid in the eyes of their colleagues. They sit quietly at their desks foolin' around until it's time to go home, then they rush back to their wives to tell them they learned how to use a computer. Sad, really. A child of four can grasp the basics.'

It's easy for you, thought Mr Canvey. People of my age have had to grow up alongside the system's development. Manual typewriters, IBM Electrics, Golfballs, dot-matrix sixteen-letter screens and BBC Wordstar, probably the least user-friendly software ever invented. In the early eighties we were still punching telex messages out on long strips of tape. The changes we've had to go through. He enviously watched the young man's fingertips feathering the keys.

'This is just the start. Things are going to get a lot smarter. In Germany they've got litter bins that order your groceries. Fridges that tell you when you're eating too much. Soon you'll be able to touch and smell and taste stuff right here at your keyboard.'

'Good heavens. I can't even type with more than two fingers.'

'In a few days you'll be typing as fast as me,' said the technician unconvincingly, but not unkindly.

'You remind me of my son.'

'He good with a computer?'

'Do you know, I—' Mr Canvey raised his knuckle to his mouth. 'I have no idea! I simply don't know. I don't know if he ever used a computer. Isn't that terrible? A man should know something like that about his own son.'

'Most people use them at work these days.'

'I don't think Tony – in Africa, you see, there was no – well, they barely had electricity. He wrote me letters. That's how I know. Sometimes the conditions were appalling, sometimes disease travelled in their tyre tracks, they weren't to know.' He saw the puzzled look on the technician's face and tried to explain. 'The health organisations sent trucks with medical supplies from village to village, but it was after the rains, and the bilharzia travelled in the tracks their vehicles left behind. Instead of eradicating the disease, they accidentally caused it to spread.'

Danny looked uneasy. He was happier working at a keyboard than hearing about someone's personal troubles.

'What I mean to say,' explained Mr Canvey, 'is that my son passed away two years ago. Sometimes you get to know more about them after they've gone than when they're here. It's terrible to lose a child, when you would have gone in their place. If I'd known – if we'd talked.' He suddenly realised that he was discomfiting his guest and tried to change the subject, but it wouldn't go away. He didn't get the chance to speak with many people beyond passing the time of day.

He missed his wife, he told the technician, but mostly he missed his son. Never a day passed when he didn't think of Tony. The boy's peculiar view of the world had coloured his behaviour so much that he had hardly ever made total sense to his parents.

'The questions he used to ask me. "Dad, why is it that the

first place you always want to touch on a cat is the only place it can't properly wash?" "Dad, what would chairs look like if your legs bent the other way?" How do you answer a child like that?' Mr Canvey poured more tea for his guest. 'Tony spent his entire childhood asking me awkward questions and never getting decent answers. My wife and I both worked, I was always too busy to help him. And what for? A few promotions in a job I didn't like. Meanwhile, Tony, well, let's just say that we didn't see eye to eye . . .'

As Tony grew older, his questions had become the symptom of a broader dissatisfaction with the world. How could his father work for a company that loaned millions to bankrupt countries at rates they could never afford to pay back? They argued all the time. Finally, the boy had left early one morning, propping a letter of explanation on the mantelpiece. He had walked away from his home, his job, his country, to go and work for a voluntary health aid service in a place hardly anyone had heard of. Mr Canvey, wanting him to be happy, had let him go. Three years later his son had died in the field, sickened and destroyed in less than two days by a virulent strain of amoebic dysentery. He was twenty-six.

'I really have to go,' said Danny, pushing back his cup.

'Yes, of course, how rude of me, going on. I'm sorry to have kept you.'

Mr Canvey saw the technician to the door, and promised to call if the computer's manual defeated him.

To his surprise, however, he proved to be rather good at using his word-processing package, his games software and his e-mail. It was the Internet he had trouble with. It made less sense because it seemed to be driven by people of alien intelligence to his own. Perhaps, like the technician, they were all simply younger and faster.

But he felt it was something beyond that. The more he

experimented with it, the more the Internet seemed a world of unnecessary information and unwanted destinations, of blind alleys and one-way cyberstreets where the fantasies of the friendless and the polemics of the mentally agitated were more intimidating than wandering the night slums of postwar Britain. As for the rest, those sites which weren't driven by the need to sell seemed to exist purely to feed the egos of their creators.

Mr Canvey was not without imagination; he could appreciate the system's uses, and had also heard the tales of its dark side; the reports of women who had formed electronic relationships with their future attackers, some going willingly to their protracted deaths, the men who had been exposed as paedophiles after foolishly downloading lurid jpegs, the lonely males who spent twenty hours a week on the net challenging each other to jousts and duels in mediaeval virtual villages, living idiot-lives in fantasy worlds, the viruses, the 'sticky' websites that clung to hapless users and could not be eradicated, the live sex-change operations filmed in California for private-view appointments by net voyeurs. The dancing cartoon animals, for God's sake.

He mainly comprehended electronic matters on a personal level. To him, e-commerce was ultimately reliant upon a postman shoving a rare book through a letterbox six weeks after it had been ordered. He had no need for Internet purchases, invisible friends, singing hamsters, webcam sex-booths, special offers he did not want or messages he could not be bothered to answer. He knew that sitting hunched at a desk staring at a screen was a poor substitute for walking in parkland after a spring rain, that fantasy and reality would always remain separate, no matter how many scientists tried to convince him otherwise.

And yet it drew him, because it was the future.

The faster-than-thought hotwire of connections, the neural net connecting millions of different minds, the sheer possibilities overpowered him. 'Surfing' was an inaccurate description – it was more like bobbing about on an electonic ocean, being pulled back and forth by warring currents. It seemed to him that the sargasso of information could do with a few beacons, shining lights that meant something more to the user than just another futile directional arrow.

A few days later, Mr Canvey walked past his old office in Truro. He did not miss working there; his colleagues had been pretty colourless individuals. It didn't pay to have too much personality in banking. Mr Canvey drove back through the tortured hedgerows to his village. After his son's death, Mr Canvey's wife had divorced him and married someone happier. His life seemed to have emptied out. He went home, turned on the computer and looked up a website he had been meaning to visit, a site for model railway enthusiasts. He thought he might find some carriages for his collection, but the site had not been updated in ages. It was virtually derelict, and most of the hotlinks led nowhere. They had been capped off, like the bricked-up streets of the village. He shoved the mouse aside and went to make a cup of tea. What annoyed him was the disparity of the world. Somewhere out there litter bins were sending messages to each other, and children were drinking from infected rivers. People talked about the hypocrisy of the Victorians. How could they dare, when everything around them was so routinely tainted?

He knew he was behaving like his son. The more he used his computer to tap into the world, the more he found himself thinking like the boy he had not understood. He found single-page websites that were little more than desperate pleas for provisions; food and clothing being bartered in the electronic ether. He found insanely elaborate interactive

sites dedicated to minor characters in television soap operas.
And he found the site of the health aid agency his son had
worked for. It had the longest website address he had ever
seen, consisting of nine separate sections.

The site took ages to download, and seemed chaotically
organised. It was separated into five main parts. **Who We
Are. What We Do. Where We Work. How You Can
Help. Diary Of A Hungry Planet.** The last section was
a log kept by various members of staff in different locations,
of their daily problems, the deprivations. You clicked on
a country, then an area, and followed different paths. Mr
Canvey clicked on Africa, then Somalia. He read about the
unstable political situation there, about the UN aid workers
taken hostage at the Balidogie airport. He read about the ban-
dits and clans, and the guerrilla kidnappings. He read a file on
chloroquine-resistant malaria, about the plasmodium parasites
that female mosquitoes left in your blood system, about the
guinea worms, the typhus, the dengue fever, cutaneous and
visceral leishmaniasis, meningitis, rabies, schistosomiasis and
the Tumbu fly, which eats human flesh and burrows its way
under your skin to lay its eggs. He read about the collapse
of the state-run health system, and how there was one doctor
for every five thousand people before young men like Tony
volunteered to run makeshift hospitals.

He bookmarked the site, but could not bring himself to
return to it, because it brought the horrors of the outside
world into his village, because it brought the death of his
son back into his life.

He called Danny at the computer shop, once to discuss
setting print margins so that the type didn't come out sideways
on the page, once because he couldn't work out how to
change to a different search engine, but he was really trying
to find out what young people like Danny were all about. He

never stayed long on the line, never asked too many personal questions.

Sometimes a young girl answered. She sounded bored and replied with quotes from an instruction manual, but when he asked her for answers which couldn't be found in the book she came to life, and tried to respond as truthfully as she could, sometimes going off and asking a colleague for additional advice.

It was just after Christmas. A watery sun hung low in the sky, barely bothering to illuminate the landscape. Mr Canvey had been playing a game on his computer which involved the three-dimensional construction of a Bavarian castle from jigsaw-like pieces. The pastime was just as boring as hunting through the pieces of a regular jigsaw, more so, because at least you had tactile sensation with a regular jigsaw.

He felt his eyes growing tired, and stopped to make some tea. He stood by the window, blowing across the top of his mug, watching the soft grey waves in fading light, looking for the beam from the unmanned lighthouse that blinked beyond the headland, but instead his eye was drawn to the bright square of the screen reflected in his window. He returned to his chair and pulled down the menu of his bookmarked sites, then summoned up the Somalian health organisation pages. There was something he remembered seeing; seeing but not seeing.

The site had not been updated for quite a long while. He ran the cursor to the end of the fifth section, where the diary entries were kept, and studied the roster of contributor names. Anthony Canvey was listed at the end, along with several other staffers from his base.

He shifted the cursor over his son's name and double-clicked. The lettering flashed from blue to red. The screen blanked, then a fresh page scrolled down and he found himself looking at a photograph of his son. Beneath the picture was a brief career résumé, a list of Tony's field interests, the things he liked and disliked about his job, and beneath this a further link; message board.

He slid the mouse and double-clicked, barely daring to breathe.

A Message From Anthony Canvey:

Hi Dad I wondered how long it would take you to find me

He stared at the message. When had this been written? How long before his son's illness? Had it been sitting here all this time, just waiting for him to stumble across it? With trembling fingers he raised his hands over the keyboard and typed a reply, not knowing what else to do.

Tony, I just learned about using this. I didn't know about this.

I left this for you Dad You were always interested in gadgets I knew youd figure out how to use it eventually

I don't understand. How can you answer me?

I have to use a laptop to enter my medical supply requisition forms I dont like using it cant sort out the punctuation never my strong point but you know that

Tony—

He realised that what he typed was not affecting the message from his son. It was coming in like a pulse from a beacon, waiting to be seen by anyone who was lost. It couldn't answer him; it could only beam out.

They have probably told you about the situation here by now many of us are sick there is a dysentery epidemic it is difficult to get fresh water because our filters are always breaking down

Can you hear me? Can you read this?

And so much of our equipment has been stolen we have to barter it back Things do not look good we are having to deal with the Mogadishu rebels in order to keep our supply routes open yesterday

*a girl here in the base died very suddenly I think what I want to
say is sorry*

You don't have to say sorry, he could not stop himself
from typing.

*Sorry for disappointing you sorry for worrying you I have to do
this its what I am*

You don't have to say this.

I want you to understand

I understand.

understand

I understand

If I don't come home

I understand

Don't be sad

I'm not sad.

*I'll be here this will always be here think of this as a light
in the dark*

There was no more. The message-board file stayed open
with its message displayed on-screen, complete and uninterrupted, an envelope in a dead-letter office that had finally
been unsealed and read. Mr Canvey found himself reluctant
to close it in case it could never be retrieved again, but
he decided to print out the message. Then he closed the
computer down for the night. He carefully folded up the
printed sheet and locked it in the mahogany box where
he kept his important papers. Finally, he made himself a
cup of tea and stood at the window, watching the crimson
pinprick of the beacon glimmering through the night mist
out on the sea.

'I wish you'd come to bed.' Fran sleepily pushed against the
pillow. 'It's late.'

'It'll just take me a couple of minutes to shut everything

up,' he called from the next room. 'I don't want to leave a path anyone can follow.'

'I don't know why you had to do it. It's . . . unethical or something. Like tampering with the mail. Probably a criminal offence. You shouldn't go upsetting people.'

'He picked up the message. There's no harm done. Nobody will bother tracing it.' Danny closed the pattern of connections and logged off, smiling as the text scrolled down to nothing, leaving just the URL. 'You know, it took me a while to place the bloke. He was in the year above me, but I remember him well. He was famous for hacking into the local bank and leaving a virus.'

'You used to do stuff like that, too.'

'Yeah, well. We all grew up a bit. This is the kind of thing he would have sent. I'm just making the connection.' Danny looked back at the top of the screen and erased the part of the address that read: /indexafr/externe/eastcent/somalia/acanvey. That was the thing with a lot of the old message-board systems. Nobody knew if you were ever who you said you were, not unless you chose to leave your e-mail address. 'I'm going to have a cup of tea with a shot of whisky in it. Do you want one?'

'Go on, then.' Fran pulled the pillow up behind her and switched on the bedside light. 'It's not like you to drink.'

'I think someone else out there is having one,' said Danny. As he opened the bottle, he looked out of the kitchen window in the direction of the beacon, and although he could not see it, he knew it was there.

black triangle

steve aylett

Four men sat around laughing it up covert style in the Cube, a surveillance-proof room two miles beneath a mountain in Bluemont, Virginia. 'What is the law but a cloven hoof embedded in a fallen child's belly,' smiled Admiral Inman, addressing a young man who, brought here against his will, sat as button-eyed as a mummified starling. Since the first time he'd scared a civilian, Inman had known this was a business in which a blank eye or a sharp chin could be required at a moment's notice. He had his career.

'We all know you're wading through cigars round here Admiral,' drawled Bobby Kimmitt, the President's errand boy. 'Shall we proceed with the briefing?'

'Sure, Bobby,' leered the Admiral, 'you're the big wheel round here. It's what we love – politicians paying a visit, quivering with altruism.' Inman flapped and stanced in his cool brass trousers, gearing up to address Kimmitt, the youngster and a stone-bald old man. 'We live in perilous times. Here at the Mount Weather complex, secrets are our stock in trade. Snow is confetti without all the dissension, candy pounds at the gullet, I hardly ever use my hair. And that's just a small selection of the secrets we have here.'

'Those are the crappiest secrets I ever heard,' Kimmitt commented.

Inman adopted a wounded and aggrieved stance. 'Well, that's as may be, but we've devoted a portion of our resources to the matter of UFOs, flying saucers, black triangles. It's in regard to our findings that we're assembled here today. I refer you to our resident expert, Doctor Wolf. Dismal beyond his considerable years, this man leaves flood-marks where he thinks, am I right Doc? Signs his cheques in Sanskrit, that sort of thing. Just this side of dead. His chakras are made of macaroni. Doctor, I throw the floor open to your damn fool comments.'

'Thank you, Admiral,' the old man responded dryly. 'That incomprehensible outburst will be your undoing. Now, we've been studying these mothers for some time and we've come to a startling conclusion. Quite simply, our visual censorship devices have escaped.'

Mr Kimmitt sat up in his tin chair. 'What the hell does that mean?'

Dr Wolf sat thinking up at the ceiling for a moment. 'What is released toward expression and blocked at the last minute, must go somewhere. We began to work it out during all the fuzzy lenticular activity over Mexico City in the nineties. Small bouncing circles in the clouds, dozens at a time. You've seen the documentary footage of immigrants being beaten up by border police? The officers' faces are always fuzzed out to disguise their identity. We discovered that the digitally generated blobs in that footage exactly matched the appearance of the objects filmed above Mexico City.

We studied the phenomenon retrospectively and it seems to have begun during the Second World War, when strike-out marks in overseas letters manifested in the sky as so-called foo-fighters. Between then and now we've had squares, circles, triangles and oblongs cluttering the sky due to document blank-outs, celebrity eye-strips and porn censorship. If one can imagine that which does not exist, surely one can ignore that which does with a similar exertion?

However, energy cannot be created or destroyed – information must go somewhere, if only as an abstract icon. A rose can't help it. There's the theory.'

The teenager sat in glum silence and Kimmitt shook his head dismally, perplexed. 'Have you guys been living entirely for pleasure round here? Keep thinking this way your head'll shatter like a vase full of meat. Wolf, your sanity's been kicked into the long grass.'

'I'm afraid not, Bobby,' said the Admiral, the only one of the three who chose to remain standing. 'It's straight from the Doc's distorted shoulder. I nearly choked on a shad myself the first time I heard about it. But you know me – if there's an envied elite, I'm there. Those in the know have smirked at you several times, but this makes it official.'

'How long has it been going on?'

Dr Wolf steepled his hands. 'Only during times of conscious and active censorship. You'll recall reports of phallic craft over Victorian London, I have a news report: *"Airships managed the wind flow with strange grace. It is an electrical, flying bid for attention. Disparage the facts and we are in retreat."* Bit of a gobful isn't it? We gaze at the sky and it fights back.'

'You know why there's so much giant triangle activity over at Area 51?' posed Admiral Inman, enjoying himself. 'Because the base in toto is shaped like a giant triangle, and we concealed it underground. Same kinda thing at Pine Gap and Rudloe. There's even a thing like a flying cube that biffs around over this place.'

'I thought you were back-engineering a couple of saucers over at Groom Lake?' said Kimmitt, his face distorted with mental exertion.

'We were but we had to stop. The fucking Digital Millennium Copyright Act.'

'The what-now?'

'Enforced system loyalty. Meant to stop people de-encrypting DVD so they can't play it on old LINUX machines, that kinda stuff. We've fallen into the same catchment with the goddamn saucers. After all we've done for the movie industry. It's irrelevant to all this but our lawyers are working on it, don't you worry.'

The kid piped up for the first time. 'The breaking of encryption is us communicating with our technology – breaking the ice.'

'So let me in on it,' Kimmitt snapped, 'why's the kid here?'

'The fact,' said Dr Wolf, 'if I can use so impressive-sounding a term, is that the number of sightings are diminishing.'

'What about last month, all the black triangles?'

The Admiral muttered awkwardly. 'That's because we put a D-notice on a news story about black triangles.'

'You mean about the TR3B?'

'Our little stealth plane? No, the story was about the goddamn giant triangles that have been appearing for years because of all the censorship about the TR3B from way back. The thing's feeding on itself now.'

'LoFlyte and ASTRA are piss-poor too,' said the kid in a voice devoid of emphasis. He seemed ferociously lethargic.

'Explain yourself, Doctor Wolf.'

'With carnal pleasure. We have found a correlation; the reduction in sightings of flying cells is in inverse proportion to the growth of the Internet. You see, whatever is censored elsewhere is freely available on the web. It serves as an overflow. The web itself is no danger; for the purpose of compression, garbage and wisdom is all of a piece there. And the trend's lucky for us, as the combination of blanket censorship in other media and the exponential feedback loop regarding the UFO phenomenon would spell disaster for our airspace.'

'The sky'd be lousy with saucers,' said the Admiral.

'So what's the problem?'

'After years of empty boasting, hackers are finally producing viruses which are a genuine threat to the web, as we've seen with bugs such as Love, Irony and Valis. With the help of this silent fiend of unguessable compulsions over here we may develop a contingency plan, to keep it secure. This lad is the famous hacker Digital Inconvenience, reputedly the greatest alive.'

Something was dawning in the face of the youth.

'That's right, my boy,' smiled Dr Wolf, 'we picked you out of the chorus for what's in that portable hell of yours.' He indicated the boy's head. 'I need hardly remind you that you have no choice. You see the pickle we're in. And from the gloomy depths of no trivial experience I assure you we are men of our word. Unlike your little gang, godlike in your refusal to accept responsibility for your actions.'

The Admiral leaned into the kid's face. 'A dead truth's the first success of an asylum, keyboard boy.'

Ever after, Digital Inconvenience assumed that one or all of the men had deliberately stage-managed the event as part of some inscrutable power play. He was young enough to think that such classically shady figures, officers of the parallel government whose career arcs were inscribed in invisible ink, would have done their research. But at the time, when he told them, Dr Wolf gave a sharp jolt he could ill afford. 'A re-set virus?'

'Of course, to be re-set every twenty-four hours or it hits the net. Every real hacker has one in case they get picked up by the authorities.'

'And you had to be free to re-set it this morning?'

'He's bluffing,' said the Admiral.

'Yeah,' added Kimmitt. 'When a kid thinks he's dangerous, it generally means he's been reading poetry.'

A uniformed flunkey came in and whispered something in the Admiral's ear, and soon they were all heading above ground in the glass elevator. Dr Wolf squawked as they emerged under a sky which was filling like a puzzle. A million cookie-cutter shapes were interlocking, zigzag seams meeting a horizon tight with data. Kimmitt began hooting like an owl as angles sheared together, clashes echoing as a titanic roof accreted. 'I just realised what we should have done,' gasped the Doctor. 'Posted the theory across the net. Simple.'

Only one gap remained, a tiny white triangle of sky. The final piece fell into place, blotting the world into darkness.

rachel, queen of the wild wide web

maxim jakubowski

He came to computers late in life. Following several decades working on a manual typewriter, the contrary spirit of independence that harboured inside him had quickly rebelled against the evangelical zeal of all his friends singing the praises of the personal computer. So, he almost reluctantly moved on to a golf ball electric typewriter, swearing under his breath whenever the damn machine couldn't keep up with the surprising speed of his two-finger typing.

He was actually quite proud to be considered a Luddite. There was a sort of badge of honour being a science fiction writer in open revolt against technological progress.

But eventually the curse of badly decipherable carbon copies, the messiness of Tippex and in-built death wish of self-correcting ribbons took their toll on his patience and he acquired his first PC.

And soon himself became a bit of a proselyte about its virtues, as well as the fact that he no longer had to do endless rewrites/retypes on every piece of work due to his annoying compulsion for a clean final manuscript.

Naturally, he wasn't the first pioneer on his block to log on to the Internet, but then neither was he a Johnny-come-lately stuck in the hinterlands of mere word-processing.

His first weeks of exploration saw him surfing away to his heart's content, checking all references to himself via the plethora of search machines, discovering *en passant* that he had a homonym in the world of real science who had authored lengthy treatises and articles on the particularities of phosphorus and, more worryingly, the fact that there was little privacy on the web and that anyone with the right determination and knowhow could find out anything about him, including his address, date of birth, details of education and more, let alone a complete bibliography of his writings, even those he had carefully cloaked under pseudonyms.

His next few months of personal research all involved typing in the word 'sex' and gladly following where the search machines would take him. The journey was a fascinating one, widely expanding his parameters of both perversion and imagination. A sheer galaxy of pornographic websites for every taste under the sun, alt.sex discussion groups, interactive areas, amateur and commercial havens where absolutely anything went and more, from hirsute as well as shaven women to anal penetration, bestiality, fatties and foot fetishism to name but a few of the more predictable kinks on open display or for sale. All this actually provided him with some good ideas for stories as a way of justifying the increasing amount of time he was wasting in front of his computer screen and not actually working. And the sizable telephone bills.

By force of necessity he also began to communicate by e-mail with his friends and acquaintances. It was so much more immediate and efficient, sparing him the envelopes, the stamps and the traditional walk up the road to the postbox. There was also a gently sexual *frisson* communicating in this way. Made letter writing so much more personal and even brought relative strangers into a risqué sphere of intimacy.

Another writer, all the way away in Australia, female, wrote him a note following a story of his in a magazine and very soon their correspondence took a most personal connotation as they began to exchange the most acutely private sexual secrets and fantasies. The medium lent itself so well to this sort of flirting.

He had heard about chat rooms but had somehow never been attracted. Had always imagined it would consist of a bunch of sad people discussing ad infinitum the minor arcana of Star Trek or Lovecraft's Cthulhu Mythos until the sorry hours of dawn. The sort of nerds he avoided like the plague at conventions, who spelled Tolkien as Tolkein or blocked the conference hotel's stairways playing Dungeons and Dragons with a satisfied grin on their pale faces. He just knew the likely conversations in chat rooms would bore him to death or, worse, make his anger rise in a wave of exasperated irritation.

An editor in Texas had asked him for a story for a thematic anthology of all-new stories about love in the third millennium. He'd agreed to pen a new tale and pencilled the delivery date in his diary but other matters, alimentary writing and the business of living had overtaken his spring and he only remembered about the promised story with just a week to spare. He usually functioned well with close deadlines, the pressure acting as a spur for his inspiration.

A sleepless night with images of countless women, past, potential and somehow forgotten, cruising through his brain like a generation ship on course for distant stars and he somehow came up with an idea. As ever, another variation on his eternal sentimental obsessions. It only took him a couple of days work in front of his screen and, two litres of Pepsi, three bars of chocolate and much scratching of his scalp later, the story was ready. 5,200 words long. He called it 'Kiss Me Sadly'.

Off it went to Texas by DHL courier service.

He hoped it would do the trick.

Five days later, the editor of the anthology communicated back by e-mail. He loved the central idea, the characters, the final twist, thought the story had really great moments, a possible prize-winner. Nebula or Hugo even. But, he did feel it required some changes. Not so much a rewrite, barely a few extra paragraphs, an editing job, no more.

He'd always known the stories he wrote were a bit left of field, far from ideal fodder for the popular American market, and it wasn't as if he got that many invitations to contribute to US anthologies. There was just one editor out there in Iowa who was keen on his idiosyncrasies. It would be nice to widen his appeal. He replied, indicating his willingness. Maybe they should discuss the required changes over the phone? When would be the best time to call?

Forget about the phone, the answer came an hour later. I see we have the same Internet server, the editor in Texas replied. It would be both cheaper and easier to do the edit on-line. Fine with me, how do we do that? he asked Neil.

Easy, he was told, and was given a short set of instructions to follow on his computer screen when he logged on at the agreed time. Find GO on your menu and type in CS3, or something of the sort.

It was a Monday, late afternoon, to cater for the time difference between north London and Austin. A series of new screen configurations waltzed across his screen. He typed in Yes twice. And arrived at his chosen destination. Within seconds – he hadn't yet got his bearings or puzzled out all the boxes or sections on display – there was a 'ping', like a sort of muffled bell, and his screen opened up and there was a line there. It just said 'Neil' and 'welcome'.

He typed in 'hi' and they began the edit. Neil explained that he was recording everything his end and would then paste the changes into the story.

The whole process took only one hour and was much less extensive than he had initially feared. Neil suggested; he agreed and furnished a new line or paragraph. It would be accepted or Neil, out in Texas, would make a further suggestion. Very quickly, he grew to appreciate the ease of on-line editing. Another wonderful use for computers, he felt.

Reminding him, ironically, how reluctant he had originally been to convert over previously! Felt like another life already.

There was only one drawback. At odd times during their on-screen conversation, that damn 'ping' sound would keep on going off. Pessimist that he was, he began worrying that something was wrong with his computer.

The edit was complete to their mutual satisfaction and they were just exchanging small talk, when he thought to query Neil about the strange, occasional noise. Being more of a computer expert, maybe he would know what the problem might be.

'Ha ha,' Neil typed. He shouldn't worry. They were in a chat room and had forgotten to go private, so this was just other people trying to contact him. I see, he remarked, trying not to betray his inexperience.

They exchanged goodbyes and Neil logged off. Back in London, he remained on-line and, sure enough, a few minutes later, the bell sounded again and his screen opened up to the chat box.

Dave: hi there

He replied:

106562.2021:   hello

The response was fast.

Dave: where are you?

106562.2021:   in London

Dave: m or f?

106562.2021:   sorry?

Dave: are you male or female?

106562.2021:   oh. Male.

Dave: ok. bye.

A line saying (Dave has left the forum) appeared on the
screen.

His first interlocutor disappeared. Intrigued, awaiting the
next call, he moved his mouse around and began to puzzle
out the possibilities on screen and soon learned he could
change his subscriber number to his name. Which he did.
Then clicked on the 'Who's Here' line and uncovered a
long list of names, many obscene, some humorous, initials,
codes, sobriquets.

The bell went off again.

9 inches: hello babe

He smiled. Answered.

Marti: how are you?

9 inches: are you dressed?

He realised that the guy at the other end assumed he
was a woman. Mischievously, he decided to play along for
a while.

Marti: not totally, actually

9 inches: great . . . do you have big tits?

Marti: no, barely A cup I fear

9 inches: no matter, i love small boobs also. looking
               for fun?

Marti: why not?

Thus did Martin enter the world of chat rooms and cybersex. And role play.

The next four months witnessed a distinct downturn in his literary output as he became badly hooked on chat room temptations. He quickly identified the most interesting ones. Adult Entertainment. Intimate Chat Forum. Pride:BI! NL Hot Chat. France Forum. Soon, he was no longer the one always to be paged and began contacting others. Female of course. Seeking out interesting names, handles that indicated a modicum of intelligence and wit. Foreign names with a touch of enticing exoticism. But still other men kept on contacting him because of the ambiguity of his own nickname and, often, he would play along for a while, despairing at the lack of imagination they displayed.

Surely, he was better than them? Within a few lines, they invariably had him undressed, spread-eagled, rubbing his clit, insisting his nipples were hard and his sexual openings moist or wet depending on the season or the time of day. He did wonder what women thought of such direct, unsubtle virtual approaches? Obviously, some would go along with the fantasies just for the fun of it, but he couldn't believe that's what women wanted.

In his own approaches, he was careful not to move on to sexual matters until well into the conversation. He was more interested in them as persons, the writer or voyeur in him fascinated to learn about their life, the reasons that brought them on to the forums. Some momentarily even became friends before suddenly disappearing with no word of warning from the virtual world (or, more likely, moving on to chat rooms with another server). He loved it. This was a wonderful way of meeting others. So easy and straightforward. He'd never been the sort of person to walk up to others in bars or at parties, and had always been too shy to begin a conversation with an attractive woman in a bus queue or sitting across from him in an underground carriage. But this was so easy. There were no barriers, no opportunities for embarrassment. Rejection, if rejection there was, was impersonal and painless.

There was the opera singer in New York. The banker in Toronto who called herself Montana and called him the sunshine of her life and sent him a couple of nude photographs of herself. She was married with two kids but had a wonderful figure. He came across a dark-haired Gypsy woman from Aix-en-Provence in the south of France, who sent him a fully-clothed photo and suggested they meet for real. After toying with the idea, he agreed and took a plane and spent a weekend there with her in a narrow hotel room. The photo had been taken ten years earlier, and instead of the single child she had admitted to, he discovered she had actually four, but no husband. The sex was good but they found they had little to say to each other and seldom spoke on-line again after they both returned to their computers. All he remembered of her later was the sublime vision of her perfectly shaped arse as she walked away from the bed to the bathroom on the first morning.

Then there was the student in south Carolina who collected photographs of men with large endowments and made it clear she wouldn't sleep with him but still enjoyed discussing the aesthetics of cocks, and the pros and cons of cut vs uncut penises and shaved vs unshaven balls. He knew that she did meet several men through the chat room during the time of their contact – she had a substantial trust fund and was free to travel places for the right fuck – as she lovingly provided him with all the anatomical details of her couplings. The college year ended and she never reappeared on the forum.

Another student in Berkshire, closer to home, was torn between her urge to lose her cumbersome virginity and her attraction to female classmates. Her name was Jenni and she also e-mailed him a photo she had taken of herself and scanned. Skinny as hell, with adorable small breasts and green thong panties and awkwardly posing for the Polaroid in her study. When the picture provoked a hard-on, he felt like a paedophile; she couldn't be more than fifteen.

And then there was Rachel.

He couldn't recall their first chat. Who had called whom first. By now, he no longer logged on as 'Marti' but as 'Writer (m)', having grown tired of all the unimaginative chat-up lines conjured up by other men.

She was American, lived in Paris where she worked for some financial consultancy organisation. She was in her late twenties, and had a daughter who was six years old. Rebecca. Her divorce was in the last throes of paperwork. From the first few conversations onwards, Martin took a strong liking to her. Her voice on screen seemed real, pleasant, quietly vulnerable.

Rachel came from a Wasp background and had been to the French Lycée in New York, before moving on to an Ivy League university. Not only did she live in France, but after a few weeks, he discovered, to his pleasant surprise, that she knew and enjoyed French culture, much as he did. Discussing films or books, she had the most amazing knowledge of peculiarly obscure writers or movies.

She had married young, a much older University lecturer who had been a friend of her family. Almost twenty years her senior. Someone she could look up to, maybe a father figure of sorts; hers had died when she was still young. The first years of the marriage had been happy despite the difference in their ages, but following the birth of Rebecca, on whom they both doted, they began to inexorably grow apart. He became increasingly jealous, abusive even and eventually Rachel felt she had no alternative but to separate.

The company she worked for on Wall Street had agreed to transfer her to the Paris office and she had now been in the French capital over six months, while the legal formalities were completed. Every two months, Rebecca would spend a couple of weeks with her father, who had not accepted the separation lightly and was seeking to gain custody of her. But Rebecca's lawyers were confident he would not succeed in this.

At no stage in their early chats, did Rachel even hint at sexual elements and their conversation soon adapted to a comfortable groove of life stories, discussion of books, films and music and a gentle flirting where much was left unsaid.

He expressed his curiosity for what she looked like. She had, in a perennial piece of Internet etiquette, provided her description and statistics earlier and the mental image Martin had fabricated of her was already well on the way to quiet perfection. Tall, blonde, gently spoken. She volunteered to send him a photograph by e-mail.

When it arrived, he opened the jpg with a nervous butterfly coursing around his stomach. But the results were enchanting. She was beautiful. Very American, long-haired, pretty in an understated woman-next-door way, pale-skinned, dark sad eyes scoring a bull's eye on his heart.

Every day, they would meet on-line in the forum around three o'clock and talk for at least an hour. Sometimes they were interrupted; after all, she had a job to do, and sometimes her answers were slow in coming and he assumed that she was also talking to others.

There were days when she was melancholy and he could sense her unhappiness invade the bright page on the screen. Loneliness, difficulties with the legal process, the child's minor illnesses, home sickness. Other days Rachel turned playful, teasing him mercilessly on his insistence to forego cybersex with her, describing her clothes in minute detail, how her office was overheated and she had taken off her pantyhose or opened her shirt, letting him imagine the delights thus uncovered. Or she would hide from him in the list of on-line names, assuming pseudonyms from books or movies which he would invariably and proudly recognise, however difficult she made the task. He would do likewise but he knew she had the latest server software and could identify him much more easily if she had clicked on his number under 'friends' and saved it; a function he did not possess.

So, following on from a light-hearted discussion about James Joyce, she would masquerade as Nora or Anna Livia Plurabelle or Dublin gal, or on another occasion adopt the persona of most of the female protagonists of *Gone with the Wind*. Once, he wasn't sure how their talk had moved on to Nabokov, she had hidden amongst the list as Dolores Haze, Butterfly or Lepidoptera. No easy Lolita for Rachel!

He could only smile, ravished as he was by the elegance of her repartee and imagination.

She even gave him her mobile telephone number.

He agreed, readily, he would never phone her unless they agreed a time to do so beforehand.

Her voice did not disappoint.

Breathy, moving from childish to pleading to joyful in the breadth of a few sentences, talking about her day, her love for her child, her apprehensions about what her erstwhile husband was up to. They tried to speak at least once a week. His heart moved with the ups and downs of Rachel's fleeting moods.

The lines on screen, the photograph saved away in his documents file, the voice. Martin was hooked.

Badly.

She knew he wrote but had never expressed much curiosity for his books or stories. On a few occasions, he volunteered to post her some copies of his books but she always asked him to wait. 'Later' she would say, as if she wanted to make the pleasure last somehow.

On the phone one day, 'I'm falling for you,' he said.

'Are you?' she answered, expressionless.

'I am, Rachel.'

'I like you too,' she said.

For the first time, the possibility of the two of them actually meeting in real life reared its head. After all, London and Paris were barely three hours apart with the Eurostar train.

He was slow to suggest it. After all, the possibility of being disappointed by her was something he was scared of. Was the photo he had actually of her? Was it genuinely taken the previous year (unlike Mireille's)? But once he searched himself, he knew that the voice on the phone corresponded so beautifully with the face on his screen. Quiet, sad, melancholy, vulnerable. All the things that attracted him in Rachel, beyond her innate culture and intelligence and the fact that conversing with her was such an easy delight.

At first, he felt all he should propose was to meet her after her day at the office and have a drink, a coffee together, maybe even a meal.

'I would like that, Martin,' she answered.

'I must come to Paris soon to see my French publishers,' he added. 'I will let you know as soon as I have a precise date for the trip.' He had no wish to reveal how much she now meant to him and the fact he was quite willing to go to Paris just to see her.

'Great.'

That weekend, he wrote her a long letter, tactfully alluding to his feelings, carefully hinting that he held her in much respect and wasn't expecting sex or an affair automatically, confessing to his previous Internet-inspired jaunt to France for the weekend with Mireille. He wanted her to know he did not think of her in the same way, that his feelings were both strong and genuine, even though the way they had met was so uncommon, nay bizarre. He polished his words endlessly over two days, putting in more rewrites to the letter to Rachel than he had done on any of his recent novels. He e-mailed it to her.

She did not respond to it and no mention was made of the letter in their on-line chats later in the week. Maybe he had gone too far, he wondered? Or maybe Rachel was exquisitely discreet and wished to spare his feelings.

But she did ask again when he would come to Paris.

They were chatting on-line late one afternoon when he suggested he could take a midday train the following weekend. She greeted the news calmly. He told her he would make a Eurostar booking and arrange a hotel and would confirm by e-mail a few hours later.

There is no need to stay in a hotel and spend money unnecessarily, she said on screen. You can stay at my place.

Are you sure? he queried, though his heart and loins danced a light fandango.

Of course, she answered. There is a spare bedroom anyway, if we don't get on.

The hint was of course present that the spare bedroom wouldn't prove necessary.

Rebecca's father would be in Europe that week and he would be taking care of her. It was his turn.

He breathed deeply. All the right elements were in place.

He logged off after some more small talk and quickly made his train reservation.

The following day he confirmed his arrangements with her and, always cautious, just in case the train arrived late and he was unable to meet up with her at the café on the Champs-Elysées, close to her office, as arranged, he asked her for her home address. She lived on the Avenue Victor Hugo, a stone's throw from the Arc de Triomphe. He noted the number.

Their next conversations saw him walking on air in expectation of Paris. It was all falling into place, too good to be true. They spoke once more on the phone and again he was enchanted by the sheer tone of her voice. He knew he was in love. Even though he'd not yet actually met her; it was illogical, crazy and wonderful. And, deep inside, he was convinced she would not disappoint, would be even better in real life.

He looked forward to the moving shades of darkness of her eyes, the small blemishes on her skin, the pale hue of her uncovered shoulders, the fragrant smell of her breath, the warmth radiating outwards from her body as they sat together at a restaurant table discussing Julien Green or Andre Pieyre de Mandiargues, both authors they had discovered they had a common liking for.

He had informed his French publishers he would be in town; some tax exemption documents had to be signed and a visit to their offices would save much time and bother.

Two days before his trip, the publishers rang with good news and bad news. The good tidings were that a major magazine had agreed to do a major interview with him as he was coming to Paris, which would be just great publicity for the translated book of his that they were publishing a few months later. The bad news was that the journalist just couldn't do this week and could he postpone his trip by six days?

He reluctantly agreed and informed Rachel. She didn't appear too distraught by the change of plan and reminded him that she would not be in Paris the following week however, as she had a business trip to Rome already set up. He did recall her mentioning this some time back. It was agreed he would come to Paris again for her a fortnight later.

There was no rush anyway, was there? Of course not, he acquiesced. After all, Rachel would always be there. Barely three hours away from him by train. The thought warmed him. The conversation moved to what she was wearing today and she teased him again insufferably, lingering insistently on the fabric of her brassiere and how flushed she could get now that summer was nearing.

By the end of their on-line chat, he had a respectable hard-on.

The interview with the French journalist was something of a disappointment. All she seemed interested in was the fact that he wrote particularly erotic stories and where did he do his research and weren't the male characters just thinly disguised versions of him, albeit in space? Still, any coverage was better than none, he reckoned.

He had an afternoon to spare before the Eurostar back to London after his publisher had lunched him. There was an alternate country CD he knew had been released early in France as the band was touring there, so he took a trip to the Virgin Megastore next to the Lido on the Champs-Elysées to purchase it. He exited the store with a further four records; he'd always been a bad, voracious shopper when it came to music. The weather was turning grey and he pondered catching a movie. Which is when he noticed the flower stall and decided to get flowers for Rachel.

Act with a modicum of elegance. He knew she was still in Rome, wouldn't be back for another two days but surely it would be a nice surprise to find a lovely bouquet on her doorstep as she returned. He carefully supervised the selection of colourful flowers until the bunch looked eminently spectacular and called a cab.

The block of flats on the Avenue Victor Hugo looked prosperous. The intercom only displayed the flat numbers and he realised he didn't know in which one Rachel lived. He rang for the concierge and the heavy wooden front door clicked open. He made his way down the darkened corridor until he found the window to the concierge's ground floor apartment. Knocked. The woman looked at him wearily; maybe she thought he was a delivery person for the flowers. He asked for Rachel. She appeared puzzled. He repeated his request, describing her, a young American woman with a small daughter, Rachel McKenna. The concierge mumbled negatively. Maybe she was known here under her married name. He inquired: Rachel Stewart? No again. The concierge was adamant, there was no American women in the whole block, he must be mistaken.

He abandoned the flowers in a wheelie-bin on the Avenue as he walked back towards the Rond-Point to catch a cab. Evidently, she had furnished him with a wrong address. Why? He couldn't fathom the answer. His heart now felt heavy. He brooded all the way back to London, in search of an answer. In vain. Rachel had lied to him.

As he emerged from the Waterloo terminal, the heavens

opened and the rain bucketed down as if it were Judgment Day.

A few days passed as he buckled down to the routine of writing and living, hesitant to log on again to the forum while the unpleasant scar of Rachel's lies festered inside him.

Finally, he could resist no longer.

Half an hour on-line later, having ignored several 'm or f?' requests, he saw her handle appear in the 'who's here' column. Rachel.

He paged her.

```
Writer(m):    hi
```

It took her a long time to respond. As if she was already immersed into a variety of conversations with other forum members.

```
Rachel:       hi
Writer(m):    how was Rome?
Rachel:       ok, a bit boring
Writer(m):    some good meals at least?
Rachel:       oh yes. You should see me in the bathroom
              mirror when I come out of the shower. I've
              put weight on. I'm gross . . .
Writer(m):    I'm sure that a few meals won't have made
              such a difference. Even fat, I'll have you
              readily . . . (s)
Rachel:       nice of you to say so. So . . . how did the
              interview go?
Writer(m):    predictable
Rachel:       oh
```

He hesitated a minute or two, waiting for her to relaunch the conversation, but she didn't. So he took the plunge.

```
Writer(m):    you know . . .
Rachel:       yes?
Writer(m):    while I was in Paris last week, I thought
              I'd buy you some flowers . . .
```

```
Rachel:        that's nice
Writer(m):     but they hadn't heard of you, Avenue Victor
               Hugo . . . why did you give me a wrong
               address, Rachel?
Rachel:        oh, that . . .
```

She fell silent.

```
Writer(m):     I understand that one has to be so careful
               with Internet encounters, but surely you
               knew you could trust me.
......................
Writer(m):     anyway, it doesn't matter, Rachel. It really
               doesn't . . .
......................
Writer(m):     Rachel?
......................
Writer(m):     talk to me, please
(Rachel has left the forum)
```

For the rest of the week, she didn't come on to the forum. Finally, he called her up. She picked up, said 'hello'.

'It's me,' he said, 'can we talk?' She hung up. He knew he had broken one of the rules not to call her on the telephone unless previously agreed. Maybe she had been in a meeting. He gave it a few more days.

He sent her an e-mail, telling her it was alright, he forgave her, but still wanted to be friends, stay in touch.

She didn't answer.

A second e-mail, which he had configured so that he would be informed when she picked it up, remained unopened in her box.

He rang her once more. By now, his thoughts were frantic, the Rachel scenarios racing through his brain, taking over his life, causing him to miss work deadlines because of the profound upset. This time, her mobile number was no longer functioning and all he got was a message in French informing him that the number had been disconnected.

One more e-mail.

It bounced back to him. She had closed her server account.

Rachel had disappeared from the Internet and his life altogether.

For weeks, he mourned quietly as he began to pick up the pieces of his life again. But just couldn't understand. Why? why? why?

The sorrow turned to anger and he carefully composed a message which he posted on the bulletin board of the forum.

```
HAS ANYONE HERE RECENTLY BEEN IN TOUCH WITH RACHEL
STEWART MCKENNA? IF YOU HAVE, CONTACT ME ON 106562.2021.
DISCRETION ASSURED.
```

He doubted there would be any comeback. As it was, he seldom even looked up the messages there himself, restricting himself to the chat room as did the majority of users and visitors who were content with hot chat or anonymous flirting.

He had to leave London for a few days and didn't take his laptop along.

When he returned, there were six messages in response to his enquiry.

All from other men who had been in regular contact with the elusive Rachel.

He began corresponding with all of them.

The sky fell.

For CK in Milton Keynes, she had been a banking executive based in Brussels. Single and without child. For months already, they had been having torrid cybersex, the best he had ever had, on a daily basis and had been planning to meet in Los Angeles a few weeks hence for a dirty weekend which had been planned in the minutest sexual detail. Thinking how reserved Rachel and I had been on-line, I blushed and cursed CK silently. She had cuckolded me with him. Virtually, at any rate.

For D (m–NYC), Rachel was an attorney in Boston. Childless, divorced, lonely. They had also been scheduled to meet up in real life very soon. He was reluctant to furnish more details about their on-line relationship.

For Lestat, she had been a bartender in Omaha. And a very hot chick.

For Ian, real–life location unknown, she had also been living in Paris but was a student and a nymphomaniac who enjoyed providing exhilarating details of her casual fucks with the men she would pick up in the Latin Quarter cafés and hinted at a future threesome if he could make the journey there.

For Michael in San Diego, she was an actress living in New York who could only get her kicks from anal sex and loved to reminisce about cocks she had known and been invaded by.

For Responsive (Paris), she had even been living in London, a lecturer at the local French Lycée in Kensington and was planning a visit to him by Eurostar soonest, with delightful hints of common pleasures on the occasion.

And, all the while, for me she had just been Rachel: demure, pretty, quietly unhappy.

If six had answered my call, I reckoned there must be at least as many others who hadn't even seen my message! It seemed Rachel, a great actress in the making, had juggled us all with dexterity and wit.

And disappeared from the forum at the same time, promises unfulfilled, bathed in mystery and possibilities.

We all missed her in different ways.

We had all been sent her photo and been captivated by her. It sounded as if it was the same photo, but I couldn't be sure. Vulnerable soul, whore, teaser, splendid creature somehow conjured by our imaginations and our personal obsessions. She had been all things to all men and briefly made us happy by providing hope of sex, friendship, lust and even love.

I was no longer angry at her. At least, it appeared I was the only man she had given her telephone number too and actually spoken to. And I knew, from the dialling code, she was genuinely living in Paris. So maybe my version of Rachel was the real one. And all the others were playful, ersatz versions of her: cruder, ruder.

I couldn't stop admiring the girl.

Sitting there at her keyboard, surfing forums with gay abandon (who was to say she didn't also roam other forums on other servers, up to her confounding tricks?), pulling our strings like a master puppeteer.

Marti? Oh yes, London, middle-aged, falling in love with me. Thinks I'm a single mother going through a difficult divorce.

CK? British businessman who likes it dirty, scenarios full of bondage and rough sex. Believes I'm single, unattached and always willing.

Lestat: likes me to talk filthy and pretend I'm masturbating. Omaha barmaid, with big sexual history.

And on and on.

Maybe she even had a little black notebook, with all of us carefully filed away, with our tastes and idiosyncrasies. If it's Monday, it must be Marti, be shy. If it's Tuesday, it must be Michael, be outrageous.

She juggled with our lives and feelings with the talent of a magician, knew what made us tick, watched us dance before her playful eyes, but did she find the circus pleasurable, I wonder? Why did she do it? Was it really only a game?

Two years later, I still have no answers and wonder daily what has happened to her. Did she retire or is she playing the same old games on some other forum, in some distant chat room I know nothing of?

She was good, I have to concede that. Give the gal an Oscar.

But if you're reading this, Rachel, my Internet queen, please get in touch, I'd still like to talk, meet.

Please?

cigarillo man

nicholas blincoe

I see her in the revolving door, pushing the glass sails with
her elbows as her fingers scramble at the fliptop of her
Marlboro Lights. Then she is on the pavement, finding
out too late that she is not dressed for the cold. But she
wants a cigarette, what can she do? Her company has a
no-smoking policy. She turns to face the wall as she lights
up. I quietly slip into the revolving door and take a whole
circuit to emerge next to her. I hold my box of Café
Crèmes open in my right hand, one finger snaking round
to hold the paper flap back. I take out a cigarillo, saying:
'Got a light?'

As she looks over her shoulder, I waggle the cigarillo
between my fingers. Her eyes move from the fingers up to
my face, making a 'y' shape in the air as she looks from my
eyes to my mouth to my eyes again. Then she turns around
and says 'Sure.'

We hold another split second look as I bend forward to

suck the flame off her Bic lighter. I inhale slowly, pausing before speaking on the exhalation.

'Do you work here?'

She nods, releasing a soft cloud of smoke. 'You too?' She knows she has not seen me before.

'I'm temping.' There is a plaque on the wall with the words BGU Insurance picked out in red. I have never heard of the company. I guess it must specialise in industrial cover or something. 'Just typing in names,' I say.

Cigarettes burn so much faster in fresh air. Hers is already half gone. I need to step up the pace.

I say, 'We're dying out here.'

'From cold or from the cigarettes?'

'I don't know.' I pause, then add: 'But I'll die happy, now I've met you.'

It is so unexpected, it catches her in mid-gesture, cigarette almost at her lips. A blush sweeps upwards and she has to consciously blink it away.

'Smooth.' She takes another soft drag, using the time to figure out a response. 'But I can't hang around being seduced. I've got work to do.'

She throws a small tight smile my way, stubs her cigarette into the wall-mounted ashtray the company has provided, then pushes at the door and revolves away. I watch her cross the foyer to the bank of lifts. She waits until the last minute before she looks back at me, doing it just as she steps through the sliding doors. I am ready: my eyes burn across the fifteen yards between us. Then she tucks herself into the hidden corner of the lift and the doors close.

I check my watch. It is ten thirty-six.

It all started from something that David, my brother, said six months ago. He works on the west side of Parsonage Gardens and in the summer the gardens are full of office workers eating their sandwiches and trying to catch some sun. I didn't have a job then – I still don't – and I would meet him during his lunch hour if I was in town.

He told me his company had closed the smokers' room.

I shrugged. 'So? You don't smoke.'

'No but when they all sat together in this horrible room, I was glad I didn't smoke. Now they've got an excuse to leave the building every hour, I'm pissed off.'

'Standing outside in all weather?' I shook my head. 'It's OK today, the sun's out. But what about when it's raining? Say there's a snow storm, they're out in sub-zero weather just to get a swift nicotine kick.'

David works for an actuarist, about the only kind of company where men outnumber women. In all the other offices around the city centre, it is completely the other way around. If you also consider that more young women than men smoke, and that what men there are tend to be in managerial roles with their own offices and control over their own windows, I realised that the people on the pavement are going to be mostly female.

The next day, I woke earlyish and stopped by a newsagent for my first packet of cigarettes. A week later, I refined my image by choosing to smoke cigarillos. A new Don Juan was born, the seducer of city workers everywhere, or at least those among them that smoked. I have been pretty successful since then.

After I tear myself away from the doors of BGU Insurance, I have an hour to kill before I meet my brother for lunch. He is always punctual and I have no reason not to be. I let him buy the sandwiches and drinks then we move to an alcove seat at the back of the bar. When I put my tin of Café Crèmes on the table he nods at them and says, 'Are you sure you can afford to smoke?'

He knows why I smoke. I tell him. 'I met the most beautiful woman just now.'

David rests his mouth on the top of his beer, his breath making patterns in the pint's head. Finally he says, 'So what's she like?'

'On the slim side but still shapely, you know. She was wearing a work suit, skirt and jacket and a white blouse. I don't know if I would even recognise her again if she was wearing normal clothes.' I take a sip. 'Except for one thing, she has this attitude. Like, she's really cool, she can throw down a one-line reply and hold your eyes while she does it. But it's all wrapped up with this nervous energy. She keeps it under control but it's there.'

'Bubbling under?' David sounds borderline wistful – the side of wistful that borders on to desperate.

'Like a *frisson,* man.' I say. 'I can't wait to see her tomorrow.'

Tuesday, I reach the corner opposite BGU Insurance block at ten-twelve a.m. There is a woman already there, smoking by the revolving doors. My pulse accelerates. But it only takes a second for me to see that it isn't her. Another few women come in ones or twos, laughing and chatting in rotation before returning to their desks. It isn't until a quarter to eleven that my target arrives. She is not alone, this time. Her work mate is smaller with a bowl haircut. I wait a moment, breathe deeply and start across the street.

She has her back to me as I say, 'You prefer smoking to working?' As she catches the sound of my voice, she turns. I continue: 'Me, I prefer smoking to anything – and I don't have anything like your style.'

Our eyes meet.

I open out a smile, making a space just big enough for the two of us.

'Hello.'

'Hello.'

'Light?' I lift my right hand so she can see the Café Crème dangling between my fingers.

The small woman with the bowl haircut asks, 'Who's your friend?'

Another look flashes between us, that *frisson* again. I love it, seeing the embarrassed shock light up her face. We have been caught in a moment of intimacy and she doesn't even know my name.

I leave it another beat before turning to say, 'I'm Andy.'

'He's temping here, Julie.'

'Oh, whereabouts?'

'Nowhere. I've just finished.' I point up the street towards the offices of the Middleton Building Society. 'I'm working up the road now.'

'You're lucky,' says Julie. 'Isn't he Debbie?'

I barely listen as Julie talks about how crap their company is. I am thinking Debbie, Debbie, Deborah. I like the name and I want to take time to shape it to the woman standing in front of me, leaning against the wall of her company, one arm lightly crossing her navy suit to cradle the elbow of her smoking arm. She holds her cigarette between her fingers in a lazy victory 'V' nodding but not speaking when Julie wants a point confirming – chiefly that their manager is a total witch.

Finally, Julie stubs her cigarette into the wire mesh that covers the company ashtray. 'But if I don't get back to work, she'll go psycho on me. Coming Deb?'

Debbie shakes her head, 'I'll be up in a second.'

I never once took my eyes off Debbie. Now we are alone, I hold out a hand and say, 'Debbie.' Then as she takes it and shakes, I say: 'Are we going to keep meeting like this?'

'I don't know. Are you allowed to wander the streets whenever you feel like it?'

'I was doing the coffee run.' It is a pre-prepared answer. Now I ask, 'Why don't you come?'

'I have to go.'

'What about this afternoon?'

She wants to, I know. I say, 'Meet here at two-thirty?'

She nods, then pushes back through the revolving doors. I look at my watch. Eleven o'clock. I have three and a half hours to waste.

I cruise the financial district for a while, buoyed along on a feeling that is equal parts warmth, excitement and smugness. No one I see compares to Debbie. Then I cut across the city to Parsonage Gardens, stopping on the way to telephone my brother from a box. I get him to promise to buy me lunch.

He spends the whole time complaining that smokers have it easy. I've heard it all before but this time he argues that it is actually healthier to smoke these days.

'How do you work that out?'

'Think about it: the smokers are the only ones getting any fresh air. We work in sealed offices, breathing recycled air, never seeing natural light. You know you need sunshine to produce special brain enzymes to stop you from going mad. Well I only get to see natural daylight during my lunch hour – and most days I eat at my console anyway.'

'You're out today.'

'Today I'm pissed off, I hate my job. It takes all my time, it's sucked up my life and replaced it with a kind of sex-free pod culture.'

'At least you've got a job.'

'You've stopped looking, that's your only problem. You let me pick up the bills while you run around trying to make out you're Don Juan — what's your total now? Five, ten.'

It is twelve since August, just half a year back. But I don't correct him, he knows my score as well I do. And anyway, he has a point: in financial terms, he is carrying me. I let him work out his aggression, counting out the number of my conquests with his fingers and then turning the gesture into a stabbing movement to make his point. Then all of a sudden he winces.

'Fuck. Ow.'

'What's up? Is it that RSI?' I know David has been having problems with the tendons in his wrist, especially in his mouse hand.

'That's another thing. Because of their addiction, smokers are programmed to take a break every half-hour. Me, I just work until my arms and wrists are fucked. I swear, I've got tennis elbow in both elbows and there's nothing I can do. It's not like I can develop a physical craving for a cup of tea.'

He is already standing, getting ready to go back and make his arms, his lungs, his brain even worse. But at least he has money — my problem, I did philosophy instead of maths at university. Most of the men working around the city are techies of one kind or another.

'Before you go . . .' I say.

He hands me a tenner but makes me feel bad by not saying anything. Even when I tell him I will pay him back he just nods. He can't even be bothered to say 'Yeah, right' any more.

Debbie touches the pavement outside her offices at exactly two-thirty. Her medium high heels rap off the kerb stones, matching my pulse rate. I run up and take a moment, pretending to catch my breath. It gives me enough time to get my pulse under control. I know Debbie will assume I have been running to make our date. The truth is I have been hiding around a corner for almost forty-five minutes.

'Debbie,' I grin at her, she sparkles back at me. 'Do you want to know where we're going?'

'On this hot date?'

'Hot date? Are you trying to seduce me, now?'

'You'll be lucky. I have to be back at my desk in ten minutes or my boss will kill me.'

I remember what Debbie's friend said about their supervisor. I hold up a flask that I have just bought from Boots and filled at the Seattle Coffee shop. 'I thought we could go somewhere quiet, so no one can report you for hanging around cafés when you should be working.'

'You're thinking ahead,' she says. 'Or being sneaky.'

Ten minutes is nothing. But planning ahead is not necessarily the same as being sneaky so I lead her to the church off Cheapside and we sit on a bench among the old gravestones, sharing a coffee out of the flask's plastic mug. I repeat a few of the things that my brother said earlier: his argument that smokers are becoming healthier than non-smokers.

Debbie says, 'Except for the cold.'

'We can huddle together.'

'And the lead fumes from the traffic.'

'We can give each other mouth-to-mouth.'

Our lips float together and dock like space craft. We kiss for thirty seconds, then for almost three minutes, and finally for a minute-and-a-half before she pulls apart. We do not even arrange to meet, everything just ends in a flustered, giggling blush and she is gone. But I know I will see her again: between approximately ten-thirty and quarter to eleven the next day.

★　　★　　★

Wednesday, I get to her office at ten twenty-nine and walk to the reception desk. It is staffed by a receptionist with a spectacular hair-do, high on top with strands plastered to her forehead in arabesques the way the r 'n' b divas wear their hair on videos. The front looks fine but the top is squashed by the telephone headset she wears as she sits in front of her screen.

I wait while she puts a call through and then say, 'Do you mind if I use the internal telephone.'

She shakes her head, saying 'Be my guest' as she places a telephone on the counter top in front of me.

I fake dialling and stand there, shifting from foot to foot as though I am waiting for a dial tone. After a few moments, I say: 'It's busy. I'll give it two minutes and try again.'

The receptionist nods and continues with her calls.

I am going through the dialling act for the third time when Debbie steps out of the elevator. I turn to face the wall but she does not look my way. I knew she wouldn't. She just stares through the glass of the foyer windows, wondering if I am already there, waiting for her.

The receptionist long ago stopped paying me any attention, but I still pretend to get a reply. I say, 'Fine . . . Fine . . . Yeah, OK . . . Five minutes.'

As I speak, I watch a man walk from the elevator bank towards the doors. As he passes the reception desk, he places a Visitors Pass on the counter. The receptionist is on a call and does not notice. And she does not notice when I pick up the pass and slip it into my pocket before exiting left, through the revolving doors.

I make Debbie jump. 'Where did you come from?'

'Inside. I'm not working today, so I thought I would roam around your office, see if I could find you.'

'They let you in?'

'I forgot to hand back my security pass, so I decided to go snooping. But I never found you,' I pull a sad expression.

'Did you try the fourth floor?'

'Uh-huh ... you weren't there. I think I saw your little friend.'

'Julie.' We pause. She is lighting her cigarette and passing the flame on to me, ready for the tip of my cigarillo. Then she asks, 'Was Julie talking to someone?'

I decide to say yes. And then, because it could hardly be someone smaller than Julie, I say: 'A taller woman.'

'It's horrible, that woman's really got it in for her.'

'The supervisor?'

Debbie nods. 'She's being really horrible to Julie today. I don't know why.'

I know I should show some sympathy, I just cannot calibrate how much. So I say, 'Every office I ever worked in – there's always an authoritarian lunatic.'

Debbie nods, sucking so hard on her cigarette I am tempted to ask if she wants a blowback. Instead I say, 'I know you would look good in anything – but office wear is really fantastic on you.'

'It's my military bearing.'

It is true, she does have a very erect posture. And her suit is cut in a thirties/forties style, kind of like the Wren's uniform. I am wearing one of David's suits a forty-two short. As I'm a forty long, it does not sit so well. The arms stop at my shirt cuffs and the shoulders and chest bag out. But it isn't that bad, I guess. Most office workers have terrible clothes. And I am supposed to be a temp, anyway – my suit is supposed to be appalling. Dressing in charity shop clothes or hand-me-downs is a sign that I haven't yet committed to the office life. Although the brutal truth is that I probably would commit if I could but I am unemployable – my degree putting me in the same boat as the lads with zero qualifications that I sometimes play pool with in the afternoons.

As we finish smoking, Debbie sighs and says: 'Well . . . back to the virtual grindstone.'

'I'm coming with you,' I flash the pass at her, my thumb covering the printed word VISITORS.

She likes the idea, I can tell, despite the hesitation. It is what a Don Juan does, he has to get under his lovers' skin and touch-read unspoken desires. The job spec. is simple – you are there to facilitate their dreams. That is all.

I nod at the receptionist as we stride for the elevators. The woman remembers me and smiles back; she assumes that I am there as a guest of the company, as I knew she would. The elevator closes on Debbie and me and the other four people inside. The elevator is brushed aluminium with underfloor lighting, like an old-style discotheque of the 1970s. I want to weave my arms around Debbie's waist and *hustle* – breathe the fresh smell of Pantene in her hair. But we are never alone, even at the fourth floor there is one woman still travelling with us.

As we step out, Debbie whispers, 'Go to the vending machines.' She gives a slight nod of her head, I follow it and see a coffee and a snack machine to the right, where the corridor turns sharply. I head towards them, past windows that frame open-plan offices, feeling claustrophobic beneath the styrofoam tiles of the low-slung fake ceiling. I reach the two machines and pretend to scan the crisp packets racked on carousels inside the snack machine. The glass-fronted case gives me a reflected view of the corridor. Debbie swishes by and stops at the drinks machine.

She says, 'What now?'

'The photocopying room?'

She nods and moves off, around the bend in the corridor. I

follow her to a grey door, noting the lock beneath the handle. These days photocopiers are among the least valuable pieces of equipment in the office and, at their weight, the hardest to steal. I cannot think of any reason why they are kept separate from the rest of an office, as though they are contagious. As I step inside the small room and close the door on myself and Debbie, I see that this room also doubles as a stock cupboard. The photocopier stands beneath shelves loaded with paper, discs and general stationary.

'Lock the door.'

I turn the chunky metal catch, one twist right. When I look back at Debbie she is standing against the photocopier, her arms spread to grip either edge. She looks both welcoming and tense. I step forward, my hands moving from her waist upwards to cradle her back, my mouth dipping until it reaches hers. We both make an intake of breath as our lips touch, welding ourselves together with warm suction. My pulse is racing. I wish I could bring the rate down a notch, I don't want to rush. I still feel that Debbie needs to loosen up. I need her to swoon into the moment. But I also have to keep the pace going. We don't have long, maybe only six to seven minutes. Certainly less than twelve.

I slip my hands under her bottom and lift her up, her weight forcing the cheeks to respond to my grip. My fingers point the direction to her labia, tensing as they ease the envelope open. I imagine the soft pink lining, swelling and blooming as it surfaces into the air. Her hands have found a way into my jacket and under my shirt. I feel her fingers flexing into my skin.

Moving through the complex series of manoeuvres of the next thirty seconds, it seems impossible that we have such perfect fluidity. I rest Debbie for a moment on the edge of the photocopier and between us we manage to ruck her skirt into a narrow band and to lose her panties completely. And somehow, my trousers are around my knees and my penis is swaying into a firm-soft erection. Then we are together, only a short pause as her tunti seals its lips around the head of my penis, then kisses open to let the whole shaft slide in. And we are riding, backs arcing and straining, hips rolling.

I hear the door handle jiggle. I ignore it. Debbie is hanging on to my neck, her mouth clamped on the soft tissue between my collar bone. She does not notice a thing – not even when a key scratches against the lock and slides into the groove.

I swing Debbie up and off me as the catch on the door turns from three o'clock to twelve. My toe pushes Debbie's panties under the photocopier as the door opens and a woman enters.

She says, 'Debbie. What are you playing at?'

Then she turns on me me, naked from my pubic hair to my knee caps.

'Who are you?'

Debbie replies first, 'He's a temp.'

I say, 'Sorry.'

'Sorry? This is disgusting.' The woman has drawn herself up to her full height, she is quite tall with heavy dark hair pulled into a tail.

'I know, it's disgusting,' I say. 'It was supposed to be a joke, then Debbie came in and caught me.'

'What?'

'I was photocopying my balls, but I forgot to lock the door. Debbie walked in.'

Debbie is staring at me. When the woman asks if that is true, she turns and nods. 'Yes, Beverley.'

'Why was the door locked?'

'I was trying to give him time to get dressed.'

'Why didn't he use it.' The woman, Beverley, stares at me

as I bend to pull my trousers and underpants up together. She carries on staring as I straighten the tail of my shirt, smoothing it into my trousers. I realise that Beverley is the supervisor, the woman Debbie and her friend detest so much.

'Why were you photocopying your balls?'

'A joke. A dare, really. It was something that started in my office,' I am running out of things to say. I tell her, 'I'm a temp.' As though that explained it.

'He works in the post room, Beverley.' The way Debbie says 'post room' it is clear that no further explanation is needed. I know my brother regards post rooms as the natural home for all that is basest in mankind. He argues that it is where the scum settles, down at the bottom of the building. David once walked in to his post room and the boys were sitting around a computer watching an M–Peg of a woman fellating a horse.

Beverley says, 'Back to work Debbie.'

Debbie leaves. Beverley stands over me while I get dressed and then goes, too. I guess that I am supposed to see myself out. I leave it a moment then step into the corridor. The only person around is a girl at the drinks machine, and she has almost finished. I watch her lift her cup, turn the corner and disappear. I walk in the same direction.

As I turn the corner, I am feeling edgy enough to keep looking over my shoulder. I do not know where Debbie or her supervisor have gone. I scan the offices to my side, trying to do it through the corner of my eyes without moving my neck. I finally see Beverley. She is standing outside on a fire escape. I pause to watch her through the glass door of the fire exit. She smooths her hair behind her ears to keep it from ruffling in the breeze. The hand she uses to hold a cigarette. I wait for her to bring the cigarette to her lips and take a long drag. At that moment, she looks my way. I smother a blush and hold her gaze. Neither of us breaks it – she just releases a cloud of smoke and it ends in a soft fade-out.

The next day, Debbie presses a 3.5″ disc into my hand.

'What's this?'

'Open it and see.'

She thinks I can open it immediately because I have told her I am still working at the Middleton Building Society. Instead, I have to wait until I get home to use my brother's computer. Even when I open the files on the disc, I have no idea what I am looking at. It is a digital picture of some kind. I am still looking when David comes home. He peers over my shoulder and says, 'What's that? Someone has scanned their face?'

I look again; he is right. It is half a face, distorted, darkened and squashed but I can make out the cavity of a closed eye, the ridge of a cheekbone and the outline of a parted lip.

'How did she do that?' I ask.

'Either a desktop scanner or a handheld one.' David peers into his screen. 'I think it was a desktop one, she just pressed her face to it, the same way you would to photocopy your head.'

We sit in silence for a while, staring at Debbie's face. The image is clear to me now, I just don't know what it means. I cannot believe the incident in the photocopy room would affect her so profoundly, she would want to replay it. A kind of primal moment. I begin to worry that I have done some kind of irreversible damage to her sexuality.

She certainly looks disappointed the next day when she gives me a new disc. I have nothing for her. After she returns to work, I telephone David from a call box and ask if he can pick up a scanner for his home computer. He tells me to bugger off. I beg, but he will not budge, saying he has no use for a scanner. He does say he is thinking of buying a digital camera. If I want to wait until the end of the month, he will buy one after he gets paid.

I tell him not to bother. I know that she prefers a photocopied quality but for some reason I don't feel like explaining exactly why photocopies carry such an erotic charge for her. Normally, I would do. I wonder whether I am falling for her.

But David seems to be ahead of me. 'You know, photographs are so clear, they have a kind of pornographic quality. I think I prefer things to be more indistinct. More abstract.'

He goes quiet for a moment. After a while, I ask if he is still there. He says he is, and he has an idea. If I photocopy myself and fax it to his home PC, care of his Internet provider, we can receive it as e-mail. Then I can do whatever I want with it: download it, copy it to disc or re-fax it somewhere else. I think about the Pakistani grocers' at the end of our street. They have a sign advertising office services so I should be able to do everything I need to in their shop. I decide to call in on my way home.

When I finally open Debbie's latest disc on David's PC, I find two files. The first is quite clear: a palm print. It looks good in itself, not just as a memento of her. The second file is harder to read, I have to stare until it resolves into a readable image. Then I get an erection. It is a profile of a breast, quite squashed but with a distinct nipple.

My physiological reaction to the breast image means that it is another fifteen minutes before I open the e-mail and look for the fax I sent from the corner shop. I am pleased to see that it has come out quite well, showing my ear and jaw line. But Debbie's breast shot has raised the stakes and I know that soon I will have to give her a more intimate picture. I save my ear to disc and catch a bus into town, running to be on time for her next cigarette break.

We sneak into the women's washroom on the third floor of her office. We don't have full sex: toilets have an intimidating effect on me. But it gets pretty intimate in the cubicle and she is soon aroused. I do what I can. Afterwards she gives me another disc and I hand her mine.

Over the next week she gives me just one more disc, of her armpit. After that, we move to e-mail. I get another breast image, this time of both boobs pressed to the glass, and a series of nipple images she made with a handheld scanner. These would be completely unreadable if Debbie had not started giving her pictures titles. Once I receive 'leftnipple 1–10', I just let my imagination flesh out the dark blur on the PC screen. She also sends me a foot, actually a sole imprint, and a navel before-and-after shot. This is how I discover that she has pierced her belly button. The next time we are in a toilet cubicle together, I kiss the sore puncture wound and let the metallic sweetness of her blood dissolve on my tongue.

I send her a foot, naked and in profile showing the slight deformity where I broke my ankle skateboarding. I also send my elbow, crooked, and my face. The face is full-on. Then I send my penis and balls as a one-shot and, the day after, my buttocks.

It is not easy making photocopies like these in a crowded corner shop. The owner is quick to tell me I should find myself another photocopier. Fortunately, I remember there is one in the local library.

I am on my way to see how Debbie likes the e-mail of my buttocks when I run into Beverley, her supervisor, again. She is sitting on a bench in Spring Gardens, smoking a cigarette. I pause, wondering whether to join her. I have not been pulling my Don Juan routine so much any more. Debbie's been taking up all of my time.

Beverley catches sight of me. She looks straight at me, saying, 'What's the problem, don't you recognise me with your clothes on?'

'Hello. It's Beverley, isn't it?'

'Yes. It's the naked temp, isn't it?'

'Andy,' I say. 'Is this where you take your cigarette breaks?'

'Yes. Either here or on the fire escape.'

'Is that the pressure of being management, you have to smoke alone.'

'I'm just glad to get away from the cows in my office,' she says. 'Though I expect they say worse about me.'

I am not going to tell her that, yes, it is true, they hate you. But I guess my uncomfortable silence gives me away.

Beverley says, 'Don't worry. It's not as though it's anything to do with you. You're not working in the post room any more?'

'No. No, I'm at Bennet Ross.' I mention the name of a group of solicitors. Then I tell her, 'Office life can get pretty tense.'

'Offices are life – who's got time for anything else.'

Debbie says something similar, a few days later. She says, 'The thing I resent is, not spending my whole life in an office, it is having no control over the people I spend it with. Personnel decides that, I just either make friends or make enemies. That's it, the sum total of my freedom of choice.'

I want to tell her that she is lucky, at least she has a job. But I haven't yet confessed all to her and she still thinks I am a temp. Anyway, I do appreciate her point. My brother once said that his sex life is entirely at the mercy of human resources, which is what the personnel department is called in his company. David sent an e-mail, cc'ed to the whole of human resources, arguing that they should advertise for women like towns used to in the old wild west.

Debbie seems a little distant. I want to get her focusing back on our romance. Her last e-mail to me was fantastic: a small patch of pubic hair, blown up about one hundred times. I tell her how much I liked it. Then ask her how she liked mine.

She waggles a hand in the air, 'So so.'

'You didn't like it?' I am suddenly mortified.

'Put it this way – it didn't do much for me.'

It was a picture of my nose – not exactly fresh meat but I have been having problems. My original idea was to copy my clavicle, hoping to remind Debbie of the way she bit into it during our first sexual encounter. But it is impossible to photocopy a clavicle unless you are a Chinese contortionist and even a Chinese contortionist would have difficulty doing it in Central Library. I am still hoping to persuade my brother to buy a handheld scanner but he has not weakened yet.

I don't bother to explain the clavicle problem. I can feel her coldness and realise I have to find a way to regain the initiative. The way she looks at me as she returns to work, I know it will have to be something startling. I finish my cigarillo, watching her as she crosses the lobby and disappears. Then I push through the doors and walk to reception. I hover over the internal telephone until someone leaves a Visitors' Pass for me to steal.

In the fourth floor photocopy room, I lock the door and undress. I begin by lying on the photocopier, navel pressed to the area marked out for A4 copies. I am starting there so that I can work outwards. My plan is to cover my entire body, pegging out my skin like an animal hide stretched on a drying frame.

I soon cover my torso, front and back, and am moving along my outspread arms, from fingertips to my face, when the door knob starts rattling. I pause. The person goes away.

I wonder whether I should jam the door shut, just to be safe. Instead, I stick out my leg and hold the door shut that way as I continue, across my face and back down the other arm. I have reached the elbow when the knob is rattled again. I stiffen my leg. The knob rattles one more time.

So far, I have kept my eyes closed. I think fear makes me open them. It is a mistake, the copier light flashes in my eyes, blinding me, then a key turns in the door. I struggle to keep my kneecap locked and my leg rigid. But I am worried about my ankle. Ever since the skateboard accident, it sometimes give way. It does now.

Beverley is standing there, looking along my extended leg, up to my bum and balls and onwards to my face. My face is still pressed flat to the glass bed of the copier. I look back along the same axis: and believe me, I am painfully aware that from my perspective, the view does not include my genitals.

Beverley says, 'What is your problem exactly?'

I stand up, grabbing a photocopy to use as a cover for my groin. 'I can't believe this has happened again.'

'You can't? I knew it would. I've been lying in wait for you.'

The words hang there for a moment. I try to make sense of them. She has been lying in wait. She wanted to catch me. I feel myself stiffen behind the white sheet of A4 photocopy paper.

I say, 'Do you want to close the door?'

'Why would I want to do that?'

'To . . . talk?' I lift an eyebrow.

She steps forward, grabbing my arm and swinging me naked into the corridor. 'You disgusting sleazebag.'

I stammer, 'My clothes, my clothes.' But she just kicks me, driving me along the corridor and round the corner at the drinks machine. The corridor is full of people, the windows at either side of the corridor crowded with faces. I do not even have a piece of paper to cover myself.

Beverley drives me on from behind, the crowds parting for me as she forces me up the corridor. Then, in the crowd, I see Debbie.

Beverley says, 'I think I've found something of yours, Deborah Slater.'

Debbie has no expression on her face. She just says, 'What's that then?'

'Your post boy.'

'I don't know him.' Debbie shrugs. 'The last time I saw him, it was with you – in the photocopy room together.'

'He was with you.'

'I found him there – but I left him and you alone together.' Debbie is stone-faced but the circle of people around her are breaking into smiles. Debbie continues, 'I don't know what happened between you and him after I left.'

The security guard makes me wait for the police in one of the offices. I am still naked, I do not know if anyone is going to return my clothes to me. It certainly won't be Beverley, she is standing isolated at one side of the office with most of the rest of the women at the other end, staring at her and nudging one another as they break into suppressed giggles.

I do not want to look. It is clear now that Debbie has discarded me. But I cannot believe she has been so cruel about it: using me one last time as a pawn in an elaborate revenge strategy. I turn to the computer on the desk in front of me, it is open at a hot-mail page. The name at the top says Debbie Slater.

I scroll down. All my e-mails are there. I open a couple quickly. My nose. My armpit. I am beginning to see why she lost interest in me.

I look at the list of the other e-mails and open another few of the ones I sent, all at random. The first is a picture of a white lily. I never sent anything like that. In confusion, I open another. It is a tiered chocolate cake. Flowers and now chocolates . . . I realise she has been accepting e-mails off another man.

Then I find a Renaissance painting of St Sebastian, pierced with arrows. And it has a text underneath. 'Andy thinks he's a Don Juan – I believe that is Juan as in Juanker.'

The e-mails are sent from David's PC. And only he and I have access to it. But even if I could not work out it was my own, bastard brother, he has helpfully signed his name.

By the picture of St Sebastian, he has written: 'I am Cupid's own dartboard. Until we meet – your devoted David xxx'

icy you . . . juicy me

pat cadigan

The crazy man was dancing around the public telephones on the north-east corner of 45th and Broadway in Times Square. Across the street, by contrast, everything was uneventful. Yellow cabs appeared and disappeared; people materialised in the crosswalk and then vanished, which meant they were walking awfully fast. Darcy wondered where they had to go in such a hurry at 5.38 in the morning. Maybe they were just trying to get out of the vicinity of the crazy man performing his ritual morning boogie. He was a pretty talented dancer for a crazy guy. Some of the people crossing at the opposite corner seemed to be watching him, or at least taking a look as they hurried to work or wherever.

It was hard to tell exactly what was going on sometimes, with the choppiness of the image progression. Even weather conditions could be hard to determine. Rain or snow was easy, but it wasn't always easy to see if it was cold or not, not even by the way the crazy guy was dressed. *Especially* that.

Even the frequency of his appearances wasn't necessarily a key – being crazy, he wouldn't always make the logical decision to stay inside when it was cold. Darcy didn't even know if he had any place to be inside. There wasn't a shopping cart full of worldly goods and chattels, but maybe he always parked it off-camera, or stashed it somewhere.

Darcy smiled to herself. Keeping tabs on a crazy guy – yeah, just another day in the life of the forty-year-old agoraphobe. The thing was, he was obviously aware of the camera; you could tell the way he performed. He always faced the camera straight on, even though the camera itself was placed at an angle meant to give the longest view down the street. You could see all the way down to the south island in Times Square with all the big screens on it, just like you could see all the way in the other direction to the north island on the other camera. Good morning, midtown Manhattan.

Darcy leaned closer to the screen, watching people flash in and out of the crosswalk, lone pedestrians giving way to groups of three, sometimes four, buses moving in and out of the frame, and, in the other window, the crazy guy still dancing around the payphones while pedestrians gave him a wide berth. She tried to imagine herself in the crosswalk, caught on camera, looking nonchalant and unaware in a dark blue parka or sid jacket or – what did they call them now? Anoraks, that was it. Herself in a dark blue anorak and white scarf, knit hat pulled down over her lank, colourless hair, hands stuffed in her pockets. On her way to ... well, somewhere. All those people outside had some place they were on their way to. Even the crazy guy.

She wondered what he would have thought if he'd known she was watching him and thinking of him as *the crazy guy*. He would probably think that was a heavy case of the pot calling the kettle a very dark colour. Depending, of course, on how crazy he was.

But the problem was that she *wasn't* crazy . . . technically. Agoraphobia was not a true psychosis. It did not qualify as R. D. Laing's sane response to an insane world. It was simply an unreasoning fear, specifically of the marketplace, in this instance.

But if the marketplace in question was Times Square at 45th and Broadway, then the diagnosis was a bit faulty. She had been watching this little piece of the world on Live Earthcam from her North London flat for, well, she wasn't sure how long. But what she *was* sure of was that she had absolutely no fear, unreasoning or otherwise, of Times Square, or at least what was visible of it going north and south from 45th and Broadway.

It was everything else between her and it that had her petrified.

She left the crazy guy and his phone booth dance on the monitor and swapped the other view of Times Square for BourboCam in New Orleans, even though she knew it would be a disappointment. The only thing you got at this time of the morning at the corner of Bourbon and St Peter were frat boys giving up and going home after a long night of drinking. They all looked like frat boys, anyway. Plus, BourboCam didn't give you a continuous on-screen image – every twenty seconds, the frame went black while the scene reloaded. She moved on.

O Street in Lincoln, Nebraska was still dark, although the view over Lincoln looking east showed her that dawn was not far away. GeekCam was dark. Badgrrl's Office took forever to load, but it was too early to see anything. Weirdcam wasn't online yet. The kitchen on KitchenCam was tidy, except for a small scattering of beer cans on some white thing with the mysterious legend *odwalla* large on the side. It was also empty. Other than that, California was cluttered up, as usual, with Nerdman, and she just wasn't interested in Nerdman today. The LivingRoomCam, which she didn't care for in the first place, played one of those awful midi tunes.

It was raining on Lower Gardiner Street in Dublin. Cloudy in Tokyo—

She was about to click on New Zealand when the Times Square frame found its way to the top of the accumulated windows on her monitor. The crazy guy was standing directly in front of the camera with his hands on his hips; the only word Darcy could think of for his expression was *provoked*.

Someone using his telephones? No one there behind him now, but most likely that hadn't been the problem anyway. If someone ever actually dared to approach the telephones during the performance of the dance ritual, the crazy guy would simply take his dancing into overdrive and that would settle the matter.

Darcy watched, fascinated, as he stood perfectly still, staring directly into the cam. It was daylight now and she could see him more clearly than she ever had. He was just a guy, only one guy of millions of guys, fifteen or fifty in a dark watch-cap, guy-shaped in a dark jacket – anorak – and jeans. Either his face was dirty or he needed a shave. Or both. She leaned closer, wishing for better resolution.

For no particular reason, she decided that underneath the dirt, his beard was a paler shade of tomcat ginger. It would suit him, she thought; all those dark colours, the dirt. He needed some brightening up.

Her gaze started to wander to the list of webcam links on the right side of her screen when he reached up and knocked on whatever glass separated him from the webcam. The knocking gesture was exaggerated, like an overenthusiastic mime in slow motion.

To accommodate the choppiness of the image progression, she realised. He was adapting his movements to the frequency of the image reloading, so they would look smoother. No denying it now, he definitely knew that cam was there, and what it was doing, and how.

Still moving in that exaggerated way, he raised his index finger and shook it at the camera in a silent scold before pointing both thumbs at himself. Then, as if to make sure, he pointed both index fingers at the camera, and then both thumbs at himself again.

No mistake; he most certainly did know about the webcam. And he knew that somewhere, someone was watching.

Well, of *course* he knew. The camera was probably in plain sight, like any other camera among the multitude of cameras in New York City. Every large city had them for traffic or police surveillance, and now, finally, for the entertainment of web surfers. Kremlin Cam – beautiful view, but too distant for Darcy's taste, too impersonal. Likewise ParlsCam, and the skyline of Lincoln, Nebraska, and a good many others. What could you watch from a panorama cam but a shifting pattern of grubby dots or out-of-focus lights? Sometimes not even that.

On the other hand, people's personal cams were just a bit too up-close for her. She had no desire to become closely acquainted with someone else's room, though she'd watch an office for a while if nothing else of interest was happening anywhere.

In the end, however, she always found herself returning to the Times Square street level cams and, thus, to the crazy guy who did his best to make sure she had something to watch.

If she had a better monitor and a better graphics card, she

wondered, watching him as he stood in front of the camera, arms folded now, his head tilted down so that he glowered into the lens from under his eyebrows, would she be able to see him a whole lot better, enough to make it worth the expense? Or would she find out that the camera, never meant to produce a continuous, flowing motion picture, was little better than the survelliance cams they showed footage from on *America's Dumbest Criminals,* pixels the size of chiclets?

Making sure the crazy guy stayed visible on her desktop, she e-mailed The Spook.

The Spook was not what he called himself but how he was known universally among his on-line acquaintances, or at least the ones Darcy knew of. He might have been a real spook at some time, or maybe he was just one of those people who always seemed to find out things that escaped other people. He ran a quirky search engine called Juicy This? dedicated to what he called I-ways less travelled. He also answered questions, but only if he thought the questions were geeky enough. This, she thought, would satisfy his urge to *neep-neep-neep.* Even better, there was a very good chance that she would be able to understand the answer. Hardware was something she seemed to comprehend better than software.

Hello. Roky: taken up webcamming in a big way. If I invest in better graphics and resolution, can I get better cam video?

She sent the e-mail and then went into the kitchen to heat up some soup for an early lunch. As she left the room, she imagined that she could feel the crazy guy's stare on her back, which was very silly. Possibly even crazy.

When she returned to her desk with a large mug of cream of mushroom soup, the crazy guy was waiting for her with a tall skinny guy wearing a black trench coat and carrying a briefcase. The crazy guy was pointing at the cam; the skinny guy was squinting up at it thoughtfully while the crazy guy told him something. The briefcase flashed from the skinny guy's right hand to his left and back again. Behind them, a fleet of yellow cabs went by, heading downtown.

'Hey, pal, if you want a cab, you better get one now, instead of talking with some crazy guy on the street,' Darcy said, giggling a little as she spooned up some soup. Who says agoraphobia's no fun?

As if in response to what she had said, the skinny guy turned around and then ran for the kerb, waving at the cabs. The crazy guy looked after him for a moment before he turned back to look accusingly into the lens again.

Maybe he thought it was a police survelliance camera, or private security. Could he have any idea that it was a webcam? Did he have any idea about the web? Were crazy guys aware of the Internet?

Were crazy guys aware of the Internet. She had to laugh at herself. Crazy guys had *invented* the Internet, conceptually, anyway. It had just taken a while for the reality to catch up with the theory. This guy had probably been performing for cameras for years. Chances were, he'd get bored eventually and move on to some other camera somewhere else. *Then* what would she do for entertainment? Hope for another crazy guy to come along, she supposed; otherwise, she might actually have to turn on the television again.

Maybe, she thought, she should try to find some other crazy guys, just to make sure she wasn't driven to anything too desperate. New York was full of webcams *and* crazy guys – surely the two had connected up in other locations besides 45th and Broadway. But as she went to choose another link from the list on the right side of her desktop, the crazy guy began jumping up and down in a frenzy, which was not much in the way of frenzy but did look very bizarre, considering.

He squatted and made large *no* motions with both arms like a baseball umpire. The message was clear: don't touch that dial. Which was completely ridiculous, of course. Maybe she had an unreasoning fear of the marketplace, and maybe she hadn't left her flat in something like two years, and maybe she just now thought webcams were the height of entertainment, but she wasn't so far gone that she believed any of the people caught in the webcam's gaze had any awareness of who was watching them. That *was* just plain crazy.

Of course it was . . . and he was a crazy guy, right?

Frowning, she pushed back from her desk and got up to take her empty mug back into the kitchen. She would use the time to wash the mug and the spoon as a screen break. *Clean as you go* was the unbreakable rule for the housebound. Let the washing-up accumulate in the sink, allow the clutter to get out of hand and you might end up as one of those pathetic minor headlines on the inside pages of the newspaper: *Local recluse found dead amid twenty years of old magazines and pizza boxes.* Being an agoraphobe was a lot more complicated than just never leaving the house, something most people couldn't begin to appreciate, Darcy thought, running the water in the sink.

And what about her crazy-guy friend on the webcam – what might *he* be able to appreciate? Even if she wasn't technically crazy, would her little problem give them some sort of common ground for relating to each other?

So, you say you can't leave the house, eh? Bummer.

Well, not really, I never get caught in the rain, for one thing.

I always do. *No choice.*

Yeah, that makes sense. So what is it with you, a compulsion?

She stood at the sink in a trance, waiting for the next line in the imaginary conversation while she rinsed the mug over and over, but it wouldn't come. She simply couldn't imagine why he danced around payphones and played to surveillance cameras. Finally, she shut the water off and placed the cup in the dishrag, but she lingered at the counter, wiping her hands on a dishtowel and trying to think. If she couldn't even theorise why the crazy guy did those few unremarkable irrational things, she certainly wouldn't be able to figure out how it was he seemed to be aware of the reactions of an observer – Well, how else stupid? Because somehow HE CAN SEE YOU.

Slowly, she turned around to look through the doorway of the kitchen into the living room. The monitor sat in profile to where she was now. She had placed it that way so that she could look up and quick-check whether she had left the oven on, or forgotten something on top of the stove. (*Cooker,* she nagged herself; *how many more years will you live here before you remember they call it a cooker?*)

The doorway to the bedroom, however, was behind where she sat at the desk. Had she ever walked around nude in front of the monitor when she'd been on-line? She came up blank, which made her pretty sure she must have done it a million times. And if he *could* see her—

Darcy looked down at herself and burst out laughing. So he saw her. At forty, she actually wasn't half bad – Pilates had been invented for prisoners, even the virtual kind. But all that aside – he was a *crazy* guy. Who knew *what* he saw, or what he thought he was seeing?

Maybe he only thought he was seeing her, period.

Tension Darcy had been unaware of drained out of her in a rush. Her shoulders dropped three inches as she sagged against the doorway, shaking her head and laughing a little. Insanity could be contagious. What did they call it when two people shared a delusion? *Folie à deux.* Could you catch it by accident? Maybe . . . if you had kind of a head start, say, with an unreasoning fear, *unreasoning* being the key word. Unreasoning as in irrational; irrational as in crazy. QED.

But not quite. Enough to be fooled briefly – and *briefly* was the key word there, thank you – but not so crazy that it would stick. Nothing that would make you take up ritual telephone dancing or trading signals with some hallucinating fool four thousand miles away in another time zone. Crazy people weren't stupid. Most had normal intelligence, some of them were quite brilliant. Her crazy guy, for example, could well be brilliance combined with experience working in the field of surveillance, prior to his going over the edge into madness.

Sure. He might have been a security guard in one of those giant office buildings, paid to watch a whole wall of monitors. That wasn't anything like just checking out a few webcams in exotic locations, that would drive anyone around the bend.

So day after day, he sat in front of his wall of monitors as people came and went and came back and went again and disappeared, reappeared, always ignoring him. No matter how carefully *he* watched *them*, *they* ignored *him*, ignored him and ignored him and ignored him, until one day, he just cracked. Sure. She could see that. She could imagine him suddenly jumping up from his chair in front of the wall of monitors and screaming at all those oblivious people entering and leaving and leaving and entering: *Goddamit. I am* here, *I exist! I* exist, *stop pretending I don't, goddam you all!*

After that, everything happens fast. Supervisor comes in, throws him out, and the next thing you know, he's a crazy guy on the street, dancing around telephones and playing to any camera he sees, doing the things he wished all those oblivious, uncaring, under-surveillance people had done for him: i.e., acknowledging the existence of the observer.

The fact that his actions had co-ordinated with her own

movements had been one of those amazing but not totally
unheard-of coincidences, a synchronicity that was perhaps a
by-product of the technology in a way that had yet to be
explained.

Yes. Yes. *Yes*. Far-fetched, maybe, and she could have
been wrong about some of the details, but the main virtue
of the little story she had just told herself was that it was
possible. That it also seemed to endow her with great insight
into the modern perils of the human condition didn't hurt.
When you didn't get out much, you had a lot of time to think
things through, to contemplate what it was to be human.

She started toward the desk and then stopped. Great
explanation, but what if he was doing something that blew
the whole thing to pieces?

Like what?

She didn't know. He was a very inventive crazy guy, she
couldn't imagine but it might catch her off guard even armed
as she was with rational thoughts, catch her so off guard that
she became too afraid to look at her own computer monitor.
What then? What if she developed an unreasoning fear of
the Internet? Except it wouldn't be an *unreasoning* fear – and
what *then?*

Well, she knew what then. Agoraphobes were tolerated,
even sympathised with a little, but technophobes might as
well go jump in a hole somewhere. Or find some telephones
to dance around, ideally not far from the cardboard box they
called home.

She gave a short laugh and then covered her mouth. And
then pulled her left hand away from her face with her right.

*Stop it. Stop it right now. There's no reason to go crazy until
– unless – there's no other choice. So far, there's always been an
alternative.*

Her gaze fell on her purse, sitting on the sideboard beside

one of the lamps she had inherited from her aunt. She left it there as if she might, at any time, just grab it up and leave the house on an errand. Just in case someday she could, or at least wanted to try just leaving the house on an errand, her purse would be ready and waiting for her, so that she couldn't use the excuse of not being able to find it or her wallet or her keys. They were all there, in a cosy heap at the bottom of the purse, underneath her make-up kit, which contained one new (mail-order) lipstick and the premium that had come with it as a reward for ordering before whatever cut-off date that had been: a rather large pocket mirror.

She took the pocket mirror out and opened it up. Her face stared back at her expectantly. She gave another short laugh, this one without a hysterical edge to it. So whose face had she been expecting to see?

Don't go there.

She would sneak up on the monitor, she decided. She would sneak up on it and hold the pocket mirror in front of it and see what her crazy friend was doing, as if in the rear-view mirror of a car.

Objects in the mirror are closer than they appear.

She opened the mirror and tiptoed across the room, refusing to acknowledge how silly the whole thing was. When she got to the side of the desk, she crouched down and raised the mirror slowly, angling it until the screen appeared in the small glass.

She saw a piece of cardboard, with large, black numbers written crudely on it: 212–669–8178.

Bewildered, she raised the mirror a little higher. It was the crazy guy, all right, the same crazy guy, and he was holding the cardboard up in front of his chest with both hands. Two women pushing a stroller appeared behind him, then disappeared as he looked back over his shoulder at the

telephones. A woman in a red coat materialised as he looked
back at the cam; he had raised his right hand to point his
thumb at the phones.

212–669–8178, she read. Easily, because it appeared in
normal hand even if it was crude. Which meant that he
had printed it backwards, as if he had known she would be
looking at it in a—

She snapped the mirror shut and scrambled away from the
desk backwards.

OK, said the calm voice from somewhere under all the
reasoning and unreasoning fear inside her, *what did you* really
see, and what do you think it means?

The calm voice was always there but tended to get drowned
out by the soundless scream of panic. Why she could hear it
now, when she felt like screaming out loud for real at full,
we-go-to-eleven volume was another one of those little
mysterious personal contradictions you could never count
on happening when you needed it.

What did you really *see?* asked the voice again.

The mental image of the crazy guy holding up the piece
of cardboard with the crude frontwards-because-they-were-
backwards numbers hung before her inner eye, daring her to
deny it.

Fine, said the calm voice. *Accepted, at least for the time being.
What do you think it means?*

Her inner eye zoomed in on his crazy face. Ginger beard
stubble, just like she'd imagined. Pale eyes, like the colour
had been washed out, faded. Badly chapped lips, so cracked
they had split in the fleshier parts. Broken nose, like a boxer's.
Filthy jacket—

But what does it mean? *That's what it looks like. What does
it* mean?

'If I knew that,' she muttered at her reflection in the hand mirror, 'I'd probably be able to leave the house.'

The words seemed to hang in the air around her. Like on the old Groucho Marx show she'd seen tapes of. *You Bet Your Life*. That funny bird that came down: *Say the secret word and win an extra hundred dollars. Well, you just said it. It's a whole bunch of words, but call it an adjustment for inflation.*

The calm voice had no reply to make, probably because it had nothing to tell her she didn't already know. If there was something you didn't know, then what you had to do was ask someone who did. Like asking The Spook about hardware and cams. She could check her e-mail and see if he'd answered yet. She could do that. That would get her back across the room to the computer, have her using it in the normal, unremarkable fashion. If she did that, she just might find that it responded in the normal, unremarkable fashion, no crazy guys holding up signs for her to read in mirrors or telling her to pay attention.

If there was no crazy guy on the monitor, she thought, she would call that doctor and consent to resume medication. *When in doubt, keep taking the tablets.* Even if they did make her drowsy and fat.

And if there was a crazy guy, she'd bite the bullet and call 212–669–8178, and ask him what the hell was going on.

But first, she would check her e-mail. First she would do the normal thing. Her calm voice would have approved, she thought, if it could have made itself heard. *Always do the normal thing first, and then go crazy.* It would say wisely. She wondered if the crazy guy knew that rule, and whether he had broken it, or it just hadn't worked for him.

She made herself get up and walk over to the desk. He was waiting there on the monitor, hands in his pockets, or behind his back, his dirty, stubbly face turned up to the camera as usual. Pointedly ignoring him, she opened her e-mail program over him. It chimed immediately; the Spook's reply was already in her mailbox. If he was this prompt, maybe she should ask him about the webcam at 45th and Broadway itself, if there was anything odd about it or—

```
Dear Friends, just to let you know I'm off for two weeks
on the beach in Florida. Not taking my laptop for a change
but there is a webcam. I'll be waving hello at 11 a.m.
eastern time every morning, so point your browser at the
following URL and give me a wave back—
```

Revolted, Darcy stabbed the delete button and shut the e-mail program without bothering to look at any of the other messages. The crazy guy was waiting underneath, the tilt of his head suggesting he was amused. The image jumped; he was looking over his shoulder at the phone. Jump; he was looking back at the cam.

Her telephone was right next to her computer on the desk. She put her hand on the receiver and just held it for a long moment before picking it up. It took another little while before she could bring herself to push the buttons on the handset, and she did it very slowly. But she did it.

There was a short delay between the time the ringing tone began in the receiver and the crazy guy signifying that he could hear the payphone ringing. It might have been the cam image lag, or it might have been that the speed of sound being slower than the speed of light. Maybe she should take notes, she thought; she might learn something of actual scientific substance.

He took his time getting to the phone, walking backwards to it as slowly as possible. Foot traffic blasted by him, men and women, in pairs, in groups, all alone, obscuring him and then vanishing, showing him untouched and the same.

It took three frames for his hand to make it from his pocket to the receiver. Before the frame changed again, the ringing cut off and she heard the relentless roar of 45th and Broadway. She waited, but that was all she heard.

And then her own voice was large in her head, in her ears, in the room: 'I see you.'

He turned away for a moment to stare at the phone before turning back to the cam. 'Juicy me?'

He didn't sound crazy. He just sounded like a guy, any guy. The guy you got when you called a catalogue to order something; the guy who answered queries about your electric bill. The guy who was stuck on the technical support hotline at 4 a.m., when only the most desperate of the desperate were awake and obsessing about some glitch in some far, dark corner of a program they only ran when they couldn't sleep. The guy at the clinic who arranged the telephone appointments with the shrink. Just a guy.

'Yeah, I see you. Do you see me?'

He giggled. The sound annoyed her.

'*How* do you see me?'

He was in profile on the monitor now, leaning on the phone box. In spite of the people popping in and out and the lousy resolution, she could see the big, goofy grin on his face.

'*How* do you see me?' she demanded. 'Is there a monitor? One, more than one? Is it that anyone who accesses that cam can be seen by – by . . .' Passersby kept appearing and vanishing in front of him, around him, making her flustered, making her flounder. '*How* do you see me? Dammit, *who is under surveillance here?*'

As she watched, he turned towards the cam again, made

a deep, formal bow, held up the receiver and dropped it. Not into the cradle to hang it up, just dropped it so that it dangled, off the hook, still connected to her.

The frame jumped and he was gone.

Darcy sat with her own telephone in one hand, waiting for him to reappear and do something else. Traffic noise drifted out of the earpiece. The complete virtual experience, you are there, webcam *and* direct phone line.

Surely someone would hang up the phone. Surely someone would.

Surely . . . if anyone had noticed. The dangling phone receiver seemed to go completely unnoticed.

Alarmed, remembering who had called whom, she slammed down the phone and counted to thirty before picking it up again.

The traffic noise at 45th and Broadway was undiminished. If anything, it seemed to be louder and clearer.

She put the phone down again and counted to sixty. Jiggled the switch-hook, pressed all the buttons. Unplugged the connection and plugged it back in again.

OK, said the calm voice. *You know what you have to do.*

'Right,' she growled. 'Visit the phone company website and report a faulty line.'

Maybe it would have worked, except the trouble-reporting area of the website refused to take any input.

'E-mail someone and ask them to call the phone company on my behalf,' she said, and sent a message to everyone in her address book.

And meanwhile, the traffic noise in her telephone went on and on and on, not terribly mismatched to the webcam frame on her screen. Sometimes the dangling receiver would swing in the wind; sometimes it was still.

Occasionally, someone used the telephone next to it and

she shouted as loud as she could, but no one heard her desperate request to hang up the receiver.

OK, said the calm voice. *You know what you have to do.*

'I'll wait,' she muttered. 'I'll wait and see if anything else works. I'll wait and see if he comes back.'

But she knew he wasn't coming back. There were a million cameras in the naked city; this was only one of them. Besides, maybe he wasn't crazy any more. Maybe he'd managed to be cured, just by getting someone to admit he was visible, he'd been seen.

You know what you have to do.

'No,' she said, but faintly, so weakly.

You're going to have to hang that phone up yourself.

'No.'

And get someone to admit they can see you.

'No—'

And then you don't have to be afraid any more.

She looked at her purse, still waiting on the sideboard for her. Pretty big errand; not the sort of thing she'd have thought of starting out with.

So what was wrong with being afraid, anyway? It didn't hurt anybody.

But that wasn't the point anyway, she realised, staring at the monitor. It didn't matter whether she was afraid or not afraid. What mattered was the cam. She had been watching, and now it was her turn to be watched. Nothing was going to be right until she took her turn. Only then would everything go back into balance. Not to mention her regular phone service being restored.

She took a deep breath. All right . . . but . . . *now?*

Plane reservations would be easy. Accommodation could be arranged via the same website. What was the big deal about going out? If you could bring it all in and put it on a computer screen – complete with traffic noise – then you were *already* out. The rest was just a technicality. Agoraphobia? Wiped out in our lifetime. Now it's *claustrophobia*.

In her hurry, she nearly forgot her purse.

only connect

lauren henderson

It's a truism that men can only concentrate on one thing at a time. Isn't that the stereotype, that women can juggle twenty different tasks at once, running from one pole to the next, keeping the plates spinning with a few swift flicks of the wrist? Men are supposed to be the opposite: so single-minded that if they try to do more than one thing simultaneously they end up messing up both. It's a neat little theory but it completely fails to account for what Dan is doing to me right now. One hand on the wheel, the other between my legs, his eyes never leaving the road, his index and third fingers stroking me through my silky French knickers. A stereotypical man would be completely thrown by the speed bumps; but Dan, far from treating them as an obstacle, is actually using them as a choreographic motif, working his fingers round the edge of the material and into me a split-second before the front wheels hit the first bump, then remaining frustratingly still, allowing each subsequent bump to drive his fingers a little deeper into me, like a wedge, so that I find myself grinding my hips in anticipation as we reach the next one, barely able to wait. Dan starts rubbing the heel of his hand against me, his fingers still inside me. The seam of my knickers, caught between us, chafes against me so successfully that it might have been specially designed for the purpose. I am moaning. Dan is still looking straight ahead – it's pretty much a point of honour – but his lips are curved into the smuggest smile I have ever seen on a man.

I'm the one here who can't concentrate on anything else. It doesn't occur to me for a moment to reach over and stroke Dan through his jeans, slip my fingers between his waistband and belly, rub my thumb down the coarse hairy line of skin to the hot, smooth, slightly damp and swollen-to-bursting head below. I am totally selfish when I'm being fingered, incapable of doing anything but lying back and letting out a crescendo of what I hope are highly encouraging moans. To be fair to me, I am just the same when I'm going down on someone; I don't want any interruptions, no matter how well meant. I like to give my full attention to the task in hand.

By the time we reach my flat I have come once and am looking almost as smug as Dan. Not quite, though. Dan's one of those strong silent types who loves nothing more – not even football – than seeing me go completely out of control. He gets excited too, of course, but only once he's already reduced me to a babbling, jelly-legged sex object with glazed eyes and rising damp.

Which is fine with me. Every relationship has its patterns and if Dan insists on making me come repeatedly before even so much as unzipping his trousers, who am I to complain? Early on, in the interests of balance as well as for my own enjoyment, I tried to buck this trend, but Dan just removed my hands, threw me over the sofa and slid his thumb into me as if he were testing me for ripeness, and I promptly forgot about everything else.

I manage to get out of the car without falling over, though my legs are so weak by now this is more of an achievement than it sounds. We walk decorously, which is to say without touching, up the steps to my front door and I am just pulling out my keys when Dan sits down on the stone wall that borders the flight of steps. He's just waiting for me to get the door open, but I look at him, his eyes meet mine, and I can't manage a moment longer without being in physical contact with him; dropping the keys back into my pocket I climb onto his lap, my bottom on his thighs, my feet on the wall for balance, and start kissing him. It's a dark night and as usual half of the streetlights are out, or at best flickering spasmodically. And the steps are high off the street, at first-floor level. We're in the shadows, a couple of closely entwined shapes, no more. What we're actually doing would be visible only to someone with night-vision goggles and a good vantage point. I hope.

Because by now Dan has what feels like his entire hand up me and is fucking me with it in slow steady strokes, fucking me actually better than he does with his cock, which is a curiosity I've noticed before but never really have much time to dwell on because my brain is pretty much fully occupied with other things, foremost of which right now is doing my best not to scream. I have what feels like my entire fist crammed into my mouth and am biting down on the knuckles in pursuit of this good-neighbourly goal, an arrangement which is amusing Dan tremendously. His hand is almost hurting me, slamming into me like a pile-driver, but I couldn't bear him to stop. I lean fully into his other hand, on my back, balancing me, supporting me so I can take the full force of what his other hand is doing to me without falling off the wall. God, this is good. There are so few moments in life of absolute transcendence. Or maybe that's an over-elevated way of putting it. I cannot think about anything else right now, anything at all; disconnected thoughts rush through my brain, gone almost before I've registered them, so fleeting that they come only to remind me that there is something outside this intense sensation, to stop me losing myself to it so completely that I can never find my way back.

Dan gives a particularly frenzied thrust into me which definitely emphasises the pain aspect over the pleasure. He's losing control. We have to get inside my flat. We have to have sex. We are having sex, of course, but I mean something more specific by that. I grab Dan's wrist as he pulls back for another grind into me, though I'm whimpering with frustration at making him stop, even for a moment. With a near-heroic effort of will I drag out my keys and get the door open. We manoeuvre past the ground-floor neighbour's damned bicycles – why was I trying not to make any noise outside? I should have wailed like a siren and woken the bastards up, the amount of times I've ripped my tights on their bicycle spokes. Stumbling past the second one I reach the stairs and hold out a hand for Dan, who is momentarily snagged on a handlebar. He drags himself free, grabs my hand and trips over a pedal, all at once, landing on the steps with a stumble that could send us both off-balance.

In that moment our eyes meet. We could recover; I could grab the newel post and brace myself against Dan's fall; but I don't. We don't. I let myself tumble back onto the stairs – which are carpeted, I'm not that much of a masochist – and Dan's weight comes down on top of me like the one thing I've been craving all my life. As soon as he lands we are scrabbling at each other's clothes, grinding into each other, every bit of our bodies that can wrap around the other's

doing so as if for dear life; feet, knees, hands all desperate
for as much contact as we can possibly manage. It must look
anatomically impossible. I have a flash of intense frustration
that I'm not completely double-jointed.

My skirt's around my waist, my knickers are down, Dan's
unzipping himself – ah, that sound, that wonderful antici-
patory sound, like a trumpet fanfare before the entrance of
the key player on the scene – and two seconds later he has
jammed himself up into me and we're fucking on the stairs.
The relief is almost unbearable. I mean, I love everything
else, all the preliminaries and the flourishes and the fanfares;
I come much more thoroughly and repeatedly before the
actual act of fucking than I ever do during it; but by God
there is absolutely nothing like it. My eyes roll back, my hips
tilt up so that Dan can get his hands under them, my feet lock
round the back of his calves, I am bracing my hands clumsily
against the wall and the stair riser, and we're fucking, thank
God, I thought I would die if we didn't manage to fuck at
this precise moment, not a second later, I thought I would
actually explode.

Dan never lasts that long, which is maybe why he dedicates
so much time to all the other variations before the main
theme. I can scarcely complain; he's already reduced me to
a boneless sex-craving wreck, dripping with moisture – how
unattractive that sounds, though it's exactly what I feel like –
and now he's taking a much briefer pleasure than mine. His
hipbones grind into my inner thighs, his fingers bite into my
bottom and with an arch of his back and a split-second pause
he sinks into me one last time, his lips curled back from his
teeth in that sneer he always makes when he comes, his eyes
almost closed, the slits of white glinting as eerily as if he were
having a fit. He collapses on top of me. That's good too. I
love the weight, and Dan isn't too big, not a great slab of meat

trying to crush me out of existence. Besides, he's completely absorbed in his own sensations, overcome by them; even as I take the full weight of his body, his entire focus is on the spasms of his cock, me beneath him a collection of body parts, the woman he loves to fuck, nothing more. I hope. Otherwise I'd feel as suffocated as if he were twenty stone of loose rolls of fat.

His cock gives a couple of convulsive twitches inside me, last moments of past glory, and then everything subsides and suddenly we can hear our breathing, which is as frenzied as if we had just done a three-mile sprint. I'm always reluctant to move, even if right now the stair riser is biting into my back as painfully as if I just had sex up against an iron joist. I like to lie here, feeling the cock slowly shrink and curl up inside me before slipping out wistfully, stickily, a sad little aftermath of what was once such a proud trophy. No wonder it was a man who invented existentialism. Think of the mood swings: how important it must be to them to live in the moment. A limp, post-orgasmic cock always provokes great tenderness in me – well, if it's just done its job to my satisfaction – but one quickly learns not to use the words 'sweet' or 'cute' about a cock, even if you have just demonstrated how much you like getting fucked by it, tucks it away immediately, almost always insists on wearing briefs in bed. I gave up trying to understand men a long time ago. Now I just go with what seems to work. It's so much easier.

Dan braces himself against the stairs and lifts himself off me. As always, the removal of his weight is sad, but immediately makes me stretch my limbs, as if to test their new freedom of movement. He hauls me to my feet. One thought has been running through my mind for the last ten minutes, almost as soon as Dan's cock slid into me; I don't want him to stay the night. This is perfect just as it is. If he even comes into my flat it will be ruined. Tactics have been running through my brain. If I were really brazen I would just wish him goodnight firmly and continue upstairs, but I can't quite manage that.

'God, I'm exhausted,' I say. 'You've worn me out.'

'Yeah?' He smirks, bless him.

'I'm just going to pass out. I'm shattered.'

I try to look regretful, intimating that I would love to ask him in but have already been so overcome by his prowess as a lover that any further bout tonight would severely damage my immune-deficiency system. This is of course a total lie – it's Dan who couldn't manage another bout; once at night, once, if I'm lucky, in the morning is his limit. But it works perfectly.

'You'd better get some rest, then,' he says, smugger than ever. 'I'll see you round.'

We kiss. He goes, climbing uncomfortably through the massed ranks of mountain bikes to the door. I sigh in relief and head upstairs. I don't even mind the fact that I live on the fifth floor. It's more distance between me and Dan.

My best friend David says that men adore being treated like sex objects and I should stop being concerned about this kind of thing with Dan. 'Just pay him lots of compliments about the sex and he'll be fine,' David assure me. I don't agree. I remember all too well the guy in college with whom I was supposed to be having a sex-only relationship who agreed eagerly the first night and then never wanted to have sex with me again. Moreover he became very bitter towards me, especially when I started going out with someone. I think this is a much truer reflection of the male psyche. Men think they want sex-only, but they are only comfortable with this set-up when they're the ones after sex while the women want something more. As soon as you make it clear that you too just want to fuck their brains out on a regular basis but not have to talk to them about their families in the interim periods, they're off faster than a speeding bullet.

My body is exhausted, quite literally – temporarily worn out, used and satisfied – but my brain is buzzing. It's partly frustration; it didn't get used much this evening. Dan insists on us going out to dinner every so often. I much prefer a film, a drink, and a swift journey to my flat, as this limits the conversational necessities as much as possible. But despite the fact that we obviously have very little in common and any occasion in which we try to talk for more than ten minutes is full of laboured questions and terrible pauses, Dan still keeps suggesting dinner. God knows why. It's another reason I part company with David. Dan's constant wish to go out to dinner with me can only be explained as a need to enact what he sees as being the tableaux of a conventional relationship, the other things men and women do together apart from fucking on staircases, as if you have to have the one to be able to do the other. I plead my way out of the dinner dates as much as I can but sometimes he just won't take no for an answer. Tonight was as awful as ever. It never gets any better.

I look at my watch. Midnight. Perfect. Plenty of time for a long, hot soak in the bath. I wish now that I had made the appointment for 1.00, instead of 2.00: I thought it would be too early. But Dan and I have managed to satisfactorialy conclude the evening's business in much less time than I had projected. How efficient we're getting. I have a long bath, make myself some coffee, pour myself a drink, and by 1.40 I'm wrapped in a big towel, wafting aromatic bath oil every time I move, logged on, in the chat room, waiting for my second date of the evening.

I know it's stupid, but there are butterflies in my stomach

as I sit there waiting for him. I know it's stupid because he'll
be there; he always is. And sure enough, at 1.56 it scrolls
across the screen:

```
>trollfan1234: Hi! So did you finish it?
```

and a lovely wave of relief and happiness floods through me
and I type:

```
lola666>sure. Disappointed though.

trollfan1234>?

lola666>it's all just the same plot isn't it? Rich boy
falls in love with poor girl/waits it out for a year or
so to prove he means it/finally the family agrees. Only
this time it turns out she's rich after all so it's OK. And
there isn't even any tension, we know from the beginning
that she's the only relative of the rich old man so when he
finds that out he'll leave her all the money.

trollfan1234>OK, agreed, it's not his strongest book

lola666>Trollope should at least have made it more of a
mystery, but we know that they'll get together ANYWAY so
it still wouldn't have helped much.

trollfan1234>but isn't there satisfaction watching the
pattern work itself out?

lola666>get more of that out of an Agatha Christie I've
read 100 times.

trollfan1234>Hmmn.

lola666>he should have fallen for someone else while he
was away all that time, create a bit of tension that way.
```

trollfan1234>Trollope does that sometimes

lola666>but you know it'll never happen, like Phineas/ Madame Goetz or John & Madeleine, the women they fall in love with in big cities are always adventuresses, then they come home to the nice girl without flashy looks, Trollope really cliched oldfashioned romantic author, why does he have an intellectual reputation?? I really don't have much to say about this book AT ALL sorry

trollfan1234>don't get started on the Joanna T v. Anthony T thing again

lola666>but it's true I really think J Trollope much more sophisticated in view of human nature, at least she sees it as protean, endlessly changeable, AT thinks everyone's personalities carved in stone

trollfan1234>do people really change that much?

lola666>oh yes I think so

trollfan1234>OK we may change opinions whatever but do our ACTIONS really change that much

lola666>Hmmn interesting maybe after lots of therapy

trollfan1234>haha

lola666>Pallisers are better

trollfan1234>well OK devil's advocate: who really changes in the Pallisers?

lola666>Hmmn I like Maud not being able to make up her mind until too late

trollfan1234>yeah but it's the right thing she didn't really love him

lola666>but she'll never meet anyone else she's too old
by their standards anyway! she would have been happy with
Silverbridge

trollfan1234>do you think so

lola666>or at least content, yeah, she'd have been a
duchess and he was v attractive

trollfan1234>funny youre arguing the way a man's supposed
to & Im more romantic (like a woman) don't think Maud
would have been happy

lola666>what about Lily Dale

trollfan1234>John made big mistake, he was always
there like a dog, should have tried to disappear/make
her jealous

lola666>so she didn't see him like the perpetual
little boy

trollfan1234>exactly, women hate men slobbering over
their feet

lola666>dyou speak from experience

trollfan1234>never slobbered! teenage years had mad
crushes on girls, made it too obvious, never got them,
cooler now I hope

lola666>youre right about John/Lily he really needed to
go away for a long time & come back as a man - you know
what I mean by that, not being sexist (he should have been
masterful, etc)

trollfan1234>no its fine we agreed that we completely

understand each other male/female stuff dont worry about
that OK?

lola666>great! forgot!

trollfan1234>interesting we always come back to
discussing relationships in AT

lola666>well I was thinking about that (am I being
stereotypical woman always talking about LOVE) but youre a
man allegedly

trollfan1234>yes, am looking at proof of that right now

lola666>not literally I hope

trollfan1234>no, wearing boxers

lola666>anyway I worked out that AT's political dilemmas
not half as interesting as emotional ones/politics used
really only to present moral choices (will X do right
thing) as are emotional ones (will he marry nice girl
at home)

trollfan1234>bit unfair, Maud has hard moral choice too

lola666>OK, true, and Madame Goetz

trollfan1234>God yeah, lots of them, and she gets rewarded
in the end

lola666>nice idea the older/more sophisticated you get
the more interesting the choices

trollfan1234>obviously I'm not old/sophisticated
enough yet

lola666>me neither mine are always brutally obvious

trollfan1234>???example

lola666>no, no personal stuff we agreed

trollfan1234>?

lola666>

trollfan1234>after all, we're analysing other relationships
all the time, we're not talking in traditional litcrit
terms

lola666>relationships in BOOKS

trollfan1234>pretend it's a story

lola666>no.

trollfan1234>sigh

lola666>

trollfan1234>OK, enough of AT, pick another author?

lola666>I know we just finished Barchester but there must
be others

trollfan1234>Minor, would annoy you even more

lola666>OK well let's do Dickens then

trollfan1234>

lola666>what?

trollfan1234>Dickens takes v long time to read, we
wouldn't talk for weeks

lola666>flattered

trollfan1234>well I like talking to you

lola666>me too

trollfan1234>pick short books!!!

lola666>we could do Dickens but split up the books/discuss them every 10th chapter?

trollfan1234>Great idea they're written as serials after all

lola666>shall we do it chronologically?

trollfan1234>no one's ever asked me that before!

lola666>funny

rollfan1234>let's start with David Copperfield I've always meant to read that

lola666>OK I'll go to the library

trollfan1234>lovely library books with hard plastic covers you can read in the bath

lola666>and that dirty, musty smell

trollfan1234>I thought you said no personal stuff

lola666>funny. Not.

trollfan1234>when's good for you next time?

lola666>Monday? 1.00?

trollfan1234>five days . . . do I have time . . .

lola666>thought you were the one complaining about not meeting for ages

trollfan1234>OK you talked me into it, I may be a bit behind

lola666>do your best

trollfan1234>yes ma'am

lola666>see you on Monday

trollfan1234>I wish!

lola666>TALK to you Monday

trollfan1234>sigh

lola666>I'm very disappointing you know

trollfan1234>me too we could be disappointing together

lola666>

trollfan1234>OK, I know, I know. Want me to talk about the weather?

lola666>will it be interesting?

trollfan1234>actually no, I never know what the weather's like, I have no idea what's happening outside right now. I'm on the 8th floor, I have double glazing and my windows aren't that clean because the landlord's lazy about getting that done, also they have these catches which slip and slam back down on your hands so I'm nervous about opening them . . . sometimes I don't even know if it's raining. I'll go out into the street and feel like an idiot.

lola666>happens to me too, most of my windows are stuck, the only one I can put my head out of is the bathroom and it looks onto an air shaft. And I have five floors/no lift, it's a nightmare working out what coat to wear in the morning.

trollfan1234>my offices are airconditioned, windows can't open, etc, even more insulated. Once I was working late

& there was a hurricane & I didn't even realise, got out
onto the dark street and it was covered with broken glass
and people with cardboard patching up their windows.
Ours were fine, we're all triple-strength glass etc. More
insulation. Shows how detached we are from the world.

lola666>my offices are like that too

trollfan1234>so we end up talking to each other through
computers – down a modem line and bounced off a server to
end up God knows where – insulation again.

lola666>that was a very neat connection

trollfan1234>thanks, I was quite impressed with it myself

lola666>have to go now

trollfan1234>OK, till Monday

lola666>bye

trollfan1234>bye

I turn off the computer and get into my pyjamas: flannel,
huge, the kind of thing you can only wear when you sleep
alone. A shot of whisky, to take to bed with me. And the
nagging annoyance: why must he always push for more?
Why does he keep asking to meet me? Can't he see that
the whole point of this is this perfect, focused connection?
Meeting would ruin everything. It's not that we might find
each other unattractive; just the opposite. What if we did?
It would ruin everything. I have everything in balance just
the way I want it and I'm not going to mess with that. It's
working. I'm happy. I take half a sleeping pill and wash it
down with a gulp of whisky. Library tomorrow. Lovely. I'm
happy. I really am.

when thought-mail failed

ian watson

It is difficult to organise my thoughts without ORGANISER 27.5. Difficult to think these thoughts without the framework for thinking that we all rely on. *Did* rely on. And *will rely* on yet again . . . ? No response to my question. Silence.

To frame these words requires will-power – the exertion of my self. My self has been submerged. In the past I have acted and voiced and interacted, yet until now 'I' did not do so. Now my identity is isolated from all other human beings. This is disconcerting. Thanks be for the nanoputer in my brain with its store of readily accessible core data. Mine is particularly data-rich.

I cannot blink-view any news, yet I fear many people may be going insane and society may be in chaos. From the main window of my homepod on buildingtree 7843 I spy men and women wandering distraught and disconnected on Avenue 78. I see a fight break out. A fight! I see a sexual assault. An assault! A man in a pod on the buildingtree opposite is banging his head against his window as if to break through a barrier that separates him from everyone else. In another pod a woman is shrieking. She is having 'hysterics'. Hysterics comes from the Greek word for womb: this datum presents itself. In a womb a baby is isolated. That woman is now in a sort of womb, all alone in her pod, consequently she is hysterical. True, she can ride the elevator down through the trunk and go outside, but she will still be isolated – as she has never been before. And as *I* have never been before.

I, I, I, I. Her, her, her, her.

My name is JackSmith527. This seems an unworthy name. It seems lacking in identity, even though it is my registered identity. It suggests a job, that of jacksmith, performed by hundreds, thousands of people. What might a *jacksmith* do? A smith is a metal worker. A jack is a lifting device. And also a prong-plug. I make neither of these. I work in Weather Management, negotiating weather. Whether the weather be wet, whether the weather be windy. By communicative consensus, impossible now. One area's storm is a more distant area's sunshine. We cannot all have the same weather at the same time. We cannot all have mild weather. Hurricanes and typhoons must be allowed. Yet where and when? The world's weather is guidable by releasing clouds of control-nanos and beaming energy from orbit but it cannot be evened out. Extremes must occur. Minimise the harm, maximise the mutual global benefit.

Weather is a super-organism. So is the human race. So *was* the human race – until today – although for the past two centuries no extremes affected the human race.

But now . . . what of that brawl on the avenue and that assault? I'm a little wary of going outside to confront other people's raw ungoverned identities.

JackSmith527 is not an adequate name. I need datum: *a nickname*. Yes, something unique.

I am not JackSmith527 but *Jazz*. Jazz was a kind of music which was mostly improvised. I must improvise myself. Improvise, from the Latin: not foreseen. Spontaneous.

Of course I know what has happened. Especially in Weather Management we foresaw the impending situation due to observations of the sun.

Solar flares, the fiercest in centuries. They bombard the earth's magnetosphere with charged particles. Before dawn today, auroras began to dance wildly across the sky. The extreme electromagnetic interference has completely disrupted thought-mail.

We knew but could not prepare for this loss. These days we have no *phones* or talking drums as our ancestors did. No need, in a world of thought-mail. Obsolete.

Of course we still have our voices, for close proximity communication. To use my voice I need proximity to other persons. I really cannot stay in my home-pod. The silence in my head is unbearably strange. I must leave the pod, the branch, descend the trunk. Shall I take a weapon to protect myself? What would serve as a weapon? An eating-knife? A fork? Their plastic is strong but might snap. Those things are small. I am much bigger. I have fists and feet. A fist can hit, a foot can kick. Hit where, kick where? I must not think of being a weapon. We do not need weapons. We need voices.

The voices in our heads are missing. I shall voice with my mouth.

As I ride down, the elevator stops at branch five. Doors open. A young woman stares at me, wide-eyed. She has short curly red hair and green eyes, and she's wearing a purple day-suit.

(Mine is beige.) On her feet, as on mine, booties, brown. I do not know her name.

'It is safe to share,' I speak. 'May I voice-mail with you?'

'You are already voicing me,' she points out. She is intelligent, relatively in control of herself, as am I, though nervous. She enters. 'What has happened?'

As we descend: 'Electromagnetic interference due to charged particles from the solar flares has blocked all thought-mail.'

'For how long?'

'A few days. A week.'

'We are free,' she speaks. 'To be free is scary. I find it hard to decide what to do.'

'You are coping.'

Doors open upon the blue-tiled foyer. A plump black-haired boy of perhaps ten years is sitting, his back to a wall, hugging his knees. He wears red.

'What shall I do?' he asks us.

'Whatever you wish,' I speak. 'But you may not do damage to things or persons.'

'I wish to run.'

'Do you live in this building?'

'Yes.'

I can see no fight or assault outside now. 'Run around the outside, boy.'

'Yes!' Scrambling up, he darts for the door, which opens for him.

'Do not run too much,' the young woman calls after him. 'If you feel tired, stop and come back.'

That is sensible.

'I am JackSmith527,' I tell her, 'but now I am calling myself Jazz.'

'That is a good idea. I am JillGreen762.'

'You are beautiful and intelligent. Your hair is red, but your eyes are green. Eyes are more important than hair.' I am voicing quite competently without any assistance.

'I think I shall call *my* self Jizz.'

'When shall you call yourself Jizz?'

'Right now!'

'Jizz is like fizz and whiz. What job do you do, Jizz?'

'I am a nurse at Hospice 7 for old people. And you?'

'I am in Weather Management.'

'Who is managing the weather now?'

'Not me. The charged particles may cause strange weather for a period. Do you have a regular sexual partner?'

'Not since last month. And you?'

'Not for two months. I had been thought-mailing a meeting room.'

The boy soon returns, panting. 'I am tired. I have not run much before. I thought I could wish to run and so be able to run.'

'Do not talk,' speaks Nurse Jizz. 'Sit down.' The boy slumps, chest heaving. Nevertheless, he manages to gasp, 'Why can I hear no voices inside me?'

'Tell him,' speaks Jizz. 'He should rest and listen to you.'

Facts are in my head. How many should I tell the boy? If I tell him many, Jizz may admire me.

'Boy, the millennia prior to thought-mail were an epoch of individualities in endless conflict. Then when thought-mail came . . . I'll start again. What year is it now?'

'2310,' speaks Jizz, so that the boy can get his breath. 'It's the fourth of July 2310 common era. Fourth of July was Independence Day in the calendar of the former United States.'

'Now we are all united,' gasps the boy.

'No we aren't, not today. Today every human being is independent. For a while. Listen to me: towards the end of the twentieth century suddenly the Gates opened, and there was e-mail. E-mail was primitive rapid electronic communication between people sitting at puters.'

'How can you sit at puters? They're too small. They sit inside your head.'

'Most of them — those are nanoputers. The first puters were as big as boxes.'

'Boxes of what?' Persistent boy!

I demonstrate with my hands.

'Very soon,' I continue, 'almost all the world was webbed and wired. Speed and capacity increased. Yet even though machines became smaller and smaller, worn on a wrist or a finger, those still communicated with other micro-machines worn externally by people. The arrival of effective nanotech at the end of the twenty-first century allowed molecular-size nanobots at last to enter the human brain. Do you understand nanobots, boy?'

'Nanotech robots. What keeps our bodies healthy till we are old.'

'You should be an Instructor, not a Weather Manager,' Jizz says to me.

'Thank you.'

Through the clear plastiglass door I watch more and more day-suited people gathering together in the avenue. They voice at one another. They make gestures with their hands.

I tell the boy how nanobots rejigged the neural network. How powerful microputers interfaced with the brain, controlled by the user's thoughts. How the brain could now function as a receiver and transmitter of weak radio signals transmitted from and detected by our smart nano-rich environment of buildings, vehicles, streets, paths, furnishings, clothing. Problems of excess heat in the brain were solved ingeniously.

'And so thought-mail commenced – the instant exchange of messages with recipients in the same building or on the other side of the world by an act of thought. Technological telepathy!'

Addresses for thought-mail were accurate since each person's neural network is as unique as a fingerprint. Silent conferences occurred in perfect secrecy. Confidential tête-à-têtes between lovers were conducted in public places in complete privacy.

The nanoputers in brains were invaluable for filtering and spooling incoming messages and for translating foreign language items, but most importantly they framed outgoing messages coherently, playing a kind of thought-checker role.

Facts are in my head. A certain Ludwig Wittgenstein observed that the 'proposition' speaks through us, and the pre-thought-mail psychologists Susan Blackmore and Daniel Dennett – such names people had in those days! – they showed that words are 'memes' competing for utterance, and that language gives rise to thought rather than thought giving rise to the words we utter. Were it not for the nano-processors mediating the framing of messages a high level of mental discipline would be needed to generate lucid thought-mail.

'Presently almost all the world was using thought-mail, even for the most ordinary activities. There were fears, boy, that young children would fail to gain fluency in language. The person calling herself "Rachel Carson the Second" thought-spammed a polemic entitled *Silent Speech*.'

'What is a polemic?'

Consult my THESAURUS 9.7. 'Argument, dispute, tirade, pamphlet, war of words. However, neo-natal injection of nanobots provided a language fix of internal dialogue as a model for speech-acquisition, and most parents were willing to speak out to their offspring. Do you follow me?'

'Somewhere,' says the boy.

'Anywhere,' says Jizz. That is encouraging.

Cut to the nub of the matter. 'Within a few years the global thought-mail network was so complex that it became self-organising and autonomous. According to the psychologist called Julian Jaynes,' (such names, such names, but I also think that Jazz is quite good) 'according to him up until the time of the Trojan War – a Trojan is a hard-working person – up until then human beings experienced hallucinatory voices in their heads, "instructions from the gods," which gave rise to automaton-like actions. One side of our brain told the other side what to do. The meme-words spoke and we performed. Full consciousness arose less than 4,000 years ago when the bicameral – that's the two-chamber – mind broke down because of the increasing complexity of life. Do you still follow me?'

'A way,' says the boy, which I don't quite understand – that's the trouble with this voicing.

'Everywhere,' says Jizz.

'Well then, in the year 2105, the human race lost consciousness once again as humanity became a hive-entity, a super-organism akin to a beehive or an ants' nest, directed not by pheromones – those are chemicals you smell – nor by instincts, but by self-generated thought-mail acting as a kind of overmind. From then on, boy, self-organising thought-mail dictated our activities and even our thoughts. Identity dwindled. Peace and utopia dawned. All was orderly and organised – until now!'

To frame these words takes will-power, the exertion of self. No voices, no assistance, no steering of my existence any longer. There's just me, I myself.

Compared with being a tiny aspect of the global network, my new individuality seems thin and two-dimensional, like the quality of light just before a solar eclipse. And yet it is everything to me.

By now perhaps a hundred people are in that slowly milling crowd in the avenue. New arrivals join it as though the crowd of itself is an answer to their dilemmas; as if it is the nucleus of a hive which will unite them and remove the need for individual decisions, though surely it is not.

'Jazz,' speaks Jizz, 'you should say these same things to the people out there. That will help them. They need a crowd manager. They need a goal.'

So we go outside, Jizz, the boy, and I. Cherry trees grow in big concrete tubs along the edge of the avenue. I clamber on to the soil of one tub.

'Hear me!' I cry.

'Only by thought-mail can we communicate speedily and globally to decide how we shall remain free,' I conclude, 'if indeed we wish to stay free! But the solar flares stop us from communicating. When the flares die down and the electromagnetic interference ceases, the network will surely resume its guidance of us all. The voices in our heads will return, once more determining what we do. So what shall we do – and what can we do? Do we wish to stay free of the voices?'

'Yes!' shouts a man. 'I'm myself at last!'

But another man calls out, 'Without thought-mail I am deaf and blind.'

And a woman: 'I yearn for thought-mail. It defined me.'

And another woman: 'I find it hard to decide.'

Yet another man: 'I do not think anything can be done.'

And: '*What can be done, Mr Jazz?*'

I must give them a goal that is possible. How to prevent thought-mail from resuming? There are no central radio transmitter-receivers, but rather a myriad of these forming a scattered network all over the world and in orbit. Thought-mail-facilitator nanos impregnate our clothing and shoes, housing and streets. The system has vast redundancy in case of any temporary local breakdowns. In the old days, the world first became webbed so that the huge armies of those days could continue to send and receive messages even if a nuclear war took place . . . Datum: *however*, nuclear bombs set off an electromagnetic pulse which fries electronic devices . . .

So where are the nuclear bombs of old? That is not the answer. They will have decayed by now. Besides, I think that setting off many nuclear bombs, even if possible (which it isn't), would cause a lot of damage and harm.

Ah, but can nanos be designed that will eat the nanoputers in our heads? Nanos that can be released in trillions for everyone to breathe in?

'How many people here work in nano design or assembly?' I demand.

A couple of hands go up. Nanos are everywhere. People involved with nanos can be found on most streets.

'Step forward,' I say. A dark-skinned woman and a blond man advance.

'Do you understand how new nanos are created?'

The man shakes his head, but the woman declares, 'I am a Designer First Class.'

'That is good.'

I need to speak with her closely but I might lose crowd management.

'Hear me!' I cry. 'We will design a new nano to destroy the nanoputers in our heads. I am in Weather Management. We will cause strong winds to spread the new nanos everywhere.'

How can I negotiate enough strong winds without thought-mail?

'No!' cries one of the objectors.

'No!' shouts another.

I must suppress opposition.

There may be much opposition. I need a band of strong supporters who will deal decisively with opposition. This will motivate those who would otherwise have little useful to contribute. They can contribute *themselves*.

'Let us vote,' I call out. 'Let us divide into three groups for ease of counting. Those who agree with me will all move over there.' I duly point. 'Those who disagree go the other way. Those who do not know withdraw to the rear.'

Ten people choose to oppose me. About forty agree with me. A slightly larger number cannot decide.

'It is agreed! You who agree with me: take those who disagree to buildingtree 7838 and push them inside. Re-programme the door to open only from the outside. Two of you stay to guard the door. Those who have no opinion must not interfere or you will also be shut up in the buildingtree.'

Those who agree with me about freedom seem happy to be told what to do. There's some shoving and slapping and twisting of arms but the forty remove the dissenters from the avenue easily enough.

While this is going on I have time to speak with the Designer First Class Woman from my podium, the cherry tree tub, about making nanos.

Jizz watches me with admiration and perhaps a little concern that the Designer woman matters more to me than she who encouraged me in the first place. With perhaps a little . . . *jealousy*? Is that the correct word for such a feeling? I suppose many feelings will be unfamiliar to us though we will feel them nonetheless.

Already I feel I am becoming a stronger individual.

* * *

The people need leadership to remain free. By noon twenty avenues are under my control. Dissidents are locked in various buildingtrees. At first, quickwalkers brought me reports; few people could run far and fast for long. Now my deputies use the underground transport system which still functions automatically. Expansion is vital at least until I control the nearest nano factory and the nearest weather-modifying station, although people's normal jobs must not be neglected for too long, and I fear they are being neglected generally. To the east a plume of smoke is rising from a conflagration somewhere distant.

Since I now control a garment assembly shop on Avenue 70 I have had bright yellow armbands made for all my supporters to wear. As support spreads, will my yellow-bands encounter supporters of another leader, similarly organised? Perhaps wearing white armbands? What could the aim of another leader be, so as to be in conflict with my own aim? Might violence ensue? Such questions cause tension in me, which I purge satisfyingly by hasty sexual activity with Jizz in my home-pod. A leader needs such release. Jizz is glad to agree to this. She speaks of power and excitement, though we soon return to the foyer, my headquarters.

Evening! I control a hundred avenues, including the nano factory and the weather-station. So far there has been no organised opposition. On one avenue I hear that a crowd spontaneously demonstrated, cheering Jazz as a liberator. I must visit there tomorrow.

The auroras dance in the darkening sky. My Designer First Class, whose name is JaneBlack772, reports that the new nanos will take two days to design and begin the manufacturing. They need to be self-reproducing – how else could they spread across the whole earth, wind-borne from one single outlet? People who breathe some in must sneeze out a hundredfold more, made from tiny amounts of cellular tissue in their bodies. Even so, will we win the race before the auroras die away? When that happens, will we simply have a liberated zone down-wind, and all the rest of the world for thought-mail to resume in? Will our new nanos continue eating away like moths devouring a curtain – or will the resumed thought-mail defend itself by commanding the creation and release of anti-anti-nanos?

Maybe kindred spirits across the world are acting similarly to me. Maybe I am not unique. We have no phones or talking drums to know whether this is so.

This makes me tense. It is not easy to be a leader. Jizz offers me release again. This second exercise within a few hours proves more satisfying to her than to me. Maybe I need to use a drug. Many former leaders used not only sexual activity but drugs and alcohol.

Unfortunately these days we only have medicinal alcohol, nor do modern drugs affect the mind, lest a person's thought-mail be disrupted. I must rely on Jizz, but only once a day.

I imagine statues to myself, fifty metres high, on street corners. One in each city perhaps.

It would be safer if I ruled the world. In the old days there was so much anarchy and conflict.

A people free at last to think freely, except about my leadership.

I summon back JaneBlack772 for a private discussion in my home-pod, having sent Jizz to her own pod. Jizz knows that I cannot have sexual activity again this evening.

'JaneBlack,' I speak carefully, 'when the solar flares stop we will need to rely for communication on radios and on phones as soon as we can make billions of them. But I think it is necessary for the freedom of the world that everyone obeys me for several years. Otherwise, people might try to restore thought-mail. Therefore I think there should also be another new nano which causes people to believe in and obey Jazz. Can you make this nano?'

She considers then speaks, 'Yes.'

'So will you make this new nano while your helpers make the anti-nano nano?'

'But you would become like a new kind of thought-mail!'

'No, because my voice will not be inside people's heads. I will issue instructions by radio and people will heed my will because they believe me. Apart from that, they can think what they will.'

'Maybe you should be named Will, not Jazz.' She does have an independent-minded way of expressing herself.

'Will you do this?' I speak to her.

'Yes,' she speaks, 'if I will be at your side as your permanent partner.'

JaneBlack772's skin is like milk chocolate. Her shoulder-length hair is raven. Her eyes are lustrous. Her nose is straight and assertive. She is quite attractive.

What about Jizz? I have only known Jizz for a few hours. Jizz will be disappointed. But Jizz is just a nurse. I think Jizz may still admire me. Besides, JaneBlack will often be busy. Jizz did indeed encourage me to address the crowd, but JaneBlack will make my vision come true.

A leader needs to make quick decisions. When I rule the world benevolently I will need to make many difficult decisions.

'I agree,' I speak. 'But you must change your name.'

She nods. 'I think I will call myself Jane Nano.'

Jazz and Jane Nano: there is a buzz to this. Thankfully there is still no buzz of voices in my brain. My statues ought to have eternal gas-torches burning from the tops of their head to commemorate the solar flares and my bright idea. I'm sure I shall have many more bright ideas, all my own for a change.

feMail

manda scott

From: Samfire <girlstalk@aol.com>

To: 'Sizecountz' <sizecountz@bigone.demon.co.uk>

Subject: RE: This is ME!!!!!

Date: Thu, 4 Mar 1999 21:56:31 -0500

MIME-Version: 1.0

Hey, you didn't have to do that, hon. I'm happy just
talking. I don't need to see what you look like. But
still, it was kind. Over here, we don't have kind. Not
that kind of kind. If you see what I mean. I appreciate
it. Really

You wrote:

>try the website if you want *real* pix of me 'n'
the lads.

I didn't do that. I don't want *real* pictures, most
especially not of anyone else, I just want to know that
you'll be there for me. Which you are. Thank you. I'm
doing my best to get hold of a digicam so I can mail you

a picture of me but I'm not sure I can afford it and I'm
not about to spend money that I could be saving towards
a plane ticket. I'm aching to see you. Really. Big, deep-
down inside aches. And it's so hard keeping it from Jake.
He's not a bad man, I told you that. But he doesn't love me
and I need to be loved. You love me. I believe that.
I can't wait to see you for real
Luv,
Sam.

From: Samfire <girlstalk@aol.com>
To: 'serpent mage' <wizzard3@virgin.co.uk>
Subject: RE: hi there
Date: Thu, 4 Mar 1999 22:30:02 -0500
MIME-Version: 1.0

Greetings. Long time no hear. Thought you'd given up
on me. Glad it's not true. Sounds as if life's utterly
appalling at your end. You didn't tell me you had a wife.
An ex-wife. I take it the newly evolved 'ex' status has
nothing to do with my imminent arrival? Good. Don't tell
me if I'm wrong, I don't want to know. What you do with
your life is your choice. Ground rules. Don't forget
the ground rules. You going to be on IRC tonight? (OK,
whatever ungodly hour of the morning it is over there when
you get on line) I'll be on undernet, #dragonslair, same
time, same nick. You? Samfire
PS You really didn't seem the married type *at all*.
Never can tell, huh? :)

From: Samfire <girlstalk@aol.com>

To: 'E.J. Reid' <Edward-Reid@1021998.1130@compu-

serve.com>

Subject: 'Morning

Date: Thu, 4 Mar 1999 23:12:57 -0500

MIME-Version: 1.0

Good morning Dr Reid.

You're in bed by now, I can feel it. Besides, it's
seriously, seriously late where you are, less than three
hours to getting up time. So, dream well and know that
I am thinking of you. The bankers draft was waiting for
me when I got home . . . You are everything you promised
and I'm sorry I threw the tantrum last week. I had a bad
day at the lab and I shouldn't take it out on my friends.
I had the necessary conversation with the Mad Professor
this morning and he's okayed my time out. God alone knows
what the rest of the retentive, reactionary, republican
fuck-wits I work with (aka my beloved workmates) will
do but that's not my problem. Not now at any rate. I have
taken your advice and been to see Ray-The-Attorney. Ray's
last big case was the Indonesian woman who came here to
escape female circumcision in her homeland. The Feds had
her in a holding camp for *two and a half years* and were
trying to send her back home to Daddy when Ray came along.
The woman got citizenship last month. I think we can
safely say that anything the grad-pack can do, we can do
better (harder, nastier, with greater venom and a lot more
legal punch). God, I'm looking forward to this. No flight
details yet, still scraping together the last few $k but
I'll let you know . . . So enjoy your day.

Thinking of you

s'later

Sam.

```
*** Topic for #dragonslair: Welcome Mages! No netsex/
christians/godbotherers of any nature. 18+ only
*** Topic for #dragonslair set by CatThorn on Weds, 3 March,
1999 4:41:42 am

#dragonslair: Sumfire Drummer Wizzzard Cronejoy
wyvern@CatThorn @Mage1 @elvenkind Shiva^
*** End of/NAMES list.
*** Mode is {+}tn
*** Channel created at Sunday, Feb 28, 1999 10:07:55 am
```

Samfire: anybody home?

wyvern: nope.
wyvern: :)

Samfire: good, thought not . . . :)

CatThorn: Fire! Long time not see. Thought you'd died and
gone to the great dungeon in the sky.
Whatcha doin' kid?

Samfire: celebrating not being at work :):):):):):)
Life is good

Cronejoy: kewl. Champagne on toast?

```
*** serpent3 (wizzard3@virgin.co.uk) has joined channel
#dragonslair
```

Samfire: Nope long hot tub and a half bottle of tequila

Elvenkind: Geez. Bad liver day tomorrow, huh?

Cronejoy: Serp! the very man, what the f** are *you*
doing here?

serpent3: cruisin', woman, cruisin'. Delighted to see you
too, I'm sure

*** PING delay for serpent3: 1 seconds

---> (private - to:) serpent3: Greetings. Good to see you.
Delay's not too bad

Drummer: So what's the Second Biggest Drug Company on the
planet going to do without you, Fire?

* (private - from:) serpent3*: the usual crowd, huh?
---> (private - to:) serpent3: don't knock them. I wouldn't
know you otherwise

Samfire: don't know, don't care, Drummer. Not my problem
any more :)

wyvern: 'spect they'll carry right on trying to rule the
world . . .

Cronejoy: nothing new there, then

* (private - from:) serpent3*: You're leaving?????!!!
---> (private - to:) serpent3: Kicked it into touch. Don't
need it. I'm heading for your side of the sea for keeps.
Don't tell me now if you've changed your mind. (or if that ex
wife isn't ex yet . . .)

Cronejoy: So what's new, Serp. Gotcha self a new woman
yet? <grin>

serpent3: maybe, dunno. ask again in a week or 3

* (private - from:) serpent3*: I *never* change my mind.

*** Signoff: Drummer (Leaving)

Shiva^: 'bye drum

---> (private - to:) serpent3: Good. I'm all set to pack in
the morning . . . OK, the one after. Make that, whenever your
wire comes through . . .

```
*(private - from:) serpent3: subtle. v subtle. I'll sort it.
Don't hassle
```

```
--->(private - to:) serpent3: fine
```

Elvenkind: you got a new one to go to?

Elvenkind: job that is . . . (we all know you have a new
man . . . :-))

Samfire: ?? who cares. Tonite I have **la femme tequila**

Samfire: gotta go, people, she calls, she calls . . .

```
--->(private - to:) serpent3: Sorry. Hangover's starting
already. Talk tomorra'
```

Elvenkind: have 1 on me

Samfire: will do. c u all l8r

/part #dragonslair

1390 Blueridge Bvd

Appt #3a

Charlottesville

VA

Friday 5th March

Dear Dr Kieland

As agreed, I am re-submitting my formal request for
sabbatical leave along the lines we discussed yesterday.
It has become apparent in recent months that certain
members of the post-graduate group are not readily going
to accept the changes that will be evident when I get
back. I wish to put on record that I have notified my
attorney and that I will be particularly attentive to
any degree of sexual harassment following my return from
Europe. I appreciate your ongoing support in this matter.
Yours sincerely,

S. E. Redmore MSc PhD

From: Samfire <girlstalk@aol.com>

To: 'Sizecountz' <sizecountz@bigone.demon.co.uk>

Subject: ME?!

Date: Mon 8 Mar 1999 18:47:02-0500

MIME-Version: 1.0

Whaddya mean >are they *you're* tits?

COURSE they're MY tits

you think i'd go downtown, spend a ****Ing fortune on

a digicam and then take pix of SOMEONE ELSE'S boobs???

YOu think i'm some kind of deviant? One more of those and

we're off dickboy. your no better than Jake. Your all the

same. I *hate* you.

Sam (see? no kisses)

From: Samfire <girlstalk@aol.com>

To: 'serpent mage' <wizzard3@virgin.co.uk>

Subject: Timing

Date: Mon 8 Mar 1999 18:49:25 -0500

MIME-Version: 1.0

Top 'o' the morning to you

Good night? Methinks Cronejoy has a thing for you.

Methinks you reciprocate and she's probably a lot closer

to home than I am. (how can I tell? Easy. She speaks like a

brit - as do you. I am doing my best to learn the language

. . . hate the idea of the two of us being separated by a

common tongue <G>) Anyways, if you don't want me to come

over, you'd better say so, otherwise the ticket's bought

the second the cash hits the can.

From: Samfire <girlstalk@aol.com>

To: 'E.J. Reid' <Edward_Reid@1021998.1130@compu-
serve.com>

Subject: 'Morning

Date: Mon 8 Mar 1999 18:53::00 -0500

MIME-Version: 1.0

Hi,

In message <183630102b30ea59c2325@[152.149.85.251]>,
Edward Reid
<Edward_Reid@1021998.1130@compuserve.com>writes
>pipistrelles, I think. They are out very early for
the time of year. Mind you, I heard the first >cuckoo
yesterday which has to be a record. We walk into the
twenty first century with >global warming a reality.
The GM food controversy still rages. The Moredun Fiasco
has >probably done more to destroy the (very rational)
arguements against Monsanto and the >Blairite Plutocracy
than any other single factor. I despair. At least with
Thatcher, nobody >was pretending we were in a democracy.
I don't think I could take much more of this if it
>wasn't for you. Do say you are coming? The days are dull
without you.

Edward. Is this true?
What can I say? I had no idea you felt like that.
Of course I'm coming. I have two or three things I have to
fix here, a few more grand to raise for Dr Strangelove and
his team and then I'm on that plane and heading your way. I
miss you hugely.
Thinking of you
with much love
S

*** Topic for #GayMarriedMen-UK: Congratulations LoVeBoY
(fatherhood calls) :>:>:>.

*** Topic for #GayMarriedMen-UK set by Siren on Weds, 3
March, 1999 4:41:42 am

#GayMarriedMen-UK: Samfire @Siren LoVeBoY linux MarilyN
Mesenfant

*** End of /NAMES list.

*** Mode is +tn

*** Channel created at Tuesday, 23 Dec, 1997 23:24:03 am

linux|: welcome home Sam

Siren: it's only a problem for you if its a problem for her

Samfire: linux| - did you go out last night?

MarilyN: how should I know?

Mesenfant: ask? or do what everyone else does - let her find
out the *hard* way <G>

linux|: what's it to you?

MarilyN: there *isn't* a hard way. She's my wife (marriage:
the ultimate turnoff:<)

Siren: And you think she doesn't know?

--->(private - to:) linux: because if you're still single
(y'know what I mean), I may be in a position to take up
your offer

Mesenfant: let her find you with The Boy
Mesenfant: she's a woman she can work out the rest . . .

*(private - from:) linux|: how so?

linux|: MarilyN - ignore her. She gets off on watching
thermonuclear war

--->(private - to:) linux: have 2 weeks holiday left

---> (private – to:) linux: = time but broke

---> (private – to:) linux: depends if the offer was real

Mesenfant: I resent that

Siren: you deserve it

Siren: 1st tantrum = kickban. Watch it

Siren: I AM da boss :)

*(private – from:) linux|: DCC?

---> (private – to:) linux: OK

DCC

linux| OK, let me get this straight. You can come over but you have no money?

Samfire: yup

linux|: how long for?

Samfire: 3 wks max

linux|: cost?

Samfire: $800 = flight fees plus kennelling for the cats plus housesitter ($10 a day)

linux|: helluva fee for a 3-week fuck

*** Signoff: Samfire (Leaving)

From: Samfire <girlstalk@aol.com>
To: 'Sizecountz' <sizecountz@bigone.demon.co.uk>
Subject: GOT IT!!!!
Date: Mon 8 Mar 1999 18:47:02 -0500
MIME-Version: 1.0

   I GOT IT!!!!!!
   I GOT IT!!!!!!
   I GOT IT!!!!!!

I GOT IT!!!!!!

THANK YOU

I love you THIS much < infinity > and more.

I'll book the flights tomorrow morning

Love you hugely

XXXXX

S

PS I do just love the pictures. The one of you and Terry (I think???) 'mooning' the lads in the bar was a gas! Can't wait to see the flesh in the flesh:)

PPS you sent so *MUCH* You want me to fly Concorde??? <huge and very evil grin>

From: Samfire <girlstalk@aol.com>

To: 'serpent mage' <wizzard3@virgin.co.uk>

Subject: RE: weekend blues

Date: Mon 8 Mar 1999 18:49:25 -0500

MIME-Version: 1.0

Hail,

Gimme a break, bigman. 2 weeks is 2 weeks. 14 days, give or take. I'm outta here on 22nd March and that's not a moveable date. So tie a knot in it. Cross your legs at the ankles. Stick an aspirin between the knees (mother's advice – the best pharmaceutical contraceptive known to woman) hold it there and don't let go. Not sure it'll work for you but, hell, worth a try. Bottom line. You shag someone else between now and April and I'm on the next plane for VA. Gotit? Good.

S

PS and if it's Cronejoy, I'll tie the pair of you to the wheels – one each – before it takes off . . . be warned. I am not nice when I'm angry.

PPS yes I got the cash. God knows what the bank was
playing at. I gave them some serious grief and - lo - it
was there all along I will be *so* glad to be free of the
all-american smartass bank clerk.

From: Samfire <girlstalk@aol.com>
To: 'linux' <jeremy@eastland.demon.co.uk>
Subject: RE: I'm sorry
Date: Mon 8 Mar 1999 18:52:25-0500
MIME-Version: 1.0
  you wrote:
  >at home. I have a friend who owns a cottage in the Lakes.
  >We can have it for 2 weeks. Give me a fortnight to sort
  >out a 'business trip' or somesuch - say first week in
  >May.
  J - You don't have to y'know. you're right. It *is* a
  helluva fee for a 3 week (make that 2 week?) fuck with some
  guy you never met before. Are you sure I'm worth it?
  S

From: Samfire <girlstalk@aol.com>
To: 'ChasTise' <roman@aol.com>
Subject: RE: I'm sorry
Date: Mon 8 Mar 1999 18:52:25 -0500
MIME- Version: 1.0
  Hey,
  Got the cash but not the books. Would be faster for me to
  order thru' amazon.com if you really think I need to read
  it before I come over. Is there something you're trying
  to tell me? Given where we met, I don't think there's
  much you want to do that I haven't done before. Try plain
  english. It works.
  Sam

From: Samfire <girlstalk@aol.com>

To: 'Femrule' <Ashling@dial.pipex.com>

Subject: RE: I'm sorry

Date: Mon 8 Mar 1999 18:52:25 -0500

MIME-Version: 1.0

I'm worried about this. lust, rust 'n' bust and all that
kind of thing. It's a well known fact that a financial
inequity causes more problems in all woman relationships
than any other single factor. (references available on
request <G>). I guess we'll cope. At least you've had the
practice. I'm sure I can get used to it . . .

Thinking of you – always – lust, no rust, long way
'till bust :-)

Sam

From: SE Redmore<girlstalk@aol.com>

To: 'Dr A Hernmeier <Ahern@ .nl>

Subject: Appointment?

Date: Mon 8 Mar 1999 19:00:00 -0400

MIME-Version: 1.0

Dear Dr Hernmeier,

You will be pleased to hear that I have now raised the
total sum required for the procedure. I have arranged to
stay with a friend in England who is familiar with the
re-assignment process and is prepared to be available in
the few weeks after the surgery. I look forward, therefore
to a precise time and date for me to arrive at your clinic.
I am sure that all of your clients say this, but I wish you
to know that this is the most significant turning point in
my life.

Very many thanks

Samuel J Redmore BSc PhD

Date: Mon 22 Mar 1999 23:44:55 -0500 (EST)

From: Mail Delivery Subsystem <MAILER-DAEMON@aol.com>

To: 'linux' <jeremy@eastland.demon.co.uk>

cc: 'serpent mage' <wizzard3@virgin.co.uk>,

'Ashling' <femrule@dial.pipex.com>,

'Sizecountz' <sizecountz@bigone.demon.co.uk>,

'Eric'<eric.olafsson@swipnet.se>,

'mesEnfant'<JYGerein@t-online.de>,

ChasTise<roman@aol.com>,

'Pollux'<Riteon@bigfoot.com>,

'Lysander' <Tesseract@lineone.net>,

'David Lyons' <David-Lyons@aol.com>

'Padraig' <killarneya5@indigo.ie>

'breakout' <dave@halley-merton.freeserve.co.uk>

'Daffyd Evans' <evans@magpiecottage.softnet.co.uk>

Drake, Alan <adrake@ingt.com>

Subject: Thank you and good night

Automated reply generator:

Nothing personal, people

S

From: Samfire <girlstalk@aol.com>

To: 'E.J. Reid' <Edward-Reid@1021998.1130@compu-
serve.com>

Subject: . . . and then he was a she . . .

Date: Tue 16 Mar 1999 12:00:00 -0500

MIME-Version: 1.0

  Ed,

  It's done.

  Don't, for god's sake, rat out on me now.

  Samantha.

pushing the envelope

jonny lewis

Yeah, I was in it from the start. Not the start, exactly, OK. I mean, that was all down to those guys in the seventies. God bless them. Great guys. But it wasn't them in the end who saw, who could see the true potential of what they were doing, what they were setting up. Setting in train, yeah, thanks. Like, um, probably the guy who invented fire just thought of it as a conjuring trick or something, something you could use to entertain your kids. Like setting them down in front of Sesame Street, y'know, like they'd put their kids in front of this fire they'd invented and that'd keep them quiet for hours. And it was only later that some other cave guy thought of putting whatever, meat or whatever, on top of the thing.

Well, OK, to use a more recent example: those guys in MIT who invented the webcam just so they could keep an eye on their coffee percolator without leaving their desks and their geek stuff. Pretty soon these things are everywhere on the net, yeah, making money, making people happy, making things happen. Whatever, because of those guys and their coffee pot. That's just an example for ya. Someone invents the technology, but the real trailblazers are the ones who work out the way to exploit it.

So these other guys in the seventies figure out a way of getting computers to talk to each other. I'm simplifying, right. You wouldn't want to get me started with the technical language, y'know, the technical stuff. I could bore you nuts when I turn on the geek talk. You wouldn't want that. My wife, when I start talking like that, she calls it alphabet souping. You know, all the acronyms: UNIX and PERL and HTM and all that. Pisses her off.

Yeah, course I'm married. Jesus, why not? There's always this bullshit myth about people who work in the industry: that we're inepts, that we just stay in our bedrooms staring at hardcore all night, that we couldn't have a proper conversation if we tried. Now maybe that was true of those early guys, the pioneers. But now we're, y'know, businessmen. Business*people*, OK, because believe-it-or-not-mister-Ripley there are a bunch of members of the other sex, right, working in our industry. OK, you knew that. Anyway, we're businesslike – and businesslike means we meet people, we talk to people, we sell to people. We go to business lunches and business meetings. That's how we get things done, same as anyone else.

So my wife, in fact, she was working for a client of mine. That was how I met her. This was way back in ninety-five, which was I suppose the big year for the web as far as corporate matters went. The big corporations were beginning to get wise to the fact that there was this thing out there which they could use to shift product on a global scale. They weren't quite sure how it could be done, though, so they got people like me to come in and figure it out for them, write the code, sort out the nuts and bolts, so forth.

Anyway, so my girl Anna was working for a clothing company, a big national outfit, no names, right? And I guess they were thinking OK this could make us some money. So they sent Anna to see me. She was like, assistant assistant to the marketing exec there. That was how we met. We met up in this cafe down on the waterfront, and straight away I thought she was the most beautiful girl. She had this really intense way of sitting – yeah, I know this sounds crazy. She sat in that cafe leaning forward with her fists clenched into little balls against her chin. But she was nervous – I guess she didn't really know what she was getting into.

Well, she told me about the company and what kind of set-up they wanted, but she was a bit vague, you know, and I ended up just saying to her: trust me, OK, I know what you want. I know what you want. And I saw her a few times in the following weeks, and pretty soon we were making hay, y'know?

But the retail website I did for her, I was really proud of that. It was the best thing I'd done up to that point. I set up this interface for buying clothes. It was pretty elaborate. It was cool, though. You'd have these studio sets, right, and they'd be made up to look like maybe a desert or a bar or a forest and you'd get webcams filming them live. And you'd have maybe ten or fifteen models working for you, and they'd be all different sizes: a tall one, a fat one, one with big tits. Men too. And the customer, whoever, would input their measurements and the clothes they were interested in and pow! This model their shape and size – better looking though, natch – would walk on to their computer screen wearing the stuff. Completely live and interactive. And remember this was ninety-five, which in web years is like the Minoan era, yeah?

Stuff like that became common enough after a while but back then it was something special.

And Anna loved it and persuaded her bosses to run with it and we got it all set up and, I tell ya what, we were getting thousands of hits every day. Those pretty models in that studio were pulling sweaters and pants and jackets on and off their hot little bodies faster than the eye could see. Man, it was amazing, exciting. Trouble was, no one was buying the clothes. People were happy enough to watch the live feeds and gawp at the outfits, but in those days folks were wary of broadcasting their AMEX number over the wire. I know, it sounds pretty weird now. So after a month or so the bosses looked at their balance sheets, panicked and pulled the plug.

Yeah, I got paid off handsomely for the termination of the contract, *plus*, right, I cut a deal where I got to keep all the equipment, the sets in the studios, the cameras, plus the rights to the interface software and so forth. So I hooked up with this New Yorker guy who was running a string of peepshows around the city and persuaded him to ship his girls west and take the operation over. I let him have the lot, the webspace, the studios, everything, in exchange for fifteen per cent of the take.

He was a cool guy, a real go-getter like I was then. He wanted to find new directions for the industry – he knew peepshows couldn't carry on just like, y'know, the low-fi way they were. And after a few years – no, scrub that, a few *months* – we've got two hundred girls working there, each with their own little speciality to suit the user. Men too. And we're clearing fifty thousand a week, which made my cut a nice little income. It meant Anna could stop working, which was great because it wasn't long after that that the twins came along.

But I couldn't just kick back my heels and stop working, y'know? Working's what I do. Sure, it was sweet when the babies came. D'you have kids? Yeah, they're rascals when they grow a little but, hey, when they're little bundles of slippy flesh. My two tiny baby boys. Man, they made me proud. I set up a site just for them: it went right through from the live feed of the birth to snaps of them growing up, audio of the first gurgles, the lot. It's still up there. You should check it out: www dot toddandskipper dot com.

But like I say, I needed to get back to work. Real work; the kind that makes foldable billpaying money. So I started touting around for business. Now this was, oh, oh one or oh two. The industry was getting crowded. There were a lot of players around, doing what I do a lot cheaper. But still I had a certain reputation around the industry because of the stuff I'd done in the nineties. I got work on the strength of that, designing some really hot sites for some major corporations. But I needed to find a new niche, right? I needed to go somewhere nowhere else was going.

Now you'll remember those days: the gun control lobby finally got the upper hand over the nation's trigger-happy citizens. After that one AK freak took on the might of the Sunnydale girl scout picnic in Minnesota the president couldn't sign the Prohibition amendment fast enough. That was oh four. And the gun people – I mean the consumers, not the manufacturers – were left with this great need, this primal gape in them. They wanted to shoot guns. It's what they'd always done, them and their forebears way back to Davy Crockett. Now if they could be provided with an outlet for their, uh, their instinct, then they wouldn't have to resort to breaking the law or going underground. Which is where we came in. We were doing the country a favour – we even got a grant from the federal government to set this site up. They begged us to do it.

We thought about having a simulation, at first, but, y'know, there was nothing we could make that would be better than the games that were coming out of Japan, the zombie shoot-'em-ups and whatever. The gun freaks could have got their kicks gaming on-line if that was enough for them. But what they wanted wasn't virtual, they wanted reality pure and clean. The kick of the rifle. The squeal of the deer. Same as sex: there were guys setting up virtual sex engines in those days with computer-modelled, artificial intelligence boys and girls; and they were super-realistic, but they never were a fraction as successful as guys like us with our cams and our actual real flesh.

So we needed to set up a cam thing, a real thing. It had to be offshore – somewhere guns were legal. Luckily a friend of one of my contacts had interests in Europe, and we got our hands on a few hundred acres of land in Poland. It was, like, wasteland – uninhabited, but with forest and scenery and a little stream and all that photogenic shit. We got a couple of thou head of deer flown out there in crates, and all over the place we set up these hides, we called them, with mounted rifles and cameras. Users could control the guns, control the cameras, all from their desktop.

Not many deer got killed. Most of the rednecks were lousy shots. If any of them did bag an animal, we could arrange to have the horns, um, the antlers shipped to their home for a hefty charge, complete with a gilt-edged certificate of gunsmanship.

Word spread quickly in the gun-loving community, course, and pretty damn soon we were making big money. We had so many users we had to expand the site – the landsite as well as the website. I had teams of negotiators on the ground talking to local landowners, farmers and so on, buying up their land so we could use it on the project. We introduced more stock as well: rabbits, birds, dogs, foxes, even bears. We toyed with the idea of introducing a lion – as a kind of mystery bonus animal – but some bright spark at the office pointed out that probably it'd kill all the other critters in no time.

Couple of years in, we'd shipped in the mobile units. We called them tracking robots, but of course they weren't your real deal because they were all remote controlled over the web. They could move at quite a lick though, and across all terrains too. They were a success. Hell, we had to expand at ten times the rate after we brought them in. We had dozens of guys getting the land and dozens more clearing it, and we even put in a plant to manufacture the hardware on site. We refined the machines, too: there were some guys got their kicks from shooting down other robots, so we put in a feature where the guns would jam if they were aimed at any other hardware.

So the site was pulling in tens of thousands of hits a day, and plenty must have been from people who'd never picked up a real gun in their lives but, y'know, they put their credit card numbers down so who's counting? I took a helicopter ride over the project a couple times. It was beautiful: these thousands of little metal tracking robots scooting all over the muddy countryside, up hills and over rivers, hunting down their prey. And each one giving a customer of mine joy, giving him back the thrill of the chase that his forefathers enjoyed.

Anna and me had a handful of disagreements around that time about, OK, animal cruelty. She always was a sentimentalist. I had to sit her down and tell her about nature red in tooth and claw and so on. And more importantly, that I was saving lives, that I was stopping Americans from going nuts and killing people from sheer frustration at not being able to shoot deer.

And then the war started. Well, you know all this. It was only two years ago now, though it seems like centuries, yeah? I thought it was so funny as well as scary, that we'd spent a whole century getting ready for a war with Russia, a century of terror and paranoia and reds-under-the-bed, and then just when we'd given up on the idea and both sides had junked their nukes in a spirit of global co-operation, just then, then it happens.

But yeah, I was expecting the call from the Pentagon. Hell, by then I had a ten-thousand-strong army of assault rifle-toting robots with no fear and no cowardice just outside enemy territory who could be controlled from an office desktop in the Washington warmth. I knew they'd need me. I surrendered control of the site to the military for ten million, on condition that I could carry on using the feeds from the webcams. Now millions of Americans are logging on to watch my boys kick Russian ass on my webspace, and I get a buck every time they do it.

They're doing OK, my boys. We lost a few hundred just after they crossed the border, and we had a little trouble early on working out how to get ammunition to them. But that's the army's job. Yeah, I'm glad to be helping my country, plus it's made me so much filthy money that Anna's begging me to retire at last. But I'm bored – I need to keep working. I got a call from Moscow last night. They sounded pretty desperate, but maybe if the price is right.

I gotta keep working. That's all.

an end to hunger

china miéville

I met Aykan in a pub sometime late in 1997. I was with friends, and one of them was loudly talking about the Internet, which we were all very excited about.

'Fucking Internet's fucking dead, man. Yesterday's bull-shit,' I heard from two tables away. Aykan was staring at me, gazing at me curiously, like he wasn't sure I'd let him crash this party.

He was Turkish (I asked because of his name). His English was flawless. He had none of the throaty accent I half-expected, though each of his words did sound finished in a slightly unnatural way.

He smoked high tar incessantly ('Fucking national sport: they wouldn't let me in fucking 'Stanbul without sufficient shit in my lungs.'). He liked me because I wasn't intimidated by him. I let him call me names and didn't get my back up when he was rude. Which he was, often.

My friends hated him, and after he'd left I nodded and

murmured agreement with them about what a weirdo, about how rude and where he got off, but the fact was I couldn't get worked up about Aykan. He told us off for getting moist about e-mail and the web. He told us wired connection was dead. I asked him what he was into instead and he took a long drag on his stinking cigarette and shook his head, dismissively exhaling the smoke.

'Nanotech,' he said. 'Little shit.'

He didn't explain that. I left him my phone number but I never expected to hear from him. Ten months later he called me. It was just luck that I lived at the same address, and I told him that.

'People don't fucking move, man,' he said, incomprehensibly.

I arranged to meet him after work. He sounded a bit distracted, a bit miserable even.

'Do you play games, man?' he said. 'N64?'

'I've got a PlayStation,' I told him.

'PlayStation licks shit, man,' he told me. 'Bullshit digital controls. I'll give you the ads, though. PlayStation ads sing sweet hymns, but you want a fucking analog control stick, or you're playing once removed. You know anyone with N64?'

As soon as we met he handed me a little grey plastic square. It was a game pack for a Nintendo 64 system, but it was roughcast and imperfectly finished, its seam bizarrely ragged. It had no label, only a sticker scrawled with illegible handwriting.

'What's this?' I asked.

'Find someone with N64,' he said. 'Project of mine.'

We talked for a couple of hours. I asked Aykan what he did for a living. He did that dismissive smoking thing again.

He muttered about computer consultancy and web design. I thought the Internet was dead, I told him. He agreed fervently.

I asked him what nanotech stuff he was doing and he became ragged with enthusiasm. He caught me with crazy looks and grinned at odd intervals, so I couldn't tell if he was bullshitting me.

'Don't talk to me about little miniature fucking arterial cleaning robots, don't fucking talk to me about medical reconstruction, or microwhateverthefucks to clean up oil slicks, OK? That's bullshit to get people on board. What's going to be big in nanotech? Eh? Like any other fucking thing . . .' he banged the table and slopped beer. 'The money's in *games*.'

Aykan had extraordinary schemes. He told me about his prototype. It was crude, he said, but it was a start. 'It's old school meets new school,' he kept saying. 'Kids with fucking conkers, in the playground.' The game was called Blood Battle, or Bloody Hell, or Bloodwar. He hadn't decided.

'You buy a little home injection kit, like you're diabetic. And you build up your own serum from the pack provided. Like when you play a wargame you choose how many fuckers on horseback and how many artillery, right? Well, you have different vials full of microbots that interact with your blood, each type with different defences and attacks, and there are miniature repair robots like medics, all of these fuckers microsize. And you make yourself a blood army, with electrical frontline, chemical attack forces, good defences, whatever you've decided.

'Then when you go to the playground and you meet your little friend who's also bought Bloodwar, and you *prick your fingers*, right, like you're going to be blood brothers, and you each squeeze out a drop of blood into a special dish, and you fucking *mix 'em up.*' I stared at him incredulously while he grinned and smoked. 'And then you sit back and watch the blood shimmer and bubble and move about. Because there's a war on.' He grinned for a long time.

'How do you know who's won?' I asked eventually.

'The dish,' he said. 'Comes with a little display and speakers in the base. Picks up signals from the 'bots and amplifies them. You hear battle sounds and your troops reporting casualties, and at the end you get a score and you see who's won.'

He sat back a minute and smoked some more, watching me. I tried to think of something sardonic to say, but was defeated. He leaned in suddenly and pulled out a little Swiss army knife.

'I'll show you,' he said intensely. 'You up for it? I can show you now. I'm primed. We know you'll lose because you've got no troops, but you'll see how it works.' The knife waited above his thumb, and he gazed at me for the go-ahead. I hesitated and shook my head. I couldn't tell if he was serious or not, if he'd actually injected himself with these lunatic game-pieces, but he was weirding me out.

He had other ideas. There were spinoffs for Bloodwar, and there were other more complicated games, involving outside equipment like airport metal detectors that you walked through, that set off particular reactions from your tiny little internal robots. But Bloodwar was his favourite.

I gave him my e-mail address and thanked him for the N64 pack. He wouldn't tell me where he lived, but he gave me his mobile number. I called it at seven the next morning.

'Jesus fucking Christ, Aykan,' I said. 'This game, thing, whatever . . . it's total genius.'

I had been curious enough to rent a Nintendo 64 console

from Blockbusters on my way home, to play the thing he'd given me.

It was utterly extraordinary. It was not a game. It was a totally immersing piece of art, a multilayered environment that passed through anarchic and biting political commentary, bleak dreamscapes, erotic staging posts. There was no 'gameplay', only exploration, of the environment, of the conspiracies being unmasked. The viewpoint shifted and changed vertiginously. There were moments of shocking power.

I was stunned. I pulled an all-nighter, and called him as early as I thought I could get away with.

'What is this shit?' I asked. 'When's it coming out? I'll buy a fucking console just for this.'

'It's not coming out, man,' Aykan said. He sounded quite awake. 'It's just some shit I did. Nintendo are bastards, man,' he said. 'They'd never license it. No fucker'd produce it anyway. It's just for my friends. The hardest thing, let me tell you, the hardest thing isn't the programming, it's making the housing. If they read off CDs or whatever, no fucking problem. But putting the software into that poxy stupid little plastic square, and making it so it'll fit in the casing with all the right connectors. That's the hard bit. That's why I'm not doing that shit any more. Boring.'

I still own it, Aykan's guerrilla software, his illicit work of art. I still play it. Two years on I'm still discovering new levels, new layers. Later, before he disappeared, Aykan translated the scrawled title for me: *We Deserve Better Than This*.

Aykan's occasional e-mails to me often included web addresses for me to look up. I say Aykan's e-mails, although no name ever appeared in the 'Sender' column, and they were never signed. Whenever I tried to reply to them, they would register as coming from a nonsense address, and the messages would bounce back to me. But Aykan never denied the e-mails were his, and sometimes even asked me if I'd received certain messages. He irritably dismissed questions about how or why he sent them anonymously. If I wanted to contact him, I had to do it by phone.

This was a time when mass-circulation e-mails were getting out of hand. Every day I'd get one or two urls to look up. Sometimes they were pornographic, with a message like 'Did you know that was possible???!!!' from some sad lad or other I vaguely knew. More often they were links to some weird news story or other. Usually they looked too dull to chase up.

Aykan's, though, I always checked. They were pretty extraordinary. Essays, art pieces, things like that.

Sometimes he provided a password to get into hidden pages on-line, and when I visited them they were incomprehensible internal reports that looked very much like governments talking to governments, or rebel groups talking to rebels. I couldn't tell if they were hoaxes, but if not, I was rather alarmed.

'What's all this shit you keep sending me?' I demanded.

'Interesting, huh?' he sniggered, and put the phone down.

It wasn't just websites he sent me. Sometimes he directed me to one or another of his on-line projects. That was how I realised that Aykan was a virtuoso of programming. He was something extraordinary. Once, on one of our infrequent rendezvous, I called him a hacker. He burst out laughing, then got very angry with me.

'Fucking hacker?' He laughed again. 'Fucking *hacker*? Listen bro, you're not talking to some sebum-faced little sixteen-year-old geekboy with wank-stained pants who calls himself Dev-L.' He swore furiously. 'I'm not a fucking hacker, man,

I'm a fucking artist, I'm a hardworking wage-slave, I'm a *concerned motherfucking citizen*, whatever you want, but I'm not a fucking hacker.'

I didn't care what he wanted to call himself. Whatever he thought he was, he left me awestruck – disbelieving, really, utterly bewildered – with what he could do.

'What search engine do you use?' he wrote to me once. 'How often does your name come up? Try it now and then again tomorrow morning.'

According to searchsites.com I appeared on seven websites, all of them work-related rubbish. When I typed in my name again the next day, I was nowhere. I looked up my company's website and there I was, halfway down the page. But when I ran my name through searchsites or runbot or megawhere, I had no luck. I had become invisible.

'What did you do, you fuck?' I yelled down the phone. I was excited, though, feigning anger badly.

'How's that, huh? I ran you through my hide engine.' I could hear him smoking. 'Don't worry, man,' he said. 'I'll take you out of it. But it's good, huh? Tomorrow I think I'm gonna run Jack fucking Straw through it, or maybe every fucking sex-related word I can think of.' He put the phone down.

If he did run those words through his engine, it had stopped working. I checked the next day. But maybe he just hadn't bothered.

I spoke to Aykan several times, but a couple of months went by without me seeing him.

One morning I found another of his unmarked e-mails in my in-box. 'HAVE YOU SEEN THIS FUCKPIG SCUM-SUCKING PIECE OF SHIT?'

I had. It was the homepage of an organisation called An

End To Hunger. I had been sent it at least twice already, as a recipient on mass e-mailings.

The site contained low-key, muted and simple graphics, with a selection of harrowing statistics about world hunger. There were links to the UN Food Programme, Oxfam, and so on. But what made it such a popular site was its push-button charity donation.

Once per day, anyone visiting the site could click a little toggle, and in the words of the website, 'feed the hungry'. Alongside the button was a list of sponsors – all very dignified, no logos or bells or whistles, just the name of the company and a link to its homepage. Each sponsor would donate half a cent per click, which was roughly equivalent to half a cup of rice, or maize or whatever.

It all made me feel a bit uneasy, like corporate charity usually did. When I'd first visited the site I'd pressed the button. It had seemed churlish not to. But I hadn't visited it since, and I was getting irritated with people recommending it to me.

I called Aykan. He was incandescent.

'I've seen the site,' I told him. 'Bit gruesome, isn't it?'

'Gruesome?' he shouted. 'It's fucking *sick* is what it is. It's fucking *beyond beyond,* man. I mean, forget politics this shit couldn't be parodied.'

'I keep getting e-mails recommending it,' I told him.

'Any motherfucker e-mails you that, reply them right back, tell them to shove it up their arses till it hits the roof of their mouth, yeah? I mean by shit almighty . . . have you read the FAQ on the website?' I had not. 'Listen to this. This is fucking *verbatim*, OK? "Can I click the 'Give Food' button more than once, and keep making donations?" "We're sorry!"' Aykan's voice spewed bile. '"We're real sorry! It's a shame but you can't do that. Our sponsors have agreed for us to count one donation per person per day, and any more would be breaking our agreement.'" He made a noise like angry retching.

'Fuck 'em, bro,' he said. He sounded incredibly sad. 'They tell us we can't be *naughty* and do it too *often*?' I didn't tell him I had donated that first time. He was making me ashamed.

I murmured something to him, some agreement, some dismissal and condemnation. It wasn't enough.

'This is fucking war, man,' he said urgently. 'This one I can't let go.'

'Run them through your hide engine,' I suggested vaguely.

'What?' he said, enraged. 'What the fuck you talking about? Don't talk horsefuck, man. I want them down and dead. Time for the big fucking guns, hombre,' he said, and put the phone down. I tried to call him back but he didn't pick up.

Two days later I got another e-mail.

'Try visiting you shitting know where,' it said. I did, and An End To Hunger would not come up. The browser couldn't find it. I tried again at the end of the day and it was back, with a small, pious note about how sad they were to be targeted by hackers.

Aykan wouldn't answer his phone.

A week and a half later he called me.

'Man!' he shouted at me. 'Go back to the bastards,' he said. 'I was . . . you know, I jumped the gun last time. Wasn't particularly clever, right? But it was like a fucking – what do you call it – I was doing a *reconnoitre*. But go back now, click the bastard button all you can.'

'What did you do, Aykan?' I said. I was at work, and kept my voice neutral.

'I don't know how long it'll last,' he said, 'so get *all* your fucking friends to go visiting. For a *short time only* the shitlicking sponsors are going to be making a reasonable fucking payout. Ten bucks a fucking click, my friend, none of this half a cent bull. So go give generously.'

It's impossible to say how much of an impact it had. Certainly for the next day or so I proselytised zealously. An End To Hunger kept it very quiet, when they found out. I like to think that it took the businesses in question the best part of a day to realise that their pledged donations had gone up by around 100,000 per cent.

I wondered when Aykan would get bored of these games.

We spoke for a long time on the phone, one evening a fortnight or so later. He sounded exhausted.

'What you up to?' I asked him.

'Waging war, man,' he said shortly.

I suggested that he was wearing himself out, that he should apply himself to other things. He got angry and depressed all at once.

'It really got to me, this one,' he said. 'It really *got to me*. I dunno why, but I can't . . . This one matters. But . . . I keep hitting the wrong enemy. "Corporate sponsors don't actually care!" "Big business is hypocritical!" That's not news to *anyfuckingbody*. Who doesn't know? Who gives a fuck about *that*?

'Do you ever stop to think about them, man?' he said. 'Them in the AETH office. What must that do to your head? Like some kind of ghouls, man. What's that got to do to you?'

I changed the subject several times, but it kept coming back. 'I dunno, man . . .' he kept saying. 'I dunno what to do . . .'

It may have been the next day that he decided, but it was a good three weeks before he could make it work.

$\star \qquad \star \qquad \star$

'Go and visit A★ E★★ T★ H★★★★★, the e-mail said. 'Click and send the poor starving masses a present. See what happens.'

I went to the site. Apart from a few minor updates, nothing seemed to have changed. I prevaricated a while, looking for some clue as to what Aykan had done. Eventually I clicked the 'Give Food' button and waited.

Nothing happened.

The usual little message, thanking me on behalf of hungry people, appeared. I waited a couple more minutes, then left. Whatever Aykan had planned, I thought, it hadn't come off.

A couple of hours later I checked my e-mail.

'How the *fuck* . . .' I said, and paused, shaking my head. 'How the *fuck*, you insane genius bastard, did you do that?'

'You like that?' The connection was terrible, but I could hear Aykan yelling with laughter. He sounded triumphant. 'You fucking like it?'

'I . . . I don't know. I'm very impressed, whatever.'

I was staring at the message in my in-box. The sender was listed as 'Very Hungry Foreign People'.

'Dear Kind Generous Person,' it read. 'Thank you so much for your Generous gift of half a cup of wet rice. Our Children will treasure every grain. And do please thank your Kind Organisers at An End To Hunger for organising their rich friends to throw rice at us – that is the advantage of employing Sweatshop labour and trade union busting. That way they can afford rice for us poor people. Whatever you do, do keep sitting back and not asking any questions of them, keep them happy, don't agitate for any corporate taxes or grassroots control or anything like that which would threaten the large profits that allow them to buy us Cups of Rice. With humble love and thanks, The Hungry.'

'Every motherfucker who clicks the button's going to get that,' Aykan said.

'How did you *do* it?'

'It's a fucking program,' he said, suddenly irritable. 'I stuck it on the website. It scans your fucking hard disk for what looks like your e-mail address, and sends off the message when you draw attention to yourself by clicking. Try pressing "Reply".'

I did. The return address listed was my own.

'It's very impressive, Aykan,' I said, nodding slowly, wishing someone else had written the letter, made it a bit subtler, maybe edited it a bit. 'You've done a real number on them.'

'Well it ain't over yet, bro,' he said. 'Watch this space, you know? Watch this fucking space.'

My phone went at five the next morning. I padded nude and confused into the sitting room.

'Man.' It was Aykan, tense and excited.

'What the fuck time is it?' I muttered, or something like that.

'They're on to me, man,' he hissed.

'What?' I huddled vaguely into the sofa, rubbed my eyes. Outside, the sky was two tone. Birds were chirruping imbecilically. 'What are you on about?'

'*Our fucking philanthropic friends, man,*' he whispered tersely. 'The *concerned folk* over at Feed The World central, you know? They've rumbled me. They've *found* me.'

'How do you know?' I said. 'Have they contacted you?'

'No no,' he said. 'They wouldn't do that, that would be admitting what the fuck was up. No, I was watching them on-line, and I can see them tracking me. They can already tell what country I'm in.'

'What do you mean?' I said. I was fully awake now. 'Are you intercepting their e-mail? Are you crazy?'

'Oh man, there's a hundred fucking million things you can do, read their messages, watch who they're fucking watching, bounce off internal memos, keep tabs on their automatic defences . . . trust me on this: *they're fucking looking for me.*' There was silence. 'They may even have found me,' he finished.

'So . . .' I shook my head. 'So leave it alone. Let it be, get off their back before you piss them off any more and they go to the police.'

'Fucking *pofuckinglice*. . .' Aykan's voice swam in scorn. 'They won't give it to the fucking police, the police couldn't find their own thumbs if they were plugging up their arses. No, man. It's not the police I'm worried about, it's these Hunger motherfuckers. Haven't you clocked what kind of people these are? These are *bad* people, man. Major bad ju-ju. And anyway, *man*. . .', he shouted suddenly, as if remembering something. 'And anyway, what the fuck you mean *leave it alone*? Don't be such a shiteating coward. I told you, didn't I? I told you this was a fucking *war*, didn't I?' He was shouting by now. I tried to get him to shut up. 'I'm not looking for *advice*, I just wanted to let you know what was going on.'

He broke the connection. I did not phone him back. I was tired and pissed off. *Paranoid prick*, I thought, and went back to bed.

Aykan kept sending his obscure e-mails, advising me of some new change to An End To Hunger.

The letter to donors did not last long, but Aykan was

relentless. He directed me to their sponsors page, and I discovered that he had rerouted every link to a different revolutionary left organisation. He created a small pop-up screen that appeared when the 'donate' button was clicked, that compared the nutritional value of rice with what was rotting in European food mountains.

He kept hinting at some final salvo, some ultimate attack.

'I keep watching them, man,' he told me in one of his irregular phone calls. 'I swear they are so on my tail. I'm going to have to be really fucking careful. This could get very fucking nasty.'

'Stop talking rubbish,' I said, exasperated. 'You think you're in some cheap thriller? You're risking jail for hacking – and don't shout at me, because that's what they'll call it – but that's all.'

'Fuck you, bro!' he shouted, excitedly. 'Don't be so naive! You think this is a game? I told you ... these fuckers aren't going to the police. Don't you fucking *see*, man? I've done the *worst thing you can do* ... I've fucking *impugned their philanthropy*, man! I've fucking sneered at them while they do the Mother Teresa thing, and that they can't fucking stand!'

I was worried about him. He was totally infuriating, no longer even coming close to conversing, just taking some phrase or other of mine as a jumping off point to discuss some insane conspiracy.

He sent me bizarre, partial e-mails that made almost no sense at all. Some were just a sentence: 'They'll love this' or 'I'll show them what it really means'.

Some were longer, like cuts from the middle of works in progress, half-finished memos and snatches of programming. Some were garbled articles from various encyclopaedias, about international politics, about on-line democracy, about computerised supermarket stocktaking, about kwashiorkor and other kinds of malnutrition.

Slowly, with a stealthy amazement and fear, I started to tie these threads together. I realised that what looked like a patchwork of mad threats and ludicrous hyperbole was something more, something united by an extraordinary logic. Through these partial snippets, these hints and jokes and threats, I began to get a sense of what Aykan planned.

I denied it.

I tried desperately not to believe it, it was just too big. My horror was coloured with awe that he could even dream up such a plan, let alone believe he had the skills to make it work.

It was utterly unbelievable. It was horrific.

I knew he could do it.

I bombarded him with phone calls, which he never picked up. He had no voice-mail, and I was left swearing and stalking from room to room, totally unable to reach him.

An End To Hunger had been ominously quiet for some time now. It had operated without interruption for at least three weeks. Aykan was building up to his final plan. I was going crazy. There was a mad intensity to everything, it was like some frenetic nightmare, every time I thought of Aykan and his plans and conspiracies. I was scared.

Finally, at ten minutes to eleven on a Sunday evening, he called.

'Man,' he said.

'Aykan,' I said, and sighed once, then stammered to get my words out. 'Aykan, man, you can't *do this*,' I said. 'I don't care how fucking much you hate them, man, they're just a bunch of idiot liberals and you *cannot do that to them*, it's just not *worth it*, don't be *crazy* . . .'

'Shut up, man!' he shouted. 'Just shut up, for fuck's sake! Listen to me!' He was whispering again, urgently.

He was, I suddenly realised, afraid.

'I don't have any fucking time, bro,' he said, urgently. 'You've got to get over here, you've got to help me.'

'What's going on, man?' I said.

'*They're coming*,' he whispered, and something in his voice made me cold.

'The fuckers tricked me,' he went on, 'they kept it looking like they were searching, but they were better than I thought, they clocked me ages ago, they were just biding time, and then . . . and then . . . They're *on their way*!' He hissed the last sentence, like a curse.

'Aykan,' I said slowly. 'Aykan, man, you've got to stop this crazy shit,' I said. 'Are the police coming . . . ?'

He almost screamed with anger.

'*Godfuckingdammit don't you listen to me?* Any fucker can handle the police, but it's this *charity* wants my fucking head!' He was in a terrible state.

He had invited me to his house, I realised. For the first time in five years, he was ready to tell me where he lived. I tried to cut into his diatribe. 'I know shit about these bastards you wouldn't *believe*, man,' he was moaning. 'Like some fucking *parasite* . . . You got no curiosity what kind of fucker lives like that?'

I managed to break in.

'What can I do, man?' I said. 'You want me to come over?'

'Yeah, man, *please*, help me get my shit the fuck away,' he said.

He named an address about twenty minutes walk away. I swore at him.

'You been close all this time,' I said.

'Please just hurry,' he whispered, and broke the connection.

Aykan's house was one in a street of nondescript redbricks, and I was staring at it for several seconds before I saw that anything was wrong.

The front window was broken, and fringes of curtain were waving like seaweed through the hole.

I sprinted the last few feet, shouting. No one answered the bell. I pounded the door, and lights went on opposite and above me, but no one came to his door.

I peered in through the hole. I grabbed careful hold of the ragged glass frame and climbed into Aykan's house.

I stood, my breath shallow, whispering his name again and again. The sound of my own voice was very thin. It frightened me, such a little sound in that silence.

It was a tiny flat, a weird mixture of mess and anal fastidiousness. The bed-sitting room was crowded with Ikea-type shelves wedged tight with carefully ordered magazines and software, all exactly lined up. In the corner was a collection of extraordinarily powerful computer hardware, a tight little local-area network, with printer and scanners and modems and monitors wedged into unlikely angles. The coffee table was revolting with ashtrays and unwashed cups.

I was utterly alone.

I wandered quickly through all the rooms, again and again, back and forth, as if I might have missed him, standing in a corner. As if he might be waiting for me to find him. Apart from the shattered window, there was no sign of trouble. I waited and moped, but no one came.

After a few minutes I saw a green light winking langourously at me, and realised that his main computer was on sleep mode.

I pressed return. The monitor lit up, and I saw that Aykan's e-mail program was running.

His in-box was empty, except for one message, that had arrived earlier that evening.

It was listed as from AETH. I felt a slow, cold surge of adrenaline.

Slowly I reached out and clicked the message, opening it.

```
We're so very disappointed that you don't consider our
mission to improve the lot of the world's hungry to be a
worthy one. We are motivated to try to help the poorest
people on earth, at a cost of nothing to our users. We
consider this to be a winning situation for all sides.
Without us, after all, the poor and the hungry have
no voice.

  It is a matter of great sadness to us that you do not
share our vision, and that you have found it necessary
to undermine our work. As you see, we have been able to
trace you, through the sabotage to our website. We do
not believe that this situation would be satisfactorily
resolved through your country's courts.

  We think it only reasonable to inform you that we take
your conduct very seriously. We have our mission to
consider, and we can no longer allow you to endanger those
lives for which we work so hard.

  We intend to discuss this matter with you. In person.
  Now.
```

And that was all.

I waited in the cold, reading and rereading that message, looking around me in that quiet flat. Eventually I left. I debated taking the computer away, but it was too heavy, and anyway, it was really beyond me. I was never more than a day-to-day user. The kind of stuff Aykan had on there I'd never make head or tail of.

I called his mobile hundreds of times, but got only a dead signal.

I have no idea where he went, or what happened.

He could have broken that window himself. He could have written that e-mail himself. He could have lost it completely and run off screaming into the night, with no one at all on his tail. I keep waiting, and hoping that maybe I'll hear from him.

He could be hunted, even now. Maybe he stays out of sight, keeps of-line, uses pseudonyms, a thief in the night, letting dust blow over his on-line tracks.

Or maybe he was caught.

Maybe he was taken away, to discuss the politics of charity.

Every week, some e-mail or other recommends I visit An End To Hunger. The site is running well. Its problems seem to be over.

on the etiquette of eye-contact during oral sex

toby litt

Posted: alt.sex.oral
Heading: New FAQ

Woman-on-Man[1]

Due to the physical construction of men, and the natural curiosity of women, it seems obvious that *accidental* eye-contact is far more likely during woman-on-man oral sex than woman-on-woman or even man-on-man. (See below.)

We, the authors, will therefore use this combination to examine the perils and pitfalls of a number of varied situations.

During Casual Sex

In our experience, we have come to regard this as potentially the trickiest of all situations. However, many of the most obvious difficulties are removed if one is aware – at the time of the fellatic act – that this is casual sex *qua* casual sex.[2]

To a certain extent, we feel, eye-contact during oral sex during casual sex doesn't matter at all. This is because no ongoing relationship is at this juncture being established. When one looks into one's casual partner's eyes, one is not looking into one's future. Therefore we should suggest that one should indeed look – as this will be one's only chance. Also, in casual sex, any clues as to the success or failure of one's performance are welcome. Remember, there may be no cosy post-fellatial chat during which to establish or confirm mutual satisfaction. It could just be bye bye baby bye bye.

At the End of a First Date

We feel that this is often the situation in which the stakes are highest. For whatever one does on a first date one will almost certainly be expected to repeat throughout the ensuing relationship. Years and years afterwards. For ever, maybe. It is important, therefore, to establish in one's own mind a clear set of principles long before one has encountered the specific situation.

We would suggest that one writes down one's 'ground rules' on a piece of paper and gives them for safe-keeping to an intimate friend – or perhaps to one's mother. Then, following the date, one's obedience or disobedience can objectively be gauged.

We realise that many things occur 'on the spur of the moment', but one must be careful not to be pricked by that spur. (Not, of course, unless one wants to be. In regard to this, consult the sections below entitled On the Etiquette of Screaming at Orgasm and On the Etiquette of Horse-play and Pony Clubbing.)

At the End of a Second, Third or Fourth Date
Clearly, if one reaches this stage without having performed oral sex, one is hoping for a serious committed relationship. We would strongly suggest that you discuss the matter with your potential partner beforehand. Perhaps in the restaurant, over coffee and liqueurs. If one is in a group of close friends, or even merely within hailing distance of a couple of vague acquaintances, then the opinions of one's fellow diners are always worth gleaning.

At the End of a Fifth to a Thirteenth Date
One should, by now, have a fairly clear idea of the potential partner's interest or lack thereof in oneself. For the would-be fellatress: if he has up until now shown no signs of desiring sexual intercourse then he is probably impotent or carrying an STD. We would advise you to steer well clear. For the fellatee: what are you waiting for? A papal dispensation? Hanukkah to end?

In an Established, Committed Relationship
In many ways, this section should be redundant. The sexual behaviour of any couple is – in the vast majority of cases – established during the first eighteen to twenty hours they spend together in bed.[3] So, as far as eye-contact is concerned, either one already does and will continue to do so or one never has and never will.

However, in an attempt to galvanise a post-spark relationship, one may start doing things in bed (or outside it) that are unprecedented. Offering oral sex may be one of these. Making eye-contact during oral sex might be another. Winking or making a comic gagging expression, we would advise strongly against.

On Your Honeymoon
In the words of Primo Levi: If not now, when?

During Extra-Marital Sex
All extra-marital sex is, we feel, defined in relation to the intra-marital sex which it is *not*. It is likely, therefore, that one's instincts will be to compensate with one's adulterous partner for what is lacking with one's tedious partner. We have no major problem with this. (Consult the section On Leaving No Clues Behind Even if Your Partner *is* a Forensic Pathologist or Sherlock Fucking Holmes.) However, one should be aware that a certain amount of honesty (or very expert deception) is always required when looking into another human being's eyes. If one is conducting an affair in which one is lying to one's partner about one's marital state then it may be advisable either to avoid eye-contact altogether (for fear they should see one's guilt) or to practise in the bathroom mirror (for a few minutes, say, every other day).

After the Birth of Your Firstborn
After childbirth, certain difficulties are almost bound to occur in sexual relations. We have found that the most common one to be involved with oral sex eye-contact is the desire to bite the penis off out of hatred for the immense pain which that member has inflicted upon one. If one believes this to be a possibility, then one had better avoid eye-contact altogether. The look on that smug sperm-slinging bastard's face may be more than you can stand without immediately chomping his dangly bits off.

During Sex with Your Doctor (or Any Professional Man)
Of course, we acknowledge that sex in this relationship will

be a total power-abuse trip. And surely most of the pleasure to be had out of such a desktop kinkfest will be to do with 'looking up' to the professional, as one did to one's father. (See the sub-section entitled During Sex with a Blood-Relation.) We[4] strongly advise you gaze long and hard into his steely blue eyes.

During Sex with a Member of a Religious Order
Supplication is a major part of all the world's religions. Therefore, to look adoringly up into the eyes of any of its celebrants, whilst at the same moment tonguing their circumcised or uncircumcised love salami, will drive them wild with blasphemous desire. A must.

During Sex with a Blood-Relation
Fathers, uncles, brothers, cousins, second cousins, it makes no difference. Incest is a consciously committed sin and an illegality to boot. To hide from consciousness of it, whilst performing it, is immature and petty. Gaze deep, sick girl. What the hell. You're already burning.

During Sex with an Animal[5]
The mechanics of the thing rules this out in the case of most animals – unless some pretty damn ingenious use of mirrors is made. We would suggest that this is only worthwhile if one finds it, in fact, the whole point of the sex in the first place.

During Sex with a Family Pet
While the issue of the greater intimacy of the relationship may be worth considering, we would still refer you sick puppies back to the section entitled During Sex with an Animal.

During the Making of a Hardcore Porn Video
Yes, definitely. But not only that. In this situation it is imperative that one also make eye-contact with the eventual viewer, through the intermediary which is the video camera. The viewer's pleasure in one's performance will be enhanced a hundredfold if one transfers to them via one's glinting gaze one's own intense delight in the act.

During an Orgy
What is the point of an orgy, we ask, if not to see and be seen engaging in depraved sexual activity? A person with their eyes closed at the orgy is like a blindfolded blind person, alone, in the National Gallery, at night, when all the lights have been turned off and the pictures removed. Get a grip.

In a Public Place
It is always advisable in this situation to keep one's eyes out for members of the constabulary. The fellatee may, we admit, be in a better position to perform this task than the fellator. However, vigilance should not be allowed to impinge upon pleasure.

With the Lights Off
Don't be silly.

During Sex in the 69 Position
Join the circus, freaks. (You're obviously in the Hall of Mirrors, anyway.)

A further Note for the Short-Sighted
The wearing of glasses during oral sex is a moot point between

us, the editors. I myself feel that it is a good thing – particularly in situations where the fellator is role-playing (as secretary, nun, school-teacher). My co-editress, who has just nipped out to buy some milk, asserts that the many advantages of contact lenses should be brought into play.

Man-on-Woman

In most cases the sub-sub-sections above deal perfectly adequately with any given situations – being written to deal with the generalities rather than the specifics.

Woman-on-Woman

Given the difference in male and female anatomy, it is far less likely that accidental eye-contact will occur. A certain effort – a certain straining of both necks – is required to achieve a woman-on-woman gaze.

The innate structural equality of the relationship establishes a further balance. Eye-contact may be less of a turn-on, given that the power thing isn't as important (unless artificially created) and there isn't quite as much to look at, narcissistically speaking. (This, we have to admit, is another moot point. But some people like looking at clouds and some hills.[6]) However, eye-contact may be more of a turn on, given that one is, in a sense, doing exactly as one would be done by.

Man-on-Man

The doing as one would be done by point also holds true here. For anyone requiring further clarification, we would refer you to the popular website 'Tip-top tips for top-tip licks'.

NOTES

1 We, the authors, have – for reasons that soon shall become obvious – decided to divide this section of *The Universal Guide for the Innocent and Unsure* into gender/gender-specific sub-sections. This policy should not be taken as implying a 'hidden agenda' of any sort. My co-editress and I are quite in agreement upon wishing to emphasise this point.

2 If one is in some doubt as to whether one will see the sexual partner again, then one should refer to the following sub-sub-section: At the End of a First Date. But one should not, of course, refer to this sub-sub-section during the sexual act itself. Reading during oral sex was permissible only during the Age of Empire – and then only the Letters and Obituary Pages of *The Times*.

3 Including sleep.

4 My co-editress in particular suggests this. Which I find slightly worrying.

5 Had we not received a great deal of mail on this subject following our first edition, we would not think it worth mentioning.

6 And some like both.

shopping

chris manby

For someone raised on QVC, Internet shopping was the obvious next step for Kara Smith. Like the progression from smoking pot to shooting up – shopping via the Internet provided a faster, more effective hit than messing about with the phone.

Now Kara didn't have to wait until her shopping channel's jewellery hour – or, heaven forbid, even miss it altogether if she had to work a late shift. She could go straight to jewellery.com at her convenience. And when she found the pair of diamond studs, or the perfect pink lipstick, or the bright orange dish drainer that would pull her look/make-up/ home together, she didn't have to face the frustration of jammed telephone lines while everyone of a like mind responded excitedly to the QVC presenter's assertion that there were just three pairs of those earrings, two tubes of that lipstick, or one, absolutely unique, orange plastic dish drainer in the whole world.

'Just click and it's yours.'

Such seductive words. And now that she had her credit card details registered with every site from Amazon to ZooAnimalsRUs.com, Kara had also managed to bypass the guilt that had overwhelmed her every time she recited her account number over the phone and had to wait while the shopping channel operative checked her credit-worthiness. In fact, Kara had even applied for a new high limit, low rate credit card via the net.

On days when she didn't have to go to her job at the insurance office, Kara started her shopping early. First she would check her e-mail. She always had mail. The on-line stores she had ordered from and even those that hadn't been able to tempt her (there were a few) were keen to keep her up to date with their latest offers. Then she hit the web with the same methodical approach with which she had once hit the high street. As a teenager her Saturday mornings had started at Top Shop and progressed from Miss Selfridge to River Island to, on a bad day, Marks and Spencer, until she found the outfit she would wear to the disco later that night. Always the same order. Kara surfed the web in the exact same way until she got that day's fix. Sometimes she found something to send for at the first site she visited. Sometimes she would be sitting at her desk until the beautiful morning she had shut out with her curtains because the sun affected her ability to see her screen became another night. But she always found something. The joy of those parcels arriving at a rate of at least one a morning was better than sex.

'You seen Jo or Lisa lately?' her sister asked one night. Kara's sister Elaine often dropped by on her way home from the office though Kara wondered why she bothered. They didn't seem to have a lot to talk about these days.

'Have you?'

'What?' Kara looked up irritably from her screen. The site she wanted was taking an age to download.

'I don't know why I bother talking to you. You're completely obsessed by that computer.'

'I am not.'

'Then why don't you turn the stupid thing off when you've got a visitor? Or at least turn your chair to face me sometimes.'

'I didn't invite you over,' Kara reminded Elaine.

'Since when did your sister need an invite? But if that's the way you feel I shan't bother in future.'

'Fine by me.'

'Oh, Kara,' Elaine rolled her eyes. 'I know you think I come round here to have a go at you but it's only because I love you. I worry about you. You don't see your friends any more. I know. I saw Jo and Lisa last weekend. They said they hadn't seen you outside the office for weeks. Anyone would think you'd been made housebound by some terrible disease.'

'I'm happy.'

'Are you really? Look at all this stuff you've been buying. Anyone would think you were trying to compensate for something.'

Elaine stroked the diaphanous skirt of a bright red dress that Kara had unpacked but not as yet even found time to try on. 'What's the point of buying a dress like this if you can't tear yourself away from the screen for long enough to actually go out in it?'

'I will. I'm staying in to save money,' Kara excused herself.

'Doesn't look like you're saving much to me. Spending money virtually is the same as handing over your card at a real shop, you know.'

'I'm not a child.'

'No. But you're not living in the real world at the moment, either.'

Kara turned towards her sister and made 'yapping' movements with her hands.

'Well, don't blame me if you end up old and skint and lonely because you won't come out of the cyber shopping mall,' said Elaine as she shrugged on her coat and prepared to leave.

'I won't. Anyway, for all you know I could meet the perfect like-minded lover on the net.'

'At saltshakersinternational.com?' Elaine asked, reading over Kara's shoulder.

'Look, I promise I'll have a look at some dating sites later on. OK?'

'Oh God,' Elaine groaned. 'I can see it now. My beautiful sister is going to end up with a geek.'

Kara ordered only a set of three nail polishes that day but the next morning the postman arrived bearing two parcels.

'I wasn't expecting two parcels,' Kara told him as she signed the acceptance for both. The second parcel was addressed to K. Smith – even if it was actually Mr K. Smith. Kara figured that she had mis-keyed her title and that this was a parcel of something she had ordered weeks before that had been out of stock.

She opened the nail polish first. Three bottles. All in the right colours.

Then the mystery box.

Kara didn't remember ordering a new mouse for her computer but that was what she found inside. Boring. But useful. Her old mouse had been becoming erratic with overuse. She plugged in the new one and was soon surfing through her favourite sites again.

The next day saw another unexpected arrival. Another parcel addressed to Mr K. Smith instead of Miss. But it was for the right address. Kara signed for the parcel without expressing her concerns that it might not be for her. Inside were a couple of CDs. One of them was the new Shania Twain release she had been coveting.

The next day, another parcel she hadn't ordered. And the next and the next. Two beautiful candlesticks. A book on Feng Shui. A box of crunchy chocolate cookies and a jar of tangy jam. A sweater from The Gap that was just her colour if not her size. She wore it to keep warm as she surfed the net into the night.

It might have gone on indefinitely. Kara felt a faint pang of guilt every time she opened a parcel that plainly wasn't meant for her but her guilt was quickly overlaid with excitement. It seemed that Mr K. Smith knew her taste rather well and what was the harm in any case? When the parcels didn't arrive at his address he could ring up the website and they would send out another one. The retailers had insurance. Mr Smith would get his purchases a couple of days late. Kara would keep the original parcels. Everybody was happy. Though Kara was just a little surprised that no one had turned up on her doorstep demanding the goods' return.

Perhaps the onus was on her. Kara tried not to think about it until the morning the little package from Tiffany turned up one Friday afternoon. Though Kara had visited their website every day for the past six months, she had never actually dared order anything from the exclusive jewellery store. Her plastic was close to melting as it was. But here was a parcel from Tiffany.com and inside was the most beautiful ring she had ever seen. A diamond as big as a peanut set in a platinum band. Kara knew as soon as she slipped the ring onto her finger that somebody would be coming to see how this particular purchase had gone astray.

Kara jumped when the doorbell rang that night. It wasn't a sound she heard often these days. She opened the door just a crack to get a look at the visitor.

'Keith Smith,' said the young man. 'I think you might have been getting some of my post.'

Kara realised that her mouth was open as she looked at the gorgeous stranger.

The ring had been for his girlfriend. She'd been angry that he spent so much time surfing the net. Even if it had arrived at the right address that morning it would have been too late to save their relationship. She'd gone off with someone she met at work. Someone who didn't even know how to turn a computer on. Keith was sad but could see the benefit. What was the point of being with someone who didn't share his passion?

Kara nodded and brought more tea.

Keith didn't leave until Sunday.

'My God, she knows how to use the phone line for something other than sending an e-mail!' Elaine exclaimed when Kara phoned her on Sunday evening. 'What's up? Has your laptop exploded?'

'Shut up and listen,' Kara commanded. 'You're not going to believe this but I've fallen in love. He's handsome, he's funny and he's definitely not a geek.'

'And you met him on the Internet?'

'Well, sort of.'

'Tell me more.'

'Elaine, I think I've met my perfect man. There was a post-code mix up . . .'

Elaine smiled to hear her sister sound animated about something other than Amazon again.

'Another parcel for Mr K. Smith.'

Kara beamed as the postman handed over a small flat parcel.

'Ah yes. But I think that this may have been meant to come here this time,' she told him. Kara signed the chit with a flourish and hurried inside. Had Keith sent her a present especially chosen for her? Kara took her special parcel-opening knife, ordered from postaccessories.com to the parcel tape and soon had the brown box open.

Inside was a video tape. Unlabelled. Kara turned the box over for a clue. But there was no clue. Only solution was to watch it. She loaded it into her player and settled down to watch.

A cartoon. Tom and Jerry. Kara wrinkled her forehead as she wondered what the significance of this clip might be. Was she Tom and he Jerry? Or she Jerry and he Tom? At one point the mouse handed the cat a Valentine's card, then hit him over the head with a mallet while he was absorbed in reading the message. Kara frowned in confusion. She started to compose an e-mail to Keith in her mind.

'Think I'm mousy, do you? Because you know that I think you're the cat's whiskers . . . Want to chase me round the kitchen.'

She soon stopped.

The cartoon came to an abrupt and unexpected end and the screen was suddenly crowded with new images. Kara tipped her head to one side as she tried to make out exactly what part of a woman she was seeing. And more to the point, what that huge Alsatian was doing with its . . .

Then Elaine's parting shot was back in her head.

'My beautiful sister and the geek.'

Kara sighed. 'Oh, bollocks.'

the last minute.con

denise danks

Jury sat in the new wing of the Science Museum eating his prosciutto and sun-dried tomato bap and contemplating Dr Philip Nitschke's Suicide Machine.

It was a curious exhibit for which the museum had paid one thousand pounds. It comprised a portable computer, which was attached to a suitcase containing a jumble of mechanical paraphernalia that terminated in a syringe.

It occurred to Jury that the 486 laptop was worth practically zero. The cheap suitcase that held the tube, bellows, syringe, cable and pin connector was hardly state-of-the-art travel technology either. It reminded Jury of those dappled Japanese-made hard shell weekend cases with razor-sharp plastic handles that were popular in the 1960s. He had seen one filled with old 45s in his grand-parents' attic.

Jury picked at a stray tag of meat that had lodged between his teeth. Any intrinsic value of the exhibit, he reasoned, had to be in the barbiturates contained within the syringe of the apparently primed machine.

It was tempting. If someone were to break the glass, jab the needle into a vein and hit the 'yes' button on the dialog box, failing a frozen Bill Gates moment, it would be all over. Jury was himself tempted. He was always tempted by death, but in this case he wasn't convinced that the laptop was actually running. It was definitely superfluous to requirements for the determined and able-bodied suicide risk. If anyone really wanted to shoot up, they wouldn't need that antiquated box of tricks. They'd just *do it*, like the corporate marketing man said. If only; Jury thought, it was that simple.

He had read the brief summary of the Suicide Machine's place in scientific history that was printed on card and attached to the inside of the glass cabinet. He remained unimpressed. There was barely any science in it, certainly nothing groundbreaking enough to earn it a place in the Museum. It was simply an extraordinary example of the appliance of science but it would have looked more at home in a chamber of horrors next to a wax effigy of some serial murderer. After all, a bath was a bath and did not become more so just because it was filled with acid.

There was no cybernetic ingenuity to marvel at in the suicide machine, merely the intent. Someone had decided to set the needle as the default output device instead of, say, a printer. That was it. The human being was the paper on which The Moving Finger placed its full point.

It had novelty although that too was debatable since Jury seemed to recall an incident where a desperate man had rigged himself to the electricity supply and programmed his computer to power on at 3 a.m. The time, the dead of morning, was, according to statistics, a popular one for suicide. Jury presumed the man had taken enough drugs beforehand to fall asleep and stay asleep. For his part, he was always awake at that time, to watch the moment pass.

The software Nitschke had written was called Deliverance, which Jury noted was also the name of a seminal horror movie starring Burt Reynolds. The film was unusual and notorious, Jury recalled, for its subversive depiction of a male rape scene rather than the more commonplace female assault. Deliverance the program was as subversive. Just as the movie wasn't any ordinary male bonding adventure tale, the software wasn't any ordinary help program.

On the face of it, it was a simple Microsoft Access application that guided the user through a series of on-screen questions that terminated in two buttons: Yes and No. However, the questions enquired if the user wanted to die. To answer, the user placed the cursor over one button or the other and pressed ENTER. The affirmative action set the computer the task of activating the mechanical bellows that depressed the morbid contents of the syringe into the prepped vein of the user. The pain of living would thus be terminated.

Any creative thought that was worth noting was in the computer's use. If it was a milestone, it was a milestone in human ethics and it let Dr Nitschke off the hook. All he had had to do was set it up. The dying patient committed suicide. Without the laptop and the retro suitcase, Dr Nitschke would have been a murderer.

The doctor, the information card said, had allowed four people to use his machine to self-administer lethal injections between 1996 and 1997 when voluntary euthanasia was legalised for a short time in Australia's Northern Territory. The law provided that two doctors had to confirm the patients were terminally ill and suffering unbearable pain before life could be ended. A psychiatrist also had to confirm the patient was not suffering a treatable clinical depression.

It was the last statement that had struck Jury as unfair. It lacked insight and understanding as to the nature and intensity of psychological pain. How could a torture that was infinite in its variations as it played across the human senses be compared to the consistent path of mere physical torment?

Jury wondered quite what advantage the defunct Australian law had provided. The common law, as it stood, was indiscriminate in its understanding of the amorphous nature of agony. It allowed for the treatment of pain, psychological or physical, and whether the doctor killed his suffering patient or not was immaterial. The doctor, by acting to alleviate his patient's suffering, was blameless and true to his, or her, oath. Common law holds that it is, after all, the thought that counts.

Jury was no stranger to thoughts of suicide. He had wanted to kill himself the first time he had come to London. He had been living in the city for six months when he decided to jump in front of a train. He was watching a grey-faced Intercity arrive from Penzance when the impulse took him and he had allowed his misery at being alone and dead at heart wash over any desire he had for living. He was sick of London and, it followed, of life. He had not been in any physical pain. He was not dying of cancer. He was not paralysed or bedridden. He had a future but it was being preceded by a present that he didn't care for.

He had moved very close to the edge of the platform but as the iron bulk of the engine approached, fear had shot through his body and shaken him to his Timberland boots. He stepped backwards at the last minute and the train passed, smearing the greasy dirt from its long journey on his single-breasted suede jacket. He had stood alone, hyperventilating in the rank fumes that escaped from the braking wheels, knowing that sheer cowardice had prevented him from taking the final exit. He would have to endure.

And what had become of him? By many measurements he had made a success of his life. He was a venture capitalist whose in-box churned two hundred e-mail alerts a day, whose pager vibrated like a cicada and whose phone rarely stopped trilling. He had offices on the tenth floor of a modern riverside development and he had incubated all manner of dot coms for highly successful market debuts, weathering two stock market corrections in the process. He had a fast car and owned a smart apartment, the walls of which were decorated with large examples of the cutting edge of Modern Art. At night, he gazed through a glass expanse across the regenerated docks, the ancient cranes and hoists of which had lifted the produce of an empire from fleets of laden merchant ships and now stood like gigantic gallows over the quiet basins.

It was true, he had an enviable lifestyle but he had no life. The pain of loneliness had ground him down like the northern wind ground the pebbles on the British seashore leaving them smooth, individual and indifferent. Jury still wished he were dead.

Twenty small companies that he was preparing for IPOs shared the tenth floor with him. All the CEOs were under thirty and dressed down in the same way. The casual talk at the communal coffee machine was of detox diets and personal trainers. Though all the companies were different, there was no way of identifying one from the other apart from their highly valued, idiosyncratic logos that hung from the acoustic room dividers. It was these logos, not the information products they produced, that defined the company and the people that worked there.

Everyone greeted him as he walked by. They said 'Hi' and

not 'Hello' and smiled as if they were all as close as family used to be. Jury would stop at random to chat to some and check on their progress, which was always good.

He did not share their space. He had his own separate office with walls of glass and an ever-open door, but separate nevertheless. Though he would have liked it to be, it was never silent. Like everywhere else on the tenth floor, there was a constant background whirr of the cooling fans within the computers that were permanently on.

He sat down and set himself a time limit of ten minutes to research his subject.

He discovered that in 1998, CBS's *60 Minutes*, television programme had screened the demise of 52-year-old Thomas Youk, a Michigan man suffering from amyotrophic lateral sclerosis. Youk had discussed his death with a Dr John Kevorkian, a retired pathologist, who had admitted assisting the deaths of more than 120 willing people with home-made devices that delivered cocktails of chemicals or carbon monoxide.

Youk prevaricated for several days before, with the patient counselling of Kevorkian, he convinced himself that he truly wanted to die. The doctor had then injected him with the narcotic, secobarbital, and enough potassium chloride to stop his heart. He then offered the tape to the networks.

There was, Jury observed, a streak of misanthropy in this apparently altruistic act and it confirmed a long-held view he had of the malignancy of physicians. He had seen more pity in the average policeman than he had ever encountered in a doctor.

Kevorkian was subsequently charged with first-degree murder and other crimes in Oakland County, Michigan and sent to prison for ten years. CBS was criticised for scheduling the tape during the November broadcast 'sweeps' when the advertising rates for the coming season are determined. The networks traditionally show blockbusters and mini-series at this time to boost the all-important ratings. Thomas Youk's last moments pulled in one quarter of the US television audience of 15.5 million households and CBS's highest rating that year. This was a telling statistic as far as Jury was concerned.

The alarm sounded and Jury logged off. What he needed now, he thought, was a business plan.

He tapped the phone and spoke into it.

'Danny? A moment, please.'

Danielle Roy, who wore baggy combats made from parachute silk and a snug synthetic gilet, was the CEO of *www.whitedot.com*. It was a so-called death site. They had got the retro name from the dot that remained on early television screens when the programme schedules had ended, usually before midnight.

The sell was insurance, legal and funeral services of any kind, burial plots, and a classified section for announcements and messages of sympathy. The draw of the site was death statistics and projections of individual dates of death based on environmental and genetic criteria for the purposes of setting insurance rates. It wasn't unique but whitedot.com had gained a reputation for fine-tuning. The punters were happy with the service and the advertisers were happy with the throughput generated by 100,000 plus hits per day.

'I want to try something,' Jury said, indicating to Danny that she should sit down. She settled back into one of Jury's soft chairs, draping one leg over the chair's arm.

He gave her the elevator pitch.

An on-line Chapel of Rest.

'People are actually very unfamiliar with actual death, you see,' he said.

'I think it's brilliant,' she said. 'Have you thought of the name?'

'How about The White Room?'

'Oh, brilliant. You don't think there'll be a problem?'

'No. It needs to be tasteful. The families will have to be convinced of that but the funeral directors will love it. It's great advertorial for them.'

It took two weeks and The White Room was indeed a great success. Copycat webcams in funeral parlours became commonplace but whitedot.com/whiteroom made the killing. The world could log on and see dead strangers dressed for weddings, their waxy faces serene, their arms folded across their chests and garlands in their lifeless hair.

For Jury, it was a softening-up process as much for him as for the on-line world. It was only a matter of time. Watching the dead would not be enough. Jury had done his figures and was sure of that.

Three months later, he presented another idea to Danielle Roy. This time, her ready smile faded. She ran a nervous hand through her lightened hair, tugging at its dark roots.

'You cannot be serious.'

'I am.'

'What about the IPO?'

'Think about it. I reckon two million hits minimum. We go for the IPO as planned but telegraph this event. Whitedot.com will come to market with a good share price but something extra will be built in. The market will be prepared for a huge number of hits, and the share price will reflect that.'

Her eyes brightened with the slick shine of greed.

'It's illegal isn't it?'

'Think about it. Who are they going to prosecute?'

'Us?'

'Where? We have mirror sites. In any case, we can argue that it's a bona fide news event. We just provide the link, exclusively.'

He handed her a single page of bullet points. Her violet eyes scanned it and a little frown creased her pale brow.

'I don't know,' she said.

'It'll be uploaded from someone's home. It's a news story. We will be contributing to the debate.'

'Who's going to take the risk of being prosecuted for assisting a suicide? For murder.'

'No one. The whole thing will be interactive. We're talking electronic votes. "Yes" for death and "no" for life. How can you prosecute a million, two million, three million people? Who pressed the button? The last person to vote, or everyone? In what nanosecond did it happen?'

Danielle looked down at the paper, her agitated fingers still pulling at her hair.

'Have you got anyone in mind for this?'

'Me,' he said, offering her a mirror on which lay a perfect line of cocaine.

Three weeks later, Jury was waiting in his apartment with a syringe in his arm and his laptop logged on to whitedot.com/whiteroom/lastminute. But for a slight ache in his stomach, he was calm and quite sure of himself.

He spoke to Danielle on his mobile phone while he watched the whiteroom.com homepage on his computer screen. The web counter was spinning like a Vegas fruit machine. The world had logged on to see and hear Jury's personal elevator pitch for his right to die.

'I'm lonely,' he had said. 'Always have been. I know lots

of people and I have lots of friends but my loneliness lies deep inside me, like hypothermia – you know, I'm kind of cold and dead inside. I can't sleep but when I do, I dream of dying. That's how I get peace. Dreaming of it. I just can't get there. I just can't do it by myself.'

The world listened and fought for his attention. Do it. Don't do it. Walk. Don't walk. Yes. No. Jury felt the thrill of the needle in his arm and watched the numbers but the outcome was never going to be in doubt.

Six months later, the three major shareholders of whitedot.com were paper millionaires and Jury was not dead. The world had decided that he had everything to live for. The millions of hits did not amount to the single telling hit and the warm feeling created by the global click of fellow feeling had rosied up the whitedot.com stock for weeks.

Jury was a little disappointed that his plan had worked because deep down, as always, he had wanted to die. But he had done his research. He knew the odds were against him. People might favour euthanasia in opinion polls, but voting for it was never popular. Since the screening, he had received death threats in double figures but thousands of proposals of marriage.

He stood in his apartment and gazed out across the silent docks in whose dark waters the multitudinous lights of a speculative metropolis glimmered. The losers in his death vote had proved one thing to him. A small percentage of the global population would have been glad to help him die. He only had to match these to the small percentage of suicides who couldn't face the task and he had a market. They only had to ask and death would come. All he had to do was build the business model.

A smile played on his thin lips.

'Cowards,' he thought.

He watched the burning lights in the banks of apartment blocks and he felt like laughing out loud. One good thing had come of it. For the first time in his life, Jury did not feel alone.

mikey's virtual million

john williams

Mikey Thompson was not a technologically minded man. He was probably the last person in Butetown not to own a mobile phone. Way Mikey saw it the last thing he wanted was to be constantly available. Specially to Tina. Bad enough getting out of the house without her calling him up every five minutes checking he was where he was supposed to be, and not running round town looking for a little bit of strange.

Tina didn't see it the same way of course. She was always on at him about getting a mobile. Obvious how she figured it, like one of the tracking devices they put on young offenders. In the end she'd given him one for Christmas, one of these dodgy ones that were floating around everywhere and never charged you for calls. Anyway she'd given him this thing and there were two reasons he'd hated it: one, the tracking thing; two, the fact he couldn't bloody understand it. All these bloody buttons you had to press, worse than the video. You know how normally it's only the bloke can set the video;

well in Mikey's house it was only their little boy Mikey Jr
who could manage it. No, technology really wasn't Mikey's
thing at all.

On the other hand making a little corn here and there was
definitely Mikey's thing. Any time he wasn't out looking
for the aforementioned strange he was likely as not thinking
about making a little deal here, bit of business there. Which
is why, when the social sent him on a training course Mikey
wasn't too bothered. Lot of the boys would just mess about,
take the piss, but Mikey had a look at what was on offer
and said he'd do the one on computers and new business
opportunities, the Internet and all that.

So Monday morning Mikey was round at Grassroots a
quarter of an hour early. You got there early you had a
chance to check out all the talent as it arrived, help find
the girls a seat, that kind of business. Mikey liked these
courses, the one chance he had to meet women without
Tina looking over his shoulder. He was even considering
signing up for hairdressing, lot of girls on that one, except
the boys would never quit taking the piss. Anyway, there
he was, bright and early, looking seriously pukka in a new
shirt he'd picked up from TK Maxx. He loved that shop, just
'cause they had those big plastic alarm things attached to the
clothes they thought they were safe. Hah!

Mikey was just having a little word with this dyed blonde
piece when in walked the lecturer, and he did a double take.
He knew the guy. He was a feller called Ozzie, old hippie
type used to be a probation officer and did a lot of stuff on
this pirate radio station they'd had going a year or so back.

'Whassup,' says Mikey.

'Hey,' says Ozzie, then pauses for a moment. 'Thompson,
Mikey Thompson yeah? Good to see you, man. Hang around
after, we'll have a talk.'

So Mikey sits himself down next to the blonde and watches the usual assembly of deadbeats file in: dumb kids, sad old blokes in suits trying to persuade you they used to be in management, single mums wondering how they're going to pay the child minder while they're stuck here on this pointless course. Same old same old.

Except far as Mikey was concerned the course wasn't pointless at all. Beforehand Mikey was worried it would all be programming which sounded far too much like hard work, but instead Ozzie starts off talking about all these dot com companies, and how much money they're making. Starts talking about this company that from the sounds of it are basically just like one of those travel agents that have their windows full of last minute bargains – two weeks in Magaluf for a tenner kind of thing. Anyway, this particular travel agent's on the Internet so they don't even need a shop and somehow or other – this was the part Mikey wanted to know more about – they start floating themselves on the Stock Exchange. And all of a sudden the value of this company is something like five hundred million pounds. That's more than a big brewery or car manufacturer or whatever. And all it is is a few computers in a room somewhere, and a few kids typing up all the information and placing the orders. Operation doesn't even make money, in fact it loses it hand over fist and yet the people who thought it up are making millions, hundreds of millions.

Be honest, Mikey didn't pay a lot of attention the rest of the session. A hundred million pounds. Mikey wasn't greedy he'd take just one little million pounds, that'd be fine. And all you needed was an idea, any old idea far as he could see, and then a catchy name with dot com on the end. How difficult could that be.

Actually it seemed to be pretty difficult. Half an hour's

concentrated thought got Mikey nowhere. He started with his own areas of expertise but had to admit that shoplifting dot com didn't sound like the kind of thing the big investors would want to touch. Though maybe you could make a game out of it like that grand theft auto thing on the PlayStation. That wasn't a bad idea as it goes, he'd have a word with his cousin Sean who actually knew how to programme computers and shit.

Then Ozzie announced a coffee break and for once Mikey didn't take the chance to hit on one of the girls over the plate of bourbon biscuits. This time he went straight up to Ozzie.

'Great talk, man,' he said. 'Inspiring, like.'

'Yeah?' said Ozzie looking gratified.

'Yeah. Christ, all you do is think up the right idea, you make millions on the Stock Exchange. Brilliant.'

'Um,' said Ozzie, 'you weren't listening to the part where I said this was potentially a total economic disaster then?'

'No,' said Mikey, 'how's that then? You mean they don't pay you?'

'No,' said Ozzie, 'I mean it's a bubble, valuing companies that don't make or do anything. It's like capitalism is completely losing any grip on reality.'

'Yeah,' said Mikey, 'like I said, great.'

Ozzie shook his head. 'The bubble always bursts in the end. Even the pretty solid success stories like the big bookshop Amazon, they lose a fortune. It's just everyone's gambling on them making a pile of money some time in the future.' Ozzie paused for a moment. 'No, as far as I know, no one's actually making any money off the net yet. Well, apart from the sex stuff of course.'

Well, that makes sense at least, thought Mikey. Everyone knows the whole point of this Internet thing is you get access to all this porn without having to like walk into Lovecraft or pick it off the top shelf, girl in the newsagent giving you a look.

And then it hit him. The brilliant idea.

'Hey Ozzie,' said Mikey. 'Any of these porn sites float themselves on the Stock Exchange do they?'

Ozzie laughed and shook his head again. 'Who knows, Mikey.'

Mikey really was inspired. He'd had a talk with Ozzie in the pub after the session finished and the guy started off a bit horrified, all this bollocks about porn degrading women or whatever – way Mikey saw it, it was not having any money degraded people. Anyway, after a bit the bloke calms down and dishes out some advice. First off he didn't reckon Mikey could just walk into the Natwest and say, hey I want to float an Internet porn business on the Stock Exchange, can I have my million pounds now please. No, first thing was you had to establish the business and far as Ozzie knew banks were a bit iffy about lending you money to go into the porn trade, so basically Mikey was going to have to make the first moves himself.

Next thing the bloke said though was a bit more helpful. He started trying to persuade Mikey to forget the porn thing and do something more 'socially useful'. Said that if Mikey like started up a Butetown keep the kids off drugs website or some such there might be some funding available, pay for the computers and so on. Oh, said Mikey, that sounds good.

And it did. The way forward was starting to open up for Mikey. Step one, get the money out of the council or who-ever and pretend to be working on some bullshit do-gooder website. Step two, get the porn site up and running. Step three, go to market and get paid. Sweet.

First thing was to find someone who actually knew how to programme computers and all that business. Mikey considered this for a moment walking back up Bute Street and smiled. He knew just the feller.

Mikey's cousin Sean was mucking about really, setting up a four PC network in his bedroom running Linux. Sean loved Linux. Who could resist a system that positively encouraged you to get under the bonnet and start tinkering, as opposed to Windows which tended to crash violently the minute you even thought about looking under the lid. Anyway there he was playing about with different skins for the desktop when the bell goes, then goes again. Annoyed at the distraction, Sean goes to the door and opens it to find his cousin Mikey standing there.

So Mikey walks in, heads through the open door into Sean's computer room, looks out the window and says great view, which of course it is being ten floors up but is hardly news and Sean just stands there wondering what the hell he wants.

'Look,' says Mikey after a bit, 'you knows I does a lot of work for the community, right.'

Sean grunted, knowing no such thing.

'Anyway,' Mikey goes on, 'I've been doing this computer business course down town like and I was thinking it would be good to have a community website, like, telling people about employment and what's on and stuff.'

Sean grunted again. He'd nothing against the idea but it still didn't sound like Mikey.

'Be money in it,' said Mikey and Sean relaxed.

'Yeah,' said Mikey, 'a lot of funding for community Internet projects and stuff. So I was wondering if.'

'I'd do all the work for you,' finished Sean, smiling. You

couldn't help smiling with Mikey around, he was such a chancer but so transparent about it too.

'No, no,' said Mikey, 'be a team, of course. I can do all the meetings if you can back up with a bit of technical expertise like, tell them what computers we need and stuff.'

Sean smiled involuntarily at the prospect of some nice new subsidised hardware. He shrugged. 'OK, you find out a bit more, we'll see what we can do.'

Next couple of weeks things ran like clockwork. Ozzie lent Mikey a hand with the application forms and before he knew it some idiot from the council was smiling and saying yes, yes, marvellous minority community Internet access, and forking over a substantial cheque to tigerbay dot com.

Second the cheque was in the brand new business bank account – signatories Mikey and Ozzie just to keep the bank happy, though Mikey had no plans to let Ozzie near the cheque book – Mikey and Sean headed down to City Road. Sean led the way into this little shop full of bits of computers and no games at all which pissed Mikey off a bit, and a couple of boring and completely incomprehensible hours later Sean was happy. Couple of days after that they moved into their new premises, third floor of a Victorian office building opposite the Baltimore and Sean got wiring the stuff up, happier than the proverbial sand-boy. Soon as that was done Sean told Mikey they needed to get a designer.

'What for?' asked Mikey.

'To design the site,' said Sean, 'make it look good.'

Mikey shrugged, thought for a moment. 'All right,' he said. 'I'll give Col a bell.'

'Col?'

'Yeah, he did the signs over Kenny's club.'

'He knows Visual Basic does he?'

'I dunno,' said Mikey, 'you could show him though I expect.'

Sean rolled his eyes but Mikey ignored him. Anyway, be good to have Col around.

And it was. Col had some nice ideas for backgrounds and colours and stuff, spent hours mucking about checking out the different typefaces and stuff. Meant a lot of extra work for Sean of course, but even though he moaned a bit it was obvious to Mikey he'd be there all night given half a chance.

So, a couple of weeks later the site was up and running, they had a resources page, an advice page, a nice little photo history page a links page and loads of the usual do-gooder guff all over the place. Mikey was well pleased with it and so was Ozzie and the people from the Development agency.

And so as Mikey, Col and Sean sat around the office basking in the glow of a job well done, Mikey decided it was time to move on to stage two.

'So how do you boys feel about doing another website, something more profitable.'

'What,' said Sean, 'you mean selling stuff?'

'Yeah,' said Mikey, 'Well, more or less.'

Col frowned as if wondering whether to say something then launched into it anyway. 'Yeah,' he said, 'I was wondering if I should make a little site for my business like.'

It was Mikey's turn to frown now, seeing as Col's little business was based around the cultivation and distribution of the most serious hydroponic skunk known to Cardiff. 'Bit risky wouldn't it be?'

'I dunno,' said Col, 'how easy can they detect where your computer is?'

'Pretty easy,' said Sean, 'least if you're plugged into the phone line it's just a question of checking where the number is.' He paused, 'Course if you had a laptop and a mobile with an Ethernet connection then it'd be pretty hard for them to trace you.'

'Yeah?' said Col, 'how much would that cost?'

'Two, three grand,' said Sean.

'You reckon the development people like to buy us one of those?' Col asked Mikey.

'Doubt it,' said Mikey, 'and anyway, it'd be the delivery would be the problem. I mean you sell it off the Internet how d'you know who's buying? Could be a copper ordering up a couple of ounces. You don't know till you go round their house and there's the Plod waiting there laughing all over their face.'

'Yeah,' said Col and fell silent for a moment before brightening up. 'I could send it through the post take the payment by credit card.'

'Yeah,' said Mikey, 'sure Barclaycard would love that. Anyway, you sell all your gear already, innit.'

'Yeah,' said Col, 'I suppose.'

'Look,' said Mikey, 'I got a much better idea. And he explained his porn site plan.

Compared to the first website the porn site was a headache right from the start. First off Col didn't want to do it. Ever since his babymother dumped him for a lesbian pimp Col had been a bit sensitive on the whole sex trade business. Sean wasn't too keen on the sex stuff either but he did say that there was some interesting technology being developed for the porn sites and Mikey said so it would be like a bit of a technical challenge then and managed to sell Sean on it that way. Next problem was the name. Sean showed Mikey this site where you could try to register a name for your site and it was unbelievable how all the filthy names you could think of were gone already. Two full days trying things out and the only name Mikey had registered was mikeyjthompson.com. He was just about ready to give up when Col comes by and says sarcastically how about Welshporn.com, no one would ever think of that. And he was right no one had. Mikey bagged it at once. It even gave him an idea for the site's gimmick: do all the girls up in Welsh girl costumes. Well, the silly hats at least.

That was the next problem of course, getting the girls. First question was what kind of girls? Mikey did a little bit of research, had a little look at the competition and he figured there were two main strands out there; glamour and amateur. Glamour meant finding cover girl types who didn't mind having sex on camera. Given that cover girl types were a bit thin on the ground in Cardiff, let alone ones keen to put out in public, Mikey figured that amateur had to be the way to go. Amateur meant girls who looked like the bird next door, filmed with an instamatic or dodgy camcorder, probably in black and white. Basically you just needed to round up a few dirty girls who liked a laugh and a few quid. This, Mikey figured, was something he could manage.

He had a word with Sean about the technicalities of the business but Sean started babbling about streaming technology and bandwidths and Mikey just tuned out. When Sean ground to a halt Mikey just said, 'How about I deliver you a couple of video tapes and a few photos and you do something with that.'

'But you want it to be live sex, right?' Sean objected. 'You'll need to set up a studio with a digital camera capable of delivering . . .'

Christ, the boy was literal minded thought Mikey before cutting in, 'Sean, live sex is what we say it is. We stick a bit of video on, the punters don't know if it's live or not do they?'

'But that's dishonest,' said Sean. Mikey burst out laughing and eventually Sean laughed too.

Another couple of weeks and Mikey finally had the stuff. And if he'd known it was going to be this much hard work he wouldn't have bothered. Must have had his face slapped more times than Ernie Wise when all he was doing was offering a bunch of not over-talented young ladies the chance of a lifetime. But one thing twenty years of being a five-foot-nothing womaniser had taught him was that persistence pays off and so it had proved.

First he'd got a few Polaroids of a girl named Gloria, big dark girl, flashing her tits right outside the pub after half a dozen Bacardi Breezers. Next he'd got a few candid type snaps of the strippers down the Dowlais before Kenny had caught him at it and chucked him out. Got a few more pics of some young girl called Lee-Ann who actually wanted to be a page three girl, let Mikey take a few snaps of her spread out on her parents' settee. So far so good, but every time he even mentioned taking a bit of video of the girl actually getting down to it, there was some serious face-slapping broke out.

He thought about asking one of the girls down the Custom House, but far as most of them went there was amateur and there was seriously bloody rough. Plus there was another problem suddenly occurred to Mikey. It was simple enough the girly mag type shots, all you needed was the girl, but for the actual nitty gritty sex stuff you needed a bloke as well. Now you might have though it'd be easy enough get a bloke ready to do the business with as many slappers as Mikey could deliver but you'd be surprised. Blokes who put it about like nobody's business suddenly turned into shrinking violets the moment Mikey suggested doing something on camera. Frightened the world might see their twelve-incher was a little less than specified, Mikey figured, or that they wouldn't get it up. Eventually he figured that if you need a job doing properly you really had best do it yourself.

Which just left the question of who the lucky lady would be. Then Mikey realised that the obvious solution was under his nose. He'd get Tina to do it. You stood back a bit, forgot that she only ever opened her mouth to give you aggravation, she was still a pretty good looking piece. Lovely big arse on her just the way Mikey liked it. Anyway there she was sitting in the living room watching bloody Holby City and worst that could happen was he got another slapping so he goes in and asks her and right away she was up for it. Made him feel a bit guilty really, like maybe he could have been doing a bit more to keep their sex life interesting and all.

In fact they had a right laugh doing it. Worked out a little scenario where Mikey carrying a camcorder pretended to pick Tina up on the street, then they got back to the flat and stuck the camcorder in the tripod and got down to it like they hadn't in years, Tina really giving it a hundred per cent for the camera.

So there he was ready to go: an hour or two of top quality video tape and a whole bunch of photos, all ready to go. He even had a nice rear shot of Tina wearing a Welsh girl hat to go on the front end of the site, bit like a logo. Mikey left Sean to it then, didn't want to embarrass the kid, and by the end of the week the site was up and running. Even had a deal with some company in California to take the credit card payments, if anyone who saw the picture of Tina's arse wanted to see a whole lot more like.

Mikey was well chuffed. Only thing left to do now was take it to the money men.

Mikey was sat in this lawyer's office in Windsor Terrace.

Not the lawyer's office he was normally sat in, his brief Terry Richards's place, wondering how he was going to get off his latest shoplifting charge, but a really smart lawyer's office, leather armchairs, modern art on the walls. Course the receptionist wasn't as cute as Donna who worked at Terry's but you couldn't have everything. Mikey was just pleased to be finally getting somewhere.

Taking his site to the money men had been a lot harder than anticipated. In fact Mikey was starting to agree with those fellers on the telly always chopsing on about how people in Britain didn't have enough business enterprise like. You offer people a sure thing – Internet porn – easiest moneymaker going, short of a lottery franchise, and they didn't want to know. You mentioned the word porn and they turned up their noses. And Mikey wasn't a political guy but you couldn't help wondering they'd have the same attitudes if he said he was an arms' manufacturer or something. Peddle a few pictures of girls quite old enough to know better and they suddenly come over all Mary Whitehouse on you.

But Mikey had persevered and finally he'd talked to one feller at the NatWest who said he didn't imagine a high street bank like his own with a public image to protect, blah, blah, would be interested, but he'd ask around, he knew one or two people interested in the more, uh, risky kinds of investment.

So a couple of days later Mikey gets a call on the phone and there's this secretary type on the line asking if Mikey would like to come in for a meeting with this lawyer feller, Ralph Cledwyn Thomas.

So there was Mikey sat in the Cledwyn Thomas's office and frankly he couldn't believe he was having this conversation. This respectable feller in a suit asking him if his porn site's dirty enough.

'Very nicely presented site,' says this Cledwyn Thomas, 'but d'you think perhaps you need more of a USP?'

'USP,' said Mikey frowning, thinking it was some computer thing.

'Unique selling point,' says the feller.

'What d'you mean exactly – unique selling point?' he asked tentatively.

'You know,' says the feller, 'something out of the ordinary, something marks it out from all the other millions of, ah, adult sites out there. Your competition.'

Mikey sat there for a moment wondering what the bloke was after. Did he mean the site wasn't perverted enough, maybe. Perhaps the bloke wanted S&M, or animals, or children, Christ. What did he think Mikey was? Well maybe he could do a bit of S&M, just play acting really as far as he could see, but the other stuff no way, he thought, feeling an unaccustomed wave of moral righteousness wash over him.

'Well,' said Mikey, 'I dunno, could have a bit of S&M on the site I suppose if that's what you mean?'

'Hmm,' said the bloke, 'yes, well, I believe that's a very popular area to explore, however what I was thinking . . .' At this point the bloke dropped his voice so Mikey had to move his chair closer to be able to hear him properly.

Ten minutes later Mikey was back outside, walking up Charles Street, past the pub that used to be the Panorama, heading back home to Butetown, and full of an unaccustomed sense of moral outrage. Bloke had obviously had trouble with his toilet training, things he wanted Mikey to get the girls to do, Mikey thought he was going to be sick. Plus, and this was the worst of it, far as Mikey could see he wasn't interested in floating the site on the Stock Exchange or whatever, he just wanted Mikey to arrange for his personal little fantasies to be carried out to order. Ended up with Mikey standing up and saying 'I'm not a pimp you know,' which was bit of a laugh really 'cause it wasn't a profession he had anything against *per se*, it was just he was trying to move up in the world wasn't he, and to get treated like some feller can lay on a freak show for any double-barrelled twat came along, just pissed him off.

He was walking through the building site at the bottom of Bute Street shaking his head at the degeneracy of mankind when his mobile went off. It was Cledwyn Thomas on the line, says he's sorry Mikey might have got the wrong impression, lays on a line of bullshit and then says all of a sudden, 'I don't suppose you could put me in touch with the young lady on your site, could you?'

'Which young lady?' asks Mikey.

'Ah, the one in the rather fetching Welsh bonnet,' says Cledwyn Thomas.

Mikey shuddered and then, without thinking, just lobbed the mobile in the path of the tarmacking machine and watched it crunch satisfyingly underneath it.

As he walked home he figured he should stick to what he knew. After all he never was a technologically minded feller.

Contributors

MATT WHYMAN is an agony uncle for magazines and a major Internet service. He is a contributor to FHM and his first novel, *Man or Mouse* has just been published. He lives in London.

STELLA DUFFY is an actress, and writes both crime novels (featuring indomitable sleuth Saz Martin) and comedies of London manners. She lives in London and runs an improvisation theatre group.

JAMES FLINT made a major post-modernist impact with his sprawling novel *Habitus*. A former technology journalist, he had written for *Mute* and *Wired*. Trained as a jazz saxophonist, he lives in London.

MARILYN JAYE LEWIS has for several years run the award-winning Marilyn's Room website and founded the Erotic Book Society. Her first book is *Neptune and Surf*. She lives in New York.

MATT THORNE is the author of three acclaimed novels, *Tourists, Eight Seconds Idle* and *Dreaming of Strangers* and a co-editor (with Nicholas Blincoe) of the controversial New Puritans anthology. He is based in London.

PAUL J MCAULEY is one of Britain's leading science fiction authors and has won several prizes in the field including the Arthur C. Clarke Award. He was trained and worked as a biologist before turning to full-time writing.

VAL MCDERMID is a former journalist who has established herself as one of Britain's major crime writers and is a winner of the CWA Gold Dagger. Her titles include *The Mermaids Singing* and *A Place of Execution*. She lives in Stockport.

STEWART HOME leads the vanguard of avant-garde/anarchist/seditionary writing in the UK. A prolific writer, he recently authored the controversial *Cunt* which, naturally, attracted much attention but is also a rollicking, subversive read.

KIM NEWMAN is a film journalist and writer whose books have almost single-handedly created the sub-genre of retro horror. A former semi-professional kazoo player and cabaret performer, his latest novel is *Life's Lottery*.

CHRISTOPHER FOWLER is a prolific short story and horror author and one of the founders of the Creative Partnership film company. His novels include *Roofworld*, *Spanky* and *Calabash*. He works in the heart of Soho.

STEVE AYLETT is fast establishing himself as a comic and witty writer whose work straddles a variety of genres with aplomb. His books include *The Crime Studio*, *Slaughtermatic*, *Toxicology* and *Atom*. He lives in Brighton.

MAXIM JAKUBOWSKI used to work in publishing and now runs and owns the Murder One book shop. A major anthologist in several genres, he is also the *Guardian*'s crime columnist and Literary Director of the Crime Scene Festival. His last novel is *On Tenderness Express*.

NICHOLAS BLINCOE has written four novels of comic noir crime, and won the CWA Silver Dagger Award for *Manchester Slingback*. A mainstay of London's young writing scene, he also writes for the *Guardian* and the *Observer*.

PAT CADIGAN is an American science fiction author who now lives in London. She won the Arthur C. Clarke Award in 1992 for her novel *Synners* and contributed to the bestselling *Disco Biscuits* anthology.

LAUREN HENDERSON has been described as the Betty Boop of British crime fiction and is the creator of sculptress Sam Jones whose exploits have graced half a dozen novels. She lives in Italy and thoroughly enjoys the local wine.

IAN WATSON is one of the UK's most respected science fiction authors of ideas ever since his ground breaking first novel *The Embedding* which won the Apollo Award, and has acquired international cult status. He worked with Stanley Kubrick on the fabled A.I. film project, now to be completed by Spielberg.

MANDA SCOTT is a veterinary surgeon and an author and the first-ever British crime writer to be short-listed for the Orange Prize for Fiction for her debut novel *Hen's Teeth*. She lives near Newmarket.

JONNY LEWIS is a young London writer, educated at Manchester University who, following several years as a buyer in the book trade, is embracing the teaching profession.

CHINA MIÉVILLE is a Cambridge graduate, studying for a PhD at the London School of Economics. He has also worked as an illustrator and a comic strip artist. His two novels so far are *King Rat* and *Perdido Street Station*.

TOBY LITT has quickly established himself as one of the most original voices in contemporary British fiction with a collection *Adventures in Capitalism*, and two novels *Beatniks* and the wicked London thriller *Corpsing*.

CHRIS MANBY was once one of Britain's youngest ever professional writers of erotica before she turned respectable and began writing comic novels of London relationship, drinking and shopping. She changes her address with frightening regularity.

DENISE DANKS is a technology and computer journalist who was the first British author to win the Raymond Chandler Fulbright bursary. She has written several novels featuring sleuth Georgina Powers, including *Phreak* which was short listed for the Gold Dagger. Her last novel is *Torso*.

JOHN WILLIAMS is a reviewer and writer who has been described as Wales's answer to Irvine Welsh! His travelogue *Into the Badlands* is still one of the best books written on contemporary American crime fiction. He lives in Cardiff.